## About the author

Christine lives in Cornwall with her husband, Jeff. She is now retired but writes full-time. (Any excuse not to do the housework).

As a believer in love conquering all, and being an incurable romantic, writing romances is the right genre for her. She really does believe that love conquers all. Consequently, all her stories of meeting, falling in love have believable endings. The stories are not always as one would have expected but heartwarming nevertheless. It would be wise to have a box of tissues handy when reading her stories.

FORGOTTEN LOVE

*Also by C.M. Bryden*

Willelm D'Anville

# C M Bryden

FORGOTTEN LOVE

Vanguard Press

VANGUARD PAPERBACK

© Copyright 2017
**C M Bryden**

A CIP catalogue record for this title is
available from the British Library.

ISBN 978 1 784652 58 6

*Vanguard Press is an imprint of*
*Pegasus Elliot MacKenzie Publishers Ltd.*
www.pegasuspublishers.com


First Published in 2017

**Vanguard Press**
**Sheraton House  Castle Park**
**Cambridge  England**


Printed & Bound in Great Britain

# Dedication

This book is dedicated to those I love. Especially to my husband of many years. He is a man in a million, but there are more like him in the world and, if like me, you are happily married to a wonderful man, then I salute you and I have only one word to say: WONDERFUL.

# Prologue

1957

It was early in the morning of Christmas day when a combination of three events occurred that would prove to have a catastrophic effect on Anna's future life. Events that would take her away from the path she'd previously believed it her destiny to tread.

First of all, there was the noise of the bedroom door bursting open, then the overhead light being switched on, which had startled her into wakefulness, followed by the sudden outburst of an angry person shouting for her to get out of the bed! To say the least, she was frightened!

She sat up, her head spinning, unable at first to comprehend what was happening. The next moment, a pair of bony hands had reached out and made a grab for her, obviously with the intention of removing her from the bed! As frightened as she was, Anna had no intention of that happening.

To stop herself from falling onto the floor, she dug her heels into the mattress, hoping to dodge the vicious blows being rained on her head and shoulders by, of all people, Paul's mother.

At the same time as she was desperately trying to ward off the hands clawing at her body, she was also struggling to keep hold of the bedcovers in an attempt to cover her nakedness; hoping to preserve what little was left of her dignity.

The shock attack had surprised her to such an extent she'd been momentarily rendered speechless, until the next assault began. Her hair was suddenly grasped in a vice-like grip then yanked and twisted with such force she thought her assailant intended to scalp her. It was only then she found her voice and screamed so loud it finally woke Paul, her bed companion who, until that moment, had been sound asleep beside her.

Once awake, although befuddled, it took no time at all for him to weigh up the situation and, with one quick bound, he'd leapt out of the bed, ready to rescue his beloved until suddenly, he realised he was naked!

In one swift movement, he bent down and scooped his underpants from off the floor and then, hopping from leg to leg, and stumbling in his haste, he managed to pull them on, before racing round the bed to intervene and save Anna.

From then on, several minutes of frantic mayhem ensued before he managed to release her from his mother's grip and she'd managed to inch her way back onto the relative safety of the bed, still gripping the bedcovers and unable to believe what had just taken place.

Paul looked at Anna who from his first quick glance he could see how spitefully she'd been attacked. He was staggered unable to believe his small and normally mild mannered mother had found the strength to inflict such hard blows, leaving him to wonder for what reason?

Paul looked at his mother, just starting to vocally vent her anger, leaving him cringing at the venom coming from her mouth.

To his and Anna's surprise the onslaught suddenly stopped. For a few moments it all went quiet and, believing the attack to be over, they relaxed, which was a big mistake, for within a few seconds another tirade of abuse had started and this time it was physical, as well as verbal as his mother sprang into action like a woman possessed!

With an almighty shove, Paul pushed his way between the two women he loved, pressing Anna back onto the bed, at the same time trying to prise his mother's hands from off his beloved's hair.

He could see the veins in his mother's neck standing out, portraying her anger and determination, until he managed to release her hold on Anna's hair. Holding his mother at arm's length, he glared at her. Mistakenly thinking he'd got the situation under control, he foolishly relaxed his hold, only for a second or two, but even that was far too long, for in a flash his mother was free of him, ducking under his arm as she tried to make another grab at Anna, this time, in one swift movement she was successful. She pulled the bedcovers off, exposing Anna's nakedness for all to see.

Paul looked at her, taking in the stricken look on her sweet face, her emerald eyes brimming with tears. For one long moment he was totally mesmerised by a solitary tear, sliding slowly down her cheek. He lowered his eyes, quickly scanning her body, looking at her breasts, those beautiful orbs he'd caressed and fondled so ardently during the night when she'd crept shivering into his bed, and he'd held her close.

Suddenly, he brought his mind back to the here and now, knowing he had to remove his mother from the room before she could inflict any more damage, but this time he was taking no chances.

Grabbing her arms, he held her tight before hooking his foot round the partly open door then thrusting her away, out of his bedroom and onto the landing, closing the door firmly behind her, and hoping that was the end!

Shaking, as much from anger as exertion, he leant against the doorframe, thankful Anna was safe from any more of his mother's wicked assaults.

Breathing deeply, he tried to regain his strength before warily opening the door, just a little. He could see his mother was still standing on the landing, leaning against the balustrade, getting her own breath back, no doubt waiting for another opportunity to continue her assault.

'What the devil was all that about?' Paul asked. His head in a whirl having never seen his mother act in such a way before.

His mother just glared in his direction, flushed from her exertions, her frizzy grey hair standing up around her head like a demented halo.

'That girl's nothing but a slut and a whore,' she screeched.

Paul wanted to shout back that Anna was neither a slut nor a whore, she was the woman he loved, but his mother gave him no opportunity, continuing to shout that he had to get Anna out of the house, straightaway.

'She'd no business being in your bed,' she yelled. 'I want her out of my house. Do you hear me?'

This last statement was emphasised by her vigorously shaking her fists at him. Paul was furious. How dare his mother treat him in such a manner?

He was no longer a child to be reprimanded in his own home, he was twenty-three years old, an adult, and in love with Anna, who he intended to marry!

Suddenly, he realised neither his mother, nor Anna, knew this.

'Get her out of here now!' his mother shouted. This time, not waiting for his reply, she went into her bedroom, slamming the door shut behind her but Paul could still hear her, even through the closed door, as she continued to rant and rage at his father who, rather wisely, had stayed in bed while his wife had been on her angry rampage!

Paul turned his attention back to Anna who, by now, was looking thoroughly miserable and humiliated as she sat huddled under the covers she'd retrieved from the floor where his mother had angrily tossed them. Her face was ashen in colour, her beautiful eyes full of unshed tears.

Paul was furious, as he reached across and pulled the covers down and saw the damage Anna had received at his mother's hands. There were dozens of red marks and raised wheals, along with several angry looking scratches, some already oozing blood, from where his mother had raked her nails down Anna's body.

Paul noticed a red mark over one eye, an obvious sign she would be sporting a black eye within the next few hours.

Looking a picture of abject misery, Anna snatched the covers from out of his hands, pulling them tightly under her chin, trying to cover her body, especially her naked breasts, but he'd already seen them and knew the damage his mother had caused. He sat down next to her and put his arms around her shoulders, drawing her close as he held her shapely body into his, trying to reassure her, nuzzling his face into the soft skin of her neck, smelling the womanly scent of her as he desperately wished the past events had never happened.

'I'm so sorry,' he murmured quietly into the sweetness of her hair.

'It's all my fault,' Anna stammered, her tears beginning to fall in a steady stream, the sight of which affected Paul greatly, having never seen her cry before. 'I shouldn't have come into your room last night, but I was so cold.' She sniffed, trying to wipe the tears away with her hands. 'I looked for some extra covers, but I couldn't find any.'

Paul bent and kissed her. 'I'm not sorry you came in,' he said, smiling at her as he wiped a wayward tear from off her face with his fingertips. 'It was the most wonderful thing that has ever happened to me. Don't you worry about my mother, when she knows we're going to be married, she'll come round, you'll see!' he said, smiling at her with a confidence he didn't quite feel.

It was at that moment Anna felt a strange sensation churning in the pit of her stomach, knowing instinctively Paul's mother would never 'come round' as he'd put it, to them getting married, she would oppose any such suggestion with as much gusto as she'd put into trying to get her out of his bed! As for them getting married, had she been dreaming?

'Married?' Anna asked, in an incredulous tone. 'When did you ask me to marry you?'

Paul laughed. 'I was going to ask you this morning... I was going to propose to you in the time-honoured fashion... you know, on bended knee? I've had it planned for weeks.' Smiling lovingly at her, he waited for her reply.

Anna looked into his eyes, trying to see deep into his soul, wondering, as she did so, if the words he spoke were true and that he did love her.

As if reading her mind, and knowing her doubts Paul spoke in a voice full of emotion. *'I love you, Anna. I will always love you. No one will ever take your place in my heart.'*

(Words that in the future would haunt him.)

Kneeling in front of her, he took her shaking hands in his.

*'Will you marry me? Will you be my wife?"*

Without having to think of her answer, Anna bent to kiss him, her long auburn hair acting like a cloak, hiding them from view. As their kiss ended, she shivered, as if an icicle had pierced her heart, unaware the fates had been listening to their vows of love and, for their own reasons, were determined to destroy the hopes and dreams of the young lovers.

'Of course I will marry you,' she said. 'I love you.'

Instead of feeling euphoric, as any newly engaged young woman in love should, Anna suddenly had an immense feeling of doom flooding through her. Morbid thoughts began to fill her mind. Desperately trying to dispel her fears, knowing it wasn't going to be as easy as Paul thought, she held onto his hands and made a silent wish.

After a while, seeing the pain in her eyes, Paul loosened his hold and pulled away, fearful, as well as concerned, because he knew it was his mother's attitude that was going to give them the most trouble. He knew his mother had to change; but at the same time he realised, although this was the 1950s, old-fashioned attitudes to unmarried young people sleeping together still prevailed among her generation; it was this attitude that was going to be Paul's biggest problem.

He could still hear his mother, ranting and moaning at his father in the next room; continuing to complain bitterly that Anna had had 'no business' going into his room, as hadn't she personally made up the spare bed for the girl?

Anna looked at Paul, fully aware of what his mother was saying.

'Your mother's quite right,' she said, gulping back the lump in her throat. 'The bed was made up, but there was only one cover on the bed. The room was so cold, I couldn't sleep!'

Paul held her close, hearing the sobs in her voice as she continued.

'I looked in the cupboard for some more covers, truly I did, but I couldn't find any. I thought if I crept into your bed once you were asleep, perhaps then I too would get warm and sleep as well!'

By now, a steady stream of tears was trickling down her cheeks that try as she might, she couldn't stop. Paul held her close, cradling her in his arms, rocking her gently, back and forth: stroking her hair, hushing her as one would a small child, thinking back to when he'd heard his door opening and then the click as it had closed. He remembered how he'd felt when her small body had crept into his bed and she'd lain very still beside him.

'I was more than happy,' he said, quietly, 'to have you in my bed, whatever the reason.'

Of course he'd known right away it was Anna next to him, he even remembered how his heart had pounded as he'd lain still for quite some time, breathing as quietly as he could as he feigned sleep, at the same time, hoping she wouldn't hear his heart thudding in his chest.

After a while, he could sense her relaxing and, at that point, he turned to face her, hoping not to frighten her away, their breaths fanning each other's faces, until he could bear it no longer and had placed his arms around her, drawing her even closer into the circle of his arms.

As Anna lay cuddled into his body, Paul could feel her shivering, mostly from the cold but also, unknown to him, at the closeness of their intimacy. She was where, in her dreams, she'd always longed to be, but had never thought possible.

Paul started to caress her, trying to bring some warmth back into her body. With each stroke of his hands Anna could feel the warmth permeating into her but, more than that, she could feel her sexual desire for him rising with each stroke, her body longing for him to caress her more intimately, hoping he would make love to her.

It wasn't long before she was following his initiative, caressing him with as much fervour; running her hands over his body as she felt the breadth of his shoulders and the muscles in his arms and the way his body changed its contours as her hands, followed the triangle of his shape as they went down to his waist and beyond, to where her hands and fingers had never been before. She could feel his erection pressing against her and, with no doubts about her actions, she'd taken her first hold of him, caressing him; loving the feel of his silken shaft and then, hearing his sharp intake of breath, as their caresses became more intimate and searching. With their dual sexual excitement reaching dizzying heights it took hardly any urging from either of them to consummate their love and, as Paul entered her for the first time, their emotions soared up to the heavens where, to their delight, they became as one.

Making love had been an exquisite experience for them both, as unexpected as it had been unplanned, yet inevitable, given they were in love. But that had been then and this was now and Anna was being banished from his home, and all because of his mother's old-fashioned values, as well as by what Anna secretly thought to be jealousy on the older woman's part.

Paul was an only son, adored by his mother, a woman whom Anna instinctively knew would dislike any young woman her beloved son wanted to marry. Something that for centuries many young women have had to face and overcome after falling in love with a young man, who might be the only beloved male child in a family.

The young lovers sat huddled together on Paul's bed, their arms around each other, listening to his mother, who was still continuing her tirade of angry words in the next room.

Suddenly, all went quiet, leaving Paul wondering if his father had managed to placate his wife, or was she plotting even more mischief against the woman he loved?

Anna knew, without being told, that she must leave the house, especially if she and Paul were to have a future together, she had to be the strong one and walk away, leaving Paul to resolve his mother's issues.

'Let's just all sit together and talk,' Paul heard his father say, 'and sort out this nonsense.'

But his mother was having none of it.'

'It isn't nonsense' she'd said, 'and there's no sorting out to do either.' Her voice rising, as once more her temper flared.

'Just get her out of this house now! Do you understand?'

'But it's Christmas Day!' they heard Paul's father say, quietly trying to reason with his wife, but to no avail, she was adamant. Once again she screamed at him.

'DO YOU NOT UNDERSTAND WHAT I'M SAYING? GET HER OUT OF HERE, NOW!'

Paul hugged Anna to his chest, loving the way their bodies moulded together. He knew he wanted to make love to her again, but even he knew this wasn't the moment to satisfy his carnal urges.

'I must go,' Anna said, hearing his mother's pronouncement.

Paul looked at her; a forlorn figure, sitting next to him on the bed. He knew he loved her and wanted to marry her; he wanted to keep her close, for always. This need was the only clear thought in his mind; he was unable to see a future without her. He knew they would have to part, if only for a short time, until he'd settled his mother and father into understanding Anna was going to be his wife, regardless of what they thought. He found it hard to believe his life had suddenly changed from one with hope for his and Anna's future, into one that was nothing short of a living nightmare, and on what should have been the happiest day of his life. Instead of celebrating her son's happiness, his mother was causing nothing but unhappiness and grief to Paul and the girl he loved.

'I have to go,' Anna said, knowing she had to get away from the awfulness of what had just happened. She was in an intolerable situation, stuck between the man she loved and his mother who also loved him. 'If I leave now, perhaps you will be able to talk to your mother and explain what happened?'

Putting her arms around Paul, she clung on, not wanting to leave, but knowing in her heart it was the only way he would be able to appease his mother. She had to be the strong one and go away.

Reluctantly, Anna moved out of his arms, but not before they'd shared a last lingering kiss, one so full of a longing they both secretly knew might not be fulfilled for some time.

Anna picked up her discarded nightdress from off the floor, wrapping it round her shoulders, trying to cover as much of her bare flesh as she possibly could. Paul watched, his handsome young face clearly showing his emotions. 'You can't go,' he insisted. 'It's Christmas Day for goodness' sake, where will you go?'

For a moment, Anna didn't answer, ignoring his plea, at the same time holding tightly to her nightdress, as well as a blanket she'd taken off the bed.

'I'll go back home!' she'd said defiantly. Then, opening the door, and seeing the landing clear, she made a quick dash for the small bedroom, which was still freezing cold and from where she'd crept the night before.

Shivering, she quickly dressed, before packing her meagre belongings into the small suitcase she'd brought with her for the holiday; leaving the Christmas gifts she'd chosen with such care for his parents on the dressing table, not wanting to take any reminders of this awful day back to her own home, instinctively knowing future Christmases would always remind her of what had happened on that day and, somehow, she felt cheated.

With her heart aching, she closed the case, wondering, as she did so, if her hopes for a bright future with Paul would ever be fulfilled?

Paul was only partly dressed when he heard Anna opening the bedroom door as she was about to leave. He hurried onto the landing, just as she was quietly closing the door behind her. As she reached him, he moved forward to take her in his arms.

'It's snowing,' he whispered. 'You can't possibly go out in this weather?' All the time conscious of his parents' bedroom door at his elbow, and that they might hear his words, well aware that at any moment his mother could, quite possibly, come bursting out of her room, ready to attack them again.

Anna stood still, giving Paul the opportunity to hold her in his arms once more. This time, she let him kiss her soundly, before wriggling out of his arms and, pushing him gently away. 'I must go!' she said, so quietly, he could hardly hear her.

Seeing the anguish in her lovely green eyes, Paul reluctantly let her go.

'I'll be right after you,' he called out, as she ran down the stairs.

Once in the hallway, Anna stopped, just long enough to put on her hat and winter coat. Wrapping her long woollen scarf round her neck, she then pulled on her gloves before picking up her suitcase. With tears glistening in her eyes, she closed the front door behind her and walked down the snow-covered path, away from the man she loved.

# Chapter 1

It was just starting to get light as Anna began her journey back to the city. Heavy snow had been falling for several hours, the first downfall of the winter and, with the temperature still dropping, the surface of the lane was already covered in a thick white layer that crunched as she walked along in her unsuitable shoes, but there was nothing she could do about them until she reached her home on the far side of the city.

Walking in snow hadn't been on her agenda when she'd left home the day before, as she'd travelled in Paul's car, never dreaming for a moment what would happen to send her away from him.

She shivered and stopped walking for a moment. Everywhere was silent, except for the beating of her heart and the soft whisper of the wind, sloughing through the trees, as snow flurries fell in front of her, momentarily blinding her.

In the menacing half-light, her imagination started playing tricks on her as she turned to look back at the road she'd already travelled. She could see snowdrifts already starting to pile up in the hedgerows making ghostly shapes. Eerie shadows were being formed by the wind as it blew across the fields. At the same time the windblown snow was obliterating her footsteps, leaving no trace of her progress.

Not for the first time, Anna wondered how long it would be before Paul joined her.

At this point, she was still confident he would do as he'd said and follow her, as soon as he was dressed. Perhaps, she thought, he'd already left? Then, berating herself, she knew she had to be patient!

Anna knew the next few hours were going to be the worst she would ever experience and, for a little while, she regretted her hasty departure, wondering if she should turn back and return to the house, until she thought back to the events of earlier and knew she'd been right to leave, knowing her presence would only have aggravated the situation further had she stayed.

As she'd walked away from the house she decided to head back to the flat she shared with Ruth, her hated stepmother, even knowing the flat would be empty. She also knew it would be cold and cheerless as Ruth had gone to stay with friends over the holiday, but Anna didn't care, being alone was the least of her worries as she trudged along, stopping every few hundred yards or so to turn and listen for the sound of Paul's footsteps crunching in the snow behind her.

Even though the falling snow prevented her from seeing if he was behind her, Anna still believed Paul would carry out his promise. Hadn't he said he couldn't live without her? Why, he'd even asked her to marry him. Or had she imagined that as well?

Plodding along, and getting colder by the minute, her mind was full of what had happened earlier that morning. She knew she loved Paul. It had been her dream for the past year for him to fall in love with her and would want to marry her and then, they would live happily ever after. But today she'd learnt a hard lesson: life doesn't always have the fairy-tale ending she'd dreamt of, and any dreams she might have had of an everlasting happiness with Paul, her Prince

Charming, had been thoroughly tainted by his mother's spitefulness and jealousy.

Anna shook her head, trying to clear her mind. Surely, she couldn't doubt Paul? He was honourable and she knew she loved him, but had she fallen in love with him because she was unhappy at home? Had she been dreaming of the impossible? Living in a world of make-believe? Trying to escape from a stepmother she hated? Was it her desperation to escape from her unhappy home life the main reason why she'd clung on to him?

Even though Paul was also young, and as inexperienced as she was in the ways of the world, she'd believed him to be her knight in shining armour: he was her hero figure. But was he really the man destined to take her away from her miserable home life? Was she so needy she'd inadvertently inveigled him into proposing to her? These were questions she constantly asked herself as she trudged through the deepening snow as she walked. The cold was already affecting her reasoning, making her senses fluctuate, between optimism and pessimism. She couldn't give herself an honest answer, at least not yet, perhaps in time she would, but not at the moment. What she needed most of all was to get home even though as unhappy as she had been, it was still the one place where she knew she would be safe.

Anna had no way of knowing Paul hadn't fallen in love with her because she was needy and vulnerable, or that she needed rescuing from her hated stepmother. He'd fallen in love with her because she was gentle and kind. She had an inner strength; a core of steel he admired. He also knew she was energetic and self-motivated and, more than that, he loved the way she took hold of a problem, shook it, and tossed it around in her head, until she'd solved it, as well as a myriad of other reasons.

Of course, he also loved her physical beauty. She was elegant and graceful, and he was the proudest of men when she walked at his side; it had certainly been no hardship for him to fall in love with her, but walking through the snow on that Christmas morning Anna knew none of this.

Paul had made his plans some weeks earlier to propose to Anna on Christmas Day. He'd even bought an engagement ring, especially for the occasion. A solitaire diamond set in gold, already languishing in a leather box in the drawer at the side of his bed, waiting for when Anna said 'yes' to his proposal. With this in mind, he'd asked his mother and father if she could stay for Christmas, as her stepmother would be away and she would be alone, omitting to tell them it was his intention to ask her to marry him. It was only after Anna had left the house he realised this had been his biggest mistake. If only he'd told his parents Anna was the girl of his dreams and of his intention to ask her to marry him. Forewarning them, especially his mother. It would have given her time perhaps to adjust to the idea her son was no longer a child, but an adult: a man who needed to marry the girl he'd fallen in love with. She might then have come to terms with the inevitable, instead of being surprised and taken aback when she'd found them in bed together, but Paul also knew his mother would never have sanctioned them sleeping together in her house, no matter what, even though his intentions were honourable. This was the fifties and the low 'morals' of the permissive society had yet to permeate from the capital to the rest of the country! Things might have changed in London and other big cities in the country but in the shires it was a different story altogether. It wasn't done in those days for a young man and his ladylove to sleep together before marriage. Any young woman found doing so, would henceforth be labelled 'fast and loose'. Perhaps in time things will change?

This Christmas holiday wasn't the first time Paul's mother had met Anna, they'd met on several occasions over the past year, it was just she hadn't realised they were more than just good friends, having accepted Paul's explanation that Anna was merely a friend from his college years. If his mother had thought Anna was more than a passing fancy for her beloved son, she would certainly never have agreed to her staying with them, Christmas or not! She would also have made it her business to put a stop to them forming any sort of a relationship, especially if she'd had any inkling they were falling in love. She wanted Paul to finish his education first and then find a girlfriend, one who came from a 'good' family, one who could advance his prospects and further his career. In her opinion, Anna wouldn't have come into that category at all. As she understood it, the girl's father had been a factory worker! Furthermore, she also believed it her 'right' to 'vet' any girl that happened to come into Paul's life, believing he should find a girl who came from a family with the 'right address' and with the 'right' connections, not one with a common back ground such as Anna's, convinced any girl like that would certainly hold him back.

Having recently completed his accountancy training and was now working at one of the big banks in the city, Paul was well aware he had to make the right choice of wife if he were to be successful. It was essential in those days. But, by then, he'd met Anna and had fallen in love with her, knowing immediately she was everything he wanted in a woman. He also knew she would get the seal of approval from his employers, even though she didn't meet his mother's criteria. Anna had been to college, where she'd trained for a professional career in catering; it was just his mother and her snobbery that was the stumbling block.

Anna continued to trudge along the country road, wanting nothing more than to reach the city centre as soon as possible and find some form of transport to take her home. She didn't want to be in the freezing cold with snow continuing to fall and no sound of Paul following on the lane behind her as he'd promised. Not for the first time she was worried!

Meanwhile, back at Paul's house, things weren't going too well for him either. He understood his mother's moods and her attitude to life, having grown up with them! At the same time, he sympathised with his father, a gentle and unassuming man, who, over the years had bravely tried to cope with his wife's unreasonableness, as well as her unpredictable behaviour, all traits, which she'd so admirably demonstrated that morning. But, before Paul could do that, he knew he had to find a way to bring Anna back into the house as he was determined to marry her and make her a member of his family. As dysfunctional as it was, it was still his family. First of all, he knew he had to pacify his mother; naively thinking once his parents knew Anna, as he did, they would come to love and accept her. But Paul hadn't reckoned with the fates, which at that very moment were conspiring to cause him and Anna nothing but trouble!

Numbed by the cold, Anna had been walking steadily for some time; her irrational fears that Paul wouldn't come after her still racing through her mind. Her main thought had he changed his mind and decided he didn't want to marry her after all? But then, perhaps his parents had persuaded him not to follow her? Maybe he thought their opinions more important than her and he was already regretting the furore that had happened earlier? Perhaps he also regretted her creeping into his bed and them making love? These were the questions that continued to plague her and for which she had no answers, unaware irrational thoughts are a common reaction from the effects freezing temperatures have on the mind, as well as the body.

Anna tried to wipe away the face-numbing snow flurries that were making it almost impossible at times for her to see the road. The hand she was using to hold her small suitcase was becoming increasingly painful, making her dread picking up the case each time she stopped to listen out for Paul following behind her. But, in spite of her discomfort, she carried on walking, all the time wishing she could be home.

Meanwhile, back at his house, Paul hurriedly finished dressing, intending to leave as soon as possible and follow the girl he loved.

Once dressed, he raced down the stairs, but was stopped in his tracks by his father, standing in the hallway and barring his way, obviously intent on waylaying him from his mission.

Paul tried to reach for his outdoor clothes but his father held him back. For several minutes they stood in silence, like two antagonists weighing each other up at the start of a fight, both wanting to break the other's will but failing, until his father spoke.

'Please, Paul, go and speak to your mother before you go,' he said, relaxing his grip just a little on Paul's arm.

Paul ignored him and made to push his way past, but his normally gentle father wasn't about to give in so easily. He looked at Paul with a steely determination in his eyes, squaring himself to do battle, albeit verbally, but Paul ignored his plea and, once more, made to go past his father's resolute figure.

'For my sake,' his father softly pleaded, 'please talk to your mother. She's much calmer now. I know you want to go after Anna, but spare your mother a few minutes of your time. She means well, even though you might not agree with her and she needs you too!'

Paul made no attempt to do as his father asked, even though he was tugging on his arm, urging him away from the front door, directing him towards the kitchen, where he knew his wife was morosely sitting at the kitchen table, staring into space, lost in her own world and thoughts.

Paul hesitated, just for a few moments, thinking on his father's words, at the same time trying to resist the urge to leave the house without speaking to his mother until, reluctantly, he gave in. There was no doubt about it, his father was right, he must speak with his mother, it would take only a few minutes for what he had to say, and it could quite possibly make a bad situation into a good one, after all, what was a few minutes out of his life?

As his father had said, it might well make all the difference and, rather naively, Paul also had the same thought that indeed the next few minutes might well solve all his problems.

'Just a few minutes then,' he had said, as he headed for the kitchen, 'because I want to go after Anna!'

Satisfied that he'd succeeded, his father shrugged his shoulders and, in quiet resignation, he watched as Paul opened the kitchen door and went in to face his mother, alone.

Once the door had closed, his father looked relieved. Perhaps, he thought, peace and quiet would at last return to the household. He was unable to understand why his wife had become so upset when she'd realised Paul and Anna were sharing the same bed. He realised these were modern times and that life was very different from when they'd been young but these days, young couples thought nothing of sleeping together before marriage, or so he understood. Why, he'd even read in the newspapers that some couples were openly living together without being married!

It was, of course, beyond his comprehension, being from an older generation. But he wasn't a dinosaur! He knew changes were going to happen. It was his wife (as he well knew) who was the prudish one. He knew she would never allow any 'hanky panky' as she called it in the house, not if she could prevent it. It was because her high morals had been deeply offended when she'd seen the small bedroom door open and the bed empty, suddenly realising Anna was in Paul's room and they were together in the bed! That had been the act that had upset her the most!

Paul's father was pleased his son had done as he'd asked. Smiling to himself, he walked into the sitting room, decked out, only a day or so earlier, with tinsel and handmade Christmas decorations, made by Paul when he'd been young.

A small artificial tree stood on a table in the corner of the room, already dressed with baubles that were shining in the glow of the fire he'd lit earlier; a reminder the day should have been special with Paul and his young lady sharing it with them. Perhaps, he thought hopefully, when Paul had spoken to his mother she would see sense and then the boy could go and bring Anna back and they could all relax and enjoy the rest of the holy day.

Paul closed the kitchen door behind him and sat down opposite his mother at the scrubbed wooden table. He poured himself a cup of tea from the pot in front of her and, sipping it slowly he studied her, waiting patiently for her to acknowledge he was there, wary of her reaction to his presence.

'I must go!' he said, after a few minutes, when his mother made no effort to speak to him. 'It is after all Christmas Day and Anna's out there alone and I want to be with her.'

This last was said so defiantly his mother stopped sipping her tea for a moment and raised her eyes, in order to give him an icy stare; a look Paul found disconcerting, to say the least.

'Anna and I are going to be married,' he said, trying to outstare her. Even to this statement there was no reaction, other than a slight shrug of her shoulders, a shrug of complete indifference.

Paul continued. 'I want Anna to be part of this family. If you can't, or won't accept this, then I will have to leave home and never come back.'

This curt statement of his intent appeared to have no visible effect on her either. She just continued to sit with her cup poised halfway towards her lips, a faraway expression on her face as she stared blankly into space, as though he no longer existed.

Sensing he was making no headway, although she did appear to be a little calmer after her frantic efforts of earlier and realising how volatile she could be, Paul knew it was time to leave her alone with her own thoughts.

He wasn't about to take any chances with her mood either; he leant forward, taking the cup away from her cold fingers he placed it on its saucer, then, taking her cold hands in his, he quietly caressed them as he told her what had happened the previous night. He told her what had led Anna to being in his bed, omitting, of course, to tell her they'd made love, that wasn't her business, it was between Anna and himself and certainly wasn't a subject open to discussion.

'Anna didn't want to wake anyone in the house,' he said. 'She was cold and, as she couldn't find any more blankets, she came into my bed to get warm and then we fell asleep, which is how you found us...' His voice trailed off.

'I don't believe you,' his mother snorted, hardly giving him time to say any more even if he'd wanted to. Suddenly, she was alert as she stared at him, her nostrils flaring, her anger quickly resurfacing.

'She was out to get into your bed. All young girls are at it these days!' she said, contemptuously, almost spitting the words out in her anger.

Paul knew at this point it was a complete waste of time trying to give his mother any more explanations; it was hopeless to even think about it. He knew he would never change her point of view on modern-day morals. Deciding he would deal with his mother later, because by now he desperately wanted to leave the house and bring back the girl he loved, he rose from his seat and made to leave.

Paul wanted nothing more at that moment than to place the engagement ring he'd bought onto Anna's finger, and then they would have a celebration. His mother would just have to accept his and Anna's plans for the future, if not, he would leave home as he'd threatened, something he knew his mother wouldn't like at all.

As he went to walk out of the kitchen he said, 'I'm going to find Anna. If I can persuade her to come back with me, I want you to promise me you will behave, or I swear to God, I will leave and you will never see me again. I'm going to marry Anna! No matter what you say!'

There was no reply. I suppose Paul hardly expected one, given his mother was a stubborn woman who had no intention of accepting he was no longer a young man who didn't know his own mind.

Gently, he placed his mother's hands back on the table and, shaking his head in disbelief, he walked out of the kitchen, leaving his mother to her thoughts, and his father, sitting alone in the front room of the house, to his!

He quickly dressed in his outdoor clothes before hurrying out of the house intent on following the route he knew Anna would have taken.

Wearing an old sheepskin coat of his father's, with a knitted muffler wrapped round his neck and a matching hat pulled well down over his ears, one that kept out all sound and, with his head well down against the force of the weather, Paul walked out of the house and headed towards the lane Anna had already travelled.

And so it was, that on Christmas Day, 1957 the fates had already started to make mischief for our young lovers.

# Chapter 2

Daylight was only just breaking as Anna left Paul's home. The country lane was familiar, it was one often walke during the summer, but this wasn't a warm sunny day, it was freezing cold, with the temperature still dropping, the falling snow turning to ice as soon as it hit the ground, making the road even more treacherous. It must have taken at least two hours, perhaps more, she thought, for her to have walked as far as she had with still a couple of miles left to walk before she reached the city limits and even then, she still had further to go to where she lived. The sky was heavy and laden with snow. It was still not completely light and all the signs were there was more snow yet to fall. With little chance of the weather improving, which only added to her misery, Anna knew she had no other option but to carry on, regardless. With the snow continuing to blind her, and the conditions underfoot becoming worse with each step, she carried on walking, but the day was taking its toll on her; the freezing cold affecting her the most, for it was mind-altering, making her mood swing wildly, backwards and forwards, from optimism to despair and back again as she went over the events of earlier, re-enacting the scene in her head of Paul's mother assaulting her as she'd tried to drag her out of his bed!

Anna couldn't understand the reason for the older woman's attack. It was as though Paul was a naughty schoolboy who'd been caught in some fiendish or depraved act, not an adult perfectly capable of deciding his own affairs. Thankfully, they were only sleeping when his mother had barged into his room, hell-bent on causing trouble. Suddenly, Anna was overwhelmed by her thoughts. Why would a mother treat a beloved son in such a way?

Thinking back to her own childhood, she could only remember the loving relationship she'd enjoyed with her parents. They'd loved her as well as each other with a love so deep she still carried it within her. They'd been childhood sweethearts, in love with each other until the day her mother had died tragically young.

Anna's thoughts flew back to those terrible days, when she'd helped to nurse her mother through the final stages of the illness that would end what had once been a vibrant life.

She remembered how distraught she'd felt, as she'd watched her mother take her last earthly breaths and then, when it was all over, how she'd tried to comfort her grief-stricken father.

She could remember quite clearly the months afterwards, as together they'd tried bravely to rebuild their lives, and what had happened next.

As young as she'd been, Anna knew her father couldn't be expected to live the rest of his life without the love of another woman so it came as no surprise to her when, three years later, he met and married Ruth, a young woman in her late twenties who worked for the same company.

By the time of their marriage, Anna was a teenager and quite happy her father had found a new love, at an age when he no doubt had thought he wouldn't be so lucky. She was looking forward to having another woman in the house, believing her new stepmother would take the place of her own late mother. It was just unfortunate for Anna that Ruth, her new stepmother, wasn't prepared to love Anna in the way she'd envisaged.

Within a few weeks of the wedding, a different side to her new stepmother's true character began to emerge as she started to make Anna's young life a misery, with her bullying and spiteful ways. An altogether different story though, when Anna's father returned home from work, when Ruth would then be all sweetness and loving, with no trace of her unkind ways, or her vicious tongue.

Walking along the country road on that Christmas morning, Anna could still remember how she'd felt, being too young and naïve to understand at the time what was happening and, with no close relatives nearby to confide in, she was unsure how to cope. As young as she was, Anna knew in her heart it was nothing more than jealousy on her stepmother's part. It would have been better if she hadn't been living with them, but there was nowhere else where she could stay. Consequently, she spent many hours alone and lonely in her bedroom, until one day, she plucked up enough courage to broach the subject of her stepmother's bullying ways and spitefulness with her father. Unfortunately for Anna, Ruth got in first, telling her father a pack of lies.

Being besotted with his new bride, her father obviously sided with his young wife, telling Anna she must have done something to upset Ruth and that it was probably her own fault for not liking her; thereby turning the tables and leaving Anna even more bereft and at a loss to know what to do next!

Anna recalled later, in great detail, how her father had even told her Ruth had complained about Anna's own surly behaviour and attitude when he wasn't around to see it for himself, even that Anna was going through what Ruth had termed as being, 'at an awkward age,' when teenage rebellions were to be expected!

That Christmas morning though, feeling thoroughly cold and miserable, all the details of her past life seemed to be magnified as she remembered how difficult she'd found life, knowing it was pointless even to try and pursue the subject, and how saddened she'd been. It was then she'd withdrawn more into herself, staying in her own room, leaving her father and Ruth to themselves; giving them the privacy Ruth so obviously wanted.

From then onwards, Anna felt she'd lost her father's love and trust, and her dislike of her stepmother deepened. It was a hard lesson to learn, especially for one so young, but it was a lesson Anna would never forget, using the experience later in her life to harden her to some of the knocks she would experience, but for now, she had to walk on and as she did so more of her memories came flooding back.

It was a year later before she'd come to realise how naïve and innocent her father had been in his choice of a new wife, having never before experienced being married to a woman with such wily ways such as the ones Ruth possessed. Anna's young heart ached for him as she witnessed the way her stepmother manipulated and abused his good nature; becoming angry on her father's behalf but unable to do or say anything. It was quite by chance, only a few weeks later she found evidence of Ruth's betrayal. Her stepmother had been having, not one, but several love affairs, none of which Anna ever revealed to her father. There was no point! He wouldn't have believed her. He thought his young wife to be a paragon of virtue!

In some ways, just knowing about Ruth's infidelities and her deceit, gave Anna the upper edge in their relationship, Ruth's actions somehow empowering her, giving her the courage to go on living with them. It was her secret weapon; one that perhaps in the future she might find useful.

In the meantime, Anna learnt tolerance and, more important, how to keep out of Ruth's way, spending even more time alone in her room. Her excuse, when questioned by her father, when he finally noticed her absence, was that she needed to concentrate on her schoolwork, knowing she had to get the best results possible in her exams, as they were going to be her escape route from her miserable home life. As young as she was, Anna instinctively knew studying hard would pay dividends later in her life.

It was as she entered her sixteenth year her beloved father suffered a fatal heart attack. Grief-stricken she felt alone and abandoned. Even in the midst of her own grief and misery she felt some degree of compassion towards Ruth, who was still quite a young woman, now saddled with a teenage daughter she didn't like, and who wasn't old enough to support herself financially, tying her down to the role of stepmother, a role she already despised. It therefore came as a complete surprise to Anna, when Ruth made an uneasy truce with her, saying she'd decided they would continue living together, or at least until Anna was qualified and able to earn her own living.

Anna couldn't believe what she was hearing, nor could she believe it when Ruth started to change her attitude towards her. The real truth behind Ruth's change of heart, and her ulterior motive, soon became abundantly clear when she demanded Anna should become their housekeeper, unpaid of course. This suited Anna. She needed somewhere to live and, believing the apartment now belonged only to Ruth, taking on the domestic chores would be the perfect way for her to live rent-free!

It didn't take long before cleaning the flat and cooking their meals became the normal way of life for Anna, an experience she put to good use, knowing it would be an invaluable lesson for when her dream of having her own business one day became a reality.

The day Anna passed her exams with distinction, Ruth was the least surprised of all; neither was she surprised when Anna was offered a free place at the local catering college on a three-year course that would give her the professional qualifications she needed.

It was simply because of Anna's easy-going temperament the two women managed to live amicably together during Anna's college years, with Ruth getting the better deal. She had someone who was not only adept at keeping house, but also one who could cook and serve delicious meals. The benefit for Anna was she had somewhere cheap to live. Even so, she still had a problem, or rather a 'no cash' problem.

Unbeknown to Anna, Ruth had kept the allowance she'd received from her late husband's will to provide for Anna's upkeep until she finished her full-time education for her own use.

Anna wasn't to know her inheritance had been stolen from her by her stepmother until many years later, by which time it was too late for her to do anything other than shrug her shoulders and sigh, knowing she would be unable to get any recompense and therefore, she had no option but to forget the past and get on with her life, letting it become a matter of complete indifference to her, but the future had yet to happen, and this was the present. It was now she was in need of money, to buy personal items, as well as extras for her college course. If none was to be forthcoming from Ruth,

Anna knew she had no alternative she would have to find a part-time job and fund herself.

With her need for an income becoming increasingly urgent, Anna began to look for work she could do in the evenings and at weekends, as well as during her holidays from college.

The first thing she did, was to enrol with an agency, one that found positions for 'catering temps,' starting off by working as a waitress at functions in the city hotels. Unfortunately, because there weren't enough functions at that time to support her needs, she then enrolled at another agency, one specialising in supplying temporary office workers.

This seemed logical to Anna. It was her ambition to have her own catering business one day and, learning how to do simple accounts and run a business seemed to be the sort of job that would suit her perfectly. It was no surprise therefore, when she was offered a holiday job in an office. Being young, intelligent and attractive all helped, of course!

To begin with, she was given the menial tasks the other workers disliked, such as filing, making teas and coffees and occasionally, standing in at break times for the receptionist. Anna didn't care what she did, she was more than prepared to do anything if it would give her experience of the working world and enable her to earn enough money to buy the extras she needed. But her main aim was to pass her college exams and qualify as a cook. After that, she knew she would be able to get a live-in job in a hotel and then she would be able to leave Ruth to fend for herself!

Anna stopped walking for a minute, putting her suitcase down on the snow as she tried to massage some life back into her body, crossing her arms and banging them against her sides, trying to get some warmth into her fingers and hands.

Standing in the eerie silence, with the wind blowing snow into her face, she listened for a while, but there was still no sound of Paul's footsteps following behind.

She picked up her suitcase and continued on her way, remembering the day she'd first met Paul. She'd recently started work as a 'temp' in the general office of the biggest bank in the city, in what she hoped would be her last temporary job as her final exams were looming. Not knowing anyone in the office to have lunch with, she'd walked down the main street to Priory Green, a small oasis of greenery in the city centre, just a short stroll away from the bank. It was a popular meeting place for the young, and the not so young at midday. It was where office workers and shoppers alike sat and ate their alfresco lunches.

Anna had already eaten her packed lunch and was just enjoying the spring day, when she saw a handsome young man walk into the park. Her heart gave a flutter as she watched him walk towards the empty seat next to hers and sit down.

They studiously avoided looking, or acknowledging each other, both too shy to speak, but each aware of the other. They sat in a companionable silence, until the young man finished eating his lunch, throwing the remaining crumbs to the waiting birds, before screwing his lunch wrapper into a ball and tossing it nonchalantly into the litterbin opposite to where they sat.

With his lunch finished, the young man stood up and started to walk away, but not before he'd given Anna, who just happened to look up at the same time, a quick glance. They'd both blushed, their eyes locking for a moment. Anna startled by the intense blue of the young man's eyes, a feature that would haunt her forever, as did her emerald eyes, that had entranced and beguiled him; not realising he'd just met the one person the fates had decided should play a big part in his life.

With Anna watching with interest, he walked out of the park, her heart fluttering in her chest. She continued to sit for a little while longer, deep in thought, wondering about the young man and whether she would ever meet him again?

With her imagination working overtime, she walked back to the bank, daydreaming of what it must be like to have a boyfriend. Especially one as tall, dark and handsome as the young man she'd just met.

From how he was dressed, she thought he had a good job; perhaps he was a junior banker! Or maybe he worked in the bank where she was working? He certainly had the bearing and the figure of a potential manager.

As the city centre was awash with banks and building societies, all taking advantage of the new prosperity happening in the country and particularly in the old city, Anna wondered if he might be one of the many young men who worked there.

She sighed and returned to her desk, wondering if the next time she went to the park she would see him again? As for the young man, he couldn't believe he'd been so stupid as to not speak to the young woman with the captivating green eyes, when he'd the chance. Like Anna, he too wondered whether they would meet again.

Anna's first week in the office raced by! Each day she returned to the park to eat her packed lunch, hoping to meet the handsome young man again but without any success. The following Monday morning she was concentrating on the job she'd been given, when suddenly, another tray of work appeared at her side. She looked up to see who'd placed it there. To her surprise, she found herself staring into the blue eyes of the young man she'd remembered from the previous week. For a moment, she was startled, thinking she must be dreaming, wondering what he was doing in the filing department. Suddenly, he recognised her and smiled and, this time he got it right!

Anna knew, straightaway, he was the young man from the park, how could she not? His eyes and face were imprinted not only on her memory but also in her heart. As for the young man, he'd recognised Anna as soon as he'd seen her, amazed to find her working in the filing department of the bank where he worked. He was shocked at first, but this time, he didn't intend making the same mistake of not getting to know her! Making one of the quickest decisions of his life and, speaking quietly, not wanting her to be singled out by the office gossip sitting just a few feet away, he spoke.

'Would you have lunch with me today?' he asked.

Anna blushed, the colour highlighting the greenness of her eyes, emphasising how attractive she was. Taken aback for a moment, she stammered, 'I have a packed lunch with me!'

As soon as the words were out of her mouth she regretted them. Her reply, even to her own ears, sounded gauche, but the young man wasn't going to be put off. It would take more than a packed lunch to stop him from getting to know her.

He knew her name from the company nametag she wore, as she did his. Mr P Adams, Anna read, memorising it, at the same time wondering what the P stood for but at the same time, knowing if she went out for lunch with him she would soon find out!

The young man smiled at her, his heart thudding in his chest. 'I've brought a packed lunch as well. If you come to the park we can eat together?'

Anna laughed softly, unaware the office gossip had pricked up her ears, But not so Mr P Adams, his antenna was fully switched on and, understanding the workings of the office grapevine regarding gossip he moved just slightly, hiding Anna from view, preventing anyone from hearing the discreet arrangements he made to meet her later outside the main door of the bank, at the time she would be released from her duties!

The rest of the morning flew by, as Anna fumbled with the trays of papers in front of her, unable to concentrate on anything as mundane as filing, willing the hands of the clock to hurry round, impatient for her lunchtime date with Mr P Adams, the young man from the park who'd been in her thoughts for days.

How wonderful, she thought, if he really did turn out to be her 'Prince Charming' after all.

# Chapter 3

It no longer mattered to Anna how cold she was as she continued on her way into the city, or that the bitter wind driving into her was affecting her senses. Every now and again, she would automatically brush away her tears, together with the freezing flakes of snow that mingled with them. All she wanted, was to lie down and let the snow cover her like a blanket, that she might sleep forever, perhaps then, she would forget why she was walking away from the man she loved.

It took all her willpower to put one foot in front of the other and to keep moving, her concentration stretched as she focused on not falling, for the narrow country road was treacherous underfoot, covered as it was with freezing snow. Surely, it couldn't be much longer, she thought, before she reached the city boundary and, if luck were with her, she would find some form of transport to take her home.

Suddenly, through the swirling snow, she caught sight of the end of the lane. At last she'd reached the crossroads where she had to turn right onto the main road. Reaching this point seemed momentous, then suddenly, a great sense of relief flooded through her and, sure enough, out of the gloom, she could make out the vague outlines of the three spires in the distance. Within minutes, as she walked down the main road towards them her spirits lifted. She'd reached the city boundary and was more than happy she'd made it this far without any major mishap, but she was still concerned as there'd been neither sight nor sound of Paul.

Anna sighed and continued on her way, her heart heavy with disappointment, convinced Paul had changed his mind!

On her left, as she walked towards the city centre, were the ruined buildings of an old priory, endowed and built in the thirteenth century, and, on her right, the road bridge that crossed the main railway line. Anna stopped to look over the parapet where she could see the freight yard. Ghostly outlines of goods wagons were all lined up, ready and waiting to be hooked to the steam engines, once the holy day was over.

Minutes later, she was standing outside the Victorian building that housed the station. Peering up at the building she tried to see the clock in its ornate tower, but its face was covered with snow, which left her none the wiser. From the amount of daylight she guessed she must have been walking for about three hours. Suddenly, her spirits rose, knowing she didn't have far to go now before she would be home. She crossed the main road and continued walking until she came to the small park known as Priory Green, a green oasis in the city where she'd first seen Paul and where they'd laughed and fallen in love. Like the rest of the city, this too was covered in a blanket of snow and, as she looked across its murky gloom, she could see the outline of the bench where they used to sit and eat their lunches. For a few heart-stopping moments, her mind played tricks as she imagined them sitting together, then, just as suddenly, the image faded away, leaving her saddened as she wondered if those love-filled days were gone forever. Wistfully, she shook her head, pulling back her aching shoulders, before she carried on walking, her thoughts filled with unanswerable questions.

She was soon walking down the deserted high street; the good citizens of the city no doubt still in bed this Christmas morning.

Even in its unswept condition, the city pavement was easier to walk on than the country lane she'd already travelled and, with her mind full of her thoughts, Anna hurried along as best she could, her feet and hands numb with cold.

Ahead, she could see a bright light shining onto the pavement from a half open door, with someone brushing snow from the pavement into the gutter. At her first glance, she was unable to determine whether it was a man, woman or child, until she got nearer and saw, to her surprise, it was a small woman, dressed in a man's long, dark overcoat that reached down to her ankles wielding the brush.

Anna looked up at the building and at the lights shining from some of its windows, a cheerful and welcome sight on this gloomy day. A decorated sign attached to the building was swinging in the light breeze, proclaiming it to be the Golden Lion, a building Anna had never been into, but knew well as one of the oldest buildings still standing in the city centre. It was one of the last few landmarks in the city to escape from being ravished in the blitzkrieg raids of the last war. As she got nearer, the woman stopped brushing the pavement and looked hard at her.

Anna stopped and looked through the partially open door into what she thought to be one of the most welcoming sights she'd ever seen, and wondered if this was the woman's home? At the same time the woman watched Anna, scrutinizing her carefully, for she could see something was wrong. The evidence was there for all to see, from the pallor of the young woman's face, to the signs of a black eye just starting to appear.

From her own experiences, during the war, the woman could see the young woman was suffering, not only from the effects of the cold, but by shock, no doubt caused by whatever had happened to give her the facial injuries marring her beautiful features. Without stopping to think of the consequences of taking a complete stranger into her home, she took an unresisting Anna and led her into the welcoming warmth of the old building, closing the outer door firmly behind them.

Holding onto her arm, the woman ushered Anna down a brightly lit passageway into what looked like the main room of the building, gently guiding her towards a huge ornate fireplace where a fire was blazing in the hearth.

Anna began to relax, her emotions raw, as she realised at last she'd reached what could be a temporary haven.

Her first impressions were of a cosy room, in spite of its size. It looked welcoming. The next minute, her heightened emotions got the better of her and, unable to halt them, tears of relief welled up in her eyes and started to fall down her cheeks. The woman seeing Anna's tears shepherded her across the room to where two comfortable looking armchairs were positioned, one at either side of the fireplace.

Holding her hands out gingerly towards the fire, Anna immediately began to feel the warmth seeping into her and, with her mind preoccupied with warming herself, she started, nervously startled for a moment, as the woman, now divested of the monstrous overcoat spoke to her in a motherly fashion.

'Let's get you out of those wet clothes, dear?' she said, immediately moving to help Anna take off her woollen overcoat already beginning to steam from the heat of the fire. The kindness in the woman's voice was more than Anna could bear and more tears began to fall, copious amounts of them, once the floodgates had been well and truly opened, simply by the woman's kindness.

Bit by bit, Anna was divested of her sodden outerwear, before being ushered to one of the armchairs. Her shoes, the last items to be removed, joined the woollen hat and scarf in the woman's arms; removed to Anna knew not where. She sniffed and wiped her face with her fingers, accepting, with a weak smile, a soft linen handkerchief taken from the older woman's overall pocket.

As the fire flamed and crackled in the grate, so the woman took a brass poker from its stand and moved the coal around, leaving Anna to take stock of the room.

Feeling safe and secure, and comforted by the warmth of the fire, she struggled to keep her eyes open; the sudden transition from freezing cold to warmth more than her body and senses could stand. With no effort at all, her eyes closed and, overcome by sheer exhaustion, Anna's head dropped onto her chest, as she finally succumbed to sleep, but not before she'd had a premonition she'd just met someone who was destined to play an important part in her future, whatever that might be, instinctively trusting the woman with the twinkling blue eyes.

Waking a little while later and feeling disorientated by the strange surroundings, Anna was unable to remember for a while, where she was, until she saw the small woman standing before her, smiling and holding a metal tray, on which stood a steaming cup of tea and a plate of hot buttered toast, which she placed on a small table at the side of Anna's chair, urging her to eat and drink.

Anna smiled her thanks at the woman, taking in her birdlike appearance. She was tiny: wiry in build, in comparison with herself, for Anna was at least a head taller than her befriender. She appeared to be a woman of an indeterminate age, although the floral work overall suggested her to be in her fifties, and then there was the frizzy grey hair, now released from the scarf she'd been wearing while she'd been brushing the pavement. It stood round the woman's small head like a halo, making her look much older. For a fleeting moment, she reminded Anna of Paul's mother, who must have been of a similar age, but this woman looked like someone who enjoyed life and immediately Anna felt drawn to her.

While she'd been eating and drinking the woman had been busy at the bar, as soon as she saw Anna had finished, she walked across, carrying a small glass full of an amber liquid, which she urged Anna to drink, standing over her until she obeyed.

'I'm Molly,' she said, by way of introduction. 'What's your name, dear?' Patting Anna vigorously on the back as the rum she'd just drunk threatened to choke her. For a moment or two, after her coughing fit had subsided, Anna felt light-headed as the alcohol in the fiery liquid hit its mark and began to soothe and warm her.

'It's Anna,' she said, her composure returning. Molly looked at her in a thoughtful manner.

'Well, dear, whatever were you thinking, traipsing through the streets in such awful weather, today of all days?'

Noting the change in Anna's colour, as the after-effects of the alcohol reached the young woman's face, changing it from its once ashen hue to a faint and an attractive shade of pink. Molly didn't really expect an answer, at least not at the time, for she could see it would be some time before the young woman would be ready to face openly what had happened to send her out that day in such awful conditions and, more than that, to explain to a complete stranger how she'd come by the scratches and bruises Molly could see on the young woman's beautiful face. As for relating her tale of woe to a complete stranger, that might be more than she could bear to contemplate at the moment, but Molly, being blessed with patience, knew her questions would eventually be answered, she just had to wait!

Her priority, at the moment, was to get the young woman warm and, from the look of her, she needed to sleep. Meanwhile, she had the bar to open, so her questions would have to wait until later.

Leaving Anna sitting by the fire, Molly continued to busy herself, clearing away the tray, then, giving the bar a final polish, she headed off to her next chore. Anna sat back in the comfortable chair and relaxed, warmer than she'd been in a long time, starting once more to feel like a human being.

A little while later, Molly came back into the room and looked at the clock over the bar. She'd changed out of her work clothes and was now smartly dressed, ready for when she opened for business. Seeing Anna was recovering, she spoke gently, more to herself than to Anna and certainly not expecting or getting an answer, 'Whatever happened lass?'

Anna couldn't answer, She was still in shock from all that had happened and now, being comforted by Molly's motherly kindness was more than she could bear. She was moved and touched: near to tears that a complete stranger was showing her more concern than she would ever have thought possible. How could she possibly tell this kind woman what had happened? For a few moments, Anna's face betrayed her emotions, showing her humiliation for looking so disreputable, leaving Molly feeling sorry she'd delved into the young woman's private life when it was obvious the girl needed more time to recover from her ordeal, perhaps later, when she'd recovered, she would

53

confide in her and tell her of the problems and trauma she'd suffered, until then, she would let the girl be!

Because it was Christmas Day, Molly was only going to open the bar for a couple of hours and, with the weather bitterly cold with even more snow forecast, she thought it unlikely she would have more than a handful of customers that lunchtime, and mostly those would be her regulars who lived nearby, especially those with no family ties.

Knowing the city was generally quiet if the shops and offices in the city were closed, it was unlikely many people would be out walking through the empty streets, so with no expectations of being rushed off her feet, for once, Molly was grateful.

There weren't many houses left in the city centre, the bombing raids had seen to that, but soon it would be different, once the bombsites had been cleared and the new apartment blocks already planned had been built, then the city would rise again, like the proverbial phoenix, rising from the ashes of a fire and, before long, it would be full of hustle and bustle, just as it had always been over the centuries.

Anna looked on with interest as Molly worked. She wanted a pub, or small hotel of her own one day and now she'd finished her catering course and was qualified, there were no reasons why she shouldn't work towards getting what she wanted. She didn't want a city pub though. She wanted one in the country. An old place, with lots of character and old beams, with a fireplace that burnt huge logs, and where lamplight and the glow from the blazing fire would shine on copper kettles and gleaming brasses, creating a cosy ambience that would entice city dwellers to travel out and eat the wonderful food she would cook for them! Molly's place had a little of what Anna wanted, but it lacked

Anna's essential ingredient, the smell of good food being cooked!

She'd looked round the room as she'd waited for Molly to finish her chores, impressed with what she saw, especially the mahogany bar with its backdrop gilt mirror that had caught her eye as soon as she'd come into the room. It reflected not only the rest of the room, but also the sparkle of the many glasses and bottles that lined the shelves and were mostly filled with coloured water as it was still not possible to get the genuine article.

As she looked around the room at the groups of tables and comfortable chairs, Anna wondered if Molly ran the place on her own, as so far, she'd seen no other person.

Molly finished what she was doing and walked across to where Anna was sitting.

'Opening times are different today,' she'd said. 'My regulars will no doubt be in soon so why don't you come upstairs with me. You can have a hot bath and get out of your damp clothes.'

Pointing to the small case Anna had carried in with her. 'You can freshen up and have a rest, while I see to the customers and then, when I've closed up for the day, we can have Christmas dinner together and listen to the Queen's speech.'

Molly could see Anna was tempted by the offer and smiled, encouraging her. Anna nodded her head and smiled in return. 'Yes, I would like to freshen up, it would be good to feel like a human being again.'

For the first time, Molly heard her laugh. 'You will feel so much better and you can go home afterwards, if you want to!'

Leading the way up the wide and curving staircase, Molly asked whereabouts in the city she lived. On hearing it was on the far side, she merely nodded her head, making no comment. After they'd eaten she would ask more but, for the time being, it was enough the young woman should be fed and warmed.

The staircase ended at a wide landing. With Anna following close behind, Molly walked to the first door and stopped. 'This is my sitting room,' she said, before continuing along the corridor to the room next-door where again she stopped, 'and this is my bedroom.' Then, pointing to the other doors on the opposite side, she said, 'and those are guest bedrooms, although there are none here at the moment. The room at the very end is the bathroom.'

With Anna still following, Molly went along to this room and opened the door onto the largest bathroom Anna had ever seen. In the middle of the room sat an enormous old roll top bath, resting on huge clawed feet. There were several cupboards and chests of drawers lining two of the walls and, next to the bath sat a round table, its top full of bottles, all filled, as Anna found out later, with perfumed bath salts. Another table, near to hand, was loaded with a pile of soft white towels. It was all very splendid and luxurious and, once Molly was sure Anna had everything she could possibly want, she left her to enjoy a bath, as well as the view of the three spires from the window, returning to the bar and her expected customers.

It didn't take long before Anna was lying back in hot scented water, admiring her surroundings and marvelling at how her luck had suddenly changed from her living a terrible nightmare at Paul's house, to finding herself in such a place as the Golden Lion with Molly, and all in the space of a few hours.

From her sanctuary in the bathroom, Anna could hear sounds of activity coming from the bar downstairs; for the second time that day she envied Molly. How wonderful, she thought, to own such a beautiful old building, full of history where she was able to live and work in such surroundings. She could well understand why Molly looked so content.

Once her cold and aching body had been soaked and warmed, and her hair washed and towelled dry, Anna made her way back to the sitting room Molly had first shown her. It was comfortably furnished and, like in the room downstairs, a fire blazed in the hearth.

It took very little time for Anna to fall asleep in one of the big chairs, not stirring, even when Molly came into the room and placed a woollen shawl across her shoulders. It was the smell of cooking a couple of hours later that finally woke her.

Opening a door in the corner of the room, Anna tracked the delicious aroma to a small kitchenette, where vegetables, already prepared, had been laid out on the worktop waiting to be cooked. It would be her gift to Molly, she decided, to have the dinner ready for when she closed the bar and, quite soon, everything was under control.

Downstairs, Molly was surprised at how she'd managed to close the bar on time, shooing the last stragglers out to the sounds of their Christmas wishes, quite sure as it was still snowing that Anna wouldn't be going home that night.

It took only a short time for her to finish cleaning the bar and, once satisfied all was how it should be, she dampened the fire and, after locking all the doors, went up the stairs.

She could smell the dinner cooking as soon as she reached the landing and, as she entered her sitting room, she gave a cry of delight, for she could see Anna had been busy.

She'd placed a small gate-leg table she'd found propped up against the wall behind the sofa in front of the fire, and covered it with a white damask tablecloth she'd found in one of the drawers of the large dresser that filled the opposite wall, along with matching napkins. The silver cutlery she'd used for the place settings she'd also found in the dresser; the table centrepiece, a silver candlestick with a white candle, she'd taken from off the mantelpiece and, as soon as she'd heard Molly coming up the stairs she'd lit the candle; to complete the ambience, she'd switched on another small lamp in the corner of the room and suddenly, the room looked festive and inviting.

Anna had found her way around Molly's small but perfectly functional kitchenette with ease, especially as Molly had prepared most of the meal earlier, therefore there was little for her to do, except oversee the final cooking, which she did to perfection. The roasted goose looked wonderful, as it sat on one of Molly's old blue and white willow pattern platters waiting to be carved, surrounded by a dish of stuffing and crisp roast potatoes, with a gravy boat half-full of homemade gravy and a dish containing a melody of vegetables, all beautifully cooked and presented, it was, beyond a doubt, a Christmas feast; followed by Molly's homemade mince pies Anna had found in a tin and had warmed in the oven, to be served with a dish of thick cream from out of the small cold box. She'd even prepared a tray of coffee for while they sat and listened to the radio, as Her Majesty the Queen, gave her annual speech to the nation.

Anna always remembered memorable and celebratory meals and that Christmas dinner was no exception, it was the first meal she ate with Molly, her newfound friend and saviour and one she would never forget. As the two women sat in front of the fire and listened to the radio, so the snow continued to fall, leaving Anna to wonder what had happened to make Paul change his mind and not follow her as he'd promised.

Looking at the grandfather clock ticking away in the corner of the room, she saw it was past five o'clock, and knew she should make her way home. She started to gather her clothes from where Molly had put them to dry, until Molly, realising what Anna had in mind, stopped her, just as she was about to pick up her still wet shoes.

'What are you doing?' she asked.

'I must be going,' Anna said. 'It's getting late and time I was on my way. I'm sure I must have outstayed my welcome as it is.'

Molly was having none of it. She certainly wasn't having Anna going out on such a night, especially this night of all nights.

'You can spend the night here,' Molly said. 'I've plenty of spare bedrooms and we can think about you going home tomorrow. In the meantime, you can tell me what happened today that drove you out in such awful weather.'

Molly never did believe in beating about the bush, believing it better to say what had to be said, aware Anna might be in need of some impartial advice and, who better than herself to give it, knowing she would admirably fill the role of counsellor, a prerequisite qualification for any pub landlady!

Knowing she was cornered and that Molly was right; it would indeed be stupid for her to venture out again, Anna gave in and sat down.

With Molly sitting in her special chair beside the fire and Anna sitting comfortable on the sofa, her long legs tucked under her, she began telling Molly everything that had happened to her at Paul's house, everything that is, except for the part where they'd made love. That, Anna decided, was her business and no one else's.

She then told Molly how Paul's mother had suddenly and spitefully attacked her for being in his bed! At this Molly made no comment, for she could see the attack must have been vicious from the evidence on Anna's face; her black eye already looking quite a sight. Molly knew she wouldn't have liked to experience such an event. As for Anna, being young and vulnerable, it must have been quite a traumatic time.

Once she'd unburdened herself, Anna felt relieved and, with her story told and urged on by Molly, she knew she should try to contact Paul, to find out what had happened to prevent him following her and whether he still loved her and wanted to marry her.

Molly went to prepare a bed, after showing Anna where the telephone was situated, leaving her to speak to her young man in private. Some minutes later, as she returned to the sitting room, she couldn't help but overhear the last part of Anna's conversation and, from how she was speaking; she could tell it hadn't been to Paul!

'What did he have to say?' she asked, as Anna replaced the receiver on its cradle.

'Nothing,' said Anna, a catch in her voice as she tried to restrain herself from weeping. 'I didn't speak to him. It was his mother who answered. She said he didn't want anything more to do with me!'

At this point her face crumpled and her tears started to fall, this time unchecked. Seeing and hearing her in such despair was all too much for Molly. In her motherly fashion, she took hold of Anna and held her close, consoling her as one would a child, but how do you console someone whose heart is broken?

'Try again in the morning,' was all she could say. 'Maybe he will have changed his mind. He said he loved you, so you must believe him. People don't just fall out of love as quickly as that, unless of course he wasn't really in love with you in the first place.'

This last part Molly more or less said to herself, because Anna was already so full of misery and desolate beyond belief she didn't need any more fuel being added to her grief.

For a while, Anna thought her life was not worth living until suddenly, out of sheer exhaustion, her tears stopped and her natural optimism surfaced. With her emotions partly under control, she wiped her eyes and blew her nose on her already tear-sodden handkerchief and then, holding a hand to her head, in a dramatic gesture, exactly as Vivien Leigh playing the role of Scarlet O'Hara had done in the film 'Gone with the Wind' and, much to Molly's amusement, she said, 'tomorrow's another day,' the words Scarlet had used when Rhet Butler had heartlessly discarded her.

Molly smiled, relieved as she saw Anna was making an effort to control her emotions and that her sense of humour was returning.

'Well, that definitely solves one problem,' Molly said, smiling at her young friend.

Anna looked puzzled for a moment.

'You're going to stay here with me, at least for the next few days. You said yourself there's no reason for you to go back home yet, so you can keep me company and you'll be nearer to your young man. You can get in touch with him again in the morning.'

It was, of course, the most sensible thing to do and, after thinking over Molly's suggestion for a while, Anna finally agreed, but only on the proviso Molly would let her help with the running of the hotel. Now she had her qualifications, it would give her some valuable experience for when she found a place of her own!

Later that evening, as they talked some more, Molly found out from Anna all about the course she'd recently finished and the exams she'd taken and passed. She also spoke of her wish to get a live-in job at a top hotel, which would enable her to leave her hated stepmother, not thinking at the time the Golden Lion might be the answer to her problems!

Molly could see for herself how bright and intelligent Anna was, an asset surely, she thought, to any business and, with a sudden flash of inspiration, she solved not only Anna's problem of her future career, but her own for expanding her business as well. Tonight though wasn't the time to speak of such ideas already forming in her grizzled head. She would sleep on them and then, when Anna had settled down to living with her, perhaps then they would discuss them, and decide together on what course of action they should take. Molly, of course, realised there was also Anna's young man to be considered and, not for the first time, she wondered whether he would, or would not, fit into the equation.

Meeting Anna, and having her in the hotel, brought back fond memories to Molly of her marriage to her late husband, the adored Paddy. If they'd been lucky enough to have a child, it would be about the same age as Anna was now and at that thought Molly had sighed. She would have liked a daughter like Anna, it was the only regret she'd had in her otherwise happy marriage. Both hers, and Paddy's families, had had lots of children and they'd loved them all, but unfortunately, having their own children just didn't happen.

Anna was in no doubt Molly had poured her heart and soul into the Golden Lion over the years, but she had yet to know of the ideas for improving it already fermenting in her head. Her latest idea would be just one part of her 'grand plan' for making the Golden Lion into one of the best small hotels in the city, but more of that later.

The Golden Lion had always been a special place in the city, changing its image many times over the years, as the wants and needs of those who stayed there demanded.

Its current name, the Golden Lion came into being barely two hundred years ago, its original name lost in the mists of time.

Unfortunately, there are no records of what it would have been like in those days when it had merely been a simple rough-hewn stone building, a resting place for pilgrims as they travelled across the Warwickshire countryside, on their way to the many and various religious shrines and monasteries throughout the neighbouring counties.

From the thirteenth century to the nineteenth, it had been an overnight stopping place for travellers and merchants; until a rich merchant had bought it and what had once been a humble resting place suddenly became the forerunner of what it is today.

It's the 1950s now and life in the country is different, and the Golden Lion has changed. Until the last war had started, it had been a proper hotel, providing accommodation for a different generation of people, but now its main function had changed, it no longer relies on overnight guests, it's become a place in the city for friends and colleagues, wishing to spend their lunchtimes and evenings eating Molly's snacks as they talked and drank. But mostly, it's become a welcoming place for those who live nearby and are in need of companionship and home comforts.

Molly was suddenly excited by her thoughts and what she might be able to achieve with Anna's help. She could hardly contain her feelings, or even believe her luck, but it all depended on whether Anna would be able to solve her boyfriend problem, before she could make any definite plans for their future, or put her 'grand plan' into action.

The two women quickly settled into their new life together over what was left of the Christmas holiday and then the New Year after Molly had told Anna of her plans for the hotel. She was delighted when Anna became as enthusiastic, agreeing to be part of her plans. They then spent hours when the hotel was closed, discussing the changes that would have to be made if Molly went ahead. She wanted to provide full meals at midday, as well as the bar snacks that were served at the moment and then later, if there were a demand, they would start to serve evening meals! It was all very ambitious, but in Anna's eyes quite doable! Molly's only concern was the type of food they should serve, and this is where Anna came to the rescue.

Being young and modern in her outlook, Anna's contribution of devising simple menus, using the best quality food available, was the main factor in Molly deciding she was on the right track. Anna was adamant. Beautifully cooked food, served at a price affordable by the up-and-coming younger generation, would be sure to draw the customers in and, after sampling some of the meals Anna had suggested and then cooked, Molly knew she'd been truly blessed the day Anna had walked out of Paul's life and into hers.

By now, Anna's black eye and bruises were beginning to fade. To start with, they'd been the cause of some consternation with the regular customers, but the simple explanation she'd fallen in the snow seemed to suffice and now, wearing a high necked jumper, one that covered the tell-tale scratches and bruises on her arms and body, she'd recovered, at least outwardly, from her ordeal and, as her natural charm and cheerfulness returned, she began to enchant the customers and one in particular.

From Christmas Day onwards, Anna tried, on a daily basis, to contact Paul, writing and telephoning but to no avail. Each time she rang, his mother answered and told her exactly the same as she'd first told her: Paul didn't want to speak to her as he no longer loved her, and he certainly didn't want to marry her!

This rejection was the only depressing part of Anna's life as she settled easily into living and working with Molly, especially knowing she no longer had to live with her hated stepmother ever again. That alone should have made her happy, but of course it didn't, it was Paul she wanted.

As she needed to retrieve her clothes and her personal bits and pieces from the flat, she said as much to Molly, not thinking she would be able to help, but Molly could see for herself Anna needed more clothes and, knowing it would be difficult for her to carry her belongings on the city transport, she arranged for Gordy, one of her regular customers, and the first to have met Anna, to drive her to the other side of the city and help with the carrying.

Molly had known Gordy since she'd first arrived in the city, when he and his wife had been a young couple, and they'd become good friends. Gordy was now in his late thirties and sadly a widower, his wife having died some years before in childbirth.

Anna liked him the first time she saw him in the bar. He was an attractive man. Funny and yet charming whenever she saw him. He didn't engage her in cheeky banter, unlike some of the other regulars. But sometimes, as she worked, she would notice him watching her with unconcealed interest that at times she found a little disconcerting.

Unknown to Anna, Gordy had fallen in love with her, a situation he didn't know quite how to solve, believing he stood no chance with the lovely young woman who'd stolen his heart.

After the loss of his wife, he'd taken to spending most of his evenings alone in his little house, which was just a short walk away from the hotel, until Molly managed to persuade him to come and sit in the bar in the evenings and enjoy the company. Ever since then, he'd taken to drinking and chatting with the other regular customers who, like him, were alone and lonely and living in the flats and bed-sits in the city centre and, like him, also looked to the Golden Lion to provide them with company and warmth. It was for these people and their circumstances Molly's plans for the hotel were pivotal and all because she wanted to provide them with more substantial and affordable meals other than the bar snacks she already served.

At the beginning of the New Year, Molly asked Gordy one evening if he would drive Anna across the city to fetch her belongings. Of course he agreed, with some alacrity, and the following Saturday he drove her across the city to finalise her life with Ruth.

Gordy could sense the tenseness in Anna as they got nearer to her old home, noting the stony expression she wore on her normally happy face. At that time, he knew nothing of any consequence of her past life, except she had a boyfriend.

He parked his car at the rear entrance to the flats and then, taking Anna's small hands in his large ones, he gave a gentle squeeze of encouragement, trying in his own gruff way to raise her spirits and comfort her, but without much success.

'The quicker we pack your stuff, the sooner we can get back to Molly's,' he said 'so, chin up, lass and smile!'

Anna said nothing, and she certainly didn't feel like smiling, she felt more like weeping but that morning she'd promised herself she was not going to weep any more for what had once been. She was going to do what she had to do and put the past behind her and get on with her new life with Molly. A life, which didn't include a stepmother who, for years, had tried to make her young life a misery.

With Gordy at her heels, and both of them laden down with an old suitcase and some empty boxes Molly had given them to use, Anna used her key and opened the door to her old home. She didn't expect Ruth to be at home, so it was a big surprise to both her, and Ruth, when Anna walked into the lounge and found her stepmother in a state of undress, wearing nothing but a diaphanous dressing gown that left nothing to the imagination, lying in a compromising position on the sofa with a man equally as undressed!

Ruth, and her man friend, who Anna assumed would soon become a resident, jumped up in surprise as she entered the room. Anna no longer cared what Ruth did with her personal life, nor was she interested.

Ignoring the fact Ruth and her man friend were practically naked, Anna introduced Gordy, standing behind her, and staring open-mouthed at the scene, merely as a friend of her new employer, which indeed he was. She then told Ruth of her intention to take all her possessions back to where she was now living as she had a live-in position in a hotel, with the prospect of a good job in the future.

Ruth looked a little bit sheepish and then embarrassed. First by Anna seeing her in a state of undress with a half-naked man. As for Anna's news, she appeared to be pleased. At least now she would be able to live her life as she wanted, without a stepdaughter to cramp her style.

As Gordy began to take the boxes Anna had quickly packed out to the car, Ruth's expression quickly turned to one of relief, happy at last the masquerade of being a stepmother was over.

To Anna's surprise, as she went to go out of the door with the last of the boxes, Ruth stopped her and put her arms around her, hugging her as she wished her well.

'Keep in touch,' was all she said when Anna gave her the address of the Golden Lion, mainly in case Paul tried to contact her; purposely making no mention of him, or the problems she'd faced over Christmas, for she knew how spiteful Ruth could be and how she would relish any chance to cause her more grief in any way she could.

Gordy was thankful the event hadn't proved to be quite as daunting as he'd been expecting, from the little Molly had told him. Neither did he make any comment as he drove Anna back to the city centre, leaving her to sit quietly next to him, contemplating her past life, with time to think about what lay ahead for her in the future.

Gordy was definitely smitten with Anna. His thoughts were constantly on her, with his feelings growing deeper each time he saw her. All he wanted was to play a big part in her new life, whether she had a boyfriend or not.

He'd even stayed away from the hotel for a few nights, when he'd first realised he was in love with her. The poor man too embarrassed his feelings might be obvious. But after four depressing evenings spent alone and lonely in his little house, with just his own company, Gordy couldn't stand it any longer. Returning the following evening to the hotel he took his rightful place at the end of the bar, which is where he continued to sit and watch the young woman he'd fallen in love with as she went about her business.

Anna at the time was completely unaware of the torment she was causing him by her very presence. Because he was much older, and believing the age difference too great, Gordy truly believed he stood no chance, but not as far as Molly was concerned!

Being an astute lady and his dearest friend, she didn't consider him to be too old at all. In fact she'd been viewing him in a speculative way over the past week or so, believing him to be a most suitable suitor for her young protégé. In her opinion, Gordy might indeed prove to be just the sort of husband Anna needed and, with this in mind, whenever she caught his eye, she would give him a small smile of encouragement.

And so it was that Gordy continued to watch and lust after Anna each evening, waiting to catch her eye as she went into the storeroom, basking in the warmth of her smile, until one evening, when he'd caught Molly watching him more intently than usual, a sudden rush of colour had travelled from under his shirt collar to his face.

For a brief moment, the normally composed and laid-back Gordy was covered in confusion and embarrassment. Molly smiled at his discomfort, an enigmatic smile on her face that left the poor man even more confused than ever.

Anna had yet to know just how deeply Gordy had fallen in love with her, or how his love would sustain her in the future.

In the meantime, what about Paul? What had become of him? Anna had yet to find out why the young man she'd fallen in love with hadn't contacted her. What, if anything, had happened preventing him from speaking to her? Why, she wondered, didn't he have the courage to tell her, face-to-face, he didn't love her or want her anymore? It was a conundrum that would soon be solved, but not in the way Anna expected!

# Chapter 4

It's time now we returned to see how Paul fared after he'd left his home on that fateful Christmas Day!

He left the house intending to find Anna and hadn't walked very far, before a car driving down the lane, its driver blinded momentarily by a swirling mass of snow only saw Paul at the last minute. Without thinking of the consequences of his actions, the driver slammed on the brakes in a desperate effort to miss him but it was too late. Predictably, he lost all control of the car as it skidded on a layer of freezing snow.

The car swerved. In seconds it had crashed into Paul, hurling him up into the air as if he were no more than a rag doll, knocking him unconscious. Seconds later, Paul landed on top of the car's bonnet, unaware of what happened, or even of what was about to follow as he was carried along, until he was catapulted up into the air, landing in the ditch as the car suddenly hit a patch of ice and overturned, thankfully, before it hit an old oak tree that had been standing at the edge of the field for at least two hundred years and was as solid as any piece of old iron.

An eerie silence followed, broken only by the sound of the wheels spinning in the light breeze that had sprung up, and the whisper of snow as it covered the scene, while Paul's broken body lay in the snow-filled ditch for a couple of hours, partly buried by the upended vehicle.

No one saw or heard the accident so it wasn't until later that morning an elderly resident, walking his dog, saw the upended car, like a ghostly statue in the ditch. Seeing the car lights still flickering, he went to investigate. This good 'Samaritan' had no idea how long it had been since the car had crashed because its tyre marks were obliterated by the snowstorm raging earlier.

It was a stroke of luck for Paul the snow had stopped falling just before the old man's dog had demanded a walk, regardless of the weather. Once the old man had seen the upended vehicle, he gingerly slithered down into the ditch to see if anyone was trapped inside. From his first glances he could see the driver had been fatally injured and there was nothing he could do to help. He was about to clamber out when he saw, what at first he took to be a broken branch until it moved. He stooped to check, to his dismay he saw it was an arm, fortunately still attached to the body. He felt for a pulse and, finding one that was very weak, he scrambled out. Calling his dog to come to heel, he walked as quickly as he could back to his house, where he alerted the emergency services of the accident, and that there was an injured man to deal with as well. Once he'd done all he could, he returned to the scene of the accident with a blanket and knelt beside Paul until he was finally removed and taken to hospital a couple of hours later, with the old man convinced the young man wouldn't survive.

Paul was lucky. He lay in the intensive care unit of the local hospital for several days, his injuries so complex and severe he'd been placed in a medical coma. His right leg was broken in two places, as well as a break in his right arm, but it was his internal injuries giving the doctors and nurses the most cause for concern during those first few days.

Thankfully, being young and fit, the prognosis was better than anyone had expected.

He was, of course, completely unaware of the drama his broken body had caused and, over the next few days, the extensive bruising to most of his body became apparent, caused no doubt from being tossed in the air, then crashing down onto the bonnet of the car before it too overturned and covered him. That was probably the most fortunate part for Paul, if you can call any part of being in an accident fortunate, because the car covering him saved him from hypothermia. His second piece of luck was being found by the old man and his dog. Without them, he definitely would not have survived at all.

It was several days before he regained consciousness, helped by drugs that ensured he was relatively pain free. Being in a coma had been a blessing in other ways as well, as it gave the doctors and nursing staff time to address some of his injuries, without causing him even more pain, drugged as he was. When Paul finally did open his eyes and was able to speak, it was obvious he had no idea what had happened, even failing to recognise his mother and father when they walked up to his bedside. As for Anna, he had no knowledge of her at all. His parents, for reasons only known to themselves, had decided not to mention her, yet another sign of his mother's disapproval at finding them sleeping in the same bed!

Once he had recovered sufficiently to be taken off the danger list, he was moved to a side room. From then on he made good physical progress, considering the extent of his injuries. His memory appeared to have returned, except he still made no mention of Anna, it was as though she'd never existed, she'd been erased completely from his mind, to the delight of his parents, and to his mother in particular, who never made any mention of her, or of what had happened that Christmas Day to have sent him out in the snow storm.

As the days progressed, so he was able to talk for longer periods of time, his first question to his parents was always predictable. Why had he been out on such a morning, and in such awful weather? And where had he been going? It was as though he was trying to clear his confused brain of a fog that covered some parts.

Each time he questioned them, his mother gave him the same glib answer, telling him he'd been going to visit a sick neighbour with a Christmas gift; a plausible enough explanation and one that seemed to satisfy him for the time being, although deep down he still felt something momentous had happened to him that day, something other than his accident his parents weren't telling him about, something important they were hiding, but what it was he had no idea.

His doctors told him it was quite possible his memory might well suddenly return. Until then, he had to be satisfied with what those closest to him told him of his past life and, as his parents never spoke of Anna, he was left in the dark, in more ways than one.

It was several weeks before he was able to return home and when he did eventually leave hospital, it was on crutches, with many more weeks of intensive treatment and physiotherapy ahead to look forward to, before he'd sufficiently recovered enough to return to work.

It was during his convalescence with his parents that Paul entered into a period of deep depression. He couldn't tell anyone how he felt, only it was as though he'd fallen into a black hole; a hole so deep he couldn't climb out, leaving him with a terrible sense of loss he couldn't explain. His doctors prescribed medication and therapy, which helped to some extent in calming him down and, over the next few weeks, he had to accept the professionals opinion it was the trauma of the accident responsible for his depression, although he really wasn't convinced, still sure in his own mind something had happened on Christmas Day that was far too important for him to forget!

Winter came and went and it wasn't until spring was nearly over he felt his depression begin to lift. He began to feel as though he was beginning a new era to his life and suddenly he had an urge to escape from his old one. Desperately wanting a change of scene the thought of going back to his old job in the bank held no pleasure for him, he not only needed to change his surroundings, he needed to change his job as well.

Paul felt stifled, especially living with his parents, as kind as they were to him, he just had to get away and restart his life somewhere different, away from the over protectiveness of his mother, who smothered him with her care and attention, all of which Paul found stultifying. It was especially the house which, after being incarcerated in for several weeks, he found it to be claustrophobic to such an extent he didn't know which was worse, losing his memory or living with his parents.

One day, to Paul's surprise, after he'd been at home for a few weeks and was finally on the mend, he had an unexpected visitor, one that was to offer him an escape from his present life, in exactly the way he'd envisaged. It was his line manager, offering him a new position at the bank.

It had been proposed by senior management that, when he was fully recovered, he should move to a small branch in the Cotswolds and take over from the current manager, who was due to retire in the near future. Then, after a spell there, he would automatically be on the list for promotions to other hierarchies of the banking world. Without hesitating, Paul accepted the offer; delighted his wish for a change to his working life had been granted.

Knowing he had a new job waiting for him, gave him the impetus he needed to exercise more and work harder at his rehabilitation. Finally, a little over six months since his accident, he was pronounced fit and able to return to work except his memory of Anna had yet to return.

Once back at work, Paul went to visit the branch of the bank he was to join. He knew he needed to find somewhere to live as well, as it was too far for a daily commute to and from his parents' house, also, he wanted to be independent and live in the community he was to serve and so, on a beautiful day in July, he drove out to the Cotswolds for a recce.

The bank was situated on the High Street of the small market town of Coombe Norton and Paul could see, right away the small town was a busy place, set right in the middle of farming country, surrounded by beautiful villages and countryside; an area fast becoming a magnet for the growing tourist industry, as well as a desirable place to live.

The buildings in the town, and the surrounding villages, were all centuries old and mostly built in the locally quarried honey-coloured stone. He was impressed with what he saw, immediately falling in love with the town, fervently hoping he would like his new job equally as much!

Once he'd made himself known to the incumbent manager, soon to retire, and had drunk a 'welcome to the bank coffee', Paul made his way up the high street to find an estate agents office doing business in the town.

Paul thought it might be a good idea if he saw some of the local properties while he was there. Within a short period of time, he was armed with details of several properties in his price range.

With the agent beside him, Paul started on a walking tour of the town, intending at first, just to look at some of the properties available. A couple of the details were of old cottages, just a short walk from the agent's office and, within minutes, Paul and the agent were standing in the kitchen of the first property.

The agent had taken him to this property first, as it had just come onto the market, being sure it would suit the needs Paul had listed.

It was an ideal property. Paul and the agent wandered through the rooms, admiring all the renovations that had been carried out and the quality of the materials used. The renovation was outstanding and very impressive even to Paul's untutored eyes. But he didn't intend to buy the first property he saw, so with the agent still at his side, the rest of the day he spent looking at every other property the agent thought matched Paul's wants and needs, even one in the next village, a newly built bungalow that to Paul had nothing special to recommend it.

Nothing he saw impressed him as much as the first cottage and, being ruled by his heart, he put in an offer, which the estate agent then put to the current owners.

Knowing the cottage had been renovated to such a high degree Paul knew he would have nothing to do except to move in and he would still be able to afford to furnish it. And that would be easy to do as well. The town was blessed with antique shops and in a nearby town there was an auctioneer's office, where monthly sales were held and where he knew he would be able to find special pieces of furniture and other objects that would enhance his new home. For a few minutes, he could see himself settled into this small Cotswold town and then, just as suddenly, the dark cloud of his depression lifted and he could see a fuzzy picture of a young woman standing at his side. He shook his head and the picture vanished. The image he was sure came from his past, or was it just an impression of what he needed to complete his new life?

Suddenly, he felt different, determined to find someone who fitted the image and then he knew he would have a perfect life!

The next morning the estate agent telephoned to confirm the cottage was indeed his and at that moment Paul knew his life, as far as he was concerned, was going to change, and for the better. He was on the road to success. At last he was on the first step to his new life.

Back in the city, working the last week or so at his old job, while waiting for his transfer to take place, Paul walked down to Priory Green, on his first full day back at work since his accident. It was a beautiful day, just made for sitting outside and enjoying an alfresco lunch and yet, as he sat there, he felt something was missing. He couldn't understand why he felt so strange. He knew the small park well enough, he'd eaten his lunch there many times in the past, but why on that day did it feel different? There seemed to be a ghostly shadow sitting next to him, someone he knew, perhaps from the past, but as to who it could have been, was a mystery Paul couldn't solve.

Later that day, Paul asked a colleague, the best place in the city for him to have his leaving dinner and was recommended the Golden Lion, as being the best hotel in the city these days for food. She'd gone there, she'd said, on Valentine's Day, with her boyfriend, who'd proposed to her during the meal. She'd laughed as she'd told Paul the story, adding that the landlady's daughter had also received a marriage proposal that same evening.

The dining room, she told him, was intimate and cosy and, in her opinion, Paul and his friends would enjoy the ambience of the newly renovated dining room, as well as the delicious food. And so it came to pass, a couple of weeks later, Paul's farewell dinner at the Golden Lion took place and, indeed, as predicted it was well worth the visit.

A table covered in a snowy white damask tablecloth was waiting for them when they arrived, it was set with beautiful silverware gleaming in the subdued lamplight, with sparkling crystal wine glasses and a small posy of fresh flowers in a silver holder in the middle of the table, finishing off the setting. It looked inviting, as did the superb menu, which was served on fine bone china plates.

Paul wasn't disappointed in any way. The Golden Lion was all he'd been led to believe and his final evening with his colleagues proved to be a big success.

Unfortunately, there'd been no sign of Anna that evening to jog his memory, as she'd taken a rare evening off to go to the theatre with Gordy and, of course, Molly didn't know Paul, so was unaware Anna's erstwhile lover had been in the hotel that evening.

As Anna and Gordy were by then married, they didn't return to the hotel either, leaving Paul never to see the love of his life, or to know how close he'd been to solving the mystery of his memory loss.

The cottage in Coombe Norton was to become his within the next few weeks, but in the meantime, he needed to find temporary accommodation in the town to tide him over. Once again he was in luck! One of the staff at the bank recommended a bed and breakfast house in the town, where the landlady offered to cook him an evening meal for the next few weeks. Paul accepted, knowing it meant he could spend his evenings getting to know the locals and, within a couple of weeks, he'd become a regular and popular customer at several of the local pubs.

Once he'd settled into the cottage Paul found he liked living in the Cotswolds and also his job at the bank, it was just right for his present needs and it didn't take long before he was implementing the changes head office demanded.

Along with the other employees, he was more than happy to do whatever had to be done. It was just the challenge he needed and, once the changes had been completed Paul's new life gave him everything he wanted.

Having better things to do with his spare time other than housework and washing, he employed a local lady to keep house for him; as for the garden, a small courtyard, he managed to do as it only took a hard broom with the occasional wash down to spruce it up.

His parents visited him almost as soon as he moved in, bringing him the extra bits and pieces he'd left behind. As much as he loved them, he was more than happy to be living on his own, although his mother was none too pleased he was no longer under her control and making no attempt at hiding her feelings.

She missed being in control of him, especially since his accident where, for a while, he'd been helpless and dependent on her; he'd eaten the food she cooked and wore the clothes she selected, but now he'd escaped her possessiveness. At last, he felt he'd gained his freedom and his life was taking on a new phase, one he dearly hoped would bring him the personal happiness he desperately craved, but only time will solve that problem!

Settled at last and doing a job he enjoyed, as well as living in a cottage he loved, Paul suddenly realised one thing was missing. A proper grown-up social life, something other than the local pub and the darts team and so he set about altering and transforming his personal life even more.

He decided he needed to meet as many young women as he could, without getting a reputation for being a philanderer or lothario. If he was to meet the right sort of young woman, he knew he had to spread himself around the area and, so it happened, girl friends came and went with great regularity, much to the amusement of his colleagues who, behind his back, referred to him as Romeo Adams!

In spite of his searching, Paul failed to find the one lady he knew was out there waiting for him. Suddenly, he became the most eligible bachelor in and around Coombe Norton, always available to make up the numbers at dinner parties, where hostesses would warn the single women attending, not to expect him to take any of them seriously. Don't bother setting your sights on Paul Adams they would be told, he's waiting for his elusive Miss Right to come along.

# Chapter 5

January passed quickly for Anna. Busy with her new life working at the Golden Lion. As for Molly, she couldn't have been happier, now one of her dreams had come true.

With Anna's help, the hotel was running smoothly and, with the first of the alterations to the kitchen due to be completed within the next few days, they would soon start serving meals at lunchtimes. Molly, having discussed the alterations with Anna, knowing she would know exactly the equipment they would need, had delegated the design of the kitchen to her, which Anna had done with meticulous care. She was now looking forward to cooking the new menus she'd spent hours devising and, with the new kitchen nearly ready, it was time for Molly to take on extra staff to help.

At last the first part of Molly's expansion plan for the hotel was about to come to fruition and, once the new dining room (made out of one of the spare rooms, found behind a false wall, when she'd first taken over the hotel) had been decorated and furnished, and the workmen had departed, the word was soon out in the city the Golden Lion would shortly be serving meals at lunchtimes. A day or two later, a new sign outside the main door, and the smell of delicious cooking, was soon enticing customers into the hotel.

This was to become the pattern of life for Molly and Anna for the next decade, with the new dining room full most lunchtimes and the two of them working flat out. To Molly's great delight, the Golden Lion was at last providing a service long overdue in the city, but even more was yet to come!

Molly enjoyed Anna's company, never noticing, or even aware of the age gap between them. As for Anna, she loved Molly. She saw her more as a surrogate mother than her employer, treating her as such and confiding in her, as Molly did in return.

Once Anna had decided to stay, Molly insisted she should have one of the large guest bedrooms, just along the corridor and opposite her own.

It was a spacious room, with two large windows giving a wonderful view of the city skyline, as well as down to the courtyard below.

Molly told her this room was in the oldest part of the building and had once been in use, as accommodation by the merchants, while the packhorses and mules would have been housed in the stables. (Also in Molly's eyes for transforming.) This was an area Anna had also looked at and knew would be a good place to use as an outdoors eating and drinking area: she smiled to herself, poor Molly was still reeling from the expense incurred by the new dining room and kitchen and here she was, making plans for yet another scheme, she laughed; Molly didn't know what she'd taken on when she'd offered her a home and a job! But of course, Molly did know, and she loved every minute of her new life. It gave her a buzz of excitement and something to look forward to when she woke each morning, a feeling she'd missed since losing Paddy. She had badly needed something exciting to fill the void his death had left in her heart, and with Anna now living and working with her, at last she'd found what she'd been looking for.

Settled happily into her new home and working with Molly; with her own room and her treasured possessions about her, for the first time since her mother had died, Anna felt truly at home, only heartsick at losing Paul. What irked her was that she hadn't been able to see him; for him to tell her, face-to-face, that he no longer loved or wanted her but, being young and resilient, she knew given time she would recover; it was closure she needed. She just wanted to draw a line under their affair and move on. But would that ever be possible she wondered, especially when she woke every day with such a pain in her heart.

Early one morning, a couple of days after the grand opening of the new kitchen, Molly heard Anna's bedroom door opening and the sound of her footsteps as she ran to the bathroom at the far end of the corridor. Moments later, as she was about to go downstairs to get the hotel ready for the day, she could still hear Anna in the bathroom. Thinking she might be ill, Molly went towards the door, just as it opened and Anna came out. Molly caught hold of her arm, afraid for a moment Anna would fall into a faint, she looked so pale.

'Whatever's the matter, love?' Molly asked, reaching out to help her back to her room.

'It's nothing,' Anna said, shakily. 'I must have eaten something that disagreed with me.'

'Rest for a while then, and if you don't feel better soon we'll call the doctor,' Molly said, full of concern as she helped Anna to lie down on the bed.

Leaving her to rest and wondering what could possibly be wrong, Molly left the room. It must have been an hour before Anna appeared. She seemed to have recovered from whatever had upset her, although to Molly, she still looked far from her normal self, with her emerald eyes even more brilliant against the pallor of her skin, startling at first glance, but Molly said nothing. There was just something about her she wasn't quite happy with, but for the moment it would have to wait.

As the new dining room was uppermost in Molly's mind that morning, she busied herself in the bar before opening time, amazed at the first day's success, trying to comprehend how much the hotel had changed since Anna had appeared a few weeks earlier, looking bruised, bedraggled in shock and freezing cold. And here she was now, relying on her for the dining room's success, even believing her to be her lucky talisman!

That particular morning though, Molly spent quite a lot of her time watching as Anna went about her duties. There was something about the young girl's demeanour that disturbed her and, for a while, she couldn't quite put her finger on what it was, but of one thing she was sure, Anna certainly wasn't suffering from food poisoning!

Lunchtime service that day flew by, with customers obviously enjoying the choice of meals on the menu. By the time it came round to closing the bar for the afternoon, Molly was exhausted. She could see Anna, as young as she was, looked equally as tired and, once the front door was locked, they both retired upstairs to Molly's lounge to rest.

Anna fell asleep on Molly's comfy old sofa almost straightaway, stray curls falling in tendrils across her cheeks that were damp from the busy lunchtime, making her look young and vulnerable: almost childlike.

As she watched Anna sleeping, Molly's heart ached for the disappointment the young woman had faced in losing her boyfriend, but then she smiled, his loss was her gain and, sorry to say, Anna's misfortune her blessing, knowing the day Anna had walked down the high street and stopped outside the Golden Lion she'd become exactly what Molly had always wanted, a loving daughter. Molly knew she could ask for no more, her cup was full and runneth over!

It was some time before Anna woke, to see Molly sitting opposite, watching her closely, and leaving her feeling strangely uncomfortable. While she'd been asleep, Molly had been doing some thinking and now that Anna was awake she decided it was time she asked her some serious questions.

'What's the matter, love?' she asked. 'You don't look your normal self these days, there's something wrong, isn't there? Can't you tell me what it is?'

Molly tried to judge Anna's reaction, noting how her complexion had become even paler than normal and, for a moment, she wondered if the child was going to faint, for she could see beads of perspiration forming on her upper lip and forehead; her mouth suddenly had a pinched look, as though at any minute she was about to throw up.

'You don't look very well and I can tell it isn't food poisoning, so, what's the problem?'

Anna looked at Molly for several moments before answering. 'I've felt sick these past few days, that's all. I'm sure it's nothing to worry about!'

Molly wasn't so sure. Perhaps there wasn't anything to worry about, but for the time being she kept her thoughts to herself, knowing full well Anna wasn't going to give her an explanation to her questions at the moment, not until she was ready to confide in her so, until then, she could do no more than be patient and wait.

The temperature in the city had started to rise steadily, day-by-day, until suddenly the freezing temperatures of Christmas and the New Year were a thing of the past. Molly thought there could be an early spring and sure enough, within a week, the city was transformed. The streets began to fill with people, all eager to breathe in the fresh air as they searched the shops in the arcades in the old city for bargains. With the city centre busy once more, the Golden Lion was full at lunchtimes, but Molly's concerns were still for Anna, who continued to look dreadfully pale and wan. It was about time, Molly thought, for her to intervene and take control of the situation.

Since Christmas, the two women had often talked late into the night after the bar had closed, first they'd talked about Anna's life and her childhood, and then the effect losing her mother had had on her, and then her life, before she'd met Paul, and how they'd fallen in love and he'd become the love of her life. And then it came to Christmas Day!

Anna had told her about the fight she'd had with Paul's mother and, knowing all this, Molly could well understand how devastated Anna had been when Paul hadn't followed her, as he'd said he would, and neither could she understand the reason why he hadn't replied to any of her phone calls and especially to Anna's heart-breaking questions of why?

Molly could see Anna was pining for her young man, but there was nothing she could do, except encourage her to keep trying to contact him, and this Anna did, several times in fact. She'd even contacted the bank where he worked, drawing a blank when a receptionist told her Paul was no longer there, which puzzled her, as his career meant everything to him. (Not knowing the girl was new, or that Paul was not at his office at the time, but more of that later.) After a while, Molly had the feeling Paul would no longer be featuring in the young girl's life and, as the days passed, even Anna seemed to realise he would no longer be playing a major role in her future and she'd best forget him, and his worthless vow that he loved her and wanted to marry her.

Gradually, as the days went by, Anna spoke less and less of Paul and, in Molly's opinion, the sooner she met someone else, the sooner she would forget her erstwhile lover and, as far as she was concerned, the sooner the better!

Molly knew it would be hard for Anna to accept this, even though perhaps in her heart she knew she must make a new life for herself. Maybe she would find another man who would love her, and want to share his life with her but at that time, it was too much in the lap of the gods!

A day or so later, after hearing Anna making, what had become her daily morning rush to the bathroom, Molly didn't hesitate to say what was on her mind.

She waited until they were both ready to go downstairs and then she confronted her.

'It's no good pretending you don't know what the matter is,' Molly said. 'I think you know, just don't want to accept it.'

Taken aback and surprised by her outburst and her words, Anna said, 'What do you mean?'

Molly continued with what she had to say, ignoring Anna's interruption. 'You're sick every morning.' Anna tried to have her say, but Molly gave her no chance and carried on. 'It's no good denying it. I hear you running to the bathroom every morning and then spewing your heart up. You do know...' she continued, emphasising her words, 'morning sickness is usually the first sign a woman is pregnant?'

'Pregnant?' Anna gasped, going pale, shocked at Molly's words. 'What do you mean, pregnant? I'm not pregnant!'

'Believe me, Anna! I think you're pregnant!'

Molly waited for a few moments, for she could see Anna was shocked and unable to speak, incapable even of understanding her pronouncement.

'First thing tomorrow morning,' Molly continued in a serious tone, 'you're going to the doctor's and he can either confirm or deny it!'

Anna looked stunned. For some time she was unable to speak and then, in a quiet voice, that Molly had to strain to hear, she said. 'You could well be right. Paul and I did make love, but I didn't think I would get pregnant, not the first time!'

Anna sat in a daze, finally acknowledging to herself, that if Molly was right, she could indeed be having Paul's baby.

Molly chuckled. Relieved at last that there wasn't anything seriously wrong. 'You won't be the first woman, nor the last, the doctor will see, who will tell him the same story! It sometimes only needs a man and woman to make love once, you know, to make a baby!

Anna was by now looking incredulously at Molly, her beautiful green eyes brimming with tears. 'Oh, Molly,' she cried. 'What am I going to do?' Her tears trickling down her cheeks as she put her arms around Molly and sobbed into her shoulder.

'What have I done? Why did I go into Paul's room that night?' A question no one could answer, not even the fates, for they were too busy making their own plans for her future!

Ever practical, and with a mothering instinct she didn't know she possessed on full alert, Molly took charge of the situation, drying Anna's tears.

'Don't you worry,' she said, hugging her tight. 'We'll sort it all out. But you're going to do absolutely nothing until we know for sure you really are having a baby. Now, you're to rest while I phone the doctor and make an appointment for you to see him in the morning.'

The next morning, still pale and a little shaky, Anna made her way to the doctors, where, after his examination, he confirmed the result to be as Molly had so rightly suspected, she was definitely pregnant, with the expected baby due to be born in September.

Molly had guessed the news before Anna had even removed her coat. She could tell, just by looking at her that the doctor had confirmed her suspicions, the glow on Anna's face, merely adding to the confirmation. It was a very different Anna now, who stood before her, from the one of the previous day who'd been upset at the prospect of being an unmarried mother but, within minutes, she was dancing around the room with Molly in her excitement. 'Guess what?' she'd said, laughing, 'I'm going to be a mother! Her eyes shining when she sat down excited by her news and puffed out by her exertions, trying to get her breaths back. 'What do you think of that, Molly?'

For a little while Molly made no reply, giving Anna time to calm down a little before she answered. 'I'm very happy for you. But what are you going to do about Paul?' Her voice was full of concern as she took hold of Anna's hands. 'He ought to be told about the baby you know.'

'What do you mean, what am I going to do about Paul? Why should he know?' she countered.

'I've tried to get in touch with him, you know I have, but from the answers I've had from his parents and his office, it's obvious he's avoiding me. As far as I can tell he doesn't want anything to do with me. Anyway, I've decided to have the baby and bring it up on my own!'

This last remark was said with such defiance that Molly was momentarily taken aback. This was a new and alien side to Anna, one Molly hadn't seen before, but it showed how, in times of trouble, she would cope.

Molly could see the girl was made of stern stuff, something she really approved of, but she had to have her say.

'It's a hard enough job bringing up children when they have two parents,' she said, thinking back to her own mother and the struggles she'd had to rear her children, without a husband on hand to help. 'On your own, it's a terrible struggle.'

Anna looked sad and woebegone at Molly's words and, for a moment or two, the excitement and happiness vanished from her face. It was at this point Molly knew what she had to say.

'But, with me to help you, you won't be on your own, will you?' she said, smiling broadly. 'Anyway, you must try again to get in touch with Paul and give him the news and then, if he doesn't want to be your husband and a father to your baby, we'll just have to find you someone else who will!'

Anna gasped, not quite believing what she'd just heard. 'What you're telling me is, if Paul doesn't want me, or our baby, I'm then to find someone else to be my husband and a father to my baby?'

'Yes,' said Molly, 'and why not? There are plenty of young men who would love to have you as their wife.' Thinking, of course, of one man in particular.

Anna interrupted her. 'Wife maybe, but being a father to another man's child, that might be asking too much of most men! What man, in his right mind, would want to marry me, especially when I'm already pregnant?'

Over the next few days, Molly and Anna discussed how best to contact Paul, as she encouraged her to try again. After several more phone calls, all ending in the same result, they both realised it was to no avail and finally, Anna accepted her fate; she was going to be a single mother, not something she was looking forward to, but she knew, with Molly's help, she would manage, somehow.

After her last effort to speak to Paul had ended in failure and, after talking it over with Molly, she decided to ask Gordy if he would drive her across the city to Paul's house, in a last-minute attempt to have a face- to- face meeting with him. This was going to be her final try at contacting him. Thankfully, Gordy agreed. There had been no hesitation, not for a single moment. Unaware Anna was expecting Paul's baby, he'd simply thought the young couple had merely had a tiff Anna wanted to resolve.

A couple of days later, Gordy drove her out to the village where Paul lived, staying in the car while she walked up the path to the front door, where she knocked on the door. Several minutes went by, before a middle-aged woman opened the door.

Gordy couldn't hear what was being said, but from the look on Anna's face he could tell it wasn't good news. With his heart aching for her, she returned to the car and sat next to him without making any comment.

Gordy drove away, at a loss to know what to say, glancing across at her as she sat huddled down in the seat, obviously full of despair, her tears falling unchecked as she quietly sobbed.

Gordy wanted nothing more than to take her in his arms and comfort and kiss her, anything to make life better for her, but he knew he couldn't do that.

It was obvious the news she'd received was not what she'd wanted to hear, but what exactly had been said, he didn't know. As he drove towards the city centre, Anna finally stopped crying and asked him, in a tremulous voice, to pull over and stop the car.

Gordy did as she asked, switching off the engine and then waited for her to speak. Anna sighed and wiped her eyes and then, with her head held high, she sat for some time in silence, staring out of the window, until she'd regained her composure. Once in control of her emotions, she turned, ever so slightly towards him, her head on one side, looking at him as if for inspiration.

'Well?' Gordy said, gently, when she appeared to have a problem saying what was on her mind. 'What's wrong? You can tell me, you know?'

In a hushed voice, Anna told him what had happened, not just the conversation she'd had with Paul's mother on the doorstep of his home, but the whole story, right down to her being pregnant with Paul's child.

Gordy sat and listened, his heart aching for her, understanding her grief at the loss of the man she thought had loved her. He wanted to reach out and take her in his arms and kiss her, to comfort her and tell her he loved her, but he held back, knowing it wasn't the time to act like a lover, he was just a friend. Nevertheless, it took an enormous amount of will power not to follow his first instinct! His thoughts flew back to when his wife had told him she was expecting their child and how euphoric he'd felt, but this wasn't the time, or place, to speak of his past.

'What did she say when you told her you were pregnant?'

'I didn't tell her that. I wanted to speak to Paul first, but she was adamant he didn't want to speak to me! I felt just like the wanton woman and the slut she'd called me...'

Anna hesitated for a moment, not enjoying the words she'd heard Paul's mother use when she'd shouted at his father to get her out of the house, but she was right, she was a slut and a whore, that's why she was pregnant!

Taking hold of her cold hands, Gordy caressed them, trying to bring some warmth into them. He wanted to comfort her, but at the same time he was afraid he might say the wrong thing. He wanted to tell her she wasn't a wanton woman, or a slut, she was beautiful, and that he loved her and that Paul was a fool if he didn't want her, but again he couldn't, it wasn't the right time. Anyway, it wasn't his place to tell Anna she might have had a lucky escape! Marrying Paul, just because she was having his child, perhaps that wouldn't be the right thing for her to do either!

Anna could sense Gordy's care, but she didn't need any platitudes and flowery speeches, all she needed at the moment was his presence; that was all the comfort she needed, for now.

They sat for some time, both lost in their own thoughts, until Gordy realised how cold she'd become and took them back to the warmth and comfort of the Golden Lion, where Molly took control, doing her best to comfort Anna over the next few days, knowing it would take time for the young girl's heartache to heal, but in the meantime, she had an idea, one she hadn't given much thought to before, but now she gave it her full attention and, by the end of the day, she'd formulated a plan in her mind that she believed might solve all of Anna's problems!

As Valentine's Day was due to be celebrated the following week, Molly suggested they should plan a special menu for the lunchtime, and one for the evening meal as well. Anna had agreed. She'd already thought of doing something special herself for the day and had drawn up several ideas for romantic menus, designed especially for lovers. When Molly saw Anna's ideas on paper later that day, she loved them and, after giving her approval, she put the next part of her plan for Anna's future into action.

Unbeknown to Anna, Molly had already spoken to Gordy and, together, they'd discussed how best they could help her through this traumatic period in her life. Molly had even confided her thoughts that Anna needed a husband, one who would be prepared to take on another man's child, at which Gordy had merely nodded and said nothing, as he had ideas of his own, that, for the time being, he was keeping to himself.

Valentine's Day duly arrived: during the course of the morning, while they were having a coffee break, the front doorbell rang. Molly motioned Anna to finish her drink and went to see who was there. Within minutes, she'd returned, carrying an enormous bouquet of flowers that she promptly placed into Anna's arms.

Anna was stunned, her face a picture of sheer disbelief. 'Who are these from?' she asked, but Molly was already busy looking for vases.

'Why don't you open the card and look?' she said, wondering if they could possibly be from Paul. Perhaps he'd changed his mind and wanted to marry Anna after all.

With shaking fingers, Anna pulled out a card from the envelope that had been tucked down amongst the flowers and opened it. For a moment or two, she said nothing, then, smiling, she passed the card across to Molly.

'From Gordy!' Molly exclaimed, reading the card and handing it back. 'Fancy that!' she said, laughing. 'He's a dark horse that man. I knew he liked you. I've been watching him for some time as he sits looking at you and you know what, you could do worse than accept his proposal!'

Anna was not only dumbfounded, but also totally shocked. She looked at the card for a second time and read it again.

It said, quite simply, *"Marry me, Anna. Please be my Valentine. I will love you and your baby always."* And was simply signed *"Your devoted Gordy."*

Anna left Molly to arrange the flowers as she sat thinking of Gordy. She knew she liked him, not only that, she trusted him. She knew instinctively, if she did marry him, he would cherish her and her baby, but would it be fair to marry him when she didn't love him, especially knowing she still loved Paul?

Molly watched Anna struggling with her thoughts and emotions as they carried on setting the dining room ready for the lunchtime service. Unable to resist having her say, Molly told her what she already knew. Paul had rejected her, his mother had confirmed this, and here was Gordy, a good and honest man, prepared to look after her, so what was there to think about?

Anna knew Molly was right, she didn't need Paul, and neither did she need his mother, whose jealous attitude towards her would always be a big problem should they marry, but was it fair to Gordy to accept his proposal, especially knowing she didn't love him, she liked him as a person but would that be enough if he became her husband?

Anna continued her mental agonising for the rest of the morning as she went about her work, debating as to what she should do, until after lunch had been served and the dining room cleared and made ready for the special evening meal, by which time, she'd more or less made her decision.

She dressed with extra care that evening; she wasn't doing the cooking as Molly had arranged for one of the new kitchen assistants to finish the dishes already prepared and, wearing one of her prettiest dresses, with an extra dab of her favourite perfume behind her ears, Anna went downstairs.

She would be serving in the bar this evening and was looking forward to Gordy making his appearance, which he finally did, about an hour later than his normal time, just as Anna was beginning to wonder if he would be coming at all.

For a few moments, she'd thought he might have changed his mind and was regretting his proposal? But she had no need to worry on that score, as Gordy couldn't wait to hear her reply!

Dressed, in what she thought must be his best clothes, and looking much younger than his thirty-six years and, with his dark hair slicked back, Gordy smiled at her, just as she'd finished pulling a pint destined for another customer, but he made no attempt to speak to her while she was working, for he could see the hotel was busy that evening, with Molly and Anna both rushed off their feet. The dining room was full of couples, sitting at tables for two, all enjoying the delicious romantic menu chosen by Anna and heartily approved of by Molly. (Tomato soup, made from the love apples of the gods; roast Spring Lamb, served with fresh vegetables and, for the finale, heart-shaped crème caramels, served with fresh cream.)

After ordering a drink at the bar from Molly, and giving her a sly wink as he did so, Gordy sat on his favourite stool at the end of the bar and watched as the two women worked, until Molly finally called "Time Please!" and the bar had cleared, the last of the night's customer's (mostly locals by then) drifting out into the night air.

Molly closed and locked the front door, leaving Anna to finish tidying the bar, before placing the washed bar towels over the beer pumps after she'd finished, in what was a nightly ritual.

Anna had hardly had any time during the evening to speak to Gordy and then only to thank him for the flowers.

To his disappointment, she made no mention of his proposal, leaving him to wonder, for the umpteenth time, whether or not he was a fool and was about to go home rejected by the young woman he'd fallen in love with.

Anna, of course, had been fully aware that he'd sat all night with his eyes fixed on her, watching her every move. Now, as she finished clearing the glasses away from the bar, she could feel a sense of anticipation building inside her, a sensation she was experiencing for the first time: a feeling of excitement she could hardly contain, knowing something momentous was about to happen, as she was about to make a decision that would set her on a new course in her life, one she hadn't previously bargained for, but which, instinctively, she knew would be right for her and her baby.

Discreet as ever, Molly, left them alone in the bar, making her way upstairs to her lounge, wanting desperately to witness the happenings downstairs but knowing she must stay out of the way, at least for the time being!

Anna hadn't given any indication as to what answer she was going to give Gordy, leaving Molly nervous on his behalf, hoping if the answer was to be "No thank you." Anna would let him down gently. So, she was more than surprised when only a few minutes later, she heard him shouting her name from the bottom of the stairs, calling for her to come back down.

Molly ran down the stairs as fast as she could, her earlier tiredness forgotten as she walked into the lounge to see Anna and Gordy dancing around the room wreathed in smiles.

Molly watched them, they looked so right in each other's arms. She could see Anna had already given Gordy her reply and, from where she stood, he looked ecstatic. It was time, she thought, to re-open the bar and open the champagne!

Gordy brought a flushed and breathless Anna to a standstill and, with a theatrical flourish, he produced from out of his jacket pocket, a small, dark blue leather box. With a slight bow, he presented it to Anna. For a moment or two she held it in her hands, sensually caressing it as Molly and Gordy looked on, holding their breaths in anticipation. Anna looked at Molly and smiled, before turning her attention to Gordy, her gaze steady as she looked into his eyes. For a brief moment, a cloud of indecision covered her eyes and then, just as suddenly it was gone, replaced by a different look, as if she'd finally made a life-defining decision. She opened the box, gasping at what she saw nestling inside. On a white silk lining sat a sumptuous engagement ring: it was exquisite: in front of her lay a square-cut emerald, surrounded by diamonds set on a golden band. Anna was completely overwhelmed, unable to do or say anything. She'd never seen anything quite so beautiful. Gordy leant forward and, taking the ring out of the box, and without any fuss, he gently took hold of Anna's hand and placed the ring reverently on her finger, lifting her hand to his mouth and gallantly kissing it!

It was this one romantic action that satisfied Anna she'd made the right decision in deciding to say, "yes" to his proposal. Not just because he was a romantic man, but because of all the other attributes she wanted in a husband. She sensed he would cherish her, but finally, deep down, she knew he would be the perfect father for her baby.

Their wedding was planned for April, when Anna would be twenty-one years of age and there would be no need for her to ask permission from her stepmother to marry.

She wasn't keen on the idea of having her stepmother at the wedding either, and when Molly and Gordy knew how

Ruth had treated her in her younger days they could well understand why! As luck would have it, Anna was saved from making such a decision by a letter arriving from Ruth telling her she was about to re-marry and intended living in Spain with her Spanish man friend. Anna wasn't particularly surprised, just pleased that Ruth would no longer be a part of her life but later, in a quiet moment, she wrote and told her stepmother she was also going to be married, omitting to tell her she was marrying Gordy and not Paul, or that she was pregnant with her ex-boyfriend's baby! It was, as far as Anna was concerned unimportant for Ruth to know that Paul was no longer a part of her life.

A day or two after they'd become engaged, Gordy took Anna to visit his small terraced house, where he'd planned on them living once they were married, if she approved. With a sense of apprehension, he showed her around but, to his delight, she liked the little house. The decoration might be a little old fashioned to her mind, but at the same time it was charming. There were treasured photographs and ornaments in all the rooms, placed in such a way Anna could see Gordy's late wife had tried to make it into a comfortable home.

As they climbed the stairs to view the upstairs rooms, Gordy surprised her by telling her that she was to have the largest bedroom, which he would decorate in any way she wanted and he would have the second, much smaller room, leaving the smallest room as a nursery for the baby. Anna said nothing, merely nodding her head, remaining silent as she looked into cupboards in an effort to cover her confusion. Was Gordy telling her he didn't want to sleep with her after they were married? Was it not going to be a proper marriage? For the first time, she felt confused and a little afraid she was about to make a big mistake.

Being a sensitive man, Gordy noticed the change in her mood as they continued looking round the house and at the small garden outside the back door. In his gruff way, he tried to reassure her the house would be her domain, and anything she wanted to change would be fine by him, she only had to say the word and it would be done!

While Anna and Molly organised the wedding, Gordy secretly planned the honeymoon, only telling Anna they would be going away for a few days after the wedding but as to where, he refused to divulge, not even to Molly.

Their wedding day arrived: a beautiful spring day, with not a cloud in the blue sky that, coincidentally, was the same colour as Molly's outfit.

Anna wore an ankle length Empire-style dress, made of silk chiffon, in a delicate shade of cream. It was a very expensive gift from Molly, who was delighted to be playing the role of mother of the bride. Thankfully, the style and cut of the dress covered all signs of Anna's impending motherhood and, with fresh spring flowers interweaved in her glorious auburn hair that she wore loose that day and, carrying a small matching bouquet, she looked absolutely stunning.

Gordy, was also looking resplendent, in a new charcoal-grey suit with a white shirt and a silver-grey tie; he looked youthful and handsome as he stood at Anna's side as they spoke their responses to the registrar and where, after making their solemn vows, they became husband and wife.

Gordy was utterly overwhelmed by the occasion, and especially so, when Anna made her responses in a clear voice, without faltering or hesitating. In his eyes she'd never looked more beautiful. He thought he would burst with pride as he placed a plain gold wedding ring on his adored new wife's finger, gallantly, once again, lifting her hand to his lips and kissing it, his eyes shining with his love.

In a strange way, Anna was happier that day than she'd ever thought would be possible. It had been a simple wedding. She might not be in love with her new husband, but she knew she liked him!

She even thought he would be a true and faithful husband, but would he ever be her lover? Not if separate bedrooms were to be believed! Then she thought of Paul, the man who should have been standing in front of the registrar with her, saying vows of enduring love and fidelity. He should have been her husband for he was the man she loved and wanted, but that part of her life was over now. She had to forget him and think only of Gordy, the man who was now not only her husband, but whom, in five months' time, would become the father of her baby!

After a simple buffet reception at the Golden Lion with Molly, and some of the regular customers, who'd become their friends, the cake was cut and toasts drunk before the happy couple left in Gordy's car for a short honeymoon in the Cotswolds.

It was an area Gordy loved and thought Anna would too, and where he'd booked them into a small hotel in the enchanting village of Broadway.

To Anna's disappointment, the bedroom had two luxurious single four-poster beds! Single beds for honeymooners! She couldn't believe it!

Each evening, Gordy would make himself scarce, while Anna prepared herself for bed, disappointed that he obviously didn't want to sleep with her, but Gordy hadn't reckoned on Anna's determination to change the status quo if they were to have a happy marriage, unaware she would soon alter that state of affairs when they returned home. He knew she didn't love him, even though he loved her and wanted her. He lusted after her so much his loins ached with his longing to possess her, wanting nothing more each evening than to remove her clothes, piece by piece until she was naked, then to kiss and caress her and finally to make love to her. His thoughts became more than he could bear, until finally, each night, he had to pleasure himself before he fell into an exhausted sleep, wanting only to have Anna in his arms.

Gordy knew he'd made the right decision in marrying Anna, his only doubt, had he been fair? She needed a lover as well as a husband to love and cherish her and, after spending three nights of having to pleasure himself, whilst sleeping in the same room, he too decided things would have to change. Like Anna, by the time they returned to their little house, he was determined to set about altering the status quo, and as soon as possible! Until then, he could only use his imagination as to what it would be like to undress her and kiss every part of her fragrant body. What he didn't know was that Anna was also nightly experiencing strange dreams, but in her case it was her hormones that were responsible as they raced around her body. Her dreams were all sexually explicit, which was surprising, for someone with no experience in lovemaking, so erotic were her dreams that she could have sworn they were real; so exciting and orgasmic, they'd left her even more determined, when she awoke each morning, to get her new husband into her bed, just as soon as she possibly could!

# Chapter 6

Anna quickly came to know that Gordy was exactly the sort of man she needed as a husband, even though only a few weeks earlier it had been Paul she'd been in love with and had wanted to marry. It was Molly who finally convinced her Paul didn't love her, if he had, why hadn't he come after her? What she needed to do (or so Molly told her) was to marry someone else. (It being a stigma in those days for a baby to be born illegitimate.) That special someone, she said, should be Gordy! And so it came about Anna did exactly as Molly had suggested and married him, believing she would have a good marriage and, putting all her thoughts of Paul and her love for him behind her, she made her vows to love, honour and obey Gordy, fully intending to do exactly that.

Having made, what was in Anna's eyes a momentous decision, it had been a big disappointment to go away on what was supposedly her honeymoon (where she had thought Gordy would at least make his claim on her body) only to find he had no sexual interest in her at all! What, she asked herself, had she done wrong? Had she made a big mistake? What was worse? Being a single expectant mother and having to endure the sneers and snide comments about her husbandless state, or married, but in a loveless relationship with a man who was obviously impotent? To say the least, Anna was confused. Perhaps Gordy was under the impression she intended treating him as second best? But Anna wasn't like that. She knew he deserved better, especially as he'd taken her on knowing she was in love with another man! For them to be happy, Anna knew she had to convince him that she was prepared to put him first and, having a physical relationship with him would surely prove she was prepared to forget Paul? All she had to do was to get Gordy into her bed, and then seduce him with her charms! As he slept in his own room, with apparently no desire to share hers, that was going to be difficult. It was going to take some ingenuity on her part to manoeuvre him into her bed, but Anna wasn't the sort of woman likely to give in before she'd even tried!

Gordy might not have made any sexual demands on her while they were on their honeymoon, leaving her to believe either he wasn't capable, or didn't want her physically, but we know nothing could have been further from the truth. He was as sexually frustrated as she was! Unfortunately, in her enhanced and emotional pregnant state, coupled with his lack of sexual attention, Anna was beginning to feel unattractive and unwanted! This, of course, wasn't what Gordy had in mind at all. He'd simply decided to give her time to adjust to being married and living with him. After all, she was so much younger and, as far as he could tell, she was inexperienced in the ways of men! He was attentive in other ways though, putting his arms around her thickening waist as he dropped a kiss onto her head, afraid to get too close, in case he lost control of his emotions!

All this made Anna feel even more frustrated, as the first stirrings of the love she was beginning to feel for him increased every day. She needed the intimacy of his lovemaking to prove his commitment to her as a husband, not an uncommon thought in new brides. Something had to happen soon, or their marriage would be over before it had even begun!

It was a couple of weeks later and nearly five months into her pregnancy when she felt the first really strong movements of the baby moving in her womb. A few days later, a momentous day, she felt its very first kick. It was this activity that made her even more determined to get Gordy into her bed and herself into his arms!

Of course at that time, Anna didn't know Gordy had fallen in love with her the first time he'd seen her, when she'd been at her most vulnerable. He'd been intrigued as to how she got the black eye and the bruises (signs of her being in a fight) and not for a single minute had he believed Molly's explanation that Anna had slipped and fallen on the ice! Because, even by then, he'd already started to worship her from a distance but, thinking he was too old for her, and therefore stood little chance of asking her out, let alone marrying her, he'd kept his feelings to himself, until the opportunity came to do both. And he certainly hadn't hesitated then.

Asking Anna to marry him, and not caring a jot whether she loved him or not, had been a high spot in his life. All Gordy wanted was for her to say "yes" and then he would woo and court her, instinctively knowing that forcing himself on her wouldn't work. He wanted to make her feel loved, before he made love to her, at least that was his plan, but the fates and Anna had other plans!

Gordy had gone along quite happily with Anna's plans for the house; doing most of the work himself, as he put her ideas into practice, even approving her modern ideas.

What he appreciated most of all though, was the respect she'd shown in keeping his late wife's treasures on show, placing the ornaments and paintings tastefully around the newly decorated rooms. It was these small things that enchanted him, as well as the concern she showed when he was late home and tired after a long day at work, when she would massage his feet for him. Then, the care she took of their home, but most of all, it was her delight in her pregnancy and the coming baby.

Gordy knew he was a lucky man; he didn't need anyone to tell him so and, for a while, he'd felt sorry for Paul, for missing out on his chance to have Anna in his life and, as far as he was concerned, what was Paul's loss was definitely his gain, a thought that even Anna and Molly shared.

While he'd been decorating the house, Anna had been sorting through his late wife's treasures; it was then she'd become curious about his previous marriage, wondering what sort of person his wife had been. Gordy had never talked about her, until that day, when Anna plucked up courage and asked him to tell her about the woman he'd been married to. Looking at some of his old photographs, it was obvious she'd been beautiful. No wonder he'd been heartbroken at her death and the loss of their stillborn baby daughter, but what was she like as a person? Anna listened intently that particular evening, as she'd shared the comfortable couch with him, looking at the old album she'd unearthed earlier, both shedding a few tears as he told her how Emma had died giving birth. He'd not only lost his beloved wife, but the child they'd both desperately wanted. It was a double blow from which he'd thought he would never recover, until Anna came into his life, not that he told her that!

There was nothing Anna could say that wouldn't seem trite, but Gordy sensed she'd been affected by his story. It was his revelation into his past that had decided her that what Gordy needed was to become a proper husband again. As far as she was concerned, their marriage wasn't going to be based on them having a brother/sister relationship it had to be a proper marriage, with them united as one.

If only she'd known the agonies Gordy experienced each night, or the lustful thoughts he had, as he imagined her getting ready for bed. It was his nightly fantasy, to be slowly removing her clothes, item by item! Then he would kiss her silken skin, fondling and caressing every inch of her luscious body from top to bottom and everywhere in between, before he finally made love to her. He even fantasized as to the manner in which he would do that! He would run his hands over her, touching her in such a way that by the time he was ready to penetrate her she would be at fever pitch with her desire for him. Poor Gordy, we can now understand why he was slowly becoming a physical wreck from his sexual frustration!

Later that same evening, after she'd had her bath and was preparing for bed, Anna felt a sudden twinge as the baby moved inside her womb. Perhaps, she thought, this was the way to get Gordy into her room?

So far, he'd been scrupulous in keeping to his own room, never making any attempt to enter hers, but not for much longer!

Anna lay down on the bed wearing nothing more than the silk dressing gown Molly had bought her. Suddenly, she felt the baby move again, much stronger movements this time. She cried out and Gordy, who was in the next room, also getting ready for bed and undressed down to his underwear, heard her calling. Sure that something must be wrong, he rushed headlong into her room, concern and panic showing on his face, until he saw her sitting up on the bed, smiling at him, propped up against the padded headboard with her pillows piled high behind her.

'What's the matter, sweetheart?' he asked, unable to believe his eyes as he saw her lying on the bed, her dressing gown open, revealing her naked body. Nonplussed for a few moments, he tried to avert his eyes from wandering over her body; from her breasts, down to her swollen belly and the mound of soft reddish-gold hair that lay between her parted legs and then back to her breasts, where her nipples were standing proud, surrounded by their rosy auroras. She was lying in such a provocative pose it made his loins ache even more; his desire so great he could feel his erection standing proud. This was the mental picture he had of her each night, when he'd lain awake in his lonely bed, wishing and hoping, and now it was for real.

'There's no need to worry,' she said. Fully aware of the effect she was having on him. Reluctantly, he moved his eyes from the tantalising sight before him to her glowing face.

'Come and sit here,' she said, her voice soft and seductive, patting the space on the bed next to her, completely unfazed that she was naked, or that she was exposing her body just for his pleasure, outwardly giving the impression she was unconcerned that he was seeing her totally undressed for the first time, when in fact she felt anything but! Was she doing the right thing, she thought, in being so brazen?

Gordy hesitated, for a mere nanosecond, before doing as she asked. Once he was lying beside her, Anna took hold of his hand and placed it on top of her swollen belly. With an edge of awe in her voice, she said, 'Here! Feel this!' At the same time, gently moving his hand across the surface, until suddenly, he too could feel the movements inside her.

Laughing, they lay side by side for some time in this manner, trying to decide whether it was an arm, leg or foot exercising, at the same time wondering whether it was a boy or girl. Anna held his hands and guided them each time she felt a movement, until all thoughts of the baby moving inside her changed, as his caresses started to excite her.

Taking the initiative, she moved closer, snuggling into the curve of his arm, guiding his free hand until it was cupped under her bump: from there she moved it downward, her sexual desire building as his hand skimmed over her pubes. Holding onto his hand, afraid to let him go, even for a moment, at the same time afraid he would find her approach too brazen and leave her bed.

With her heart thumping, Anna moved his hand downwards, encouraging him to stroke and caress her most secret place, already moist, her body longing for him to bring her to orgasm.

By now, Gordy was equally as excited. His desire to make love to her had aroused him to such an extent he was unable to do anything other than let her take the lead, knowing it would take very little encouragement for him to make love to her. Suddenly, he removed his arm from around her and got out of the bed. Anna was distraught! What was happening? And then she understood, he was simply removing his underwear! The next minute, as he turned, so she was faced with his erection. A sight she found to be both tantalising and exciting.

She claimed it and, holding him gently, she guided him back into her bed, at the same time lifting her face, waiting for his kiss. And Gordy didn't disappoint her. He pulled her into his arms, kissing her, enjoying her kisses in return, his tongue searching her mouth, teaching her how to make love.

By now they were both fully aroused, with Anna caressing him in such an intimate way, he thought he might at any moment explode.

Suddenly, he moved away, afraid her caresses would bring him to his climax, something he didn't want to happen yet awhile. For a moment, Anna looked surprised! Unused, as she was, to the ways of men and women enjoying themselves in bed!

Had she embarrassed him with her brazen ways? Had she been too bold and presumptuous? She only knew she didn't want him to stop. She wanted him to make love to her properly: to hold her close: to continue stroking and caressing her.

With Gordy now taking the lead, Anna followed his example, moving her hands over his body, loving the broadness of his shoulders and the feel of the muscles in his back, marvelling at the tautness of them and how they rippled as he moved, and then the way his torso tapered down to his waist. Catching his breath, Gordy held on to his self- control for several minutes, before he straddled her, something he'd wanted to do for a long time. Anna held him close, loving the way his body felt against hers. Like Gordy, she was in heaven. If this was a foretaste of their future together, she knew she'd made the right choice of husband!

As Gordy explored every nook and cranny of Anna's body, so she explored his, running her hands down to the roundness of his buttocks and, clasping hold of them, she pulled him in even closer, pressing herself against his erection, that was hard against her, kissing him all the while, deep kisses, that left them both breathless and gasping, until they had to come up for air. Between gasps, Anna whispered her one desire, 'Make love to me, Gordy! Make my baby yours!'

It took little or no persuasion for Gordy to comply with her wishes and, with Anna's hands guiding him, they made love for the first time as husband and wife.

Satiated by their lovemaking, they lay together, both sexually satisfied and happy: euphoric even, that they'd finally made love. Gordy looked down at Anna's naked body with unashamed adoration, reaching out once more to touch her; her glorious hair tousled and spread over the pillow, her lips swollen from his kisses. Silently, he gave thanks to the gods for their gift in giving him this wonderful creature to love and care for and, for once, the gods smiled back on the man who loved Anna, more than she would ever know.

Anna was also giving thanks to those unseen fates, for her luck in finding a man so gentle and caring. She knew she had to repay him, she had to make him happy; it was her duty. It was the least she could do. Even though he'd taken Paul's place in her life, she knew her life had to be dedicated to her husband from now on, as he'd become more than just her saviour and husband, he'd become her lover, and for that she would always be grateful. It was then Anna made a solemn promise to herself, she would forget Paul, and all he'd meant to her, from now on, the only man in her life would be Gordy.

'You're going to be a wonderful father,' she said, stroking her husband's hairy chest, interrupting his reverie. At that moment, Gordy wanted for nothing, he was a king, with his queen at his side.

From then onwards, after that momentous first night of lovemaking, they never slept apart. Each night they would sleep in each other's arms, where Gordy would caress her breasts, that were more pendulous and heavy in his hands as the days went by; her once slim body becoming more rounded and fulsome with her impending motherhood, her increasing size making no difference to his sexual desire for her, or for that matter, to Anna's. In fact, if the truth be told, her changing shape and her racing hormones enhanced her desire, leading them to make love often, in every room of the house, they were unable to get enough of each other's bodies, so hungry were they for sex, their hunger only assuaged, once their joint passion had been satisfied.

Anna's lovemaking techniques were blossoming as the weeks flew by, becoming ever more inventive, especially when her increasing size made making love conventionally uncomfortable. For a while, to Gordy's amusement, Anna thought she was in danger of becoming a nymphomaniac. It was as though she had an itch that needed constant scratching!

Needless to say, Gordy was delighted by his young wife's appetite for sex. Making love became an activity they both found to be a mutually satisfying experience, right up to the final week of her pregnancy when, even then, she would be waiting for him to come home from work, eager to get him into bed as soon as possible, and equally reluctant to let him out of it the next morning!

Poor Gordy was exhausted as he tried to keep up with her demands. Not that he would have admitted as much, rightly guessing that once the baby arrived she might not feel quite the same way!

Anna had temporarily retired from working at the Golden Lion a month before the baby was due but, within a few days of being at home and alone, she found she missed Molly and the other staff, as well as the hotel's regular customers and went back nearly every day, just to say "hello", because they'd become such a big part of her life. The Golden Lion had become her home and refuge, at a time when she needed it the most. As for Molly, she'd become more than just Anna's saviour, when she'd walked out of Paul's life. Her present happiness was all down to her, knowing she'd been blessed that Christmas morning, when she'd taken her in and cared for her. Anna knew she'd found, not only a home and a job, but also a surrogate mother, with Molly treating her like a much-loved daughter. It was this mother/daughter love between them, along with the expected baby, that had been responsible for Molly at last having a reason to live and, like Gordy; she too couldn't wait for Anna's baby to be born.

Molly had watched the newly-weds relationship with concern when they'd first arrived back from their honeymoon. Wondering if she'd interfered too much by her matchmaking. She was dismayed when she'd seen the look on Anna's face when they'd arrived back. A look that showed all was not well between them, making Molly unhappy for them both, especially knowing Anna had married Gordy merely as a marriage of convenience, to prevent the stigma of being illegitimate attached to her new baby. It was Molly's female instinct that first told her their marriage hadn't been consummated, until one morning, when Anna arrived at the hotel with her face beaming and Molly knew all was as it should be. She never enquired, but it soon became obvious they'd fallen in love. She could tell they were lovers from how they acted towards each other, especially as Gordy couldn't keep his hands off his new wife!

It was obvious to everyone that he was looking forward to becoming a father. Whether it was a boy or girl he didn't seem to have a preference. But Molly was concerned. She could see beneath his '*bonhomie*' exterior that he was getting more and more nervous as the weeks went by. She knew his past experience, of tragically losing his first wife and daughter, was the main reason for his nervousness. As for Gordy, all he wanted was the safe delivery of a healthy baby and for Anna to be safe as well but he was unable to voice his concerns, as Anna would have laughed off his worries, totally convinced all would go as planned and that she would deliver a healthy baby, with no problems at all!

It must have been a nerve-racking time for Gordy, unable to think what he would do, should he lose Anna and the baby he now truly believed to be his. As for Molly, she couldn't wait to get her hands on the baby, which she'd already claimed, to Anna's delight, as being her grandchild!

With all thoughts of Paul firmly at the back of her mind, as well as being sexually satisfied with Gordy, Anna's contentment with life seemed to be the perfect antidote for her previous disappointment in love! Her life with Gordy was calm and tranquil (except for when they were having rampant sex!) and her happiness at being pregnant was apparent for all to see, along with her serenity, which was at odds with her young years, but that's how life is sometimes, especially when you've experienced trauma and disappointment, such as she had known.

It was planned for the baby to be born at home, unless there were any complications, in which case Anna would go to the maternity ward at the old hospital in the city, but for Gordy, remembering how his late wife's pregnancy had sadly ended in tragedy, the tension started to mount the nearer Anna's days moved towards the date marked on the calendar hanging in the kitchen. She didn't appear bothered at all, quite the opposite, confident that giving birth was going to be easy, a natural occurrence for a healthy woman and one she fully intended to experience by delivering her baby at home, regardless of what anyone else had to say on the matter.

Gordy tried to hide his fears and remain calm, unlike Anna, who was in her "nesting mode." Like most pregnant women, as her due day came nearer, she bustled around the little house, making sure everywhere was spotlessly clean and ready for the new arrival. Her only concession to Gordy's worries was an emergency bag packed and waiting by their bedroom door, "just in case" she had to go into hospital, except that Anna had no intention of having her baby anywhere, except in her own bed, with Gordy at her side and possibly, with Molly there as well!

As luck would have it, her waters broke on the date she was due to give birth. It was a Saturday afternoon and believing all was well, Gordy had gone to get some extra shopping from the city centre. When he returned home, he could see the baby was on its way and that Anna had already started having contractions. The midwife arrived soon after Gordy's anxious phone call and, after checking it wasn't a false alarm, and telling them it would probably be some time before the baby was born, she left them to see another new mother, saying she would be back later, leaving Gordy, who was trying hard not to panic, in charge.

And so they settled down to wait for the birth, with Gordy lying on the bed beside Anna. Sponging her hot body and rubbing her back in his effort to share in her pain and discomfort. He cuddled her for some of the time, speaking words of love and encouragement, until the contractions became more and more frequent and it was evident the birth was near. To his relief, the midwife arrived only minutes later, closely followed by Molly, who'd closed up the bar and shooed out the stragglers faster than usual in her haste to get to Anna, there being no way she intended missing out on the excitement of her new "grandchild" being born.

Finally, at two-thirty the next morning, Anna and Gordy's daughter came into the world, red-faced and squealing!

Gordy was the first to hold her, while the midwife made Anna comfortable. He kissed the baby's head, admiring the mass of dark hair and then it was Molly's turn. It was only after that, that Anna got to hold her daughter, unable to believe how beautiful she was. She unwrapped her from the towel the midwife had hurriedly wrapped her in, checking everything was correct! Ten tiny fingers, ten tiny toes, Anna counted them twice, before looking at the small nails on the end of each finger and toe, marvelling at the markings on each tiny palm.

The midwife smiled as she looked at them, three people, all of whom had fallen instantly in love with the new arrival, or perhaps besotted might be a better description!

As for Gordy, he felt as though he'd won the best prize in the world. Anna was safe and had given him a beautiful daughter. What more could any man want?

Molly was the first to ask the one question she'd been eager to know the answer to for ages. What name had they decided on for the new baby? Gordy, sitting on the bed next to Anna, with his arms around her shoulders also wanted to know. They'd never discussed possible names, as Anna thought it unlucky to give a child a name before it had opened its eyes on its new world, so it was a complete surprise when she said, 'I would like to call her Emma!'

Molly gasped in astonishment, as for Gordy, his face was a picture of complete joy.

'Are you sure?' he asked, his voice choked with emotion.

Molly said nothing, like Gordy she too was full with emotion; unable to believe her beloved Anna was naming her new daughter after Gordy's late wife, knowing how much he'd loved her and the sadness he'd suffered when she'd died.

'Yes,' Anna said. 'I want to call her Emma.'

And so Molly watched, delighted and satisfied with the outcome of the long night, but it was time now she left her new family to their much-needed rest, for that was how she thought of them. With Emma, their new baby daughter sleeping in the Moses basket at the side of their bed, Molly knew how blessed she'd been the day Anna had walked away from one life and into hers.

So there we have it, another human has been born and one the fates are already favouring!

# Chapter 7

Molly walked through the silent streets of the city to the Golden Lion deep in thought, her thoughts on the time when she'd first moved out of London and had gone to live with her friend, Jean, in the Midlands. She smiled to herself as she thought of how they would dance the night away and then go to work the next morning, as if they'd had hours of sleep! These days though, it was a different story, she was many years older and needed her sleep. Staying up late to be at Emma's birth had exhausted her and then the excitement of watching the baby being born, and the emotion she'd felt as she held the tiny mite for the first time. Real stirrings of love had gone through her, as though the child was her own, and then her delight for Anna and Gordy that all was well, and how they'd looked at each other as they held their daughter. Molly knew she would never forget that night, neither would she forget Gordy's expression, ecstatic at being a father, as though the baby was indeed his; his face showing not only his love for the child, but also the deep love he felt for Anna. It had been a magical time and one Molly knew she would never forget.

Now she had help with running the hotel, she planned on sleeping in a little later that morning, perhaps taking another nap after lunch, as she intended to visit Anna and the baby before she opened the bar for the evening trade. As she waited for sleep to overtake her, she mulled over the previous day's events, her mind wandering to when Gordy had been newly married to his first wife and his excitement at the prospect of becoming a father, only to have his hopes dashed and his life shattered, when his wife had died in childbirth a couple of years later. She'd been there to console him and it was then they'd become really good friends, both lonely and alone, even though Molly had the Golden Lion, which was as demanding as having a husband and children would ever have been.

When Anna needed a husband, Molly knew immediately Gordy would be perfect for her. He might have been several years older but in terms of reliability and constancy, he was definitely Molly's first choice and she made it her business to be instrumental in arranging their marriage! Telling herself, there are times when couples need someone not emotionally involved to see how right they are for each other, as being blinded by lust often hides defects in personalities that, after a while, can cause insurmountable problems and quite possibly lead to divorce!

Molly closed her eyes but it was impossible to sleep, her imagination was too much on fire as her mind raced, her thoughts going back to when she'd fallen deeply in love with her beloved Paddy and had married him. Oh and how she'd loved him! He was her mad Irishman! A part of her life since they'd both been born, only months apart, their mothers being each other's best friend and their families coming from the same Irish backgrounds.

Molly and Paddy were each the youngest child in their respective large families: Molly, the only girl in a family of six brothers and Paddy, the youngest of five, the older children all girls, all of whom acted as his surrogate mother, spoiling him in the nicest possible way. They'd laughed, many times over the years, saying they'd been born and raised for each other! Which in a way I suppose was true!

Nineteen hundred and nine, the year they were born, was a time of great poverty in Ireland and not much better in England but as there was no work in Ireland at the time, their fathers decided to go across the North Sea to find work in England, believing it to be marginally less poor than Ireland!

They'd also heard if they went to Liverpool they would be able to find work as navvies, working on the new railways and roads being built, confident they would soon earn enough money to be able to send for their families.

At this time, most families in rural areas of Ireland relied on each other, not only for friendship, but financial support and so it was with Molly and Paddy's families. They were from a second generation of poverty, their ancestors also having lived in a time of great hardship and famine, when their only means of escape was either death, from hunger or disease, or leaving their homeland to travel to other parts of the world; to go where a man with muscles and a will to work, could find employment. This, sadly, was just how it was at the time. The only way their fathers could see for them to support their families, was for them to go from their homes in Ireland, leaving their young wives to bring up the children as best they could, sharing their meagre possessions, as only those who have little do, with the men sending money home as and when they found work.

Molly finally fell asleep; her dreams filled with a sentimental yearning for Paddy and what had been, even though the past life they'd shared had been hard.

Her dream then changed to the vision of the day when finally there was enough money hidden inside the big brown pot in Molly's mother's kitchen for the two families to get to England. And then, at last there came the arrival of the long-awaited letters from their men folk telling them they had jobs and a house.

And so, with great excitement and knowing a house was waiting for them in England, the two wives along with those children not yet old enough to be left behind in Ireland, boarded the mail boat and sailed away from the country of their birth to find their fortunes in a new and alien country.

By 1914, England was at war, a worrying time for both families. But by then Molly and Paddy were both six years old. They'd clung to each other as their fathers enlisted in the Irish Guards and were marched away to serve their adopted country. Sadly, both men were killed in 1918, during the last stages of the Great War, that most awful war of wars that robbed millions of women in Britain and Europe of their husbands and sweethearts, leaving thousands of children fatherless, and the men's bodies left to rest in the graveyard of a war-torn foreign country.

While their mothers grieved, Molly and Paddy had to grow up quickly and play their part in keeping their families fed and watered. With no money saved and no prospect of them ever returning to Ireland, even if they could have afforded the fares, they had to stay in England and make something of their lives and gradually, somehow, they survived, with Molly and Paddy growing from being the two youngest children in their families, to two young adults who'd suddenly fallen in love, which was no surprise to their families, who always knew they would. Eventually, in 1929, despite the economic state of England, and the rest of the world, they were married, as predicted by their families, in the local Catholic Church.

Even though the world was suffering an economic depression, they struck lucky, finding work together, as servants to an Irish peer, a city banker, who lived for most of the year in a large mansion house in London. Molly was to become a lady's maid to his imperious and haughty wife and his two older daughters, as for Paddy? He became his Lordship's trusted valet and so Molly and Patrick's good luck continued.

His Lordship and his wife often travelled to Dublin, where the family had a house in the country, taking some of the London staff with them and it was this continuing good fortune that enabled Molly and Paddy to keep in touch with their older siblings who'd been left behind when their mothers first left Ireland for England.

Between 1919 and 1939 they travelled farther afield with the family, going to France, Spain, Italy and even to Germany, when the family went on holiday, or on business. It was on these travels across Europe and beyond that helped to finish Molly and Paddy's meagre school education. Being intelligent, they took every advantage of this opportunity to enrich their lives and gradually learnt the customs and languages of France and Germany, relishing being able to converse in these languages as well as being able to discuss the arts and cultural differences they saw on their travels. It was because of this 'finalization' to their education that they both progressed in later years.

They were lucky too in other ways. Being married they had the use of a small flat at the London mansion where they worked and, although their wages were poor, they still managed to save a little, as well as helping their mothers, who at the time were both living in London.

As for the other children in their respective families, they'd all left home long ago, leaving the two mothers deciding to live together, which everyone thought to be a good idea, but it was Molly and Paddy who insisted on buying a small house for them to share, knowing when the two women eventually died it would then become their home.

The only disappointment and sorrow Molly and Paddy had in their marriage, was their inability to have children of their own. Being good Catholics, they'd made no attempt to prevent themselves from becoming parents and, although Molly hadn't become pregnant, she made no effort either to find the reason why not. As far as she was concerned, it was an act of God if a married woman failed to conceive and, being religious she never questioned the reasons as to why she didn't have babies of her own.

The years passed serenely for Molly and Paddy, until another war in Europe was declared, when by then both their mothers, being elderly had died. The little house had finally become theirs, but times were changing! Their employer decided the time had come for him and his family to return to Ireland, at least for the duration of the war and, as Molly and Paddy had no children of their own to worry about, they decided to enlist in the armed forces and serve England, knowing they would never return to Ireland to live, a momentous decision for them both and one they'd not taken lightly but, putting their worries behind them, they went, arm in arm, to the enlisting office to sign up, determined to do whatever was necessary to help Britain win the war!

In different ways they both enjoyed the war. Not that any war is enjoyable. It was the companionship and camaraderie of being with like-minded people that they enjoyed!

Molly found herself working as a transport driver, a world away from being a lady's maid. As for Paddy, after his initial training, he was transferred into what was to become known after the war as 'Churchill's secret army.'

It was during this time he earned the nickname, 'Mad Paddy,' his 'devil may care' attitude to life being partly responsible for its creation. Yet for all this, his attitude to his work in the army was completely different. He was extremely careful in everything he had to do, not reckless in any way; taking no chances that would lead his team into disaster but his greatest asset was, without a doubt, his ability to speak both French and German. It was because of his linguistic abilities his life, and those of his men, the main reason they were saved when they were cornered and nearly captured, leaving Paddy thanking his lucky stars and counting his blessings for the time he'd spent travelling abroad with his Irish master.

Like many other couples at the time, Molly and Paddy were separated for months on end during the war years and, although their everyday lives were filled with the excitement of their work, they still missed each other enormously, being as much in love as when they'd been young and newly married. They adored each other, living only for the day when they would finally be together at the end of the war, until then, they had to make do with their infrequent leaves; although few and far between, the days they spent together then were even more precious.

It was towards the end of the war, during the last two months in fact that life changed. Molly was on leave and staying in their house in London's East End, waiting for Paddy to join her for some shared leave, when she was visited by two army officials bringing her dire news.

They were sorry, they said, '*regretted*' I believe was the official word they'd used, but they had to tell her, that her beloved Paddy was dead! Killed in action! To say Molly was devastated was an understatement of her feelings.

Paddy, her dearest love, the young man who'd been so precious to her, so full of life and laughter was gone, taken from her by foreigners from across the channel.

Heartbroken, she carried on with her work in the army, until she was no longer needed and was demobbed. With no idea of what she wanted to do with the rest of her life, once she'd been freed from the regimentation of army rules and regulations, or even of how she would fill each day, she decided to return to the little house they'd bought for when the war was over and spend some time there but, to add insult to injury, a stray bomb, falling over the city in the final hours of the war destroyed it, and the rest of the street, just before she arrived, leaving her homeless and even more bereft.

With Paddy gone, and now all her possessions as well, there was no reason she could think of for her to stay in London, and she certainly didn't relish the idea of being a servant again, in any case, the gentry were finding it hard to finance and maintain their large houses and, with new fashions available, genteel womenfolk were no longer in need of personal maids. There was never going to be a return to her pre-war life for Molly so what was she to do?

She thought long and hard. She had no relatives left in England, her family, as well as Paddy's were scattered all over the world, some gone to America and Canada and some even to Australia. With no family left in Ireland either, she didn't relish the thought of going back there and being alone. Her only real friends were the girls she'd worked with in the army and, one in particular, a girl called Jean, who came from an old city in the Midlands.

Knowing Molly was now on her own, Jean asked if she would like to live with her and her family and find a job in the city, where work was supposed to be easy to find. To

Molly one place was as good as any other, especially when she no longer had a home, or a family to call her own.

Together, the two friends went to work in a new factory on the outskirts of the city: going into the city at weekends to go dancing, or to visit a cinema, and then afterwards, going for a drink with their new friends from the factory. The place they went to most often was a run-down hotel in the city centre, called the Golden Lion. Run at that time by an old man, who'd tried since the war to run it single-handedly after most of his family had been killed in an air raid.

He didn't run it as a hotel these days, unable to understand why his hotel had survived the bombing when all around him houses, shops and offices had been razed to the ground. He was amazed the old building was still standing, albeit on an island, surrounded as it was by bomb-damaged and derelict buildings where once medieval houses had proudly stood.

To Molly, the hotel, as well as the city, were places that could and should be saved; it took hardly any time for her to realise she'd fallen in love; hook line and sinker, not with a man, but with the city and especially the old hotel. It was a building she could see needed a woman's touch and an idea began forming in her head.

She'd never thought of becoming a licensee, and neither did she have any experience of running such a business, but she knew she loved the old place, even in its run-down state and verging on being 'seedy.' She could see it had potential. It just needed bringing back to life.

One Saturday evening, enjoying their drinks at the bar as usual, Molly and Jean became aware of some consternation amongst the regular customers. There was talk the old man was going to sell up, as he wanted to retire. To

Jean's surprise, Molly began to show a keen interest in this news and later, when the old man had closed the hotel for the night, she stayed behind to help him.

After a short conversation, the old man told her that yes, he wanted to retire and, on a sudden impulse, and without any prior discussion with her friend Jean, Molly decided to put in an offer for the hotel and its contents, her reasoning later to Jean were that she needed the old place as much as it needed her and, before the old man could change his mind, and because he liked the look of her, Molly had his agreement to the sale!

Jean and her other friends at the factory all thought she was quite mad, taking on a building that only by the grace of God had managed to come out of the war years for the most part unscathed. And the hotel was certainly not profitable, as her lawyer went to great pains to point out to her before she signed the final papers making the Golden Lion hers, but Molly wasn't worried: she had every confidence she could turn it around. She had a little money put away for her old age and now was as good a time as ever to spend it. Her reasoning? Who could possibly say whether she would ever reach an old age, look what had happened to Paddy? All she instinctively knew was that it had the potential to become a fine business, and with her special touch, it was going to be the best in the city.

A few weeks later, the Golden Lion took on an entirely different appearance. Surprising even Molly when she saw what elbow grease and lots of hot water could do. She'd worked wonders. After the hotel closed at night she could be found on her hands and knees scrubbing the grimy floors and washing nicotine-stained walls and woodwork. For the time being, the rest would have to wait, until her shoestring budget improved and she could afford to employ someone else to help her, other than the old barman cum handyman, she'd inherited, along with the building.

The hotel had changed many times since it had first been built, starting its life as nothing more than a simple dwelling, gradually progressing through the centuries until the present day, when its outer appearance was more Georgian than anything else. Molly was at least thankful the building had come safely through the bombing. Even the old leaded windows had miraculously survived and, after a thorough washing and polishing, they once again became the smiling eyes of the old place. The next step was to transform the interior and, like the city centre that was rising from near dereliction to live again, so did the Golden Lion.

Most of the downstairs walls were covered in nicotine-stained paint, or hideous wallpaper, peeling off in places. When all of this was stripped away, Molly did a dance of joy for, to her surprise, there was some fine Georgian panelling hidden behind the nicotine-stained dross. Once cleaned and polished it looked wonderful.

The bar took hours of cleaning and polishing, before the true colour of the rosewood and mahogany it was made of was finally revealed. All this took weeks of hard labour for Molly and Ned, the old barman. But the end results more than made up for her aching arms and body.

New curtains were made and hung at the front windows, as well as new seat covers in red leatherette (the material found by a retailer in an old warehouse that had miraculously survived the bombing raids on the city). With a new red patterned carpet (from the same warehouse) fitted in the lounge area, at last the public rooms looked comfortable and welcoming, exactly as when Anna had first seen it, the morning of Christmas Day when Molly had brought her in from the snow.

Molly loved the Golden Lion. She'd lavished all her care and attention on the old place, until it became the child she'd never had, that is until the day Anna walked into her life and became her much-loved daughter!

Later that day, when she went back to visit Anna and her new baby, Molly looked at the little family she now considered to be hers, knowing it must have been her destiny to arrive in the city and to buy and renovate the hotel. How strange, she thought, that one's destiny is determined by outside forces we humans have little control over.

It had obviously been her destiny to travel a different path through life, regardless of what her original plans might have been had Paddy lived; maybe she'd been chosen to see Anna achieved the destiny the fates had decided for her?

# Chapter 8

Paul's move to Coombe Norton in the Cotswolds had gone
smoothly and he'd made good progress, amazing his
superiors with his enthusiasm and motivation. Since then,
he'd been promoted to manager at a much larger branch in
Gloucester, but his eyes were set on something even better,
such as becoming a financial advisor at the bank's
headquarters in London!

He decided it made financial sense to keep the cottage
he'd bought in Coombe Norton and not just because of
sentimental reasons, it being his first independent home, but
because he'd paid off the mortgage and it wasn't sensible to
leave the old cottage empty or to just to use it for the
occasional holiday or weekends. His financial acumen won
the day and he decided to rent it to a young couple in need
of a first home.

As his latest promotion came with a substantial increase
in salary, he decided to buy another home, this time in a
village on the outskirts of Gloucester and commute the
twelve miles to work each day. It was a totally different way
of life, having to travel to his office, instead of just walking
down the street, but he enjoyed his morning drive through
the beautiful Gloucestershire countryside and the return
journey home in the evenings was just long enough for him
to have shrugged off the stresses of modern-day banking.

His new house was substantially larger and modern,
totally different from his old cottage in Coombe Norton

that he'd furnished with antiques that suited the age of the property; his new house needed something different. It was fortunate that in nearby Broadway there was a company making beautiful modern pieces of furniture, which Paul judiciously mixed with his growing collection of fine antiques. This time though, he did have to find a gardener; he could no longer sweep this back garden clean as the two acres of land that went with the house needed someone with green fingers, and a strong back; also, gardening didn't appeal to Paul one jot, he wanted a social life!

To the outside world, he appeared to be content, but to his old friends he often seemed deep in thought with a problem he wouldn't, or couldn't talk about.

When his father died suddenly of a heart attack, a year after Paul's move to Gloucester, he knew he had a bigger problem to solve! What was he to do with his mother? He tried (after his father's funeral) to persuade her to move in with him. His house was large enough, but she steadfastly refused to budge from her own home and, much to his consternation, it was obvious she wouldn't be able to cope without his father: it was also a problem he didn't need at the time as the bank was enlarging its facilities and services and he needed to be there to put the new systems into practice. He continued to make the journey every week to see his mother and, at each visit, he tried in vain to get her to change her mind and go back with him. It was an impossible situation! His mother was a stubborn woman and nothing he could say or do would make her change her mind, until one day, when fate stepped in and did it for her!

For a few months, she'd appeared to be managing quite well on her own until the day arrived Paul had been dreading. A phone call from his mother's neighbour told him his mother had been taken to hospital because she'd fallen while shopping in the town and had broken her hip. Unfortunately, within a couple of days, she'd contracted pneumonia and, with Paul at her bedside, holding her frail hands, she finally passed peacefully away.

Paul was heartbroken. First he'd lost his father and now his mother. Full of grief and regret he hadn't been able to prevent her death, he was guiltily convinced she would still be alive had she been living with him. It was a trying time and it affected him so badly he fell into a deep depression.

As an only child, he had all the arrangements to make for his mother's funeral and then, as executor of his parents' wills, along with the family solicitor, he had to sell the family house and finalise his parents' lives. To do this, he had to go through all their possessions and this was one part he knew he wasn't going to enjoy.

Full of grief and guilt, he decided to take some compassionate leave from the bank to sort out his life, but before he could do that, he had to finalise the bank's big expansion programme he'd already set in motion.

He decided to live in his parents' house while he went through their belongings, intending to get rid of what he didn't want to keep, before selling the house. He took his time to get settled in until one day, he knew he had to get down to doing what had to be done; he couldn't put it off any longer. Sitting on the floor in his parents' bedroom he made a start; upending the contents of drawers and boxes he'd taken from out of the cupboards onto the floor in front of him. He'd sorted through some of the articles, discarding most and keeping others, until, at the bottom of the pile, he came upon a small bundle of letters, together with a small box that seemed familiar to him. He opened it and stared in amazement at the contents, a gold ring, set with a solitaire diamond lay before him. He felt his body go cold, even though the room was warm. He picked up the bundle of letters, staring at the writing on the outside of the envelopes and, with his hands shaking, he took out the first letter, his heart thudding as he started to read. He couldn't believe the words that spilled out of the pages, shocked by what was written. One by one, he opened all the envelopes, reading every page until he'd finished and the final piece of his personal jigsaw had been put in place. Suddenly, the fog from his memory was lifted. He was holding in his hands the explanation as to why he'd felt his life was missing something of vital importance. He couldn't believe what he'd found. He'd known immediately the letters had come from Anna, the young woman he'd wanted to marry. He held his head in his hands, grief-stricken at what his mother and father had done to him, and to her.

Paul looked at the ring as it sparkled in its box and his anger rose with a vengeance. He looked at the dates on the letters, angry that so much time had passed since Anna had written them. He wondered where she was now? It was obvious from her letters she had no idea he'd been in an accident that Christmas Day. And only now did he remember himself what had happened that morning. It suddenly became clear. He could see it in his mind's eye, his mother yelling and fighting like a mad woman as she'd tried to get Anna out of his bed, and then the state Anna had been in, when he'd last seen her as she'd walked down the stairs and out of his life. He suddenly remembered how he'd tried to talk to his mother, and how he'd tried to persuade her Anna wasn't the slut and whore she'd accused her of being, and the way she'd ignored him, refusing to listen to his explanation of what had happened.

He could see himself leaving the house, intending to follow Anna, and then walking in the snow down the lane after her. After that, there was nothing! There was a complete void in his memory. The next few weeks were also blank, until the day he'd finally come round and found he was in hospital, so badly injured he had to spend quite some time in intensive care and then the many more weeks he'd spent recovering.

And all the while his parents lied to him, by their omission. They'd deliberately made no mention of Anna at all. It was as though they'd whitewashed her out of his life, easy to do once they knew his memory of her had vanished.

Sitting on the floor that day, going through his mother and father's life, he was desolate at what he'd lost. Suddenly, the pent-up emotion inside him exploded and real tears, hot and scalding fell until exhausted, he couldn't cry any more: clutching Anna's letters and the ring box, he climbed onto his parents' bed and slept.

It was some time later before he awoke, but then he was determined to find Anna and explain what had happened and, with this resolve firmly in his mind, he continued clearing away his parent's lives, just as they had tried to clear away his love for Anna.

Once he'd finished he'd calmed down, relieved in one sense that at last he knew it had been Anna who'd been missing from his life. She was the shadowy person he'd been unable to see, at the same time, other parts of his missing memory returned but, more importantly, he knew he still loved her and fully intended telling her how he felt; all he could hope for was that she still loved him and felt the same way!

With his mind made up, Paul decided he would go into the city the next day and find her and make her understand it was the accident that had caused his memory loss, and his parents who'd been responsible for not bringing her to see him in hospital, quite certain that had he seen her his memory would have immediately returned.

The following morning, he drove across the city to the outlying suburbs, to where Anna used to live with her stepmother, hoping she would still be there. His mouth was dry, and his palms sweaty, by the time he arrived, wondering whether he was doing the right thing or not after so many years. Apprehensively, he rang the doorbell, crossing his fingers that someone would be at home. To his surprise the door opened just a little, as an elderly lady peered cautiously out at him from behind its safety chain.

'I'm looking for a Mrs Ruth Spencer.' Paul said, his smile charming the old lady. 'Does she still live here?'

Looking at him closely and weighing him up until she was finally assured by his handsome good looks, manners, and his natural charm that he was a nice young man and not a rapist or murderer, the old lady said, 'No, I'm afraid not. She's been gone for some years and now lives in Spain. I believe she married a Spanish gentleman and is not called Mrs Spencer any more. I'm sorry but I don't know what her name is now.'

Feeling sorry for the young man standing in front of her with the crestfallen expression on his face at her news, she trustingly took the safety chain off the door and invited him in. She could see he was upset at her news and wondered what relation he was, if any, to the awful woman from whom she'd bought the flat.

Paul sat for a while with the old lady, drinking the coffee she'd insisted on making for him, as he tried to regain his composure. His hostess watched him with some considerable interest, answering his questions as best she could, until he asked about Anna, the young lady who'd lived with Mrs Spencer and whether she knew where she was now? The old lady immediately poured cold water on that line of questioning, telling him she'd never seen anyone else in the flat, except for Mrs Spencer. Seeing this was unwelcome news, she suggested he contact her solicitor, who might have a forwarding address. Thanking the old lady, Paul took his leave, deciding he would have to make several phone calls when he returned to his mother's house.

It took another couple of weeks before he'd finally cleared the clutter of his parents' lives and, in the meantime, he'd put the house up for sale and written to Anna's stepmother in Spain at the address he'd obtained from the old lady's solicitor, hopeful a reply would be waiting for him with an address for Anna when he returned to his own home.

Paul waited impatiently for a reply from Ruth, wondering if Anna still loved him? Or had she forgotten him and moved on with her life? Being busy at work, setting up ever more new systems helped, and the days flew by.

Each evening, as soon as he returned home, he would empty the post box; disappointed when no letter, with a foreign stamp, sat waiting for him, until a month later, when the long-awaited letter finally arrived.

Ruth's letter was short and to the point, her vindictiveness and spite against Anna still apparent, even after all the years that had elapsed.

Her answer: Anna's last address was the Golden Lion, but she didn't advise him making contact with her as Anna was married; she didn't think there were any children but by now that could have changed.

Her only other comment; Anna's husband might not take too kindly to an ex-boyfriend turning up wanting to make contact with his wife!

Paul was shocked! Anna married! He couldn't believe it. He'd imagined her still to be waiting for him! He couldn't imagine why she would have forgotten him so quickly, failing to realise several years had passed with no news from him!

As he sat and thought about the contents of Ruth's letter he calmed down a little, until a sense of reasoning returned. He hadn't contacted Anna for years, therefore she had every right to believe he didn't want her, and was free to marry whomsoever she pleased, especially, as she'd said in her letters, she'd assumed from his silence, he didn't want anything more to do with her!

And then her last letter, the most poignant and heart-breaking of all; when she'd said how disappointed she was by his mother telling her he didn't want anything to do with her and why couldn't he have told her himself? Paul could only imagine how Anna must have felt as she'd written those words. What he couldn't understand was why his mother and father had wanted so badly to spoil his life? What did they have against Anna? They hardly knew her. Sadly, he put Ruth's letter back into its envelope, unsure at that moment of what he should do next.

Later that evening, as he sat thinking about Anna, and her letters, and especially the one he'd received from Ruth, he realised Anna had obviously made a new life for herself, one that didn't include him but he still couldn't believe, no matter how hard he tried, that she no longer loved him. Putting his doubts behind him, he decided he would go back to the city and visit the Golden Lion and see if he could find her. He wanted to know how she really felt about him and then, he suddenly remembered, she might have children! If this was so, then it must mean she was in a proper married relationship and maybe she had forgotten her love for him?

Another two months were to pass before he was able to get away from the demands of his job and return to the city. As he had to see the solicitors who were finalizing his parents' estates, he thought it an ideal time to try and meet Anna.

It was his intention to go to the Golden Lion for lunch after his appointment and, once the final papers were signed, he left the solicitor's office and walked down to the park where he used to meet Anna for their picnic lunches. He wanted to sit and watch the hotel, and its customers, as they were going in and out, to see if he could catch sight of her. His feelings were different now. He was the one afraid of being rejected and this time, by the only woman he'd ever loved.

Paul sat for some time on the seat he and Anna had always thought of as being theirs: watching the comings and goings at the Golden Lion, at the same time going over in his mind what he would say when he finally came face-to-face with her after all this time. Would she be prepared to listen as he explained his absence of the past few years? Would she believe him? He would have to tell her of his accident; that was the first item, and then, how his family had kept him in ignorance of her, when he'd been ill and his memory of her had gone. But, more to the point, what would she say when he told her he still loved her and wanted to marry her? Would she leave her husband and go back with him to Gloucester? But what if there was a child, or even children? Would her husband let her take them away with her? All these questions gnawed at his mind until, with a purposeful sigh, he left the park and walked into the hotel, his heart pounding in his chest as he went into the bar.

At his first glance, there was no sign of Anna and, strangely, he felt relieved. It gave him the chance to have a look around and weigh up the place. He stood at the bar and ordered a drink, watching through the mirror at the back of the bar, the comings and goings of the staff as they waited on the tables in the dining area. He was disappointed. There was no sign of Anna. To be certain she wasn't there he ordered a meal, just to be sure. Paul wasn't to know Anna had taken Emma to the children's hospital that morning to see the ear, nose and throat consultant and would be working during the evening, instead of her normal lunchtime duty.

It was Molly who noticed the good-looking young man sitting on his own eating his meal. He seemed to be watching the activity in the pub with more attention than she thought to be usual, and wondered if he was from a rival's premises, trying to steal her and Anna's ideas.

Molly was already suspicious, as this had happened in the past. She knew it would make Anna laugh, when she told her they'd had someone else in the restaurant she'd thought fitted their idea of a spy!

It was only a few minutes after Paul left, convinced Anna wasn't going to be there that day, that she returned with Emma, full of the morning's events at the hospital.

While Emma went to have a late lunch with Molly, Anna checked the bar and kitchen, ready for the evening's session. She had some extra cooking to do as tomorrow was Emma's fifth birthday; they were going to have a party and she needed some extra items for the buffet she was planning.

Anna looked thoughtful as she prepared the food, her mind on Paul, as usual when it was Emma's birthday and, as usual, she wondered where he was and what he was doing and what he would have to say if he knew he was a father? She felt his nearness, as she always did at this time and wondered if he was happy with his life, but she no longer wished to change hers, she was more than happy with

Gordy, who'd often proved to be a wonderful husband and father. She might have lost Paul's love, and he'd no doubt forgotten his love for her, but that was all in the past; it was best she tried to forget what she couldn't change, but even so, she still had a feeling that day she couldn't describe: a strange feeling in her heart she couldn't explain.

Paul made another visit to the city a couple of weeks later; this time he went straight to the hotel and up to the bar, catching a fleeting glimpse of Anna as she made her way into the kitchen. His heart jumped. He recognised her straightaway. She was still stunningly beautiful and, from the pounding of his heart, he knew his feelings for her hadn't diminished in any way over the years, but had hers?

With shaking hands, he took his drink and went to sit in the far corner of the lounge, a vantage point from where he could observe the doorway to the kitchen as he waited for her to re-appear.

He ordered his meal and, when it arrived, he ate it, without seeing any sign of Anna. Later, with his coffee in front of him, he opened his newspaper and pretended to read, wondering, as he hid behind it, whether he'd changed much physically over the past five years since Anna had last seen him, leaving him wondering whether she would still recognise him. But where was she. Surely, he thought, he couldn't have missed seeing her go out.

Molly had been working in the bar when Paul had first walked in. She'd watched him through the mirror at the back of the bar as he went to sit in the far corner of the dining area and suddenly, she recognised him as the 'spy' from his previous visit. As he finished drinking his coffee, she walked across and stood looking down at him. 'Did you enjoy your lunch?' she asked, innocently picking up his empty cup and saucer.

'Yes,' he answered. 'It was delicious. But then the food you serve here always is!' Wondering if he really was from the opposition Molly said, 'Yes! We try to do the best food in the city and, judging by the amount we sell, we must be getting it right!'

Paul nodded his head in agreement. 'I came here five years ago, just as you were starting to do lunches. It was my leaving lunch. I thought then you'd be successful and today's meal has proved me right!'

He wanted to say more, but Molly had moved away, having seen Gordy walk in and go to the bar. To Paul's surprise, he suddenly saw Anna standing at the bar. She must have come out of the kitchen while he'd been speaking with Molly, and where she'd shielded him from Anna's view.

Paul's heart lurched for a minute as he watched her. From the way she was standing, with her arms around the man's waist, he could see they were more than good friends. At that moment, the man pulled Anna close and kissed her. It was this one simple act that made Paul realise he stood no chance of Anna ever being his. He lifted his newspaper and hid his face, pretending to be engrossed in reading, waiting for Anna, and the man, who by now he was sure was her husband, to leave the bar and, for the second time to walk out of his life.

Molly saw the young man leave. He'd seemed such a pleasant young man but was he a 'spy'? She smiled to herself wondering whether she would see him again and then she remembered, she'd forgotten to point him out to Anna!

Paul's thoughts were troubled as he left the hotel and walked back to his car. Seeing Anna with the man he believed to be her husband had been upsetting, but he knew he had to accept it and that it was time he too made a new life. He had to find someone he could love and marry, but how he wished, at that moment, he could move time back five years to that fateful Christmas morning, when his and Anna's lives were irrevocably changed forever. He knew now he shouldn't have taken her to his home, but then, maybe that was his destiny, to have loved Anna and then to have lost her!

Paul felt sad as he drove back to Gloucester, his mind full of 'if only and what ifs?' Unable to understand why his memory of Anna and the events of that fateful Christmas Day, when his mother had thrown the biggest tantrum he'd ever witnessed, had returned so suddenly. Why hadn't his memory come back while he'd been in hospital? He could only assume, being so traumatised by his accident and his injuries, his mind had literally closed down, shutting itself off from the events that had happened. His doctor had told him that losing his memory was his body's way of repairing itself. Paul didn't know if this were true or not. He wasn't a 'mind doctor' and neither could he say with any certainty why it had happened to him. Whatever the reasons, his gut instinct was to believe only what he felt now. His life was now going to go on a course different from the one he'd originally planned when he'd proposed to Anna. Perhaps this new life plan was merely yet another part of his destiny.

Paul read Anna's letters, over and over again, until he could stand it no longer and finally, he placed them, along with the diamond ring, in a secure box that he hid in a seldom-used drawer. He would keep them for always, but for now, he had to get on with his life, as Anna had obviously done with hers!

And so the weeks and months passed and, to some degree, Paul came to understand his mother, and her attitude towards not only to Anna, but also to any young woman he might have brought home. Before Anna had come into his life, his mother had encouraged him to concentrate on his studies and, being a dutiful and loving son, he'd agreed. His parents making it quite clear only by studying and getting a qualification would he succeed in life. They even managed to discourage him from getting romantically involved with any girlfriend he'd known before Anna. He knew getting a good job in finance was his big ambition and he didn't intend, as he constantly assured them, in getting involved with anyone, until he could be a proper provider and the right person came along. Only of course, the right person did come along in the guise of Anna and, as so often happens, his and Anna's hormones had taken over before his parents were ready to lose him, whether she was the right woman for him or not! Paul felt sorry his parents hadn't been able to accept Anna as being a suitable wife for him, because he knew she would have been a wonderful life partner, as well as a loving and caring daughter-in-law, but it wasn't to be. Everyone could see she was beautiful and intelligent, as well as talented; her skills as a cook were proof of that.

Paul had fallen in love with her the first time he'd set eyes on her and he knew, from the first day they'd had lunch together in the park, she was going to be the one special lady in his life. He knew, even then, he wanted to marry her and had taken his courtship of her slowly, not wanting to rush her into making a wrong decision. He wanted her to be sure she loved him. His plans to propose to her, and then for them to announce their engagement on Christmas Day, should have been the culmination of all his plans, but they'd been destroyed, and all because of his mother's old-fashioned values and, through all that, he'd lost the love of his life and the chance to be married to the only woman he wanted.

With his box of memories stowed away, Paul hoped he would be able to forget Anna and get on with his life, but it wasn't going to be that easy. He couldn't rid his mind of the image he had of her standing at the bar with her arms around the man he thought to be her husband. He wondered if this was how his life was going to be from now on. Thinking of Anna and her husband all the time. He had to ask, what sort of man was she married to? Did he make her happy? And, the final cruncher, how soon after she'd left him did they meet?

He felt the familiar feelings of jealousy rising inside him as he asked himself another question. Did Anna really love her husband? And how could she, when she'd sworn that fateful Christmas morning, after he'd proposed to her, that she loved him?

It was with a heavy heart he acknowledged he would never know the answers to any of these questions and, regardless of the old adage, that time is a great healer, he knew he was going to find it hard to believe it to be so!

It took several months before he could get through the day without Anna constantly invading his thoughts, until finally he knew he had to change and thankfully slowly he did. As his working life was fully involved, he gradually transformed his social life, by asking some of the girls he met at his various clubs and meetings out for meals and theatre visits, looking at them differently now he was seriously looking for a wife; always hopeful he would find someone who would take Anna's place in his heart.

It was the following year he met Angela at a local hunt ball. She was an attractive divorcee in her late twenties with an adorable six-year-old daughter called Zoe she shared custody with her ex-husband, who'd moved away from the area when he'd gone down south to live with his new partner.

Paul liked being a part of Angela and Zoe's life and, quite soon, he'd become a surrogate father to the young girl. It wasn't long, before he sensed Angela had fallen in love with him, at the same time hoping he'd fallen in love with her!

It didn't take long before Angela became frustrated at Paul's reluctance to take their relationship a step further into marriage, unable to understand, after they'd been an item for several months, the reason why he shied away from making a long-term commitment to her. It was obvious he liked her and adored Zoe. So she was at a loss to know how to get him to make that final commitment. It even gave her a crisis of confidence for a time: especially knowing she was an attractive woman with a good personality. She made no demands on him financially, having a well-paid job of her own as a financial advisor in a building society in Gloucester that made her independent. She certainly wasn't looking for a man to keep her and even having a daughter hadn't in the past seemed to be a problem. Paul gave all the signs of liking her and Zoe enormously yet she was still unable to get him to say the words, '*I love you! Please marry me.*'

Paul was well aware he'd used Angela, as he had all the other young women before her. Selfishly, sleeping with them whenever possible, without giving anything emotional in return.

It was Angela, out of all his other women, he'd led the most into believing he had fallen in love, except when in they were in the throes of lovemaking, when she sometimes thought his mind was elsewhere, that he was thinking of someone else! As for Paul, his thoughts did stray. Sometimes he would be thinking of Anna at the critical moment. It was then he felt guilty and ashamed, knowing he didn't love Angela in the same way and that he was mentally cheating on her with his thoughts. Sadly for Angela, Paul's need of physical contact and his desire for womanly companionship far outweighed his ethics, but how much longer would it be before Angela realised he was just using her for sex and that he had no intention of ever asking her to marry him?

Paul was about to find out, as Angela finally made her decision!

# Chapter 9

In Gordy's eyes, Anna grew more beautiful as the years passed. He knew how fortunate he was to have her as his wife and how much he loved her, but the jewel in his crown was Emma. He adored her. It never occurred to him she wasn't his child and, if it did, it certainly didn't bother him. What really mattered, was he believed she was his daughter, and had done so ever since he'd made love to Anna for the first time. And neither had he given a moment's thought to the man who was her biological father: as far as he was concerned, Paul was in Anna's past and, as she'd never given him the slightest inclination she ever regretted her decision to marry him, Gordy had the capacity to disregard the fact Paul had ever existed, being was truly confident in his own manhood. So, once he'd possessed Anna, he gave her no opportunity to want her past lover. Adoring her as he did, and being a truly wonderful lover, Anna soon thought less and less of Paul, although her deep-seated love for him never disappeared.

The years were passing too quickly for Gordy's liking. Emma would be nine years old soon and Anna, within a few days would be celebrating her milestone thirtieth birthday. With Molly's encouragement, he began making secret arrangements for them to have a short holiday in Paris to celebrate. As always, Molly was looking forward to having Emma to stay, like Gordy, she too adored the child and, as her adopted grandmother, would get to spoil her for a few days. As for Emma, it was just another opportunity to twist Grandma Molly even further around her little finger.

Gordy couldn't wait for Anna's birthday to arrive. He wanted to see her face when he gave her the tickets to Paris, knowing it was the one place she'd always wanted to visit and where he intended to make it a memorable time for them both.

Her surprise was wonderful to see as she saw her presents on the kitchen table, arranged earlier by Emma. Of course, Emma's parcel had to be opened first!

It was a picture she'd drawn and coloured, which Gordy had had framed. They were both watching intently as Anna ripped open the wrapping paper and took out the picture and saw how thrilled she was.

Anna cherished all her talented daughter's artwork and that day was no exception: her heart swelled with pride and love at Emma's latest creation, as beautiful as her previous ones, knowing Emma's childish drawings were just the beginning of something special.

Gordy's gifts were next. After kissing her, he took one of the gift-wrapped parcels, a long slim envelope and placed it in her waiting hands. Anna looked at him with loving eyes as she took hold of it and slowly tore it open, unaware Gordy and Emma were holding their breaths. She took out a sheaf of travel documents from a travel agent's wallet and read the destination on the first ticket, then gave a shriek of delight, reaching out to take Gordy in her arms, hugging him in her excitement. 'Oh, what a wonderful present! You're such a lovely man! Paris in the spring!'

Delighted by her approval, Gordy held her close and kissed her, knowing how much he loved her.

'Open the next one, Mummy.' Emma said, passing a small gift-wrapped parcel from the table into Anna's waiting hand. Trembling with excitement, Anna struggled to unwrap the parcel, finally revealing a small jewellery box. She lifted the lid and for a moment was speechless as she looked in amazement at the contents.

Emma stretched across to have a look. 'OOH, Mummy, aren't they pretty?' she said.

With shaking fingers Anna unclasped the earrings from the box. 'Yes, darling they are,' she said, her voice full of emotion and near to tears. 'More than pretty, they're beautiful!'

Gordy reached across and took them from out of her shaking hand. Moving her hair to one side, revealing her delicate ears, he proceeded to fasten them into Anna's small earlobes before standing back to admire them.

The earrings he'd chosen with such care looked stunning, each earring holding a square-cut emerald, surrounded by diamonds, matching the engagement ring he'd given her.

Anna was thrilled. She looked at herself in the small hand mirror Emma handed her, admiring her reflection, feeling humble and overwhelmed by Gordy's gifts. She already knew how much he loved her and, at that moment, she knew she loved him equally in return. Deciding to marry him had been by far the best decision she'd ever made, at that moment, Paul Adams was far from her thoughts.

Next she opened Molly's gift; a pendant, hanging from a fine gold chain that matched the earrings from Gordy. A perfect emerald surrounded by small diamonds that also left her speechless. Feeling blessed, by their love and kindness she kissed them in turn, tears of happiness spilled onto her cheeks.

The trip to Paris was scheduled for a couple of weeks later for, as Gordy had said, 'Spring is the best time to see the most romantic city in the world.'

He'd chosen a luxury coach tour that gave them the chance to see other parts of the surrounding countryside, as well as excursions to the Louvre, Montmartre and the Elysee Palace.

Their hotel was situated in the centre of the city, so they had the pleasure of seeing and hearing the sounds and sights of Paris, as well as wonderful views from the small balcony of their room, where they would sit each morning to eat warm, buttery croissants and drink the aromatic coffee that gave Anna a buzz for the whole day, before they went off to explore. Mostly they walked around the city, enjoying the sights and sounds of springtime, but sometimes they went by coach enjoying one of the excursions included in the holiday. At each stop they would buy gifts to take home for Emma and Molly, but the days in the city were the ones Anna liked best. After lunch, eaten at one of the many pavement cafés, they would sit and watch the world go by and then return to their hotel room to enjoy a bout of lovemaking that seemed even better than usual: only then would they have a short siesta and rest!

In the evenings, they would go out and eat at one of the small and intimate restaurants they'd found earlier. But the culmination of Anna's evenings was always the time when she was being held close by Gordy, when he would kiss her and whisper words of endearment, caressing her, before bringing her to a climax so intense she often cried a little, her love for him overwhelming her emotions. Rarely did she ever think of Paul and what might have been and certainly never when in the throes of lovemaking with Gordy. Her thoughts then were only for him, the man who'd skilfully managed over the years to diminish any thoughts of Paul she might have had, at the same time, blocking out any comparison between them, especially of the only time they'd made love and she'd become pregnant. Gordy had definitely overwritten any thoughts she might have had of Paul with his own brand of passionate lovemaking, leaving Anna never regretting her decision to marry him.

All too soon, their short holiday in Paris was over and they had to return home, but good and happy memories linger on and that's exactly what happened with Anna and Gordy. Wonderful memories that would sustain Anna in the years to follow!

Life at the Golden Lion had become even more demanding since they'd started doing meals at lunchtime as well as the evenings. They were so busy since then they'd both been working fulltime and even Gordy could see Molly was getting tired. She'd confided in him one evening of her longing for retirement, leaving him to wonder what Anna would do if Molly sold the business as she'd threatened, and then he'd thought, what would Molly do without the city centre hotel that had been her life for so many years? So far, she hadn't discussed her desire for retirement with Anna, and this left Gordy in a quandary; should he warn Anna, or wait and see how Molly felt in a few weeks' time, when the rush of spring and summer visitors to the city had abated.

He knew how much Anna loved her work and how she never seemed to tire of the business, in fact she seemed to thrive on hard work. She would even spend what little spare time she had experimenting with new dishes to add to the menus: using her considerable skills and ingenuity to make the meals more interesting, as well as cost effective for the business, all without sacrificing the quality expected by their customers. She was a woman driven at times with her pursuit for perfection, a fact that not only Gordy noticed but Molly as well, but were both powerless to alter.

To accommodate their ever-increasing numbers of customers, Anna finally managed to persuade Molly to have the dining room extended into the courtyard, adding a brick and glass conservatory, they decorated in white and pale green, and where Anna placed an abundance of green plants, along with tables and chairs all fashioned in fancy white painted ironwork, with comfortable cushions on the metal seats. Once finished, the new room looked fresh and inviting and it didn't take long before the conservatory became the most asked for area for eating in by their customers.

The next year passed as quickly as all the others, since Anna had arrived to live and work with Molly, and soon it was nearly time for Emma's tenth birthday.

Gordy wanted to organise another party for her, as he'd done for all her previous birthdays, but Anna was concerned for his health. She'd noticed over the past few months how he seemed more tired than usual: she'd even suggested he make an appointment for a physical check-up, but of course he'd scoffed at the idea, telling her that there couldn't possibly be anything wrong with his health, trying to soothe her fears by telling her he'd just been extra busy at work and all he needed was a short break, and then he'd be fine. Before that happened though, he wanted to organise Emma's party and no amount of persuasion on Anna's part could convince him to do otherwise.

Emma solved the problem herself. For her birthday treat she wanted to take some friends skating at the new ice rink in the city centre, with just a small buffet tea party afterwards.

Anna had watched Gordy's face as Emma told him what she wanted: amazed at the child's insight as to how he was feeling. She'd sat on his knee, explaining to him she was 'all grown up now' and that his magic tricks and party games were far too babyish for her and her friends. Anna could see the disappointment on Gordy's face and it took quite a lot of their teasing, before his normal sunny mood reappeared until eventually he agreed to Emma's wishes, albeit rather reluctantly, and so the matter was closed!

At least Anna was thankful he would be able to relax on Emma's big day, instead of being so involved, he ended up exhausted, even if he was happy!

Molly, in her role as grandmother, had of course attended every party since Emma's birth ten years ago and this one was not going to be the exception. Like Gordy, she absolutely adored the child, by now a smaller edition of Anna in looks, with her elfin face and green eyes. Anna had told Molly years ago, when they were alone one day, Emma had Paul's hair colouring. As Gordy was also dark-haired no one ever thought or suspected Emma wasn't his child.

The day of the party arrived. While Emma and her friends had gone skating, with Gordy as their minder, Anna and Molly arranged the buffet tea. By the time they'd finished, the table was groaning with plates of sausage rolls and finger rolls filled with egg and cress, a selection of small iced cakes and biscuits and fancy-shaped jellies, and a blancmange in the shape of a rabbit, along with the mandatory birthday cake, made and iced, as always by Molly. The cake itself was covered in the palest of pink icing with the model of a ballerina poised in mid-twirl in the centre, with ten candles arranged around the top, ready for the birthday girl to blow out once Gordy had made a big show of lighting them.

Anna could see, as soon as they arrived home from the skating rink, Gordy wasn't feeling well. As usual, he refused to allow Anna to fuss over him, saying he just felt tired and would feel better after he'd had his tea and a piece of cake!

It was some time later, after the party was over and Emma was tucked up in bed, and Molly had gone back to the hotel to close up, Anna really began to worry about him. He was sitting opposite her in his favourite chair, looking pale and tired. Suddenly, he clutched his arm to his chest, gasping in pain. In a flash Anna was at his side, worry for him etched on her face.

'What's the matter, darling?' she said, alarm welling up inside her as she knelt on the floor in front of him. She could see he was in pain, grimacing as another spasm travelled from his chest, down his arm. 'I'm going to call the doctor!' she cried out, rising to her feet, intent on running into the hall to phone the doctor. Gordy reached out to stop her as another more painful spasm ran down his arm. 'I think that would be a good idea,' he said, 'I really don't feel so good!' Bending forward, as yet another spasm racked through him, holding his arm tightly to his chest.

For a moment, Anna was in a dither, undecided between wanting to stay with the man she loved, at the same time, wanting to get to the phone to get help. Getting help won and she quickly ran into the hallway, dialling the doctor's number, as fast as her shaking hand would allow.

It seemed to take forever for the phone to be answered. While she was waiting, she heard the noise of Gordy falling on the floor, obviously trying to reach her; she could hear him calling her name. As the phone was picked up at the other end, she just managed to tell the doctor what had happened, when she heard Gordy again, this time he gave a cry of desperation, in a panic, she dropped the phone and rushed back into the room, to see him lying on the floor where it was obvious he was having a heart attack.

Anna screamed his name and knelt down beside him. Hearing the commotion, the doctor understood all too well what was happening and had rung off to call for an ambulance. By now, Anna was beside herself with worry, hoping against hope the doctor would come quickly and help her dearest husband.

The doctor and ambulance crew found her, minutes later, as they'd hurried into the house sitting on the floor, with Gordy's head cradled in her lap, tears silently flowing down her cheeks knowing they were too late to save his life. Gordy had died in his beloved Anna's arms as she'd tried to give him the kiss of life. There had been no hope of her reviving him the doctor had told her, he'd died instantly, after suffering a massive coronary. Anna was dumbstruck. How would she carry on without him? But more than that, how was she going to tell Emma her beloved daddy had died and was gone forever?

Numb with grief, Anna didn't remember the funeral at all. She felt like a zombie just going through the motions of living, feeling dead herself.

Molly understood her grief and despair, remembering how she'd felt at losing her own beloved Paddy. She knew it would take many months before Anna and Emma would come to terms with their loss, all she could do in the meantime was to comfort them in the only way she knew how, with her own brand of loving kindness, and by offering them a temporary home with her. This helped, of course, as Anna and Emma couldn't face the thought of living in the little house without their beloved Gordy.

The next few months passed in a blur, with all of them merely going through the motions of celebrating the festive season of Christmas and then the New Year. More for Emma's sake, and their customers, they decorated the hotel, as usual, but were both relieved when the celebrations came to an end and they could take them down and pack them away in boxes and put them into storage for another year.

With the New Year started, Molly began to think it was time she talked seriously to Anna about their futures. Before she'd gathered enough courage to say her piece, Anna received a letter from Gordy's solicitor, asking her to make an appointment as soon as possible to see him regarding Gordy's will.

A few days later, she was sitting in the solicitor's office, with the man who'd looked after Gordy's affairs over the years, full of anxiety for she'd never been involved in their finances and wasn't sure what to expect. Her main fear, was her home safe? She'd always thought the little house they lived in was rented! Maybe, she thought, panicking slightly, she would have to find somewhere else to live.

To her surprise, the man who sat in front of her looked at her kindly for several minutes, fully aware of her nervousness as he sorted through a pile of official-looking papers, finally extracting one single sheet of paper, which Anna could see was covered with closely-typed writing. The solicitor adjusted his glasses and, after clearing his throat, commenced the task of altering Anna's future.

To her surprise, Gordy had left her a small fortune! Not only did she own the house they'd lived in since their marriage, but several others as well, along with stocks, shares, bank accounts and investments in building societies. There was more than enough money for Anna never to have to work again and for Emma to be educated. He'd even set money aside for Emma's future, in his own words he'd left his beloved daughter a dowry.

Anna returned to the Golden Lion in a complete daze. Her mind a jumble of thoughts as to what she should do with her inheritance. She knew she would have to consider what would be the best for them all, as now she felt responsible for Molly, as well as Emma.

She also knew Gordy would want her to be happy. At that moment though, happiness didn't figure very large in Anna's world. She would have given everything she now possessed to have him back. Without her dearest husband she felt bereft. She also knew she had to work her way through her grief before she could make any firm decisions as to her future and that of Emma and Molly's as well. It was up to her now to decide the best path they should all take, a daunting prospect at first, but one she knew Gordy must have thought her capable of doing or he wouldn't left her a legacy that had made her very rich!

What about the fates? Were they looking down and smiling favourably or were they going to cause further mischief for her? What is the best way forward for Anna?

# Chapter 10

Grief stricken, and still in a daze at their loss, Anna and Emma were reluctant to move back to their own home and so they continued to live with Molly. Anna, ostensibly to be on hand to help run the hotel, but Molly knew the real reason was neither of them could bear to live in the little terraced house without their beloved Gordy.

Unaware of the scale of Anna's inheritance, Molly thought it was time to discuss both their futures. She'd hoped having Anna to stay would give them the chance to talk about her own plans for retirement; plans so far she hadn't discussed with anyone, other than Gordy and he was no longer alive.

By now it was spring and any talk of Molly's retirement still hadn't taken place and neither had Anna made any attempt to return to her own home, not that Molly didn't want her to stay. She just knew if she wanted to retire she would have to sell the Golden Lion to fund her retirement and Anna would probably leave to work elsewhere and she didn't relish the thought of living without her and Emma.

Events took an unexpected turn a week or so later. The two women were sitting in Molly's upstairs lounge, drinking a nightcap after they'd closed the hotel for the night. They always talked over the day's events before bedtime and that evening was no exception, except that earlier in the day, Molly had made up her mind to finally broach the subject of her retirement with Anna. It was therefore a great surprise when, before she could have her say, Anna started telling her of her plans for her future; plans that happily included her.

Anna tried hard not to cry as she sat holding her nightcap drink. She'd cried copious amounts of tears since Gordy's death and her emotions were still raw, her grief heightened at the very mention of his name making her tears always near to the surface, but that evening she wanted to talk about hers and Molly's future and tried hard to hold her feelings and tears in check.

Sitting with Molly, Anna suddenly felt an inner peace settle on her. It was as if Gordy was with her, approving the plans she had in mind; perhaps he was telling her the time had come for her to dry her eyes and get on with her life; to stop wallowing in her misery.

Anna looked across at Molly and smiled. It was time she knew to take on the challenge of being wealthy, young and intelligent. Time, she knew, for her to use her talents constructively and make a good life for them all.

As Molly listened to Anna's plans she too smiled, shaking her head in wonderment. Anna's dreams weren't of taking a luxury cruise or buying jewellery and a large house in the country, what she planned on doing with her legacy was to buy a business! And not any old business if you don't mind, but a country pub! Molly, of course, loved the idea. For a while she was speechless, as Anna told her what she planned on doing with her life, using Gordy's money of course! It was exactly as Molly would have wanted for herself, had she been younger. She was thrilled Anna would get to live her dream and, best of all, she would still get to live with the two people she loved more than anything else in the world!

Anna had been well aware of Molly's desire to retire for some time. She'd seen for herself how she'd been getting ever more tired each day. It was no mean task running a successful hotel, as Anna knew only too well. It took hard work to make it look easy! But now the time had come for Molly to stop working and enjoy her remaining years in comfort and let someone else do the worrying for her. And that was exactly what Anna had in mind.

Since she'd first gone to live with Molly, Anna had never thought of Molly as being anything other than her surrogate mother and her guardian angel! And for that she was grateful. The fates must have been looking kindly on her when she'd been most in need, choosing Molly to be her saviour and now Anna intended doing the same for her!

Molly sat and listened intently as Anna told her she was keen to buy a pub in the country, in a village not too far away from the city, making it quite clear from the start Molly was to retire from being an hotelier; her role in the future would be to provide them with her own brand of loving care. She was the one who was to be the homemaker! To make a home for her and Emma, where they could all relax and enjoy life as a family, leaving Anna to run whatever business she decided to buy.

Molly had sighed, past thoughts of a retirement spent on her own vanishing, as she envisaged a new life with Anna and Emma, instead of being alone and lonely, not a prospect she'd been looking forward to. She'd never wanted to live out her days without Anna and Emma nearby, and that evening, listening to Anna's plans meant she would be with them all the time. They were her family, especially as her own family of nephews and nieces were scattered across the globe and were no longer interested in her, or her life.

The two women sat companionably as they talked about Anna's hopes and her dreams for the future. At the same time, Molly wondered what the outcome would have been if Anna had married Paul all those years ago. If she had never entered what had once been her mundane life. And how her life, since that Christmas Day, ten years ago had been enriched when Anna stopped outside the front door of the Golden Lion, complete with scratches and a black eye, her dreams of love and a future with her young man dashed, and all because of an older woman's spitefulness and jealousy!

Molly often wondered if Anna had thought of Paul over the years. If so, she knew Gordy would have taken her mind off her ex-lover. It was Gordy's love, as well as his astuteness with money that was now going to enable Anna to make a new life for them all and, in all likelihood, still being as attractive as she'd been ten years ago, she would probably find a new husband into the bargain!

Over the next couple of weeks, whenever they could get away in the afternoons from the hotel, Anna would drive them around the nearby countryside to visit different villages that appealed to them both, not just as potential places to buy a business, but where they could make new lives for themselves.

Towards the end of the second week, Anna drove them out to the Cotswolds, where, by sheer chance, she came across exactly what she'd been looking for!

She'd driven into the market town of Coombe Norton and parked the car. Immediately liking the town and where, just as if the fates had planned it, in the window of an estate agent's in the main street was a photograph and details of a dilapidated country pub. From the look of the faded photograph and the details, it was obvious the place had been on the market for some time. Molly grimaced, quite sure Anna was mad to even contemplate such a property but then, she didn't have Anna's vision!

Anna felt both nervous and excited as she went into the estate agent's. It was as though it was meant to be.

With Molly clutching the details and tut-tutting now and then to herself, Anna followed behind the agent as they drove out to the village of Little Coombe to view the old building that, according to an inscribed stone over the door had been built in 1542. In Molly's opinion the building had been sadly neglected over the years and probably hadn't had much done to it since!

Thankfully, Anna was blessed with a vivid imagination and could see beyond its present state. It certainly needed more than just renovating but she could see it had potential. She viewed the old building from all angles, making a mental list of all that needed to be done. First of all, most of the stonework needed urgent attention and the roof definitely needed replacing.

Walking slowly through the rooms, Anna viewed the whole of the property, her heart beating fast. By the time she'd seen all there was to see, she knew she would have to spend a great deal of Gordy's money to get the old place up to a standard she would be happy with and, after a final look, they all trooped outside.

The agent, having shown them over the entire building, as well as an attached and semi-derelict cottage, took them to meet the owners. He'd already assured Anna and Molly the couple would probably accept any reasonable and sensible offer they made, as they wanted to retire and move back to the city to be near their families, none of whom were interested in taking on the old property, especially as it needed virtually rebuilding in parts to bring it into the twentieth century. The old building might have been Anna's dream property, but to Molly, it looked more like a nightmare!

Anna had been unsure of buying in the Cotswolds, as she thought the area too expensive, even for a woman of her means, but the village of Little Coombe was so pretty and romantic she couldn't resist it and, succumbing to its charms, she just knew she had to buy the pub.

As a business it seemed ideal; she wanted a property that would attract customers and the Ring O' Bells, as it was called, certainly had plenty of charm, perhaps hidden from view at the moment, but once revealed, it would certainly be an attraction.

Molly couldn't see its potential at the time, but she trusted Anna's judgement completely. As for Anna, she already knew if the renovations were carried out sympathetically the pub would look splendid. The attached cottage needed the same amount of work as the pub and Anna thought if that were done first, they would at least have somewhere to live, while the pub was being tackled.

Next, they explored the huge garden attached to the cottage, and this was where Molly's eyes finally lit up. Even though it was knee-deep in weeds, with a couple of old apple trees in need of severe pruning, and a tumble down greenhouse that needed replacing, she could see in her head the garden in full bloom and, like Anna with the pub building, her head started to buzz with ideas for what she could do to the garden and, at last, Anna had an ally for her plans.

There was a large car park on the other side of the pub, full of ruts and potholes at present, also another large and overgrown garden at the rear that she knew, once it had been tamed and redesigned, would become one of the pub's best features. She could visualise it with a pergola, covered with climbing roses and a honeysuckle, making it into a shady area, set with tables and chairs for those customers wanting to sit outside on sunny days.

Anna's imagination had been working overtime as she explored further, finding an overgrown pathway leading down to the river. There was a riverside walk going off in both directions. In her imagination she could visualise small river craft coming up the river from Stratford-on-Avon, mooring at a landing strip she would have built, bringing customers from the town and villages upstream. Perhaps in time, even small pleasure boats could be hired from a quay she would build further upstream, which she knew could well be another feature for her customers to enjoy.

Anna said very little as she went back to join Molly, the realisation that she wanted this building more than anything else in her life had rendered her, for once, totally speechless.

The agent quite expected Anna to take him to one side and tell him, as other potential buyers had over the past few years, that the place needed far too much money spending on it to be viable, but then he'd never met a woman like Anna before. He didn't know, or understand, she'd fallen in love, totally and utterly in love, with her whole being, with a crumbling and ancient building that had stood for over five hundred years and, that she wanted nothing more than to own it and bring it back to life.

Molly could see from the determined expression on Anna's face she intended to buy the ancient wreck. So it was with quiet resignation, she accepted their roles had fundamentally changed. From now on, it was going to be Anna doing the leading and she the one doing the following, supporting and helping her in any way she could. From that moment on, Molly began to look to the future with different eyes, and an optimism for her future she hadn't thought possible as she felt herself being drawn further and further into Anna's dream of a new life for them all, in a centuries-old building, in one of the prettiest villages in England.

As they walked away from the agent to talk over what they'd seen, Molly knew, from how Anna was talking, she'd guessed right, Anna wanted this property and, come what may, she was going to have it!

Anna's decision to buy the pub and the attached cottage had been made with her heart, her business head hadn't come into her thoughts at all and so, it was with a great deal of hope in her heart, she instructed the agent to offer a price she considered to be fair and reasonable. If her offer were to be accepted, she would take on the pub and put everything she could into making it the place of her dreams.

The next morning, the estate agent phoned to tell her the offer she'd put in had been accepted and, laughing with joy, she'd danced round and round Molly's sitting room with her arms around Emma and Molly, until all three of them fell exhausted onto the squashy old sofa in Molly's sitting room.

Getting the Ring O' Bells renovated and a new two-storey extension built to house the new kitchen and bathroom at the cottage, seemed to take an inordinately long time, as well as a huge amount of money, and that was only the start. Because the buildings were so old, they had to be treated accordingly. Being bound by rules and regulations demanded by the local council and preservation groups, Anna had to show patience, which for someone with her boundless energy and enthusiasm she found to be quite irksome. As they still had the Golden Lion to distract them, they carried on working as usual while they waited for the wheels of the planning department to slowly go round.

The cottage, as planned, was finished first. The new kitchen and the upstairs bathroom and bedroom extension, blended in with the old building as though it had always been there. Molly was then given the task of choosing the interior colours she wanted for the new farmhouse-style kitchen and, once it was finished and had been fitted with a new cream Aga (installed in an alcove made especially for it) the kitchen was just as Molly imagined it to be, with enough room for a large pine table and chairs in the centre, and a huge pine dresser on one wall for all their treasures to be displayed. Molly instinctively knew this room would soon become the favourite place for them to sit and talk as they ate the meals *she* intended cooking and serving from now on.

Between them, they chose the colours and soft furnishings for the rest of the cottage, to compliment the antique furniture they were going to take from Molly's sitting room and bedroom at the hotel. The rest of the furniture was to come from Anna and Gordy's little house, along with some of the treasures that had belonged to his first wife and had been Gordy's legacy to Emma. They all knew the cottage was going to be lovely and Molly couldn't wait for the day to come when they moved in, but there were still a few hurdles to jump before that day arrived!

The village was beautiful, just five miles, or thereabouts, from its big sister, the market town of Coombe Norton. Like the market town, all the buildings in the village had been built in the same locally quarried golden stone as the pub. Over the centuries it had weathered, turning to a soft golden hue. For the new work at the cottage and the pub, all the stone used came from redundant farm buildings, so that when it was all finished, the old and new parts were indistinguishable from one another.

Anna was absolutely thrilled with the final results of the cottage and, with the quality of the workmanship being outstanding, the Ring O' Bells looked superb, better than

Anna could ever have imagined, and all due to the materials that had been used, making this once old and crumbling wreck of a building into one of the loveliest in the village, which not only delighted Anna, Molly and Emma, but the locals as well.

The old oak front door they'd kept, flanked as it was on either side by stone mullioned windows. The door colour had changed over the centuries and had weathered to a silver grey, all it needed, after the ingrained dirt and grime had been removed, was a coat of wax for its natural colour to be enhanced.

Tubs and baskets, all full of colourful plants and flowers, stood at the entrance and, with the renovations nearly complete, Anna set about getting some help in running the place, knowing opening the pub and running it would entail more work than she could cope with alone.

With Molly's help, she interviewed several couples that had answered her advertisement in a trade magazine for a barman and assistant cook. Jim and Monica Davies were the youngest couple out of the ten that applied. They were in their early thirties and, liking them both immediately, Anna and Molly selected them to come and work at the pub.

Anna had made up her mind that, apart from this once, Molly was no longer going to be part of the working team and, to Molly's relief, she was now relegated to being Anna and Emma's housekeeper, with strict instructions that from now on she was to enjoy her retirement!

Jim and Monica planned on moving to the Midlands from the Welsh valleys, after Jim had been made redundant from his job as a coal miner in the village where they'd both been born and bred. They decided to look for work away from Wales; preferably somewhere they could work together, intent on gaining experience with the ultimate aim of owning a business of their own in the future. Thankfully, Jim was already an experienced barman, his knowledge gained from working at the local miner's social club in their village and Monica, according to Jim, was the best cook in Wales. Taking them at face value, mainly because she liked them straightaway, Anna and Molly thought they would be ideal; Anna particularly liking Monica and, because of this, she offered them the jobs immediately after she'd interviewed them!

It was quite fortunate that only a few days previous, one of the builders working on the pub had told Anna of a pair of cottages in the village that were up for sale and could do with her kind of treatment. Knowing any staff she employed might possibly need accommodation in the future, Anna bought, not just one cottage, but both, so continuing Gordy's investment plans and it was into one of these cottages, once renovated, Jim and Monica moved, a couple of weeks before the pub was due to re-open.

The day finally arrived for the grand re-opening of the Ring O' Bells with the old place looking every bit as Anna had first imagined. The old roof had been replaced, as had a fair amount of the crumbling stonework, which had either been repaired or replaced. There was fresh woodwork, plaster and paintwork throughout the building and a new and up-to-date professional kitchen had been installed. The inside of the pub had altered drastically and was now much better in terms of attractiveness and practicability. Even the car park had been set in order, as well as the garden.

All the locals had been invited to the grand opening and they couldn't wait to get inside and see for themselves what had changed. Needless to say they were all amazed at the transformation. The interior, especially the bar, had been done in a tasteful manner, with a new bar fashioned out of old oak that, to anyone who didn't remember what the old one looked like, would have assumed it to be the original. A new floor had been laid throughout the downstairs, using old reclaimed flagstones that added to the authenticity of the place with under-floor heating. Sensitive to the feelings of the locals, Anna had kept as much of the old furniture as she could, adding to the pub's character and charm, with other antique pieces she found in the local sales room.

Along with a log fire laid ready for lighting on the first cold day, and vases full of flowers, the pub looked superb. The final finishing touches to the pub's ambience were those Anna had dreamed of long ago; highly polished copper kettles and brassware, gleaming on the bar counter and windowsills, along with some of the paintings and ornaments from Molly's old hotel spread around, as well as some from Anna's own collection. With the pub finally dressed in its finery, the old oak door was ceremoniously opened, ready and waiting to welcome its first customers.

Anna was confident it would be the ambience of the place that would at first draw in the customers. But to keep them coming, she knew she would have to supply really good food to tempt them back again and again. She wanted her pub to be on the list of best places to visit for eating and drinking, but most of all, she wanted her customers to enjoy the experience and its charms and advertise it, by word of mouth to their friends.

Molly, of course, performed the opening ceremony.

After declaring the pub open for business, all the villagers and other invited guests, friends of Anna and Molly from the city, they were soon enjoying tasters of the food and drink that were going to be available in the future.

It didn't take long for Jim and Monica to settle into their new life in the village and, working at the pub, they too soon became essential members of Anna's 'team'. All looked set fair for the Ring O' Bells and its future and, for the first time since Gordy's death, Anna felt exhilarated and alive.

At last she was her own woman, independent and so far, in a small way, successful. She looked forward to the future; to seeing where this venture would take her, as did Molly and Emma, all thrilled that so far, all had gone according to Anna's master plan!

# Chapter 11

Anna had been thirty-one years old the year Gordy died. By the following spring she'd bought the Ring O' Bells in Little Coombe and started a new phase in her life, at the same time realising a long-held ambition to run a pub of her own. She had never thought her dream would come true and yet, here she was, the owner of one of the prettiest pubs in the Cotswolds, in one of the most beautiful villages she'd ever seen.

In a remarkably short time, her new venture became successful and, with Molly and Emma settled into the cottage and happy with their lives in the village, all was well in Anna's world. At last, she began to look at life with more optimism than she'd felt for a long time. But she missed Gordy. With her every waking hour accounted for, it wasn't until late at night, as she lay in her bed, when she would think of him and talk to him in her mind, telling him of her plans and dreams, sharing with him her fears and doubts and her wishes, imagining him in bed with her, his arms around her, until exhausted, sleep finally claimed her and Gordy's image would fade away as she slept.

The pub was Anna's only interest. Nothing else, apart from Emma and Molly interested her. Along with Monica and Jim, she set about making it the best country pub in the area. If her artistic skill inside the pub had impressed everyone then so did the garden design. Not that she did the gardening! She'd designed it for her customers to relax in, with rustic tables and chairs set out under the trees and under the pergola she'd been so determined to have; already covered with rambling roses and sweet-scented honeysuckle, making it a shady area where her customers could eat and drink when the weather was fine.

A newly gravelled walkway meandered through the garden, down to the hedge and beyond to the riverside, where she'd had a landing built to take the expected river craft. There was even a separate area set aside in the garden for children, with swings and a slide and, at the back of the bar, a family room she'd had built especially for children to play in; a new innovation in those days, as children were not allowed into the main bar of public houses.

Anna had come to realise early on how few pubs in the area catered for children or families and it was her insight into how family attitudes to their leisure times were changing that made her business so successful, her undoubted foresight just one of the many reasons for her success. Families could now eat in the pub, with their children's needs catered for as well. The 'Ring O'Bells' was an eating-place that welcomed them, as in France and Italy.

As Anna knew well, times were changing in the country, and she embraced these changes, especially those that gave a challenge for her mind, as well as her heart.

She really enjoyed her life working in the pub with Monica, as she had at the hotel in the city with Molly, throwing herself wholeheartedly into getting the most out of it, and now she began creating new recipes and special dishes, adding to those they already served.

She'd always made savoury and sweet pastries while working with Molly and, since opening the pub, she'd started making them for her own customers. Her chicken and mushroom pies, and then her steak pies, were soon to become legendary and the most asked for specialities, with people travelling miles during summer evenings and at weekends, when the garden and pub would be full of customers, especially to eat them.

Being a sociable person herself, Anna loved the atmosphere of the pub and, on balmy summer evenings, with a glass of white wine in hand, she would wander through the garden, talking and listening to her customers and watching as they enjoyed themselves.

By the end of her first year in the village, Anna found she couldn't keep up with the demand for her pies and had to resort to getting some of Molly's new friends in the village to step in and make extra ones for her. This helped a little to fill the gap, but she knew the time had come when she must look at the problem in more depth and try to solve it another way. And so, it was the success of her pies that was responsible for leading Anna in another direction, enabling her to take on yet another challenge!

Talking over her problems with Molly, after a particularly busy evening, Anna bemoaned the fact she and Monica couldn't cope with the demand for the pies, even though she'd since taken on another cook to help out. As astute as ever, Molly offered her a solution to the predicament. She'd realised herself what Anna needed to do was to off-load some of her present workload. As far as she could see, she had two choices, one, to fail in giving her customers what they wanted or secondly, to expand the business, not just by taking on more kitchen staff, but by getting her pies and other popular items made elsewhere to her recipe!

It was talking over these options with the ever-sensible Molly, that made Anna think even harder about what she wanted to do. She wasn't very keen on getting someone else to make her pies, but after having what she thought of as a 'light bulb moment', perhaps setting up a business to make the pies elsewhere, in a purpose-built factory, would be the answer. Doing this, she knew would enable her to expand not only her existing range of pies and pastries, but into other products, convinced there was a bigger market for these products, but first, she knew she needed to find premises, somewhere away from the pub, where she could make the products she needed.

Convinced by now of the feasibility of what she wanted to do, Anna thought it would be a good idea if she appointed Jim to be the pub manager, with him taking over the daily running of the pub and Monica taking charge of the kitchen staff and all the catering, as they'd both proved during their first year of working for her that they were more than capable of running the place and, after they'd both agreed and approved her ideas, Anna was at last free to make her new plans become the reality she envisaged.

By doing what she was best at and being creative, Anna was gradually turning her ideas into reality.

It was only a matter of days before she came to know of a small factory unit that was available on the outskirts of the village. After looking at the building and the site it stood on, she thought it would be ideal for what she wanted. This would be the only big mistake she was ever to make in any of her ventures; not anticipating the future, or the demands for her products, a lesson she would soon learn well!

As it was, she formulated a plan for what she wanted to achieve to start with and, as she'd never believed in using Gordy's inheritance frivolously, spending only when necessary, her aim for the future was for the business to be self-financing and as quickly as possible.

After talking over her plans with Molly, Anna went to see her bank manager in the city to discuss her ideas and obtain his financial help. The serious young assistant manager, charged with taking on her account, quickly became impressed with her business acumen, as well as with the detailed business plan she'd put before him; after discussing her proposal with a senior member of the bank, it was agreed the bank would back her venture, leaving Anna delighted, of course.

Along with her own financial input, and that of the bank, she arranged to buy the lease on the factory unit and purchase the equipment needed to get the business started.

Once the plans had been given the go-ahead, she couldn't wait to get back to Molly, her dearest friend and advisor, to tell her of her success and, with little or no delay, Anna set about planning and organising the next phase of her life, turning herself, within a very short period of time, from a successful pub landlady, into a highly successful businesswoman, which in the late 60s was no mean feat!

Anna knew she would need professional help in getting her new catering business up and running, something she'd talked over with her business advisor at the bank. He'd advised her to employ someone with experience in large-scale food production and, as luck would have it, a few days later, she saw an advertisement for a local catering exhibition to be held in Birmingham, where, quite by chance, she came across the very person she needed, in the guise of a young man called Andrew White.

They met, just as she was looking, somewhat bemused, at one of the large commercial ovens she thought she would need to buy. Andrew was working as a temporary salesman at the show. He approached her, to give her information and hopefully to sell a cooker, until he learnt of her plans and then told her of his! It was after their conversation Anna knew the fates were really looking after her!

After she'd walked around the rest of the exhibition and looked at all the other equipment available, she met up with Andrew to have a coffee and a talk. He told her it was his intention to move down from the north of England, where work was in short supply, to the Midlands, where he believed there to be more jobs than people! Trusting her instincts, Anna invited him to visit the site before he returned home, to advise her on what she needed to install to set up the factory, of course, Andrew jumped at the chance, travelling down to the village the following week, this time bringing his wife and staying at the pub for the weekend. Anna had a feeling, when they both saw the village, with its lovely old stone cottages (one of which she intended to make available for them, should he accept her offer) and the surrounding area, they would be smitten, and then, if they were, perhaps she would then have the production manager she needed!

Within a month, Anna had taken Andrew on and, along with his wife and three small children, they were soon ensconced in the second renovated and modernised cottage and into the village way of life, and she had another member for her team.

Leaving Andrew to organise the ordering and installation of the huge stainless steel ovens and overseeing the food preparation areas in the new factory unit, Anna turned her attention to finding someone to sell the excess products and again the fates stepped in, this time in the shape of Lesley, an old friend from her college days.

Lesley had left college at the same time as Anna, and had gone to Scotland to work in a large hotel. It was while she was there that she'd met, and quickly married, a man several years older than herself.

Unfortunately for Lesley, the man she thought she'd fallen in love with turned out to be abusive and cruel. Even though she tried hard to make her marriage work, and to provide a happy home life for him, she lived in fear and dread of his terrible moods. There was no reason at all, as far as she could see, for these mood swings, he would just suddenly change and begin to attack her verbally, often just on a whim. It soon became a daily ritual, finally changing to physically abusing her after a while, until one day, after a really vicious attack, she was left unconscious on the floor of her bedroom. Fearing he'd killed her, he'd cradled her in his arms, swearing he would change and, once his anger had abated, he would beg her forgiveness, swearing he loved her and couldn't live without her, pleading with her to give him another chance, begging her not to leave him and that he would get help for managing his temper.

At the beginning, and still believing she loved him, Lesley did forgive him, even thinking he would change, believing his outbursts of violence were her fault but, as time went on, she knew without a doubt he would never change, that she was living in a doomed marriage, one that quite possibly, might lead eventually to her death at his hands.

Lesley continued living with him until she became pregnant, which delighted her, as she thought a baby might be the answer, until a few months into her pregnancy when her husband attacked her again; this time so badly she lost her expected baby. Doctors then told her the worst news of her life. The injuries she'd sustained during her husband's latest violent and unprovoked attack meant she would never be able to have another child. Devastated by this news, as well as the loss of her baby, and the violence she'd endured during her marriage, Lesley found, from somewhere, deep inside her, a smidgen of courage and finally she escaped, leaving her abusive husband and divorcing him as soon as she was able.

A few months later, she left Scotland and returned to the city of her birth, to make a new life. It had been on an evening out with friends, who were keen to visit the popular Ring O' Bells in the Cotswolds Lesley met up once again with Anna and where, she not only rekindled her friendship, but found a way back to sanity with a job thrown in as well.

Anna was delighted to have found her old friend and, once she knew the circumstances of why Lesley had returned, she offered her a position as her assistant, and finally, Anna's company 'Pies & Goodies Galore' was born.

Emma, meanwhile, was enjoying village life and especially her schooldays. With her artistic talents flourishing, Anna decided it was time to put them to good use, persuading her daughter to draw the designs for the company logo, as well as the artwork that would adorn the first two delivery vehicles she ordered. Anna was proud of Emma's contribution to the venture and, not for the first time, she thought her business might one day become a family affair!

Once the factory was fully equipped and local suppliers found for the ingredients they needed, Molly duly performed the opening ceremony, just as the first of many pies came out of the ovens!

Within a couple of weeks, the new company was forging ahead, the factory busy with the orders Anna had obtained from local pubs in the Cotswolds and Warwickshire areas.

Lesley was now responsible for selling these products and her idea to take some to local catering fairs, as well as to the large wholesale suppliers. She also visited much smaller places as well, armed with a small selection of the factory's other products. She made it her business to visit every pub, restaurant and café in the Cotswolds and then in Warwickshire, with details of the ready prepared food range; before long, her order books were filling up, with more orders coming in daily. It wasn't long before Andrew was pleading with Anna for a bigger unit, as the original one was hard pressed to make the amount they needed.

His request, that Anna would soon need to find an alternative factory, if the orders increased any more, was met with her eyebrows raised in surprise, knowing she had some hard thinking to do.

Being confident the business was heading for success, Anna agreed with Andrew and Lesley the next factory needed to be nearer the new motorway, which would then enable the products to be delivered as soon as possible after they were made. With all these factors at the forefront of her mind, Anna once again approached the bank for their financial advice, as well as the city council.

Thankfully, there was a new and much larger factory unit available on the outskirts of the city; one that this time Andrew assured her would be ample for their needs. By providing the new factory at a reasonable rent, the council reasoned it would not only be prestigious for the city, but would also provide much-needed employment. It was this forward thinking by the city elders that helped Anna's company achieve the accolade of 'Business of the Year' a couple of years later, the first of many such awards the company would attain over the following years, to be swiftly followed by Anna being awarded 'Business Woman of the Year', an accolade she believed to rightly belong to her team because, without them, and their hard work and support, she would still be serving pints behind the bar at the 'Ring

O'Bells' and relying on sandwiches to feed her new customers in the pub!

It was enough for Anna to have her products available at the pub but quite soon they were also to be found on the shelves of the new supermarkets being built, as well as in all the pubs and clubs in and around the city. Her company, 'Pies & Goodies Galore' had invaded everywhere, to Molly, it seemed everything Anna touched turned to gold, except for her personal life!

Not a day went by when Anna didn't think of Gordy and thanked him for his faith in her. Mostly she missed his common sense approach to life and its problems: but even more than that, she missed having his loving arms around her at night and the wonderful sex life they'd shared. She would sigh wistfully as she remembered the past, wondering if she would ever find anyone to replace him? She'd thought even less about Paul as the years had passed; convinced he must be married by now and have children of his own. She'd even convinced herself he couldn't have been in love with her, even though he'd sworn he was. Her mind would race back over the years; to the day when she'd walked away from him and returned through the snow to the city, sure she'd lost the love of her life! But even after all the years that had passed he still had a place in her heart, and always would, because he was Emma's father. And even though she wouldn't have admitted it to anyone, she knew, deep down, he would always be her forgotten love!

With the second factory soon working at full capacity, Lesley became Anna's right-hand woman, their relationship going from strength to strength as they ran the business together. Anna relying on Lesley for much more than her ability as a saleswoman, she was the sounding board Anna needed, as her mind raced from project to project. It was

Lesley's common sense approach to life, along with her dedication to the business that kept her on track. Being divorced had mellowed Lesley's attitude towards men, but she was still scared of making the same mistake twice, until the day she met and fell headlong in love with David, who, as well as being Anna's financial advisor, was now her bank manager. He'd also become a personal friend and often visited the two factories and the pub on business. It just so happened that on one of his visits he met Lesley, and he too fell instantly in love. He'd arrived unannounced, unaware Anna had gone to visit a supplier, leaving a very flustered Lesley to deal with him alone!

As usual, he'd made his way through the factory to Anna's office, where, instead of finding Anna sitting in the chair behind the desk, he saw Lesley. He'd felt something happen to him that morning that he'd never expected to happen, being too engrossed in his career to even look at another woman, let alone thinking he might find one to marry, having been deserted by his previous wife, that was, until lightning had struck them both at the same time. They were twin souls, who'd waited a lifetime to find each other.

The moment they were struck by the thunderbolt of love, they'd been unable, by the constraints of business, to voice how they felt, so it was several days before Anna had any inkling of what had happened to her friends.

She knew David had visited the office while she'd been away, as Lesley had told her, the 'dishy' bank manager had visited, and she'd dealt with him.

Anna had looked at her friend; aware from Lesley's tone of voice something momentous must have happened. She smiled, trying to hide her amusement, as David had been on the phone only a few minutes earlier, asking after Lesley, after he'd dealt with the business side of his call. She was unable to resist telling her friend of David's interest in her wellbeing and, seeing her reaction, Anna knew for certain they were two adults, interested in each other but too scared and afraid of rejection to approach the other.

After her next visit to the bank, a few days later, Anna noticed how David had reddened at the mention of Lesley's name when she'd deliberately brought it up in conversation! It looked as though Anna was about to become a matchmaker, just as Molly had been to her and Gordy! Glad her friend was at last no longer quite so cynical about men, could it be, Anna wondered, if Lesley really was falling in love with David, one of the nicest men she'd ever met. She thought them to be well suited as they had much in common, him being a divorcee as well and, like Lesley, he'd had to learn to trust again.

David, had taken an instant liking to Anna the first time he'd met her at the bank, he'd been drawn to her, not only to her looks, but by her personality as well. He'd sensed immediately though he stood no chance of her falling in love with him, someone else had captured her heart and, until he met Lesley, he'd never found another woman he wanted to spend his life with.

Realising Lesley and David had fallen in love (but were too scared of admitting it) Anna took the matter in her own hands and engineered a social evening for all her employees and business associates. To her delight, they found each other, leaving Anna wondering whether she should add match making to her growing portfolio of businesses.

It was on one of David's next visits to the factories, and after seeing the amount of office work they had to do; that he'd suggested it was time Anna employed a professional accountant to run her offices. This would free Lesley to concentrate her talents on selling the products, which she did brilliantly! Also, he had an ulterior motive. If Lesley could get home earlier in the evenings he might get to see more of her! To his surprise, Anna agreed, with no demurring either on her part, promptly promoting Lesley to be the company's Sales Director, before setting out to find someone qualified to be the company's chief accountant.

Administration was always the one part of the business Anna liked least of all, it was, as she'd often said to Lesley, the devil on her back. She'd much rather be in the test kitchens at the factory, devising and making new products, such as the ready meals she and Andrew had added to their current line of products, rather than sitting in her office, checking accounts, even if it was her money!

Setting up her businesses, then seeing them take off, had given Anna a tremendous adrenalin buzz, a feeling she loved, but once everything was up and running she was looking for the next challenge. It was in her nature, something she couldn't alter. Her father, and later Gordy, had both understood this part of her make-up, saying she was possessed of a butterfly mind, not knowing where to settle next.

Being creative and decisive was just the way Anna was, she never could understand how anyone would want to sit at the same desk, in the same office, for forty years, doing the same boring job, especially when there was a whole world waiting to be explored and conquered. Lesley liked to tease her, telling her, it was the people who were prepared to do the boring bits that enabled Anna to run her business as successfully as she did! A point Anna had to agree with! She didn't dispute what Lesley had said for one minute, it was just that she didn't do boring!

The day arrived when a bundle of letters lay on Anna's desk awaiting her attention. They were from the employment agency she'd appointed to help find a suitably qualified person to become her chief accountant, someone who would be in charge of her financial empire!

Her schedule that day was busy and, having no time to look at them, she decided to take them home and read them later. After a quick shower and a delicious supper, prepared as usual by Molly, and with a chilled glass of white wine on the small table at the side of her armchair, Anna finally sat and read through the letters and the accompanying CVs.

As she sipped her wine, savouring its crispness, she read through each letter in turn, until sometime later, she'd whittled them down into two piles, making a mental note of those she was interested in, the ones where the resumes sounded right for her. But one letter in particular stood out from the rest, and this she placed on top of the pile.

Some of the applicants, in her opinion, had no idea of the dedication she needed from them if they were to perform the duties outlined in the job prospectus and, it was apparent, from just looking through them that some were just looking for an easy ride until they reached retirement age.

Anna had read through one particular letter twice. It was signed Paul Adams. Her heart had leapt in her chest as soon as she'd seen the name. She opened his curriculum vitae, intrigued to know if this was her Paul Adams or not? Unable to believe she was holding in her hands a letter written by the man she'd fallen in love with years ago, or even that he was applying for a job in her company. She tried to think rationally. Of course, she reasoned, he wouldn't know it was *her* company because he didn't know she was married.

Suddenly, she was in a quandary. She needed someone qualified to take over the reins of the company and steer it into the future but did she need it to be him? Unsure what she should do, she read through his letter twice more, until she knew it by heart, all the while pondering on what she should do. Would her brain win? Or would it be her heart?

Paul's letter and curriculum vitae had definitely impressed her, as did the positions he'd held throughout his working career. But she couldn't believe he could possibly be serious in wanting to leave his present position with the bank, and take, what for him would be a backward step, into an insignificant job in comparison. He must, she thought, have a good reason for wanting to leave the bank, one he wasn't admitting to, so it would be interesting to hear what he had to say and, making up her mind, she placed his letter on top of the pile, intending to offer him the job should he want it!

Sleep was a long time coming that night, as her mind raced over the day's events and she tried to clear her mind, until at last, her eyes closed and sleep descended, but that night, restful sleep eluded her, as her mind kept going back to when she'd been a very immature twenty-year-old and, unknowingly had become pregnant, and then abandoned, by the self-same man who now was applying for a job with her company! She'd waited a long time to find out why Paul Adams had behaved as he had and now it looked as if she was going to have the opportunity to ask him!

Anna knew that although she'd loved Gordy deeply and they'd had a happy and loving marriage, she also knew Paul had once been the man she'd wanted. She'd never forgotten him, or the one and only time they'd made love.

He would always be a part of her life because he was Emma's father and, thinking back to that fateful Christmas, she felt her body respond with its familiar longing for him, a longing that she'd put to the back of her mind once she'd

186

married Gordy, but now she remembered how she'd fallen in love with him and had wanted nothing more than to live her life with him at her side. She remembered how he'd taken her in his arms that night all those years ago and how he'd held her, changing her from an inexperienced virgin into a fully-fledged woman. Not only had he made love to her, but also he'd made her pregnant with the child that so far he had no knowledge of.

The next morning, Lesley could see something momentous had happened to Anna from the look on her face as she entered the office. It was unusual for her to be so sombre and abrupt with her work colleagues and, with Lesley especially. It took the better part of the morning before Anna got round to apologising to her friend and finally telling her what had happened.

It wasn't a short story, as Lesley had no previous knowledge of Anna and Paul's relationship, but Anna knew she had to tell her friend everything; even down to the fact that Paul and not Gordy was Emma's real father.

Haltingly, Anna had begun. She could see Lesley was shocked at first by her revelations. Not shocked in a disapproving way, but out of concern and love for her friend and, after the story was told, and the initial shock had worn off, Lesley showed her true friendship by hugging Anna and holding her close. 'Do you think it would be wise to see him again?' she asked, concern for her friend uppermost in her voice.

'I really don't know,' Anna said, full of anguish. 'I want to see him! But his letter and CV made no mention of a wife or children and I wouldn't want to do anything that would cause him to have a problem in his private life.'

'I don't see what your problem is then,' Lesley said. 'Just tell them at the agency he's not the sort of candidate you're looking for!'

'I can't do that,' Anna said, forlornly, 'because he's exactly what I am looking for!'

'Well then, you'll just have to bite the bullet and see him!' Lesley replied, rather prosaically, for Lesley was nothing, if not practical in her outlook. To her, black was black and white was white, no shades of grey ever clouded her thinking, not after the stormy and violent relationship she'd gone through.

Anna knew her friend was right, she couldn't refuse to interview him; his qualifications and business experiences were exactly what she and her expanding business needed, especially if in the future the business expanded even more. Her thoughts were, if she didn't go for the best, she didn't deserve to succeed and, being afraid of a situation, or of something that had happened in the past, was not one of the options open to her.

Making her decision, Anna wrote Paul's name at the top of the list knowing she could do no more than wait and see what happened.

She grimaced, so the outcome to her life was once again down to the fates, and to the hand she'd been dealt!

A week later, the agency contacted her with the proposed dates for the interviews, by which time Anna was nearly a nervous wreck with the anticipation of seeing Paul again. Even Molly, when Anna had told her what had happened had been astounded by the events.

Anna rarely discussed business with her these days thinking it only right her old friend should enjoy her retirement, without having to share the problems or the worries that running a large company brought with it, but this time, knowing she needed to unburden herself, who better was there than to her dearest friend to share her thoughts with, knowing instinctively Molly would understand, for without her support, she would never have married Gordy and brought up Emma, or even contemplated buying the pub. Her only fear now, as she confided in Molly, was that Emma would one day have to know who her real father was and, when that day came, and she finally knew the truth that it hadn't been Gordy who'd fathered her, what would she say then?

How could she begin to explain to Emma her real father had forgotten the love he'd once professed to have for her mother, and that her marriage to Gordy had, to start with, been just a marriage of convenience?

Deciding to meet Paul was a momentous decision and one, which Anna didn't know if she could face.

# Chapter 12

Angela had been flattered when Paul first asked her out. What woman wouldn't? He was your stereotypical tall, dark and handsome man most women dreamt of and she was no exception. Ever since she'd been a teenager, finding a man such as Paul had been on top of her wish list. Unfortunately, the man she chose, her now ex-husband, had none of Paul's physical attributes! Although, he'd been quite good-looking when much younger: of medium height and build and fair of hair already starting to go thin on top. Finally leaving him completely bald, a couple of years into their marriage. Angela had at first thought, being naïve and vulnerable, his masterful and controlling attitude towards her was wonderful, but once he'd courted and won her, (and she'd become pregnant with Zoe) his masterful attitude soon turned into vicious bullying. By this time, she'd started to dislike him intensely, wondering what she'd ever seen in him until, after one spectacular incident so vicious and cruel, her love for him finally died and she knew she would have to leave him.

Up to that point, Angela had tried to be the sort of wife he obviously wanted, subservient and willing at all times to appease him, regardless of her own wants or needs. As for his bullying ways, they gradually became more abhorrent and Angela's dislike of him grew, to such a degree, that after a time, she found it impossible to live with him, which of course led to even more arguments, until eventually, she couldn't stand being in the same house with him, let alone the same room and, with no regrets, she left, taking Zoe with her and filing for divorce, citing his unreasonable behaviour, as well as his physical and mental cruelty, backed up, of course, by photographs taken by the police when they'd been called to the house after he'd done more than slap her around once too often. So that was the end of Angela's dream of wedded bliss!

She'd been divorced for some time before Paul sailed onto her horizon, meeting him through her business connections. This time, being older and wiser, she formed a much truer picture of his personality and was delighted when he made a play for her. But, being extremely vulnerable after her divorce, she was wary of making another mistake, yet at the same time, she longed to find a lifelong partner, a soul mate, so when he came into her life, Angela thought at last she'd found the very man!

After they'd been out several times as friends, Paul's physical needs finally won her over, but several months later he was still only a part-time lover, with no mention of a commitment from him at all.

Zoe absolutely adored Paul right from their first meeting; in her eyes he was the perfect father and it was his affection towards her daughter that Angela thought might well have made him want to marry her, if only to be the child's father, but their relationship progressed no further, until one day, in a fit of depression, she finally made up her mind. She knew she wanted more from their relationship and decided it was time to force the issue.

Angela was angry, not with Paul, because he'd never intimated marriage was on his mind, but with herself, for assuming that sooner, rather than later, he would ask her to spend her life with him. It was at this point she decided she needed to find out whether she was wasting her time with him or not and, with confrontation on her mind, she asked him to supper.

Paul liked Angela, and eating supper with her was something he did quite often, staying overnight for a session of lovemaking afterwards; it was this intimacy that always left her wanting more. Even then, Paul only ever spent the night with her when Zoe was staying with her father or friends, as she was that evening.

It seemed an ideal opportunity to make Paul face the fact she wanted more than occasional sex; she wanted him to make a decision, one way or the other as to whether they would get married or not and become a family.

As well as being very fond of Angela, because she was attractive, intelligent and good company and because she was always a pleasure to take out, Paul was also astute enough to know his behaviour towards her had been unfair. As it was he enjoyed her company and knew if he lost her friendship, and the sex they both enjoyed, his life would become dull and boring.

Angela seemed unusually quiet that evening when she greeted him, which bothered him, as mostly she was full of life. She'd been his partner at formal dinners and social evenings for several months now, but this evening, he had the feeling she had something on her mind she wanted to say, and quite possibly, it was going to be something he wasn't going to like.

With her mind made up, Angela knew it would be either the beginning of a new relationship with Paul, one that would see them married, if he proposed, as she hoped, or it would be the end and she would be on her own once again.

With supper finished and the dishwasher loaded; a mug of coffee in hand, and with her feet pulled up underneath her, Angela sat and looked across at Paul. She loved everything about him, from his handsome features to his masculinity, and the undoubted virility that seemed to ooze from his every pore. His very being thrilled her and, as always, her heart and senses ached with her love. That night though, she had a feeling of great sadness, especially when she thought of the time and emotion she'd invested in their relationship, but she'd prepared herself earlier for what she thought might possibly be the inevitable. It hadn't really been wasted time, not as far as she was concerned, because she'd had some wonderful times as his companion, but now she wanted and needed more from him, more than perhaps he was prepared to give. She wanted a commitment, but could she be asking for too much?

Paul looked away, unable to give Angela the eye contact she wanted, fully aware of her, yet ignoring her questioning looks. Suddenly, she started to speak, in the quiet and controlled way she used to such good effect in her work.

Desperately trying to hold back her emotions, Angela told him how she felt and Paul let her speak, knowing his behaviour over the years had not been wholly that of a gentleman.

He was well aware he should have finished, what he considered to be a lukewarm affair, with her a long time ago, knowing he'd merely been using her. Treating her badly, not as her ex-husband had in an abusive way, but by enjoying the sex they'd had together, when all the time he'd been aware she wanted more than just a casual sexual relationship. He also knew she loved him and, like most women in love, she wanted the committed relationship of marriage. At the same time he knew he didn't love her, at least, not as she deserved.

For a long time he'd put off making the decision to finish their affair, even though he knew he should, but sitting with Angela that evening, he felt ashamed for not making it clear sooner, he had no intention of making a commitment to her, or to her young daughter. And, for that alone he felt a great sorrow, at the same time knowing he had to tell Angela it was the spectre of Anna holding him back, and this had been his biggest shame.

Angela could see Paul's emotions in his eyes as she waited, but her patience was wearing thin. She wanted to know his answer.

'Do you love me, Paul?' she asked quietly. 'No hedging now, Paul, not any more. No dodging the issue. Just tell me the truth?' Angela could see he was trying to give her an answer, one that was honest, but the words wouldn't come out. He was temporarily speechless.

With her heart jumping and a terrible feeling in the pit of her stomach, she issued her ultimatum. 'I want to know how you really feel about me and whether you intend to marry me or not?'

Speaking out, and getting him to give her an honest answer would be the only way Angela would know exactly where she stood with him.

For a long time, she'd gone along with the casualness of their relationship, but not anymore! If Paul gave the answer she wanted, she would be ecstatic, but deep down she knew this wasn't going to happen.

Paul still didn't reply.

She could see from his facial expression he felt trapped; he was cornered, like a hunted animal and, even before he could put into words he didn't love her enough to marry her Angela knew their affair was over!

It was a moment of truth for Paul as well, knowing he couldn't prevaricate any longer. He had to be honest and open his heart and tell her about Anna and that there could never be anyone else for him but her!

Angela had cried as Paul told her what had happened years ago and how he'd since found out Anna was married to someone else. He kept nothing back from her. Telling her all that had happened after his mother had assaulted the woman he loved and how Anna had left his home and how he'd been involved in a car accident, resulting in his head injury, which had been responsible for his memory of Anna being completely obliterated.

As he recounted his story for the first time, Paul relived the experience and, for only the second time in his adult life, he cried. His loss of the woman he loved still as painful. As his tears fell, so he released pent-up emotions that had lain dormant for a long time, ever since he'd found Anna's letters and the ring, that by rights she should be wearing. Angela cried as well, not only for Paul but also for his lost love and mostly for her own self, knowing for sure he would never be the love of her life. There was no way she could compete with someone who, in her eyes, was only a distant memory.

Wiping away her tears, Paul kissed her a tearful goodbye, promising he would always be her friend; leaving Angela knowing her life would be different from then on and that she had to put Paul Adams to the back of her mind and make herself believe there was a special man somewhere, who needed her as much as she needed him!

Several months passed since Paul had parted company with Angela. Without her company, his life had become boring, until, one day, whilst skimming through a banking and finance magazine he'd picked up on his travels, his eye was caught by an advertisement that intrigued him. It was for the position of chief accountant at a catering company in the city. Thinking it might be a good idea to do something completely different, he did some research into the company and found it was a relatively new company, one that was expanding in a big way. From the job specification he'd received from the agency a few days later, it looked as though it could also offer him the new challenge he needed. He knew he'd not only come to a crossroads in his personal life but, being bored with his present job, he knew he needed to make some changes, perhaps leaving his safe office at the bank and doing something different might be just the fillip he needed.

Paul had no idea of Anna's married name, and therefore he didn't make any connection to her when he wrote his letter of application, the first in years as all his previous jobs so far in his career had been gained because he'd joined the bank as a trainee accountant and, after passing his examinations, he'd gradually moved up the promotion ladder at the bank, until reaching the position he was at now. Knowing he would have to move to London, to the bank's head office to gain any further promotions, he read the job description and decided it could be the move he needed to revitalise him. Somehow, he felt weary and mentally tired of doing the work he did. He needed to do something different; something that would excite him and re-charge his inner batteries, to re-motivate him. He knew his next promotion at the bank would be as a senior manager, but was that really what he wanted?

The job advertised at Anna's company sounded particularly interesting and Paul definitely saw himself as a possible contender. It would be a demanding job as well. He had no doubt it meant steering the company on to greater success, just the sort of challenge that appealed to him and, with his optimism for life renewed, and before he could change his mind, he sat down and filled out the application form.

It took him a long time to write out his curriculum vitae as he'd not written one of those in years. By the time he'd finished, it was late but, for the first time in months, he went to bed feeling excited, and more optimistic about his future.

A letter asking him to attend for an interview came within a day or so of his application being received; the agency explaining they would be conducting the interviews, with their professional staff acting for the company, but the company owner, Mrs Anna Grey and her deputy, Mrs Lesley Reynolds, would be involved as well. Paul was staggered, Mrs Anna Grey, could it possibly be his Anna?

Later that day, he did some research into the company, where, to his horror, he found out his suspicions were well founded. Mrs Anna Grey was definitely his Anna! There was only one thing he could do, and that was to pull out of the interview. He couldn't believe the love of his life was the owner of a successful business, one he'd hoped to work for, but knowing she was married (to his regret his research didn't show she was a widow) he decided he couldn't show himself to her. As far as he was concerned, if Anna and her husband were the owners of the company, he had no alternative but to forego his wish to work for them. He couldn't possibly contemplate taking a job working for her, not while she was married and he still loved her. Sadly for Paul, he missed the opportunity of meeting Anna and finding out the truth. It was as though the fates were still conspiring to make mischief for them, determined to deny them a happy ending.

Anna and Lesley checked the final list of candidates together and, sure enough, one of the prospective applicants, the one Anna had particularly chosen to see, was missing from the list. She checked with the agency to see if there'd been a mistake. But no, they assured her, there was no mistake, the candidate had phoned with his regrets and apologies; he would be unable to attend and asked for his name to be removed from their list of interviewees.

By way of explanation, Paul had told the agency his present employer had offered him a huge and unexpected promotion which, after due consideration, he'd decided he would be much wiser to accept instead. His explanation was quite true.

When he'd spoken to his senior line manager and told him he was looking for a new challenge, as there was nothing on the bank's promotion horizon, and that he would have to look outside the bank, his manager was happy to tell him on that very day, he'd been advised, confidentially, of course, of a promotion coming up and Paul was the man they were looking to fill it!

Unhappily for Anna, she had to be satisfied with the agency's explanation.

She was free to fall in love and marry, but it obviously wasn't going to be Paul Adams, not unless he came into her life some other way!

# Chapter 13

As we already know, Anna's company, 'Pies and Goodies Galore,' had taken off like a rocket! With the second factory unit on the outskirts of the city up and running with new orders coming in daily making it difficult at first to keep the production lines running, as the demand for all the products exceeded even Anna's wildest dreams. Within a few weeks, the factory was running twelve hours a day, seven days a week. Anna was not only thrilled with the production figures, but also with the staff she'd chosen to work for her. They were an essential part of her business and, without their co-operation and dedication, which she fully acknowledged, she knew neither of her ventures would be as successful as they were.

Gordy, she knew, would have been proud of her achievements; she also knew she would be forever grateful to him for his legacy. Her only sorrow? To achieve her success she had to lose him. There were many times when she'd wished he were with her, to share in the pleasure his money had brought, not only to her, but to everyone else involved. It was only when she was tired and alone she wondered if she would ever find anyone else as wonderful as he'd been to share her riches and her life.

In the meantime, the interviews for Chief Accountant went smoothly. Anna had done well to hide her disappointment at Paul not being amongst the candidates, but she managed, along with Lesley and with the input of the agency staff, to agree on one particular candidate, a fifty-year-old man called John Summers, whom they'd unanimously chosen from the half-dozen men they'd interviewed.

John Summers told them he was looking for a new challenge, after being at the same company all his working life, and after being turned down once more for promotion on account of his age, (although this hadn't been the reason his company had given him.) He'd therefore decided, on the spur of the moment, to apply for the job the agency had advertised.

His present company had insinuated he was stuck in his ways and they needed someone more dynamic, which to Anna seemed a strange requirement for a position as chief accountant. She wanted someone who was solid and diligent, with her company's interest in his heart.

John told her he'd felt used, after spending years of studying in his own time and rising, by sheer diligence and hard work, to his present position. Being turned down by his company, for what he considered a justified promotion, had been a slap in the face. It was this that finally decided him it was about time he had a change and, within a few weeks he'd finally found a position in Anna's company where, instead of being bored, he would be more stimulated than he'd ever thought possible!

Anna and Lesley liked everything about him, as did the agency staff doing the interviews with them. He'd been honest when he'd told them why he wanted the job. He wanted to use his intelligence and expertise in financial management to help to take the company into the future, (as he'd done for his present company) and that everything he'd read about 'Pies & Goodies Galore' intrigued him.

When asked how he felt about working for a woman, he'd looked shocked!

'Why should working for a woman be any different from working for a man?' he'd asked.

It wasn't the gender of the one in charge that mattered to John Summers, but how honest and dynamic they were!

To Anna, John Summers was anything but a boring fifty-year-old accountant; he had an air of quiet unflappability about him that instantly appealed to her and, in some ways, he reminded her of Gordy, in as much as he was solid and trustworthy, a man of honour. They learnt he was married, to Julie, with one son, Matthew, who was two years older than Emma. It was his previous experience and his personal manner that appealed to both Anna and Lesley and, when the agency staff gave their thumbs up as well to his appointment, after he'd left the interview room, and they'd finished interviewing the rest of the applicants, it was unanimously decided John Summers was the right man for Anna's company!

Anna, of course, insisted on him being notified straightaway and, later that same afternoon, the agency phoned to tell him of his success. With this piece neatly fitted into the company jigsaw, Anna began to feel her team was almost complete.

One of the reasons she'd liked John Summers, right from the start, was his attitude to working for a woman, this and his obvious ability to be flexible in what he would be prepared to do during his working day.

All her employees did not only their own designated jobs, but anything else that needed doing to make the company a success; this was the reason Anna had instigated a profit sharing bonus scheme that appealed to everyone, especially as it was paid out just before Christmas!

And that was how John Summers, instead of Paul Adams, came to be Chief Accountant at 'Pies & Goodies Galore'.

John's first task, was to set up a new and easy to use accounting system, and to update all the working practices in both factories, all things Anna thoroughly approved of. Gradually, over the next few months, John took over more of Anna's workload, leaving her to rely on his good sense a great deal and soon counting him and his wife as being part of her small circle of trusted friends. At the same time, John Summers came to realise his role in the company was important and finally, he became a man of substance and more than happy to be working with such a woman as Anna Grey.

Matthew, John's son, and Emma, were expected to earn their pocket money and therefore, whenever they were on vacation from school they had both been found jobs at the factory and, being about the same age it was inevitable they would become firm friends.

Anna was soon harbouring secret thoughts that Matthew, being a presentable young man, might find Emma attractive enough to fall in love with him, making him, in Anna's eyes, an excellent candidate as a future son-in-law. It was just unfortunate Emma didn't quite see Matthew in the same light as her mother, especially after he'd told her he was gay, not that Emma ever told her mother this.

Taking John Summers on had given Anna more freedom to devise and test recipes and to invent new products and, it wasn't long before she'd started travelling to trade shows around the country with Lesley, selling and promoting them. It was after one such show Anna decided the company needed a professional sales team; giving Lesley more time to run the sales department she'd already set up in the factory. Once again Anna struck lucky. She met Mark Thomas at a social function, introduced to him by a business associate as being a super salesman. After talking to him, and being charmed by his outgoing personality, she persuaded him to leave his present company and join her company as its Sales Manager. Once Mark was on the payroll, she promoted Lesley to Sales Director and so Anna's small empire continued apace.

The company was growing so fast, Molly began to worry Anna was running, before she could walk, and spoke of her concern, asking her if she might be over stretching herself, but Anna had merely laughed, dismissing her fears, telling her that her products were exactly of their time. She even brought home the latest sales figures to prove it and a pile of reviews from newspapers, all extolling the virtues of 'Pies & Goodies Galore'. After that, to Anna's relief, Molly gave up worrying and left her to do what she'd obviously been destined to do.

Mark Thomas was a natural-born salesman. He was single, thirty-five years old, extremely handsome and mad about golf.

When not working, and occasionally when he was, Mark could be found playing golf at the local course. It was on his first Saturday morning off, after joining the company, and out on the golf course, he did a deal for his first big order for the company, signing up the catering department of the golf club to a contract for purchasing half of 'Pies & Goodies Galore' steak pie production for the next year. Anna thought it all very impressive, even amusing, leading her to offering to buy him some replacement golf clubs if it improved his sales technique and brought in more orders!

Feeling more than satisfied with her working life, and with her business on the up and up, Anna decided it was time to address her personal life that was, in her opinion, in the doldrums!

It was the one area she felt she needed to change, not that she was desperate for a man, or even that she intended to actively look for a new bedmate, but it still irked her she hadn't met Paul again but, being the optimistic person she was, she simply put that upset behind her and carried on with her life, at the same time knowing something had to change.

Many times over the years, Anna had said how fortunate she'd been to have Gordy as her husband and lover. He'd made it possible for her to live her life with dignity and, loving her as he had, he'd helped her to put Paul to the back of her mind. He'd not only usurped Paul as her lover, but also as Emma's father!

It was a fact of life she had loved Gordy and had never regretted, not for a single minute, their life together, she just wished he could be with her now, but that wasn't to be, and she knew she would have to live her life the best way she could, with or without a man, and take whatever the future might bring.

Molly and Emma, in their different ways also worried about her, especially knowing her social life was more or less non-existent, mainly because she worked too hard and for too many hours. Of course it didn't bother Anna. Her work was her life.

To Molly, it wasn't natural for an intelligent and good-looking woman, such as Anna to be on her own. As far as she was concerned, she spent far too much time with balance sheets and experimenting with her recipes, rather than going out to the many functions she was asked to, and where she might meet someone new to take Gordy's place. Not that Anna would have agreed. She didn't have the time for 'dating' she was far too busy making a living for her employees.

Molly though was convinced Anna should make an effort to socialize more and then, maybe, she would then find the soul-mate she was quite sure was somewhere around just waiting to find her!

It was Anna's fond hope Emma should eventually follow her into the business and, with this in mind she actively encouraged her to work at the factory with Matthew during the holidays. It was during this time the two young people became firm friends and, as we already know, unhappily for Anna, it was to be no more than that.

It was Anna's intention Emma should learn money was hard to come by and that one day she would have to earn her own living. She wanted her daughter to learn the value of money before she came of age, and inherited her considerable 'dowry' from Gordy.

Knowing it was a large sum of money, which would give Emma a good start in life, Anna had been adamant the money wasn't to be used for frittering away and had wisely invested it.

She also knew how fortunate she was in having Emma as her daughter for, with Molly's help, she was fast becoming a beautiful and graceful young lady, with an inbuilt compassion for others and, of course, Anna was inordinately proud of her. Emma enchanted everyone, including Matthew, but not enough to persuade him girls were better for him than boys!

It was about this time Anna decided Emma should learn the business from the ground floor upwards, at the same time, John confided he too wanted Matthew to do the same, even though neither of their children wanted to go into the business!

It was a work ethic and discipline measure both parents thought essential for their beloved children, and so it came about, that Emma, and Matthew started off by being cleaners at the factory.

Once they'd learnt how to clean the offices, and then the factory, they were promoted to work together in the staff canteen, which was where Anna tried out her newly designed products, using the company staff to taste them. She even called it her research laboratory! It was about this time the two young people became not only best friends, but each other's confidante as well.

Emma, thought of Matthew as the brother she'd never had and, in turn, she became a surrogate sister to him and so it was to him Emma agonised over her decision as to whether she should go to Art College, and use her talent in the way she wanted, rather than do the degree in business studies she knew her mother favoured?

It was Matthew's support and encouragement Emma was most thankful for, especially in her final year at school, when her subjects for college had to be chosen and her mother was putting pressure on her to study subjects she didn't want to do, knowing she would be making the wrong choices, a discussion that nearly ended in tears, until she finally got her own way, much to her mother's chagrin!

Being older, Matthew couldn't wait for the summer to end so he could start his degree course at university, which made Emma unhappy. For the first time in her life she was going to lose not only her best friend, but also her ally and, for the next two years, while she did her 'A' levels at college, she worked on her own.

With both factory units and her team working full out, Anna was definitely proving to be a woman with a million ideas. She finally found time for trying and testing some of the old recipes she'd collected over the years; making an executive decision one day, to incorporate them into the production line of ready prepared meals, already being made, if they were suitable.

From then on, she would spend her weekends trying out the results on Molly and Emma, getting their feedback and suggestions, but it was at one of her weekly team meetings, Anna and the team decided the small factory unit, (Anna's first acquisition after the pub) should be where her experimental ideas needed to be tested and tried, before being produced, leaving the second and largest unit in the city, to concentrate on producing the main products they couldn't make enough of, such was her success!

It was Anna's research into new products, along with her collection of old recipes that were soon to become the basis for the first of several cookery books, but that is still for the future.

Molly was much older now, in her seventies, yet still agile. She loved living in the cottage, and her life in the village. It was indeed a dream come true for her, although some days, she'd started to feel her age. She was an active member of most of the village clubs and was always at the forefront of any activity being organised. She was a founder member, and the present chairperson, of the village garden society and, each month, she could be found in the ancient church, even though she was a Catholic, helping to arrange the flowers, many of which she'd grown herself in the now flourishing garden at the back of the cottage. The years since she'd first met Anna had flown by as quickly for her as they had for Anna, with no regrets either she'd once taken in a stranger in need of her love and protection.

With both factories in full production, life was hectic for Anna. She was only spending weekends at the cottage now, arriving late on a Friday afternoon and staying until Sunday evening, when she would return to her penthouse apartment in the city, loaded down with Molly's home grown produce.

She'd bought the apartment at Molly's insistence, when the second factory had opened on the outskirts of the city. Molly had seen for herself how exhausted she was at the end of each day, working long hours, and then travelling back to the village late at night, to be up early the next morning to make the return journey back to the factory.

'Enough!' Molly had told her one weekend. 'Get a place near to the factory and come home at weekends.' And that was how it happened.

This particular weekend though, the atmosphere at the cottage was a little tense. Emma was waiting for her 'A' level exam results to arrive; results that would determine whether she would be going to university or not!

She'd finally decided, to her mother's dismay at first, to follow her heart and take art as her chosen subject, and was now hoping her results would be good enough for her to get into the university of her choice and study for a fine art degree and so it was with fingers crossed, she waited for the postman to call!

Once Anna had finally accepted Emma would never follow her into the business, she'd supported her in every possible way, so when the results landed on the mat later that morning, she was shaking as much as Emma.

They both stared at the white envelope, neither of them daring to reach down and pick it up. Anna hoping it would hold good news for Emma, yet knowing the day when her beloved daughter would leave home was getting nearer but, like many other parents, she knew she had to give Emma a long lead. Teenagers leaving home for the first time were like young puppies; they had to be allowed to run and Anna, like these others, knew she couldn't chain her beloved daughter down, she had to let her make her own mistakes and fly her own course, no matter how upsetting it might be to her and Molly to lose her.

Ever since Emma had been born, Molly had been like a second mother, never having had children of her own and, needless to say, she loved and adored her, as though she were her own child, almost worshipping the ground the child walked on; giving her the same unconditional love she gave to Anna.

To Molly, Anna and Emma were the sun, moon and stars in her life and especially now, with Emma grown up. She looked physically much like Anna, both being of medium height and slender and with the same elfin-shaped features, the only difference between them, the colour of their hair. Anna's was still the same glorious auburn, falling in deep waves onto her shoulders, the same as when Molly had first met her. Emma's though was exactly like Paul's, dark brown and curly, fortunately, it had been just like Gordy's too, which, given the circumstances had been a blessing.

Anna and Emma both had similar coloured eyes. Emerald green, cat's eyes were Paul's description of Anna's. They'd entranced him from their first meeting, as they had Gordy. The difference? Anna's held a hint of hidden laughter, while Emma's glowed with mischievous anticipation.

As for their personalities! Emma was just like Gordy, a trait Anna put down to his love and nurturing, as he'd tried, successfully, to be the best father Emma could ever wish for. Sometimes though, Anna was reminded of Paul when she looked at her, so like him in many ways, yet very much hers and Gordy's child.

Anna loved nothing more than to drive away from the city and return to the countryside on a Friday evening to be with Molly and Emma, where they would often eat supper at the 'Ring O'Bells' with Jim and Monica, sitting in the original dining area, which Anna had enlarged into a conservatory, reminiscent of the one at the Golden Lion, and fast becoming a favourite place to sit and eat one of Monica's 'specials.'

When Monica had taken over the cooking from Anna, she'd extended the menus, using some of Anna's new products and adding in some of her own specials, keeping up with the original standard set by Anna.

Since then, the Ring O' Bells had been voted the top place to eat in Gloucestershire, not only by the locals, but also by the tourists who came in their droves at the weekends and holidays, as they searched the area for the historical places written about by Shakespeare.

But the village history went back even earlier than Shakespeare's time, to a period in history Anna loved the most. It was one of the reasons why the village held such a fascination for her.

It was atmospheric, with its rows of medieval stone cottages, and of course the pub, older than all of the other buildings, even older than the church itself. Starting out as a simple stone building built to house the stone masons, and the other tradesmen who were building the church, as happened in most villages throughout the land. If you see a church in an old village, invariably you will find a pub such as the 'Ring O'Bells'.

When Anna had first taken over the old pub, she'd been intrigued with how the original inhabitants of the village, or hamlet as it was then might have lived, and the sort of food they would have eaten. It was this interest in its past history that led Anna to write her first cookery book, the recipes a modern take on the old recipes she found in old record books or from some of the locals, who were more than happy to donate old recipes that had been passed down through the generations. The fun part for Anna, Molly and Emma was locating similar ingredients to those that would have been in use in those far-off times, and then Anna cooking them with an original twist!

Over the years since her original renovations, the Ring O' Bells had turned into a glorious old pub, a place to visit at any time of the year and Monica took full advantage of this, making two of the bedrooms available to those wanting bed and breakfast holidays.

Weekends in the winter were the times when city folk would book the rooms, and then, during the spring and summer months, holidaymakers from all over the world would come to stay, all clamouring for a chance to sleep in one of the two antique four-poster beds that added to the atmosphere in the luxurious accommodation. Monica, of course, kept the pub in the same wonderful condition Anna had originally envisaged, with log fires burning in the inglenook fireplaces at the first hint of a chill in the air: with the copper and brass kettles gleaming in the firelight and the smell of wonderful food being cooked.

Anna loved the old place with a passion, and especially its peaceful atmosphere, which soothed her soul. At the same time, the countryside that surrounded it invigorated her. There was nothing she liked more at weekends, after a long walk in the country, than to sit with a glass of her favourite white wine in her hand and, with Molly at her side, watch as the river gently flowed past. For Anna, the pub and its gardens had become the perfect antidote for relaxing after the stresses of her working week, and the visitors who continued to come in their droves to eat and drink, obviously agreed!

The main garden had become an extra special place, with its colourful boarders and shrubs, and was the perfect setting for the wedding receptions Monica had started to organise now there was room for a marquee.

As with most mothers with daughters, it had long been Anna's dream for Emma to find a nice young man to fall in love with, and then for them to marry in the village church, with the reception afterwards at the 'Ring O'Bells' with Monica cooking her wonderful food!

On one such Saturday afternoon, when the weather was not kind enough to sit outside, Anna and Molly were sitting in the cottage, chatting together about each other's week. They started to reminisce about the past and, somehow, the conversation turned to Paul. Anna took his first letter from her briefcase and showed it to Molly, the letter she'd received when he'd applied for the position of chief accountant at the factory, and then his second, rescinding the job even before his interview, giving Anna no chance to meet him.

With Anna speculating that he must be married, Molly was equally as mystified. She'd remarked that perhaps, when he'd realised it was Anna's company, he'd decided to keep away. Her suggestion, that Anna should write to him at the address he'd given and enquire as to how he was, had been met with a snort of derision from Anna and the remark she could never do that! If he were married, whatever would his wife think? It might cause him endless trouble if she believed he was having an affair, especially from an ex-girlfriend, and she certainly didn't want to be the cause of any problems, no matter what had happened in the past. In any case, eighteen years had passed since they'd parted and maybe he'd changed and she wouldn't love him if she knew him now! As it was, she still had her old memories, along with her past hopes and dreams to remember him by and, more importantly, she didn't want Emma to know he was her father, not yet! Gordy had more than proved his worth as her father and that was good enough for Anna, for the time being!

She'd shrugged her shoulders and put his letters away. Perhaps at this stage in her life, with her businesses and her other interests, it was better for her to be single! She didn't have to consider anyone else except Emma and Molly and, with that explanation, Molly had to be satisfied.

# Chapter 14

As Emma grew to young womanhood, she knew two things for certain.

First, she was truly loved, and second, all the women she knew worked for their living, not relying on a husband or a partner to provide for them.

She also knew her father would have been more than happy had her mother wanted to stay at home and be just a housewife and mother but, being the fore runner of the modern man, he'd had enough intelligence to know Anna would have been bored without the interest of her work at the Golden Lion to occupy her, even though it was demanding and exhausting at times. Working and using her brain had made her into the businessperson she was later to become, when Gordy was no longer with her, and thankfully, Emma had the foresight at the time to understand this.

She also knew she'd been lucky in having a mother and a father who'd looked after her with no problems over childcare, unlike some of her school friends, whose mothers had to work, leaving their children to arrive home to a cold and cheerless house. Her mother's working hours at the hotel were planned for when her father was at home, and then, of course, there had always been Grandma Molly on hand and only too willing to help.

These three adults were the most important people in Emma's young life and, when her father had suddenly died, they were all, without a doubt, equally as grief-stricken, for he'd been an exceptional man; one who'd loved her and her mother deeply; his very life and existence revolving around them.

At least she knew she could look back at her young life knowing how much her parents had loved each other. It was this knowledge that had taught her about the emotions involved when two people fall in love. She'd learnt, first hand, what falling in love means to the two people involved, and that was in part the reason why she'd been surprised her mother had never remarried, especially being such a loving woman and one who blossomed when being cherished.

It was a sad fact of life that her mother cared nothing for the attractive, and often wealthy admirers who tried, at every opportunity to coerce her into going out with them. She had no regard for looks and wealth, she wanted much more than those attributes; she wanted love, it was as simple as that!

Like her father, the men who'd thought they were in with a chance had been beguiled by her looks and personality. Unfortunately for them, none had ever come up to her expectations! It was as though her emotions were locked away. She just wasn't interested in making a commitment to another man, or so Emma heard her say one day to Grandma Molly, leaving Emma certain it was the businesses her mother ran that were the root cause of her disinterest in the opposite sex, perhaps it was because she had a flourishing business career, in what was mostly a male dominated world, a career that demanded so much of her attention she'd decided not to commit herself to another personal relationship.

And so it was Emma had watched her mother coming to terms with not only losing her husband, in itself a heartbreakingly difficult time, but also coping with the stress she inflicted on herself, by buying a run-down building, then devoting herself to its renovations until finally, she'd turned it into a wonderful place to eat and drink, making it into a huge success and then, of course the other businesses that had quickly followed!

Without a doubt, buying the Ring O' Bells had been her mother's first big success, and then her next project, which had been spawned, by the success of the food she'd cooked at the pub, another business, making her pies. These were such crowd-pleasers she couldn't keep up with demand for them in her own kitchen, more or less forcing her to take over the first factory. When that had taken off, she'd then been forced to change her plans yet again, going from being just a pub landlady, into a fully-fledged business woman, eventually running two factories, and all because she needed somewhere to make the products her customers loved!

Over the years, Emma had marvelled at her mother's courage, and her business acumen, admiring her faith and self-belief, knowing she was unstoppable. Her mother was a woman who believed in her own abilities, a woman she knew would be successful at whatever she chose to do. Emma wondered if she would ever have the same self-belief when she finished her studies and, if so, would she recognise opportunities when they came her way? Would she also have the same mental and physical stamina, or indeed the same amount of motivation to grasp opportunities as her mother had grasped hers? But this was all in the future; she was still young and had yet to pass her examinations and then she would see what the fates had in store for her.

Her final year at school had been difficult; she missed Matthew, mostly for his common sense approach to life and his advice, and for the laughs they'd shared. Instead of moping for what had been, she applied herself to studying, and then came the agonising wait for her results to arrive.

Apart from losing her father, this was the second most stressful time in her young life and how she'd wished, many times, her father was still alive to offer her the comfort and unfailing love he'd excelled at. How she missed him and wished he was still with her, the very same thoughts Anna often had when she arrived back at her apartment after a long and arduous day, wanting nothing more than to be in his arms as they made love. She missed their intimate moments most of all, especially the way he would caress her and bring her to a climax just before he entered her and how, since his death, she'd often dreamt of them making love only to wake up on the verge of climaxing, with her emotions about to explode; her mind and body realising there was no Gordy to satisfy it.

Emma knew her present moodiness was of great concern to her mother and Grandma Molly. They weren't used to her being anything other than happy, and so they'd watched over her carefully, excusing her moodiness, which was totally out of character, as just being part of her growing up, for she was normally a sweet-natured child.

They'd both been sympathetic and encouraging in their own ways, as they tried to keep her happy, both agreeing they too would be more than happy when she had her results and knew what her fate was to be!

Emma's creative flair and artistic talent in Art and Design had proved to be the subjects she'd excelled at in school and so it was obvious they were to be her choice to study at college, even though Anna had originally had dreams of Emma following her into the business.

Emma's choice made Anna wonder if she would be able to make a living from being an artist, or even if her talents were as good as she thought. Would Emma's work be commercial enough for her to make a living? But Emma had no doubts.

She quite liked the idea of working with children and had thought of combining her love of art and her love of children by becoming a teacher, thinking this could be a good career choice, but of course it all depended on whether she passed her exams or not!

Discussing Emma's choices later with Molly, Anna agreed working with children would be a good way for Emma to combine her two loves and then she would have the best of both worlds. It was at times like this Emma dearly wished she hadn't been an only child, she would have loved a brother or sister to talk over her future plans with but with Matthew away at university, and no longer available, except by phone, she had no one to bounce her ideas off. Her mother and Molly were fine, up to a point, but they could only give her advice based on their past life experiences. They didn't understand young people! Or so she thought!

Emma wasn't to know that not having more children had been a source of great disappointment to her mother, who would have loved to conceive a baby with Gordy. To give him a child of his own would have repaid him, in some small way, for the love and devotion he'd given to her and then Emma. He'd proved himself to be the most admirable father Emma could ever have had, and no child could have had a more devoted parent, but even so, Anna always felt guilty when Emma discussed her father with her, knowing she should have told her who her real father was immediately after Gordy had died.

Not for the first time, she felt afraid of Emma's reaction when she finally knew the truth, knowing full well her daughter would be angry for her mother holding back a vital part of her existence. This left Anna wondering whether she was not only being unfair to Emma, but also to Paul, for not giving either of them the chance to know one another. It was a dilemma she'd debated many times over the years and more so, since Gordy had died.

It was of course, a problem only she could solve. But how was she to tell Emma that Gordy hadn't been her real father? And then, how was she to tell Paul he had a daughter? Should she write and let him know?

These were her dilemmas and responsible for her thinking, more often than she liked, of Paul. Sometimes at odd moments she would find herself wondering where he was, and what was he doing and if he was happy. But, most of all did he ever think of her, or had he really forgotten their love? Also, what would he say, when he knew he had a daughter?

Anna made a point of being at the cottage the night before Emma's exam results were due and therefore had been standing next to her the following morning as the dreaded white envelope fell through the letterbox.

Emma gingerly opened the envelope and pulled out the slip of paper, reading its contents twice, before passing it across to her mother.

Anna smiled and then looked at Emma, still reeling from the shock of having passed all her subjects with top grades, knowing, without a doubt she would now be able to go to the university of her choice.

Happy for her success, Anna took her daughter in her arms, hugging and kissing her in her delight. 'Well done, my darling,' she said, tears in her eyes.

'You can make your choice now, can't you?'

'I think I'll take up the offer from Exeter and do a fine arts degree there! What do you think?'

'Sounds like a good idea to me, but what about the London College? They offered you a place as well, didn't they?'

'Yes, they did, but I much prefer to go to Exeter! What do you think, Grandma?'

Molly just smiled. It was Emma's decision and hers alone. The only sad part for Anna, was not being able to share the news with Gordy who would have been thrilled to know his beloved Emma was about to set out on her own path to success.

Emma must have been thinking the same, for she put into words her mother's feelings. 'What do you think Dad would have said?'

At that point, Anna just couldn't hold back the tears. She'd been fighting her emotions all morning, knowing her daughter was now grown up and would soon be leaving home. She tried, but couldn't stop them, they overflowed and fell, unchecked, as she held Emma in her arms, holding onto her as if her life depended on it and, for the first time in months, she felt a release from the pent-up emotions she'd held in check for so long, ever since she'd realised her baby was about to head out on her own road to independence.

Emma wiped her own and her mother's eyes. 'I'm sorry Mum,' she said, 'I didn't mean to upset you.'

Anna shook her head and laughed. 'I'm not upset,' she said, 'I'm really proud of you and you know I cry by the bucketful when I get emotional.' At that moment, another surge of sadness came over her, was it thinking of Gordy that had caused such an emotional outburst, or was it something else?

Molly, of course, was equally as delighted at Emma's news, at the same time unhappy she would be leaving home. She would miss her, and her school friends from the village, who would also be leaving their homes and going off to their various colleges.

Once Emma had gone away to university, and with Anna working and living in her city penthouse, except for her weekend visits, Molly knew she would be the lonely one and, for a few moments, she felt as though she was being abandoned. Her only consolation, Exeter wasn't that far away and they could always drive over and see her, but how, Molly thought, would Emma manage without her?

Anna had the same thoughts. Would Molly be lonely on her own in the cottage? Should she take her back to the city and let her share the apartment? But Molly was her own woman, and fully intended to be the one to make any decision as to where she should go. The following weekend, when Anna tried to broach the subject, Molly was adamant, there was to be no more talk of her moving out of the cottage, and she certainly wasn't going to go and live in the city. Her life was here in the village, and that was where she intended to stay, reminding Anna, she also had her garden to look after! She also had a nice young man from the village doing all the heavy work and she could still enjoy pottering in the greenhouse and growing plants. In any case, as she hotly informed Anna, she had her committees and flower arranging at the church to organise: how could Anna possibly think she would leave it all and go to live in her city apartment, as lovely as it was, when there was no garden? Or even to leave behind all the friends she'd made since living in the village? In the end, Anna reluctantly gave in, with one proviso, that Molly had someone in to do the housework. As for shopping, she could go with Monica when she went into Coombe Norton.

Eventually Molly gave in gracefully, for she knew Anna's concerns were for her safety and perfectly valid, and then, of course, Anna would still be coming home at weekends and sometimes Emma as well.

Emma spent most of her last summer holiday working at the factory in the city, earning extra money for university, staying with Anna in the penthouse, thus giving Molly a trial run of living on her own in the cottage, but each weekend, Molly could be found waiting patiently for Friday evening to come, and for Emma and Anna to come bounding through the door.

Gradually the summer passed and it was nearly time for Emma to start her new life as a student. On one of her visits to Exeter, looking for somewhere to live, she'd met, quite by chance, another would-be student, Sam Noakes, who, like Emma was also going to be on the same fine arts course. They'd liked each other right from the start and had decided to share a flat in the city.

Anna distracted by problems at the factory when Emma phoned to say she'd made a new friend called Sam, and that they would be sharing a flat. She hadn't realised Sam was a boy! As for Emma, she kept quiet!

The day finally arrived when Emma left home for Exeter. After tearful goodbyes from her mother and Molly, she left the village without a backwards glance, heading west in her new little Mini, having passed her test a few months after her seventeenth birthday.

The car was piled high with her belongings and, driving down the motorway, she suddenly felt grown up, excited at the prospect of at last having her own independence: especially looking forward to sharing a flat with Sam, an arrangement that suited them both, for various reasons. Their pre-arranged plan was for Emma to do most of the cooking, with Sam being the cleaner cum handyman! But, more importantly, they'd agreed to look after each other!

Several weeks passed before Emma returned home again for the weekend and, it was during this first visit she asked if Sam, her flatmate could come home with her the next time.

No problem there, as Anna and Molly were keen to meet Sam and to get to know her! But Emma still hadn't thought to tell them Sam wasn't short for Samantha, but for Samuel. At least it would be a weekend full of surprises, especially for Anna and Molly!

Time flew by and the proposed weekend finally arrived. Anna was delighted at the thought of seeing Emma again and had arranged for them to eat at the pub that evening but first she couldn't wait to see if Emma had changed!

Together with Molly, Anna waited impatiently, for what seemed like ages that evening, looking out of the cottage window, excited at the prospect of seeing her darling daughter again until suddenly, they saw her Mini coming down the lane and turning into the car park. Craning their necks to see if she'd altered physically over the past weeks and, with some interest, at the new flatmate she was bringing home, both wondering what she would be like.

Emma's small car came to a halt. Unfolding her long slim legs from the driver's seat, she climbed out, followed, to Anna and Molly's joint astonishment, by a tall, very skinny, red-headed young man! Anna turned to Molly. 'I thought she said she was bringing her flatmate home?'

Molly shrugged her shoulders, as bemused as Anna. 'Hmm, that's what I thought as well. Perhaps she changed her mind? You know what young people are like these days!'

Emma and the young man headed for the cottage where, after hugging and kissing her mother and Molly, she turned and introduced her new flatmate. 'Mum, Grandma, this is Sam!' pulling the skinny young man into the cottage.

It was only her good manners that prevented Anna from choking on her surprise; Molly just stood beside her, openmouthed and staring.

'Hello Sam,' Anna said at last, remembering her manners and holding out her hand to greet him. To her surprise, Sam took her hand in his and held it to his lips, kissing it gallantly, repeating the same gesture with Molly who was suddenly overcome with love for this young man. He reminded her of her beloved Paddy when he'd been at the same age, complete with the same red hair.

Of course Sam immediately won them over and, as the evening wore on, it became apparent the two young people were indeed just friends, enjoying their time at university, sharing a flat and studying together. Emma, it seemed to Anna, had at last found what she'd always wanted, a surrogate sibling!

After being concerned, when she first knew her daughter was sharing a flat with a young man, Anna soon changed her mind, as she realised Emma wasn't viewing Sam as a possible sexual partner. As she'd stressed to Anna and Molly later, 'sex before marriage wasn't what she wanted!'

Anna had felt her colour rising as Emma made her pronouncement, wondering what her daughter would say when she found out she'd been conceived out of wedlock!

The word *hypocrite* sprang to Anna's mind. She'd always told Emma, *marrying the man of your dreams was always better if sex was delayed until after the marriage certificate had been signed*!

Somehow, she'd managed to convince herself this was true of herself and Gordy. It was certainly true she didn't have sex with him until after they were married, conveniently forgetting, that by that time, she was already pregnant, and by another man!

That weekend was one of the most enjoyable Anna had spent for some time: hurriedly changing the sleeping arrangements, when Sam turned out to be a young man instead of the girl friend she was expecting.

Sam had Emma's old room with Emma sharing her mother's bed, as she'd done often when growing up, and had been small and frightened and when she would creep into her mother and father's bed.

The two young people went for long walks, taking Anna with them one time, when they walked along the riverbank towards Coombe Norton, the market town just a few miles away.

The one disappointment for Molly and Anna was their failure to elicit any information from Sam about his family, other than his father was a financial advisor in a bank, with no mention made of a mother, or of any brothers and sisters. Leaving Anna to wonder if his father was a widower or divorced!

After realising the young man didn't want to discuss his family, or lack of one, Anna wisely kept her own counsel, quite sure Emma would find out all there was to know if the past was anything to go by, knowing she would confide in her later, as she'd always done! Perhaps, this time, Anna was due for a disappointment?

Like Molly, Anna liked Sam, right from their first meeting. He was a cheerful young man and thankfully, one who seemed to be level-headed.

Now they were sure Emma was safe in the flat with Sam, they were happy but, to make sure all was indeed well, Anna decided to make a visit to Exeter and see for herself, her excuse, taking Emma a small freezer, a gift from Molly as a flat warming present, of course, Molly went as well.

Once Emma had showed them around the small flat and they'd found her possessions were in one bedroom, and Sam's in the other, they were both relieved and happy and, satisfied at the arrangements, leaving Emma to live her university life in her own way and by her own rules. This was a good thing because, had she known Sam had already tried to get closer to Emma, she would certainly have been worried!

It happened one evening, not long after they'd moved in together. They'd eaten a meal and drank nearly a full bottle of wine, a gift from some friends a few weeks earlier. Unaccustomed as they were to drinking large quantities of alcohol, it had gone to both their heads and, in a moment of madness, Sam made a grab for Emma and tried to kiss her.

To his disappointment, he was firmly rejected and pushed away. There was to be no hanky-panky Emma told him. As far as she was concerned, there would be plenty of time for that malarkey when she was qualified, as for Sam, well he hoped he would still be around!

Emma and Sam's university years sped by. As they each had different projects to do, Emma would mostly go home to the cottage alone at the weekends, when she was able, and occasionally, Anna would visit her when the two of them would go shopping and talk of Emma's plans for the future, while they ate out in one of the many cafes in the city.

Finally, Emma was coming to the end of her course, where it was predicted she would get a top degree and, having given her future a great deal of thought, she'd decided to do her teacher training as soon as she could.

Anna had always known Emma to be a compassionate young woman and therefore, was very sensitive in her attitude to her daughter's future plans. Emma often talked of her plan to work with children with special needs and, as she'd spent some of her spare time at university working at a local school in Exeter, she knew it was exactly what she wanted to do.

As for Sam, as far as Anna could find out from Emma, he was going to live with his father and work in London. If he obtained a good result, his ambition lay in design: a company he'd sent some of his designs to were interested in taking him and had already approached him so, sadly, the two friends were due to part at the end of the term.

By this time, Sam was no longer the skinny boy he'd once been, but a strikingly handsome young man who, under Emma's influence had finally tamed his red hair. As for Emma, she'd grown into a younger version of her mother, the only difference between them, the colour of her hair, not at all like the vibrant auburn of her mother's, but a dark glossy brown, that waved and rippled on her shoulders as she walked.

Anna and Molly both attended Emma's graduation. Although they only saw Sam in the distance, he'd waved to them but there had been no sign of anyone from his family at the ceremony, not as far as they could see, and this saddened them, especially Anna, who'd been looking forward to meeting Sam's elusive family!

By the time Emma finished her teacher training and had started her first job, she was nearly twenty-four years old.

She'd applied for a position at a school in Birmingham where, to her delight, she'd been accepted, which meant she wouldn't be too far away from her mother and Molly, but any thoughts they might have had that she would be able to spend more time with them were quickly dashed, especially once she started her new job.

Using some of her inheritance from Gordy's 'dowry', that her mother had wisely invested, Emma bought a stylish new apartment, in what had once been an old warehouse; equidistant to where she would be working and the city.

It was near to the renovated canal, in an up-and-coming area of the city that buzzed with life, being well blessed with shops and bars as well as a theatre and an art gallery. It was, she assured her mother, the 'in' place to live if you were young and upwardly mobile and it didn't take long before she'd settled in and started to make friends in the multicultural neighbourhood.

Emma loved her new job at the special needs school and the work she was doing with the children. In her free time she'd started designing clothes for herself, having decided she couldn't afford the designer clothes she would have liked on her salary.

As there was a warehouse near to where she lived, where she could buy reasonably priced fabrics, it didn't take long before her beautiful clothes soon caught the eyes of her colleagues and friends and, before she knew it, what had started out as a necessary hobby was fast heading towards being a fulltime business.

By word of mouth, she was being feted as the one to ask if a special outfit was needed. Of course Emma was delighted with her success, as limited as it was, and maybe in the future this will all change and she will become like her mother, a businesswoman!

Ever since she'd been a young girl, she'd been designing and sewing clothes, making them first of all for her dolls and then, as she was growing up, for herself. At one time, she'd even thought of going into design and fashion; as it was now, she had the best of both worlds; she was doing a job she loved and making clothes she and her friends liked to wear.

Of Sam, there'd been no word. Not since they'd left university, until she received a letter, forwarded to her by Molly, saying he'd managed to lose her new address.

There was no mention made of the letter, when at the end of the month, she went home for a long overdue weekend visit to the cottage. Anna and Molly didn't dare pry, knowing from her past behaviour she would only tell them in her own good time what Sam had to say, until then, they would have to have patience and wait, something neither of them was keen to do.

They'd both been speculating, that now Emma and Sam were young adults, perhaps they might get together romantically, something Anna would have liked to have happened for herself, but this didn't seem likely to happen either, resigning herself to remaining a singleton forever. She still longed for Gordy and especially his love, but even this she knew was in the past and that she had to look to the future for any hope of a romantic entanglement, but so far, nothing had happened to convince her she would in time find someone new.

Strangely enough, over the past couple of years her mind had turned more often to Paul. If only she knew if he really had forgotten her and the love he'd once professed to have for her. But was this just wishful thinking on her behalf!

She'd often wondered whether he was married, or not. But as there was no way, or so she could see, for her to find out, she had put the matter to the back of her mind. It was only the fates that knew the answers to her questions and, so far, they weren't willing to let her know what those answers were!

# Chapter 15

Emma and Sam's young lives could not have been more different. Emma had grown up as the main star in a loving and caring family with her mother, father and grandmother, Molly, all adoring her. Sam's childhood had been quite different. He'd grown up in different circumstances to Emma, as she was much later to find out. His parents had met at medical school and were both doctors, doing research into tropical diseases and working abroad for a medical charity. They'd decided not to have children as soon as they got married, but to wait until their tour of duty was over, knowing their chosen careers would take them away for long periods of time to foreign countries. Unfortunately, Sam's mother unexpectedly found herself pregnant and, rather than abort him, she'd given birth and then abandoned him to her parents to look after, which they did willingly while he was a baby. This arrangement worked fine, until, during one tour of duty, when the country was besieged by rebels, intent on overthrowing the ruling party. Sadly, the insurgents invaded the clinic where they were working, brutally murdering them and their colleagues. Thankfully, Sam was too young at the time to fully understand what had happened and remained with his grandparents who were his legal guardians. As he grew up, so they were getting older and, inevitably, they began to find it increasingly difficult to deal with an eight-year-old boy, especially one as truculent and demanding as he'd become; clearly Sam had been badly damaged by the loss of his parents, so reluctantly, his grandparents decided to send him to boarding school, where it was hoped he would be disciplined, as well as educated, as his parents had always wanted.

Paul Adams was Sam's parents' closest friend. He'd always taken an active interest in Sam since the boy had been born and, not thinking anything bad would ever happen, they'd appointed him to be Sam's godfather and guardian, along with their parents, should they die before their son was of an age when he could be independent. They had never envisaged such a tragedy would ever happen to them, of course had they known, Paul would still have been their obvious choice as their son's guardian.

Unfortunately, at the time of their deaths, Paul had not been in a position to have Sam live with him, as he also worked abroad at times and, without a wife at home to help, regretfully he had to agree to Sam going to boarding school, no matter how hard the young boy pleaded not to go. Paul also thought Sam ought to learn how to adjust to his new life and how to cope so therefore the argument was closed and Sam had to remain in his hated school.

During his school years though, he often stayed with Paul in the holidays and came to idolise him, looking on him as his surrogate father. By this time, Sam had calmed down and was no longer quite as truculent or rebellious. He'd turned into a likeable young man, considering how traumatised he'd been, a fact that at the time no one seemed to understand or care about, it had merely been a case of 'get on with your life, Sam, there are plenty more worse off than you in the world!' Of course, he had done just that, not knowing the trauma of his parents' deaths was clearly the reason for his earlier wilful and rebellious behaviour. Being a naturally optimistic soul he gradually learnt how to change.

Eventually, his grandparents became too old and infirm to care for him. Sadly, during one of his school holidays, and within weeks of each other, they both died and at last his guardianship fell to Paul.

Sam continued his education at boarding school. To his delight, he now spent all of his holidays with Paul, or with the occasional school friend should Paul have to be abroad on business. These arrangements lasted until he went to university, by which time Paul was based permanently in London, and Sam had grown up to be an independent young man.

After talking over his university options with Paul, Sam made up his mind to go to Exeter, where he was looking forward at last to having his own flat, or at least that was his plan, until the morning he met Emma and fell in love!

Theirs was an auspicious first meeting: like Emma, he too had applied to do a fine arts degree and, coincidentally was spending a few days in Exeter, intending to seek out accommodation. His first port of call that morning, like Emma, had been the student housing office in the university building. It was there he'd been given loads of information, as well as a handful of leaflets, listing available bed sits, flats and houses, all suitable for students to rent.

He'd been standing in the outer office for some time, thumbing through the leaflets, when Emma had walked in and suddenly caught his eye. It looked as though she was also going to be a student and Sam couldn't wait to know who she was and what course she would be doing. And neither could he take his eyes off her. She had to be the most gorgeous girl he'd ever seen, with her long dark hair and enviable figure. There was no doubt about it, she was stunningly attractive and Sam was immediately smitten.

He watched her, surreptitiously for a while, from behind a brochure advertising flats he knew were too expensive for him, weighing her up, at the same time, hoping they would be on the same course and studying together.

Emma picked up a sheaf of leaflets from off the desk, the same ones as those held by Sam. Taking the initiative, he walked across the room to stand next to her.

Emma turned and looked up to find herself staring into two of the palest blue eyes, fringed with golden lashes, she'd ever seen. She stepped back a pace to look him over properly; appraising him, taking in his bright red hair and the mass of freckles covering his face. He looked back at her without the slightest embarrassment, holding out a skinny hand. Emma smiled at him. It was at that moment Sam fell headlong in love.

Emma, unfortunately, failed to get the same feeling. She'd looked him up and down; only aware he was someone who would always stand out in a crowd, with his long and lanky frame and his mop of red hair, a beacon of colour.

Sam smiled at her in return and blushed, suddenly overcome with shyness.

'Are you looking for somewhere to live?' he asked, at last finding his voice. His mischievous eyes widening as he looked at her, his admiration apparent.

Emma blushed at his direct scrutiny, taken aback for a moment as their eyes suddenly locked. It was Sam who found it impossible to unlock his eyes from hers; colouring even more with embarrassment at being found openly and rudely staring into the greenest pair of eyes he'd ever seen.

Emma continued to smile at him. She liked him. There was an honesty and openness about his manner she immediately understood and trusted.

'Yes,' she said, answering his question. 'I am. What about you, are you looking for somewhere as well?'

'Sure,' he said, holding out his hand to introduce himself. 'Sam Noakes, prospective first-year student, hoping to do a fine arts degree! And yourself?'

'Emma Grey,' she said, holding out her hand to shake his proffered one.

Sam held onto Emma's hand, for just a fraction too long for her liking, before pulling it away sharply from his grasp.

'The same course,' she said, smiling and returning to the leaflets she'd been given, but Sam was not going to be put off.

'Would you be interested in a flat share?' he asked, watching her reaction closely. 'It's much cheaper than trying to run a place on your own,' he said, rushing headlong with his thoughts, not giving her a chance to interrupt, 'and, it's not so lonely either. I'm looking for someone to share a place with me, if you're interested?'

That wasn't strictly the truth. Sam had thought being able to live on his own would be the greatest thing ever, especially after spending years in a boarding school with little or no privacy and here he was offering to share with someone he didn't know and on his first day of starting to look! Whatever was the matter with him? From the way his heart was pounding in his chest he knew instinctively what the real reason was. It was this lovely creature standing before him. He'd fallen in love but, being a callow youth, he had yet to be able to put his feelings into words. If he had been able to express his feelings, he knew he would have frightened her away and that was the last thing he wanted to do.

Emma looked at him, studying him closely for a while without speaking, weighing him up. He certainly looked all right; perhaps it would be a good idea to do a flat share, she hadn't thought of that before, but with a boy? She wasn't over certain on that score either, but she could give it a try, for a term at least. Sam would be able to protect her, and then she laughed to herself, from the look of him it might be her doing the protecting!

They spent the rest of the day together, companionably looking at bed sits and flats, finally choosing one both agreed would be the most suitable. It was near the campus and within walking distance of most of the facilities they'd previously agreed they needed. It was the sort of place they both had in mind. With the deposit paid and the lease for the first year signed, they parted company, agreeing to meet and move some of their belongings in before the start of their course.

Sam phoned Paul later that evening, just to let him know he'd found somewhere to live in Exeter, even telling him about meeting Emma and, that night, he spent most of it awake, thinking about her as well.

Paul's only laughing comment when he knew Sam was sharing a flat with a girl had been, *"lucky dog, got yourself a girlfriend, and a flat and you've not even started your course yet!"*

Sam admired Paul. He looked up to him, especially being young and in need of a father figure. He would have liked to call him Dad, but it didn't seem appropriate at his age, but sometimes he did use it, only jokingly, a joke that one day, unfortunately would misfire.

Over the years, Sam had met many of the women Paul seemed to have in his life with great regularity, but there had never been one particular lady staying for long, leaving Sam to realise Paul, as much as he liked the ladies, was really married to his job!

As he'd got older Sam sometimes went with Paul if he had to work abroad during school holidays. By then they'd become quite close, more like a father and son and, confiding in Paul seemed the most natural thing in the world for him to do. Needless to say, Sam was delighted, when Paul promised to come and see the flat, as soon as he could and meet the fabulous Emma!

Meanwhile, Emma continued to work at the factory with her mother during her last remaining weeks of her holiday, visiting Exeter and meeting up with Sam as they organised their little flat for when the new term commenced. Emma came to know Sam quite well, soon realising his red hair didn't signify a fiery nature at all: in fact she found him to be the calmest and gentlest young man she'd ever met, but so far, she hadn't been infected with the same love bug!

Going to university and doing the same art course was going to be the most exciting thing that could happen and neither of them could wait for their real lives to begin so it didn't take long for them to suss out each other's talents. Sam's artistic and creative ability was equally as outstanding as Emma's and, like her, he was an innovative and hardworking modern artist, conscientious and also like Emma he was also expecting to finish his course with an honours degree. Except with no idea at the beginning, what he would like to do once he'd completed his course, unlike Emma, who knew exactly her intentions for the future.

Sam fell deeper and deeper in love with Emma the more he got to know her. He loved everything about her from her physical beauty, of course, being the first thing that had attracted him, but then, as he got to know her better, it was her compassionate nature and especially her determination to work with children less fortunate than herself.

After their first few weeks together, Sam decided, when he qualified, he wanted to work in a design environment, one that stimulated his creative juices, as well as being interesting. Most of all, his work had to satisfy him. By this time there was no doubt in his mind Emma was his first love, a fact that, thankfully, at the time, she was completely unaware of.

It was soon time for the Christmas vacation, which Sam planned to spend with Paul, at his flat in London. Working, for a couple of weeks at the advertising studio, owned by the father of his old school friend, where he hoped he would gain a valuable insight into design, as well as getting some essential work experience, at the same time, working on the first of many assignments he had to complete over the next two years, as part of his degree course. Emma, of course, returned to the cottage to her mother and Molly, spending her vacation working on her assignments in the comfort of her home.

Those first few months at university had seen Emma marking the boundaries of her relationship with Sam. There was no doubt in Sam's mind he loved her, nor was there any doubt in his mind that, so far, Emma had not fallen in love with him. It didn't upset him in the least, for one of Sam's many talents was patience!

Emma was as driven by her ambitions as he was and, until she qualified, there was going to be no room in her life for a romantic entanglement. Sam knew that, and had decided he could wait, just as long in the meantime, no other young man put in an appearance and tried to queer his pitch!

On their return to university, after the New Year, all was going well, until one night, after they'd eaten a wonderful dinner, cooked by Emma, and drunk nearly a whole bottle of wine, a flat warming gift from friends, when Sam had put his arms around her. Being the less inebriated of the two, Emma had promptly pushed him away and, in no uncertain terms, told him there was to be none of that malarkey!

The next day, being sober and full of contrition Sam apologised profusely, promising, with his fingers crossed behind his back, he would never again to try to compromise her; he would keep his distance and, because she had a forgiving nature, Emma was satisfied, for the time being.

As for Sam, it was a time of both agony and ecstasy living in the same flat with the woman he loved, but as agonising as it was, he wouldn't have changed places with any other student in the university. At least he was living with his beloved and if she was beginning to have any romantic feelings for him, Emma, rather wisely kept them to herself.

Occasionally, Sam would visit Little Coombe for the weekend and it was there he fell in love with another woman! It happened on his first visit to the cottage, when Emma's mother had first come into his life and he'd fallen completely under her spell, not in a lustful way, he just wished she were his mother!

His thoughts of that first meeting were how wonderful it would be if Paul could find a lady like her, sure they would be well suited to each other, even though they were both wedded to their careers. Paul, to his banking life, and Emma's mother, to her food production companies. And now, according to Emma, her mother was writing cookery books as well, with a new career in television in the offing.

Sam was impressed. He couldn't imagine him or Emma running a business, or for that matter appearing on television, but he could see Anna loved every minute of her life and, like Paul, she seemed to thrive on hard work. They were both driven by their ambitions, to the exclusion of their social lives, leaving Sam to wonder sometimes what it was that was missing from their personal lives that drove them so hard.

Emma and Sam's university years passed quickly, three wonderful years suddenly gone in a flash!

As they got ready for their graduation ceremonies and started to pack their belongings, ready to move on, it was an emotional time; one not only of sadness they would be leaving their little flat and their carefree lives as students, but exciting as well. They had passed all their examinations and were now officially professionals with degrees.

Emma had decided she was going to do her teacher training in Exeter, as for Sam, he had an offer from Mark's father in London to work full time in his studio and so, after promising to keep in touch with each other, they finally parted company.

Six months passed before Sam heard from Emma. From her first call, she told him how hard she was working on her teacher-training course and how she had to do work experience at different special schools as well, she also told him, as she was so busy, she wouldn't be able to see him at the moment, leaving poor Sam gutted. Being optimistic, as well as stoical, he knew eventually he would get his woman!

Another year passed, with little or no communication between them except for cards on their birthdays and at Christmas, until Emma finished her course, when she wrote and told him she'd been accepted as a probationary teacher at a special school, just outside Birmingham.

Although it would have been easy enough for her to travel each day, to and from, her mother's apartment, or even the cottage in Little Coombe, Anna thought it a better idea for Emma to use some of the money from her 'dowry', to buy a place nearer to where she was to work.

In the meantime, Sam had been making good progress at the London design studio, so good in fact, the company wanted him to open a new studio for them in the Midlands.

With Emma constantly on his mind, and knowing it was about time he made a play for her before some other fellow did, he agreed and, within a week or so, he'd installed himself into a rented flat, unknowingly at the time, near to where Emma lived. As far as he was concerned, he'd given her more than enough time, now it was up to him to get her into romance mode and pursue her, absolutely believing it was his destiny to be with her!

Sam had never been with another woman, even with all the distractions available in London. And neither had he ever been unfaithful to Emma, how could he, when he loved her as deeply as he did? It was then, not knowing her new address he'd written to Molly, asking her to forward his letter. Of course, Molly had duly obliged, mainly because she liked Sam and thought he would make a good match for Emma and, to his surprise, just a week later Emma phoned him.

It had been an even bigger surprise to Emma to hear from Sam. She'd thought he'd vanished from her life but on hearing his voice, her heart did a little skip and, unknown to her, Sam's was also doing a little skipping of its own.

They arranged to meet the following evening at one of the many cafes near the renovated canal basin!

Sam was already waiting when Emma arrived. She'd physically changed since they'd last seen each other; she'd grown more beautiful, if that were possible. She looked sophisticated and elegant, and she blew his mind away! He was even more in love with her than when he'd last seen her!

As for Emma, it was a shock seeing Sam again. She hardly recognised him. Standing in front of her, instead of the boy she'd last seen, there stood a handsome young man. His once skinny young body, topped by a mass of red hair she remembered so well had gone and, in its place, was a well-honed body, which obviously owed much to the gym. With his hair changed into a much less fiery red, its colour tamed by age and by being beautifully cut and shaped. To Emma, Sam looked devastatingly handsome and well groomed, even dressed as he was in a casual and understated way.

Emma suddenly became aware of her heart beating faster than usual. Her mouth had gone dry. For a few moments speech was impossible as she took in Sam's transformation. He now looked elegant and suave, something she found to be quite disconcerting.

Her first glance had been a shock, expecting to see him as she remembered, not as he was now in his designer clothes and with his well-modulated voice. She began to wonder, what had happened to the callow youth she'd once known? Where had the old Sam gone? The young man she'd known had certainly disappeared and, thankfully for Sam, Emma at last felt the first stirrings of love beginning to take place in her heart.

Sam's feelings for Emma were exactly the same as they'd been the very first time he'd seen her. This time though, he wasn't going to let her escape his clutches! Emma, though, even with her heart leaping each time she looked at him, was in no hurry to get involved, taking several months of being 'just good friends', before they shared their first kiss, one that was to change both of their lives, forever!

It happened on a weekend visit to the cottage to see Anna and Molly. As usual, Emma had shared her mother's bed, while Sam had slept in her old room.

They'd all had dinner at the pub and, afterwards, enjoyed drinking at the bar with Jim and Monica. Not being used to drinking alcohol in such large quantities, Emma and Sam were more than a little tipsy, when, much later, they arrived back at the cottage!

Anna and Molly, both pleading tiredness, had left the pub earlier and gone to bed, leaving the young ones to follow. It was then, back at the cottage, supposedly making a bedtime drink, with their inhibitions weakened by the quantity of wine they'd drunk, they found the courage to say how they felt about each other and, before long, they were in each other's arms and kissing as though they would never stop.

At last Sam had the girl of his dreams in his arms and was going to make the most of it. Being less drunk, Emma halted the kissing and petting before it got out of hand and anything more serious took place. Rather sensibly, they went to their respective beds, but not before promising that in the future, they would take each other seriously, with Sam insisting from now on Emma was to understand she was his girl!

Being in love suited them both. They were happy to let their love grow and mature. It wasn't until they'd been a 'couple' for some months Sam surprised Emma one evening by going down on one knee and asking her to marry him. To his delight, Emma had thrown herself into his arms and accepted.

The next day, being a Saturday, the lovers went to the jewellery quarter near to where they lived, which is where Sam bought Emma an engagement ring they'd both fallen in love with, a second-hand ornate Victorian gold band, set with diamonds and sapphires. He also bought her a wedding ring at the same time, but this he kept in its box, waiting for the day when they would marry and he could place it on her finger.

They decided to keep their engagement a secret for a while, until Sam had formally asked Anna's permission for her daughter's hand in marriage.

To this end, Emma arranged for her mother and Molly to come and visit her in Birmingham a couple of weeks later. Sam, of course, did the same with Paul, who he'd kept informed of his romance, right from the beginning.

The fact Sam had fallen in love with Emma had not surprised Paul at all as he'd met her briefly on a couple of occasions. She had a familiar look about her but he couldn't place how he knew her, thinking at first it must have been Sam's over-the-top descriptions of his love for her being the reason she seemed so familiar. Of course Paul was especially looking forward to meeting Emma's mother, as Sam had said she was a widow and equally as attractive as Emma.

Not for one moment, did Paul realise Emma was his daughter, or even connect her to Anna, who was still the love of his life. And neither did Paul or Anna know they were about to walk back into each other's lives, which goes to show just how busy the fates must have been, manoeuvring them into position for the next instalment of their lives.

And neither did any of them realise the path of true love sometimes fails to run as smoothly as they would like, as Emma, Sam, Anna and Paul were about to find out!

# Chapter 16

Since Sam had moved to Birmingham, his visits to Paul in London had become less frequent. He was, of course, in touch by phone, keeping him up to date with his romance with Emma, a romance Paul wholeheartedly approved of, secretly wishing he could find a similar one for himself.

As for Emma, she went to the cottage at least once a month for a long weekend, whenever her university work allowed, mainly because she missed Molly, who by now was getting older and increasingly frail, but also because she missed her home and her mother.

As usual, Anna was leading her own hectic life; busy with her flourishing business interests, along with her second career of writing cookery books, as well as a weekly cookery column for the local newspaper, all of which took up quite an amount of her time. There had also been yet another request from her publisher, for a second 'Pies & Goodies Galore' cookery book, which she had started working on.

It wasn't the writing that was time consuming, it was experimenting with all the new recipes and this is where Lesley's cooking skills came into play.

Anna dreamt up the 'goodies' and Lesley cooked them, the bonus being when they'd finished, the factory had a new line of products waiting to be incorporated into the range it already produced.

For Anna, it was definitely a win-win situation. At times even she had to pinch herself, unable to believe her luck, and all this thanks to Gordy, and his wonderful legacy.

Emma was always amazed at how much her mother achieved in her working day but she too was concerned maybe she was doing too much. She'd begged her many times to slow down, but Anna seemed to thrive on hard work and so it was pointless to keep asking.

Even Molly had asked her to reduce the hours she spent at the factory, but Anna had just scoffed at her concerns as well but, at the back of her mind, she did think the day was coming when she would soon have to relinquish a little of her power and let someone else take over the business, but not yet! She still had too many ideas in her head she wanted to work on and see through!

Earlier that month, she'd been approached by a television company, to host a series of weekly lifestyle programmes, scheduled for transmission in the autumn. Shows that incorporated cooking, along with other homemaking skills, with a line-up of celebrities, who would participate and provide the chat on topical issues. According to the producer and the director Anna had already spoken to, many stars of stage and screen had already been provisionally booked to appear.

Of course, should it prove to be a success, more stars would be clamouring to appear alongside her as well, which was all rather mind-boggling, leaving Anna to pinch herself to make sure she wasn't dreaming. She wasn't in the least worried, she just seemed to take it all in her stride, delighted to have yet another string to her bow.

The hardest part was trying to organise her already hectic schedule, knowing television would be the perfect showcase for not only her talents as a cook and a writer, but that it would bring more business into her companies.

Anna was as excited about her future prospects as if she was just starting out on her career, rather than getting to the end! But Emma, even thinking her mother should retire, had of course scoffed when Anna told her that! Knowing it would be impossible for her mother ever to give up work, or to even admit she was getting too old, never!

Emma had been quite envious when her mother had told her about the television programme and could well understand why the company had chosen her.

For a woman in her middle-forties, her mother was still stunningly attractive, and colour television would show off her good looks brilliantly. Her hair was still the same glorious auburn it had always been, as for her eyes, her best feature; they were still like the glittering emeralds she often wore in her ears and on her fingers.

Emma was biased, of course, as she'd always thought her mother had film-star looks and soon, television viewers would see it for themselves. As far as she was concerned, the general public were in for a real treat, if the show ever went on air!

One evening, after they'd been secretly engaged for a couple of months, Sam had pulled Emma into his arms, when he'd finished kissing her soundly, he told her it was about time they got married! He was getting tired of going back to his lonely apartment each evening after supper. He wanted to be with her all the time. Much to his surprise, Emma agreed, without any demurring on her part, because she wanted the same for herself. It was decided they would get their respective parents, and Molly, to come for a weekend visit, when Sam would then formally propose to Emma at a family dinner! All they had to do was to make sure Anna, Paul and Molly would all be able to come the same weekend!

Since moving to London from Gloucester, Paul had travelled almost constantly and, after his weekly chat with Sam, he agreed to adjust his diary for the next month and travel to Birmingham to join him for the proposed weekend. Sam had told him over the previous months of his romance with the wonderful Emma, but not that he'd actually proposed. For the time being, he kept that to himself, wanting it to be a surprise!

A week later, while walking down Oxford Street on his way to a meeting, Paul's attention was drawn to a display of books piled high in the window of a well-known bookshop. To his utter amazement, stuck on the inside of the shop window, was a poster of Anna, the same photo shot as on the covers of the books.

Paul was shocked! Without hesitating, he immediately went in and bought a copy, which he thrust into his briefcase. When he returned home that evening, his first thought was to read the book and see if it gave him any idea as to where she was living but, after skimming through it, there were no clues as to her personal life at all, only that she was a businesswoman.

It mentioned her factories although at first he didn't connect her with the 'Pies & Goodies Galore' company he'd sent his CV to a few years ago. He certainly knew the products though. Over the years of being a lone male, he'd eaten and enjoyed many of them, and then suddenly, he remembered the interview he'd turned down at the company!

Looking through Anna's book, and reading the personal notes at the beginning, it told him very little about her private life. There was no mention of a husband, or children, and this made Paul wonder whether she'd ever married? But he knew that not to be true, because he'd seen her in the Golden Lion, when the waitress had told him the man with her was her husband so, what had happened to the husband? Maybe he kept himself in the background, allowing Anna's talents to shine through and perhaps, at this very moment was sitting at home eating her scrumptious food!

The following weekend he was due at Sam's for the planned meal, except his flight into Birmingham was late arriving, which made him angry, as he'd wanted to be back in plenty of time to have a fatherly talk with the young man, but this wasn't to be. By the time he'd collected his hire car, and driven across the city to Sam's apartment, there was only enough time for a quick shower and change of clothes, before they had to leave and meet Emma and her family.

Meanwhile, Emma was experiencing a similar event at her apartment. Her normally punctilious mother, who hated being late for any appointment, was also later arriving than she'd planned, waylaid by a smooth-talking television reporter who'd insisted on obtaining a story on her reaction at being chosen to host the new television show.

She'd rushed into Emma's apartment with barely time to change, quickly explaining why she was late, as she headed for the bathroom.

Thankfully, Molly had spent the day with Emma.

With barely any time before Sam and his father were due to arrive, Anna changed into her evening finery, warned by Emma the previous week Sam was going to ask her permission for them to marry, which had made Anna laugh, especially as Emma had turned twenty-five years old and didn't need anyone's permission to marry the man of her choice.

Emma's only disappointment, that Gordy wasn't there to witness her happiness, but she knew he would have approved of Sam. He would have seen for himself how kind and loving he was. He was a man who would cherish her when they were married, just as her father had cherished her and her mother.

Anna was really happy for Emma and was looking forward to her getting engaged and married, especially as she liked Sam. She'd met him quite a few times since that first weekend, when she'd been expecting him to be a 'her'.

After that first visit, whenever Emma and Sam came to stay, she'd got to know him better and had always thought he would make an ideal partner for her beloved daughter and, this night, she knew, was going to be the start of their new life together.

Emma had chosen to wear a long silk dress she'd designed and made for herself. It skimmed over her slim hips, its neckline showing off her pert breasts, its deep carmine colour the perfect foil for the darkness of her hair.

Molly, her beloved grandmother, was wearing a silk dress and matching jacket in the palest lilac, bought especially for the occasion, prompted by Anna with a hint as to what might take place later.

As for Anna: as always, she was elegant. Her choice for the evening, a coffee-coloured silk trouser suit. Her auburn hair piled high and, wearing her emerald earrings, pendant and engagement ring, she looked exactly what she was, a successful and wealthy businesswoman, with the world at her feet!

The three women, dressed in their finery, had been waiting barely five minutes for Sam and his father to appear, when suddenly, they heard Sam's voice, calling out as he raced up the stairs to where Emma was waiting, with the door open ready to greet him. With their arms around each other's waists, they entered her apartment.

Sam bent to kiss Anna's cheek and then turned to Molly to do the same. As he stepped aside, so Anna saw the man who'd entered, just behind him. As soon as she saw, face on, who it was, she turned deathly pale, gasped and, clasping a hand to her chest, promptly fell to the floor in a dead faint. For a moment or two there was complete silence in the room, until the others realised what had happened.

In a panic, Emma, Sam, and Molly tried to revive her, thinking at first she might have suffered a heart attack. Paul meanwhile stood and watched, unable to move as he too was in shock; suddenly realising Emma's mother was his Anna!

Emma, worried something was dreadfully wrong tried to rouse her mother. Within a few minutes Anna had roused herself enough to sit up and had been helped onto a chair, by which time she'd partly recovered from her shock of seeing Paul.

Emma was all for calling off the meal but Anna would have none of it, telling her it was nothing more than exhaustion. Her busy day had taken its toll, at the same time, attempting to keep her face averted from Paul's, afraid to make eye contact with him.

Meanwhile, Paul managed to greet Molly and Emma and now Anna appeared to be recovered, he was intent on greeting her!

He bent down and took hold of her hand, just as Sam was about to start on his prepared introduction, saying, 'It's a pleasure to meet you again' to the surprise of everyone in the room including Sam. His formal words gave Anna the courage to act as he'd done and make out she'd met him some time before, maybe on business, but neither she nor Paul made any other small talk.

With Sam and Emma keen to get to the restaurant, if Anna was sure she was well enough, they made their way out of the building, with Paul deliberately holding onto her arm, his touch burning her skin, the touch she'd loved all those years ago and thought would never feel again.

Her heart had leapt in her chest when she'd first looked into his eyes as he entered Emma's flat, unable to believe he was the man Sam always referred to as his father. And now, dear God, she thought, whatever's going to happen next, as the realisation struck her! If Paul was Sam's father, then Emma's to-be husband, must be her brother! Anna was dumbstruck and quite unable to voice her thoughts.

As she walked into the restaurant, she felt quite ill, knowing there was a death sentence on her daughter's impending marriage, even before the engagement had been announced!

It was painful for her to sit and watch how happy Emma and Sam were, on what should have been her happiest day as well, celebrating her daughter's engagement to the man she loved, instead, she'd sat at the table, moving the food, that tasted like pulped cardboard, around her plate, her normal healthy appetite deserting her, until the moment when Sam stood and asked if he could have her daughter's hand in marriage.

Anna felt as though she would faint again and could only nod her head, too emotional to answer. When their glasses had been re-filled, Paul had proposed a toast; Anna, could do no more than take a sip of the expensive liquid, that to her dry mouth, could have been almost anything!

It was the most dreadful evening of her life and one she wished would end with Paul vanishing from the face of the earth, taking his son with him!

Emma, meanwhile, was completely oblivious to her mother's discomfort, but not Paul. He'd been watching her during the meal, concerned that for some reason he couldn't quite fathom, she seemed to be upset by the engagement, but why, he'd asked himself?

Emma and Sam were proudly showing off Emma's engagement ring to Molly, leaving Paul to move closer to a silent Anna, her face a mask of inscrutability, her one thought, how could she break the news to her beloved daughter the man she wanted to marry was her own brother? And even worse, how was she to tell Paul, Emma was his daughter!

Anna never did know how she managed to get through the rest of the evening, it all passed in a blur and, on her part, it left her with not only a pounding headache, but also with her heart aching, bitterly sorry she hadn't disclosed Paul's relationship to Emma before. Regretting now she hadn't found her voice and told them all at the restaurant, that neither the engagement, nor a marriage could take place, and the reasons why.

Anna knew there could be nothing in the future for Emma and Sam except for despair, and unhappiness, as well as the awful recriminations she would have to face, when she broke the news.

For once in her life, she knew she wasn't looking forward to the future!

# Chapter 17

Anna had often thought of Paul over the years, he was after all Emma's father and her first love. He was embedded in her heart and there she'd kept him locked him away, having decided long ago it was no good living with regrets for what might have been. And so she'd got on with her life. She had her marriage to Gordy, where her love for him over the years had blossomed and grown. There were no regrets either that she'd become pregnant, without being married or that she'd married as a convenience and given birth to her darling daughter, Emma. And neither did she regret the friendship and love she'd found the day she walked into the city and met Molly, who over the years had become her dearest friend, as well as a beloved grandmother to Emma. Anna had no regrets as to how her life had turned out, except for her loss of Gordy. She missed him most of all. Especially his physical presence, as well as the constant love and encouragement he'd always given her. It was because of his love and her inheritance, she was now a woman of some substance, as well as the owner of a flourishing business, with her mind still full of myriad ideas for the future.

For all of these blessings, Anna was immensely proud. And all this had happened since the day she'd walked away from Paul's home and had travelled through the snow into the city, into a new life. Her experience at his home had changed her, from a naïve and gullible young woman, into what she was now. She knew it was during those first few weeks of living with Molly her true personality had started to sparkle and she'd come alive.

Paul had always known she was wonderful; it was the reason he'd fallen in love with her, especially when allowed to be herself. It had been her life with her stepmother that had kept her repressed, of that he was certain, but he also knew, once they were married, and she was away from her old life she would blossom into a vibrant young woman, and he had wanted to be with her when that happened. Like Anna he too had his own dreams for their future, but that was before the accident happened, the one thing that was to change both their lives.

If one's destiny is pre-ordained, it doesn't really matter what one does, or which path one takes, the outcome will always be the same. And so it was with Paul and Anna. Except it was Gordy who was to have the privilege of seeing her grow into womanhood, and who would be the one to help her to achieve her successes, and the route she was to take through her life. It was Gordy who'd been the one to see her change into the special person she'd become. It was his love and nurturing that had been responsible, but what now of her destiny? Was she forever destined to always remain on her own, or was there someone in the future waiting for her?

Before she could think of herself and her future, Anna knew she had yet to solve one big problem, and that was Emma's engagement to Sam. How was she going to prevent their wedding from taking place? She knew what she should do, but it was the 'how' she found so difficult; afraid she would lose Emma if she made a mistake.

For someone normally so clear-thinking her thoughts at that moment were in a jumble, leaving her indecisive. What should she do? This was the one question she'd constantly asked herself, ever since Paul had walked into Emma's flat and back into her life.

Should she contact him, and confront him, before the young ones became even closer, and let him share the burden and responsibility? But first, how was she to tell him Emma was his daughter? Should she wait a while, in the hope Emma and Sam might possibly fall out of love? But even she knew this was unlikely to happen; they were too much in love for that! Anna knew she had to talk to Paul.

If telling Emma and Sam they couldn't marry wasn't bad enough, because they were brother and sister, she then had to tell Sam, Paul was Emma's father and then, worse still, she then had to tell Emma!

With her heart heavy and full of foreboding. It was as if the past had come back to haunt her with a vengeance, Anna asked herself, over and over again, how was she going to break the news to Emma, who was already puzzled by her mother's behaviour since her engagement to Sam had been announced. As for her mother fainting when Paul had arrived, Emma could only put that down to her mother overworking, as usual.

Anna spent the Sunday after the engagement dinner, walking alone along the riverside, deep in thought as she wrestled with her dilemma, leaving Molly and Emma to enthuse about Sam, and his father, and excitedly starting to make plans for the wedding Emma planned on them having in the village church, later in the year.

By the time Anna left to return to the city in the early evening, Emma thought her mother had recovered and was back to her old self, if perhaps somewhat quieter and more subdued than usual. She'd tried to discuss the wedding plans, but each time she began, her mother had changed the subject, which seemed strange to Emma, considering how keen her mother had been in the past to get her married! Even Molly could give her no explanation, though she did have her own suspicions, which for the time being, she wasn't about to divulge. If she was right, then it was up to Anna to tell Emma!

Emma's first impression of Sam's father was that he was handsome and charming. He was quite tall as well. With his dark hair flecked with silver at his temples, he looked exactly what he was, a distinguished banker! There was something indefinable about him Emma had instinctively liked and trusted, right from the minute she'd first met him when her and Sam had been at university and he'd come to visit Sam. He'd shaken her hand, holding on to and looking deep into her eyes, so like her mother's it was surprising he didn't realise then she was his daughter.

As he'd held her hand Emma had immediately felt a sense of 'knowing' him. For a few seconds, her inner senses recognised him, but from where? He was so unlike Sam in looks and personality she'd presumed Sam must follow his mother for his looks and red hair.

Sam had told her his mother had died when he was young, without elaborating on the circumstances and, being compassionate and caring, Emma didn't intrude on what was his personal grief. Perhaps later, she would regret not asking, but who can tell?

Over their time together at university, Emma had grown to understand Sam and knew, given time, he would confide in her.

Sam had always referred to Paul, as his father, leaving Emma no reason to believe otherwise. He couldn't bring himself to open old wounds, not even to his beloved Emma, so it never occurred to him that, unknowingly, he was making a huge problem for them all.

Liking Paul as she did, Emma had already created a romantic notion, whereby she and Sam got married and then afterwards, Paul and her mother would fall in love and get married as well. All very cosy, but from what was about to happen, Emma wasn't going to have the fairy-tale ending to the romantic scenario she wanted.

After much heart-searching, during the first few days of the following week, Anna finally plucked up courage and rang Emma, asking her to go down to the cottage the following weekend, ostensibly so they could be together, which Emma took to mean her mother was prepared at last to discuss wedding arrangements.

Emma, knowing she would be free that weekend, had no reason not to say no to her mother and enthusiastically agreed.

Molly loved the weekends when her two favourite people came to stay. She would make the cottage even more welcoming with fresh flowers from the garden in their bedrooms and the fridge and larder full of home grown fruit and vegetables, ready for the meals she'd already planned.

It had been a few days after the engagement dinner Molly suddenly remembered when and where she'd seen Paul!

She'd been taken aback when she first met him at Emma's flat, knowing his face was familiar, but how she knew him she couldn't recall. As usual, it was, once seen, never forgotten for Molly and, sure enough, days later, her mind suddenly focused and she remembered. He was the good looking young man she'd at first thought to be a 'spy' from one of her rivals! If only she'd known then he was Anna's Paul. Not that she would have been able to do anything about it, as Gordy was on the scene by then and Anna seemed more than happy living with him. There would have been no point in upsetting their lives. So this was just another case of 'if only' but unfortunately, that is the way of the way of world!

On this particular Friday evening, Molly sat anxiously watching out of the cottage window for the sight of their cars coming down the lane. Roly, her little King Charles spaniel, a gift from Emma when she'd left home to go to university so Molly wouldn't be too lonely without her, sitting by her side, with his ears pricked every time he heard a car stop outside the cottage, knowing full well, if visitors arrived, he would be in for a few long walks. For Molly, it was a worrying time as well.

Anna was the first to arrive and, after changing out of her business suit and into her weekend casuals, she sat with a glass of her favourite white wine and talked to Molly of her week. Molly could see something was troubling her. They'd been talking, mostly about Anna's latest book and the television series she was about to start, until Molly asked the question she'd been thinking about all day. In her usual forthright way she said, 'I know there's a problem between you and Emma and I want you to tell me about it.'

Anna looked taken aback for a minute or two, her shoulders tensed, her normally smooth forehead lined with a frown. An action Molly had seen many times before, when Anna had been faced with an awkward situation.

'You need to talk, and there's no one better than me at listening!' Molly had said.

'I know,' Anna sighed, 'I just don't know what to say to Emma that won't cause more problems than there are already!'

'Perhaps telling her the truth might be the best way to start?'

Anna's eyes filled with tears. 'Oh, Molly, what am I to do? The truth is, Sam's father is Emma's real father!'

With the dreaded words spoken, her voice broke and her tears started to fall. To Molly's alarm, Anna sobbed, as though her heart would break.

'How am I to tell Emma?' Anna said, through her tears, desperately trying to stop crying.

'Crying isn't going to help,' said Molly. 'You need to stay calm and think carefully about what you're going to say to the child.' Her reply, always the pragmatic one that sometimes hit home deeper than Anna would have liked.

In Molly's eyes, Emma would always be a child, as Anna would always be the daughter, she'd never had. To Molly, they were both her children and, like all mothers, she was on hand to help them solve their problems and, if necessary, pick up the pieces if their lives were shattered by misfortune.

Anna finally calmed down and began to talk about Paul and how she had fallen in love with him, but Molly knew most of the story, especially the attack his mother had made on her, for she'd seen the results. She even knew how Anna had tried to get in contact with him and how he'd refused to return her calls or answer her letters. Perhaps, if Anna could have told him she was pregnant, he might have changed his mind, but that was merely conjecture on Molly's part. Anna had been a different person then to the one sitting next to her now. Twenty-five years ago she'd been gullible and naïve, as well as frightened, because in those days, society was quite different to how it was now and, without Gordy's marriage proposal, she would have carried the stigma of being an unmarried mother throughout her life, which in many ways would have affected Emma as well.

Anna's main thought now was, how would Emma see her, when she knew the facts? What would she think of her as a person, once she'd revealed the facts of her birth, and told her who really was her father?

At that moment, Anna fervently wished Gordy could be at her side; she missed him so much, his wise counsel, and the unconditional love he'd given her throughout their life together, and the way he'd taken her in marriage, never once reminding her she'd made love to another man, or the child she'd been expecting wasn't his. He'd always said Emma was his child and, in time, even Anna had come to believe him!

By the time Emma arrived at the cottage that evening it was getting late. Being in love suited her. She was looking even more beautiful than usual; a younger version of her mother; her dark hair hanging loose on her shoulders, the only reminder of Paul. Nothing was said that night and, after a light supper, they all went to bed. The only one to sleep soundly though was Emma. Molly slept very little these days, existing, Anna was certain, on catnaps. As for Anna, she was too strung up and emotional to sleep; consequently, the next morning there were black circles under her eyes that showed her tiredness, that not even a slick of judiciously applied make-up could hide.

It was now or never, Anna told herself later, as she sat with Emma, drinking the remains of the pot of coffee Molly had made earlier.

Molly, deep in her own thoughts had cleared away the breakfast dishes and left them alone, to go out into her garden.

Anna looked across the table at Emma, unable to speak for a moment, her throat tight and dry. Mentally rebuking herself, she cleared her throat, while Emma continued her daydreaming, until suddenly, she looked up and saw her mother looking at her in a strange way; her face tired and wan, her emerald eyes full of unshed tears, the dark circles underneath emphasising their brightness.

Molly suddenly came back into the kitchen and sat down at the table, waiting expectantly for Anna to say what she had to say. She knew she could only sit and listen, and then maybe, afterwards, try to use her wisdom to heal what she already knew would be a rift between the two people she loved more than her own life. The suspense was agonising, until at last Anna spoke, her voice soft and clear. 'Emma, darling, I need to tell you something that may hurt and surprise you.'

Emma looked up, her attention fully focused now on her mother, wondering what she could possibly say that would hurt or surprise her. Anna paused for a few moments, obviously gathering her thoughts. When next she spoke, she chose her words carefully.

'I want you to get married.'

At this statement Molly gasped. Whatever was Anna saying? Had she gone completely mad? This wasn't what she'd thought she was going to say, more like, I don't want you to get married!

Before Molly could interrupt, Anna was speaking. 'But not to Sam!'

'What do you mean, not to Sam?' Emma asked hotly. 'I thought you liked him? You said he would make a wonderful husband!'

'Yes,' said Anna. 'I do like him and I know he will make some girl a wonderful husband. But not you!'

Anna placed her hands over her eyes, her weariness and anguish apparent in her gesture. There was a stunned silence in the room, until she spoke again. 'You can't marry him because...' At this point, she paused, her carefully chosen words gone momentarily from her mind, until finally, she blurted out the dreaded sentence. 'You can't marry Sam, because he's your brother!' There was a gasp from Emma, but Anna hadn't finished. 'Sam's father is your father!'

Anna couldn't look at Emma; she couldn't bear to see the look in her beloved child's eyes; to see the hurt and anger she knew would be reflected there. When she did raise her eyes to look at her, she could see Emma was looking thoroughly stunned and ashen.

'I don't believe you!' Emma said. 'It can't possibly be true. My father's dead! You're only saying this because you're jealous of me; jealous because I'm getting married and you're not!'

The look on Emma's young face was almost one of hatred. 'Emma, darling...' Anna tried to speak to her.

'Don't Emma darling me!' she snorted. Her voice and attitude portraying her anger and disbelief at what she'd just heard. 'You're only saying this because you don't really like Sam!'

Anna reached across the table, intending to take her daughter's hands in her own, but Emma snatched them away and stood up, leaving Anna sitting alone with her own misery.

Molly, unable any longer to bear the anger she was hearing from Emma, or the despair she could see in Anna's eyes, merely watched, as Emma fought back her tears, but wisely, she kept her own counsel, for the moment saying nothing.

Anna tried to explain how she and Paul had been young and in love and were indeed her parents, but Emma refused to listen, unable to believe Gordy wasn't her father, at the same time, Anna kept insisting Paul really was her father. Finally, Emma burst into tears and ran from the room.

Anna made to follow her, but Molly, in her wisdom, reached out and stopped her, holding onto her hands.

'Sit down and leave the child alone,' she said. 'Let her be. She needs to work this out for herself.'

Anna nodded. Molly was right, as always.

Emma would have to come to terms with the facts in her own way and in her own time. There was nothing she or anyone else could do or say that would lessen her grief.

Seeing Emma heartbroken, Anna couldn't believe she'd caused her child so much unhappiness, especially at what should have been a joyous time in her life, but she knew Molly was right, she had to let Emma come to terms with all she'd told her in her own way, however long it took.

Anna and Molly were still sitting in the kitchen when they heard Emma's bedroom door opening, and then closing behind her, as she came down the stairs. For a moment, they both looked towards the door, expecting her to come in, but Emma opened the front door and, before they could stop her, she'd gone.

Anna went to the front door to follow her, but by then Emma had tossed her holdall into her car, had climbed in and, before either Anna or Molly could get to the car park to stop her she was already driving up the lane, away from the village, without a word of goodbye.

Anna sobbed, as though her heart would break for most of the day; sure she'd lost her daughter forever, remonstrating with herself for not handling the situation better. Suddenly, the cottage became a place of sadness, as though there'd been a death and the family were in deep mourning. Every car that came down the lane had Anna or Molly jumping up to see if it was Emma returning, but without any success.

With Sam away for the weekend, and not having any knowledge of Paul's address or telephone number, Anna had no way of getting in touch with either of them to let them know what had happened.

Several times during the day, she tried contacting Emma at her flat where the phone would ring, and then the answerphone would click into use, giving her no idea as to whether Emma was at home or not. As the day drew to a close, Anna knew in her heart her daughter wasn't going to ring and let them know she was safely home, as she normally did, let alone pick up and talk! As for Molly, she tried her best to soothe and console Anna as the longest day of both their lives gradually passed into night.

Molly could well understand Anna's grief. She could see how she was fretting over Emma's swift departure, but it wasn't until Anna decided she should inform the police that she stepped in.

'The child's just licking her wounds. She knows full well you're bound to be worried sick about her and she's making sure she gives you a hard time! When she's calmed down, she'll get in touch, you see!'

Anna didn't have Molly's convictions and neither was she sure she was right. She knew how stubborn her daughter could be, and knew that this time, she was the one to blame.

She should have told Emma the facts of her birth years ago. And definitely she should have told her who her biological father was after Gordy had died, but they were all too grief-stricken then, and she couldn't have taken away Emma's belief that Gordy was her father, for the child had idolised him. There was no way she was prepared to take responsibility for destroying Emma's love for the man she truly believed to be her father.

Molly tried to comfort and console her, but nothing she said made any impression and so the rest of the weekend passed, without a word from Emma.

It was soon time for Anna to return to the city and, with Molly's loving wishes ringing in her ears, she drove back to her lonely apartment. For the first time since she'd moved into the penthouse apartment she felt alone and afraid; afraid of her emotions. If only Gordy had been with her, they would have been able to explain together how he came to be her father and then, maybe, Emma would have understood and forgiven her.

Anna tried several times that evening to phone Emma, each time getting the same mechanical message, demanding she leave her name and number and Emma would return the call, but of course there was no return call and Anna wondered if her life and her relationship with her daughter would ever be the same again.

Meanwhile, Emma was also going through her own torment. Why, she asked herself, hadn't her mother told her before that Gordy wasn't her father? She'd adored him and she knew, without a doubt, he adored her in return; surely only a true father could have been so wonderful to her.

As for Paul, how could he have been her father, as well as Sam's? She found it impossible to believe what her mother had told her. Perhaps when Sam came back he would have the answer she needed. Until then, her mother could wait and worry!

# Chapter 18

Emma had driven back to Birmingham completely unaware of how she'd managed to arrive at her apartment without mishap, considering her confused and unhappy state of mind. She was not only angry, but upset; troubled by what her mother had told her and unable to get her head around the fact the man she'd always thought of as her father was in truth not! Neither could she believe Sam's father was hers. It just didn't make sense. As she calmed down, she made up her mind that as soon as Sam arrived back she would talk to him and then maybe, between them, they would find the truth.

As she'd opened the door, and entered her apartment, the phone was ringing. She let it ring, knowing the answerphone would click in and take a message, but she knew, even without listening, it would be her mother. At that moment, Emma had nothing to say to her. What was there to say?

The phone rang several times over the next few hours, each time with another message from her mother, all of which Emma ignored. Her head aching from the stress of what she'd been told, along with the tears she'd cried since leaving the cottage and driving home. Suddenly, she had an idea; she went into her bedroom and opened the cupboard where she kept the mementoes of her childhood. As she sat looking through the albums of photographs, studiously ignoring the phone whenever it rang, she slowly turned the pages of the album; staring at the photographs taken over the years by her father, mostly of her mother and herself.

Looking closely at the photographs of what she remembered as being an idyllic childhood she could see her resemblance to her mother. They shared the same elfin features, then, looking closely at those of her father, she could see how she followed him for her colouring. They both had dark, wavy hair, but there the resemblance ended. Then, thinking of Paul, she knew he was also dark haired but there the similarity to him ended as well.

To Emma it didn't make sense. Why would her mother marry the man she'd always thought of as her father, when her own was still alive?

Paul was about the same age as her mother, whereas the man she thought to be her father had been much older.

Her mother had said her real father had wanted to marry her, but that was before he knew she was pregnant. Before she could tell him, he'd changed his mind and abandoned her. It was then Gordy had stepped in and married her instead, preventing her from being shamed by society.

By the time Sam arrived back from London the following day, it was late in the evening. Emma had calmed down a little, although she was still not answering her mother's calls.

She was so relieved to see Sam, she almost knocked him over in her hurry to get him into her apartment, hurling herself into his arms as soon as the front door was closed, dragging him into the room.

She gave him no time to tell her how his weekend had gone, before she was rushing to tell him their wedding was off.

Sam couldn't understand what Emma was saying. One minute she was in his arms kissing him until he was breathless, wanting more than kissing, and then, the next minute, she was telling him the wedding was off! Whatever was the matter with the girl?

Emma, by then with her emotions simmering at a high-octane level, was by now ready to explode. To Sam's utter astonishment, as she'd suddenly blurted out, 'I can't marry you, Sam.'

'What do you mean you can't marry me?' he said, totally stunned by her statement, as well as puzzled, wondering what on earth had got into her? He knew she loved him but at that moment, he could see she would have been quite happy to see him gone, so what on earth had happened over the weekend to get her into such a tizzy?

Emma walked away from him, trying to calm herself down and gather her senses, knowing they had to talk if they were to find a solution; but it wasn't going to be easy.

Sam hadn't expected her to be in such a state when he'd arrived. It was obvious she was wound up about something and, the best thing he could do, was to find out what the devil was wrong with her, and why she'd suddenly decided she wasn't going to marry him?

Before he could say anything, Emma clutched his arms and pulled him down onto the sofa.

'We can't get married...' she said, hesitating for a moment, tears welling up in her eyes, 'because... you're my brother!'

Sam's face was a picture of incredulity. He wanted to burst out laughing, but from the look on Emma's face he changed his mind. 'Don't be so ridiculous!' he said, trying to suppress a laugh.

'Who told you that rubbish?' he demanded, when the seriousness of her statement suddenly struck him.

Emma, all keyed up with her emotions, was about to burst into tears and, for a moment or two, Sam was filled with dread, he hated it when Emma cried.

'My mother told me yesterday. She said your father is also mine!'

'I'm quite sure my father never met your mother!' Sam replied, aghast at Emma's comment. 'And,' he continued, 'more to the point, when could your mother have ever met him?'

'I don't know,' Emma answered, gulping back her tears, 'but they must have had an affair for me to have been conceived!'

It was the only explanation she could give him, and a feeble one at that. She wiped her eyes and looked at him.

'Okay, let's think calmly about this for a while shall we?' said Sam, taking Emma in his arms and holding her close. 'Let's sit and work this whole thing out?'

Emma sat quietly, cuddled into Sam's arms, with him soothing her hair away from her tear- streaked face.

'Right,' he said suddenly, in his no-nonsense manner, 'you were born in 1958? At that time, my mother and father had been in Canada for two years and they didn't return until the October after you were born, so that I could be born in England. My father was working at a hospital in London then and, after that, he and my mother started to travel throughout Africa, doing their medical research, so how could he possibly have had an affair with your mother, either before you were born, or even afterwards?'

Sam's attitude was, I told you so, but Emma still wasn't convinced. She looked at him, puzzled, as she digested his words.

'I thought your father lived in the Midlands? That's where my mother said he lived, with his mother and father.'

'Not my father!' said Sam, wondering if Emma had been listening to what he'd said. 'Perhaps we ought to take my birth certificate and my parents' marriage certificate to your mother and she can see for herself I'm telling you the truth. It seems to me your mother has made a big mistake!'

Emma clung onto him, her head spinning. She knew he would have the answers! He was such thorough man when it came to facts and figures!

At last Emma got the message, the man Sam called his father wasn't! So how come he'd said he was?

Sam was beginning to understand how the misunderstanding had taken place. It was entirely his fault for referring to Paul as his father, when he was nothing of the sort. He was his godfather certainly, but that was as far as the name 'father' went.

Emma understood. 'Because you introduced him as your "father", my mother wrongly assumed he was married to your mother?'

'I guess so,' said Sam, proceeding to tell her the story of his childhood and what had happened for Paul to become his surrogate 'father'. Once he'd finished, Emma seemed happy her nightmare was over, relieved that at last the mistake of Sam's parentage had been rectified.

As it was so late, Emma decided to ring her mother early the next morning and explain what had happened, until then, she and Sam had some catching up of their own to do, all involving their own love life!

Anna had many business commitments and functions that often took her away from home and that week was no exception. Emma had spoken to Molly and told her the outcome of her conversation with Sam, asking her not to tell

Anna when she phoned, as she wanted to break the news herself.

It was just pure coincidence Paul also happened to be working in the south of England the same time as Anna and, like her, had decided to stay overnight, little realising she would be staying at the same hotel!

Paul saw her first, as she entered the dining room that evening. He was taken aback at seeing her, wondering for a few moments why she was there, but then he realised, quite rightly, as a businesswoman she was possibly doing business in the area, as he was and, after all, she had to stay somewhere and eat. As soon as he saw her, he signalled the headwaiter to bring her across to join him at his table in the far corner of the room.

Her look of surprise when she saw Paul at the table made him smile. For a moment or two, she thought he looked like the cat lapping cream and, for a few seconds, she was tempted to ask the waiter for a table for one in another part of the room, but something stopped her, suddenly realising here was an ideal opportunity to find out about Sam and his mother, for she was intrigued as to where and when Paul had met her and, who was she?

Paul stood up as she arrived at the table and held out his hand in greeting.

'How nice to see you again,' he said, formally, as Anna briefly shook his outstretched hand, before sitting down.

'I didn't expect to see you again, and so soon,' she replied. Her curt reply softened by her heartstoppingly beautiful smile, 'we need to talk and I suppose now is as good a time as ever!'

Paul looked at her closely. She was still as beautiful as she'd been when she was twenty years old and he'd first fallen in love with her. In his opinion, she was as captivating now as then and no other woman had ever made his heart pound as she did. He could feel it now, thudding in his chest, leaving him wondering if she could hear it from where she sat across the table. Little did Paul know Anna was experiencing the same reaction to his presence, the tell-tale stain of her emotions rushing up her neck giving her away.

'Why don't we eat first and then we can talk?' he said. 'I don't know about you, but after my day I'm starving. What do you say? Eat first? And then talk?'

Anna was indeed hungry and it made sense to do as he said, after all, she had plenty of time to tell him he was Emma's father!

Paul ordered wine for the dishes they'd chosen, without consulting her, and that had made her smile at his chauvinistic manner, or was he merely being gallant?

Paul often stayed in this hotel and knew the food was superb, but for the life of him, he couldn't have told anyone what he'd eaten that evening. He only knew his hunger had been assuaged, and that was as far as he would admit. Anna felt exactly the same.

Their talk at the table had been of inconsequential things, the sort of chitchat two strangers thrown together might have.

As the waiter cleared away the dishes, Paul ordered coffee for them, to be served in the upstairs lounge, without giving Anna a chance to make other arrangements. Before she knew what was happening, he'd risen from his seat and was helping her from hers, escorting her from the room with his arm around her waist in a proprietarily manner, his touch burning her flesh through her clothes as they retired to the lounge. The electricity flowing between them almost tangible, as it had been when they'd been much younger and, as Anna thought, deeply in love! But that was all in the past.

Sitting with their coffees, and a brandy each, Paul asked Anna about her work. Knowing a little, as Sam had told him something of her working life, but even he hadn't realised quite how big her business interests were.

She told him of the pub and the factories and how it had all started. He made no mention though of applying for a position at her company as Chief Accountant, or even that he'd turned it down before having an interview! For a moment, he briefly wondered what would have happened had he turned up and met her then. But Anna was already ahead of him in thinking the same!

They sat for some time in the lounge, drinking their coffees and sipping at the brandy, surreptitiously watching each other, until Anna took a big breath and, bolstered by the alcohol, blurted out, 'Sam and Emma can't get married you know?'

'Why ever not?' was his laconic reply.

'Because...' Anna hesitated for a moment. 'Emma's your daughter!'

Paul's face was a picture of shock, and surprise at her words, he even went pale. 'Emma's what?' he said, incredulous at her statement.

'She's your daughter!'

'I don't believe you,' he said, by now not only pale but also shaking. 'Why didn't you let me know?'

'I did try to get in touch with you. I phoned your house, but you wouldn't speak to me. I wrote to you as well, but I never received a reply. I even went to see you, but your parents said you weren't interested in seeing me anymore.'

Anna paused for a few moments, giving him some much-needed time to absorb her words. 'I knew I was pregnant by then and, as Molly and Gordy were my only friends at the time, they looked after me. When Gordy knew you didn't want me, he offered to marry me instead, to give my baby a name.

Paul reached out and took her hand. 'I'm so sorry. I did know you'd written to me and that you'd come to see me.' Seeing the shock on her face, he knew he'd upset her by what she must have thought to be a callous statement, but he continued speaking before she could question him. 'I didn't know any of this at the time, not until some years later, when I was clearing out my parents' house after they'd died. Perhaps I should tell you what happened after you'd left the house that Christmas morning?'

Anna nodded, and then, calmly holding onto her hand, he told her what had happened after she'd left the house on that awful morning. He told her of how he'd spoken to his mother, trying to reason with her, and how eventually, he'd left the house and walked down the lane after her. Of his accident he could say very little, as he could remember nothing about it at all, except the evidence the police had gathered from the stranger who'd found him under the car. He then told her about his long stay in hospital and the fact he'd lost his memory of her, even when he'd recovered physically and was back at home. He told her it wasn't until he was clearing out his parents' house he'd found her letters and had tried to find her.

Of course, he'd said, when he found out she was married he knew he'd lost her. He had to let her live with her new husband, without trying to get her back. Not, he was quick to assure her, that he hadn't wanted to.

Anna was stunned. So he hadn't deserted her after all, but that still didn't explain Sam being his son!

Paul laughed. Gently, he explained Sam was in fact his godson. The son of his best friends, who'd both been killed while working in Africa and he'd taken on the role of father to the young boy, giving him the stability he desperately needed, at the same time, explaining calling Paul his father, was Sam's security blanket.

By now, he was caressing Anna's hands, smoothing her fingers between his, his eye caught by the emerald and diamond ring she still wore on her finger, along with her wedding ring.

'I'm sorry. I forgot you were married,' he said, looking pointedly at her ring finger.

'Yes' she said. 'I was married, but my husband died, several years ago. It was through him I went into business.'

Without elaborating any further, she pulled her hands away, afraid of having contact with him as it was affecting her breathing.

Taking a deep breath, she tried to regain her composure and started to get up from her chair. 'Well, Emma will be pleased. Now she can go ahead and marry Sam.'

'Yes, I suppose so,' said Paul, looking quite dejected, knowing Anna would be walking out of his life again, unless he said or did something quickly.

Finally knowing the mystery of Paul's past life, and the problem of Emma and Sam being resolved, Anna wasn't about to fall into his arms, contrary to what her heart was telling her to do. She had her independence and it was no longer in her nature to let a man lead the way. If Paul still wanted her, he would have to woo and court her. In her usual and decisive way, and with her mouth dry with nerves and her heart beating twenty to the dozen, Anna rose from her seat and wished him goodnight. She'd waited a long time to meet him and to know the truth, surely, waiting a while longer could do no harm to either of them?

Paul looked at her in amazement. Unable to believe she was going to leave him when he wanted her so badly.

What she really wanted, was for him to stop her, and take her in his arms and make love to her, instead, he merely wished her a brief goodnight and watched her walk away towards the lift, without so much as a backward glance in his direction.

He sighed. At least he had an excuse to see her again. Their daughter, and his godson were going to be married. All he hoped for before then, was that he and Anna would be more than just reconciled, if he could possibly arrange it?

As Anna walked towards the lift, her legs were shaking. She'd desperately wanted, on the one hand, to stay with Paul, yet on the other, she knew she had to leave and let their emotions settle down for, like Paul she was no longer young and impressionable. She smiled to herself, knowing she was only trying to convince herself she was a sensible middle-aged woman, with her own businesses, as successful, as he was, and certainly not a woman to be tangled with!

Which was exactly Paul's opinion of her as the lift door closed behind her! He also knew he had his work cut out if he was going to improve the situation to his advantage.

Having at last met the woman he'd fallen in love with over twenty-five years ago, when in his early twenties and thought he'd lost her forever, he knew he had to work out how best he could get her back into his life and, more to the point, back into his arms and then, as fast as he could, into his bed.

It was something Paul had yet to fathom, but he hadn't climbed to the top of his profession by being indecisive.

He had all the qualities needed to be successful in business, so he just hoped that now he had enough of these qualities to woo Anna and convince her he still loved her.

He knew he had to get a strategy, as it was obvious she was no pushover and not, as far as he could see, in her business life either!

# Chapter 19

Anna walked into her hotel room, her head aching from tension; she needed time to herself, to relax and take in all Paul had told her; not that she disbelieved him. What she found hard to believe, was his parents' attitude towards her, unable to understand the reason why they'd felt so vindictive towards her.

What, she wondered, would they have said, or done, had they known they had a granddaughter? Would they have felt differently then? These were all questions she knew she would never have the answers for. As for Paul he'd looked stunned when she'd told him Emma was his daughter, even questioning her as to whether she was indeed his, which had made her angry, especially as he knew she'd been a virgin when he'd made love to her. Once she'd assured him Emma was indeed his daughter, she could see he believed her, but she could also see he was shocked, unable to believe making love just once could result in a baby being conceived!

Paul had made no attempt to take her in his arms while they'd been sitting in the lounge and neither had he made any physical contact, other than to take her hands in his, making Anna wonder whether he did still love her? Or was it that he had indeed forgotten he'd ever done so?

Her own question, did she still love him was easy to answer, she'd never stopped loving him. She didn't have any doubts on that score, but what the future held for them she couldn't answer. Should she follow her heart and declare her love for him? Or follow her head and keep him at arm's length?

Meanwhile, in his room, Paul was trying to take in all Anna had told him. He had known she was married, but not that she'd had a child. Nor that her child was indeed his! He still couldn't believe Sam's wonderful Emma was his daughter, his own flesh and blood. He'd been utterly stunned at Anna's revelation and even now he still couldn't quite believe it.

He wondered if Sam and Emma knew the truth. He wished he'd asked Anna before she went to her room, but he'd seen how weary she'd been looking, her day obviously as tiring as his own and then, being confronted by him, must also have been a strain. He'd rightly guessed he was indeed the last person she would have wanted to see that evening. But at least they'd talked, even if he hadn't been expecting to have his life turned upside down in quite such a way! He also knew his feelings for her were exactly the same now, as they'd been twenty-five years ago, when they'd both been young and starting out in their careers. He knew he still loved her of that he was certain and he still wanted her to be his wife. As they'd sat talking, he'd had to fight the urge to scoop her up in his arms and hold her close to his heart, to reassure her everything was going to be fine, but age and experience told him he would have to give her time; he would have to play a waiting game; to court her and to woo her, all over again. He just hoped there were no other suitors waiting in line!

That night, neither Paul nor Anna slept well.

Paul was up early and in the dining room as soon as it opened, but of Anna there was no sign. When he asked at the reception desk if she was breakfasting in her room, he was told Mrs Grey had checked out early and, with this disappointing news, Paul had to be satisfied. At least he knew they would meet again, even if he had to wait for Emma and Sam's wedding day!

Anna had purposely left the hotel early, not because she wanted to evade Paul, but because she had an appointment in London for a meeting at the television studios. And after the previous evening spent with him, she didn't want him confronting her when she had work to think about; he wasn't on her agenda yet. But she knew from now on he would be playing an important part in her life, especially as he knew he was Emma's real father and therefore, it was inevitable she would see him again.

Part of her wanted that to happen, just as soon as she could possibly arrange it, but another part wanted for them to give each other time and space, to assess what had happened and to take it easy before they rushed into resuming their relationship. At their ages, a full-blown love affair might not be the right move for either of them!

Thoughts of Paul filled Anna's mind as she arrived at the studios where she was to meet the producer, and the team, for the new show she'd been signed to appear in. There were further meetings scheduled for the rest of the week as well and, with her nerves already taut, she tried to comprehend exactly what it was she was letting herself in for.

As she sat waiting in the studio reception hall, she agonised, over and over again, as to how she felt about Paul and her life in general. For the first time in her life, she wondered if she was up to starting a new career, or even a love affair, even debating whether she was too old for either.

It had been the events of the past week, then seeing Paul again, as well as her problems with Emma, that had not only dented her confidence, but her enthusiasm for living her life to the full. It hadn't killed it, but it had certainly doused it a little. At the moment, all she wanted to do was to hide away and recoup her innermost resources; somehow she needed to rekindle her verve and zest for life and the only way she knew how to do that was to keep herself busy and being at the studio seemed the right place to be.

She'd made no attempt to speak to Emma while she was away, but she did phone Molly, who couldn't wait to tell her Emma had been in contact and had solved the problem of Sam being her brother! Molly relayed the bare details of his birth parents to Anna, along with the news Emma appeared to have forgiven her, at this Anna gave a sigh of relief, at least that was one problem solved.

After a visit to the powder room, before the producer appeared and, with a judicious amount of fresh makeup applied, Anna managed to cover the fact she'd slept very little the night before. With a slightly forced breeziness to her manner, she managed to sail successfully through the day.

The following few evenings she spent on her own at her hotel, dining quietly, followed by restless nights, having given in to the demands of her heart by spending her nightly hours dreaming of being in Paul's arms and them making love, feelings that left her not only frustrated, but wanting desperately for him to be in her life!

By the end of the week, she was more than ready to go home, but instead of driving to the cottage, she returned to her apartment and stayed in the city, where she continued to wrestle with her thoughts, knowing the time had come to be decisive about her life. She had to stop dithering and make a decision, should she give up all her business interests and just concentrate on her writing and her new venture in television?

Just one of many questions she had yet to answer. Another? What should she do about the Ring O' Bells she still owned and was presently being run by Monica and Jim as her managers?

Anna knew they would like to buy the pub, they'd told her so many times over the years, but she was loath to part with the old place, mainly for sentimental reasons, it being the first major investment she'd made with Gordy's inheritance. It had also been the springboard for all her other businesses and even now, going into television, was the direct result of her starting out in the old pub in Little Coombe.

It had been cooking for her customers and experimenting with recipes that had been the start of everything. Leading to her writing career as well, using the cookery books she always wrote her recipes in as the basis for her first book, and how that had been a big success.

It was just one thing leading on to another and then, before she knew it, she'd leased the first factory, where at first all the pies had been made.

It had been Gordy's wonderful legacy, multiplied now many times by her judicious investments that had indeed been like a golden egg and responsible for making her life into a circle of success. Everything she'd done since his death had started because of his legacy. First of all there was the pub, and her days as a pub landlady, which had led to her becoming a successful businesswoman. And now she was an author, with a fourth volume nearly completed of her successful cookery books and then, yet another opportunity in television that loomed ahead and all because of Gordy. It was as though he was guiding her but it was at times like these she missed him the most, not only his physical presence but his good sense. For a while she felt sad and alone.

Anna knew she must think carefully about her future.

Perhaps Paul would be able to give her some advice, especially if they had a future together. Meeting him had definitely been a shock to her system and, if she was really honest with herself, it was a shock she was finding difficult to come to terms with. Ever since she'd met him again, there had been a big question mark hanging over her life but one she'd already answered.

Even when married to Gordy she'd never forgotten her first love, it might have been put on the back burner of her life for the past twenty-five years, but now she'd decided she was ready to have its light re-ignited!

For some people this must be difficult to understand, but not for Anna. The love she'd felt for Gordy and Paul was different. Gordy had been much older than Paul and was also more experienced in the ways of women, and this had showed in how he treated her. He'd been a gentle and caring man, loving her and cherishing her but when it came to lovemaking, he was passionate and, she could honestly say she'd never once thought of Paul in her most intimate moments with him. Had Gordy lived, Anna knew she would never have left him for Paul and that puzzled her.

Once she'd married Gordy, Anna managed to accept her love for Paul belonged to another time, he was in her past, maybe now was the time for them to move into another dimension and for their destinies to merge, allowing them both to find the fulfilment they desperately wanted as they finally came together.

Vanity and self-importance had never played a large part in Anna's life, as she wasn't that sort of woman. She was well aware of the physical effect she had on men. If anything, it amused her. Her women friends equally liked and admired her, and even her married friends trusted their husbands in her company but now she wondered idly, did Paul have a girlfriend, or possibly a lover? The idea this might be a possibility made her heart race as a jealous pang rose within her. Mentally shaking herself away from these disturbing thoughts, she knew all she could do was to wait and be patient and take each day as it came, until the day arrived, when she was sure all her questions would be answered.

Once her mind was set on an idea and a course of action, Anna set them in motion. First of all she planned to speak to Emma, then Sam. Then to Molly, for surely, between them they would have the answers she needed. They would then all get together and make plans for the wedding. As for Paul, she would have to consider how she was going to handle him!

In another part of the country, Paul's life, like Anna's was fully taken up with work and travelling; not a problem while he'd been single and footloose, but not ideal if he managed to get back into a committed relationship again with the mother of his child. Anna wasn't back in his life yet, but she was definitely permanently on his mind, so much so, he found work to be an irksome duty. He wanted to be with her, to hold her in his arms and tell her how much he loved her and, more than anything else, he wanted to make mad passionate love to her.

The one advantage of getting older, he thought, was at last he'd acquired some patience, especially where Anna was concerned.

He was prepared to wait, but for how long was that going to be?

Let's hope the fates will be gentle with Paul, and his fair lady, and that at last, our hero and heroine get to claim their prize!

# Chapter 20

Emma was relieved when her mother rang during the weekend and told her she'd seen Paul and he'd explained his relationship to Sam. With mother and daughter once more reconciled and their relationship back to normal, they had much to talk about. Once Anna was satisfied Emma was not too unhappy to have Paul as her father and, with Sam eager to marry, it was agreed they should meet at the cottage the following weekend and start to make plans.

Not only were Emma and Sam keen to get married, they were equally as keen to get Anna and Paul together; taking Molly into their confidence, they agreed to invite him down for the weekend without telling Anna.

As usual, Monica and Jim at the Ring O' Bells came up trumps, with the two visitors' bedrooms available for Sam and Paul and, with Molly included in the conspiracy, the matchmakers waited impatiently for the weekend to arrive.

Paul hadn't asked if Anna would be at the cottage when Sam issued the invitation, he wanted his surprise at seeing her again to be genuine, if and when he did see her, and, being two steps ahead of both Sam and Emma in their scheming, he'd packed the original solitaire diamond ring he'd bought years ago into his weekend holdall, the ring he'd found hidden in his mother's room, just in case he had the opportunity to get Anna on her own and into his arms!

Sam and Emma were the first to arrive, only to find Molly in a high state of anxiety. Emma suddenly realised

Molly had never kept a secret from her beloved Anna before and here they were expecting her to be a conspirator in their matchmaking efforts, not that Molly disapproved of the idea; she was all in favour, having decided Paul was the ideal man for her beloved Anna, especially since she'd heard the story of how he'd been in an accident and lost his memory of her. Molly thought it the most romantic story she'd ever heard and, as far as she could see, there was no reason for them not to get together again and if all it took was a white lie here and there to make it happen, and it helped in Sam and Emma's plans, then she was only too happy to oblige.

The two young ones, along with Paul, who'd also arrived early and had parked his car at the back of the car park, were all in the pub when Anna arrived at the cottage.

Molly managed not to blurt out that Paul would be staying for the weekend and, as soon as Anna had changed out of her business outfit into her usual casual weekend clothes, a relieved Molly, and an unsuspecting Anna, walked the few yards to the pub next door to join the others.

Anna noticed Emma and Sam as soon as she walked into the pub, but as Paul was shielded from her view by the layout of the room, it wasn't until she'd turned to go into the dining area she suddenly set eyes on him.

She felt her legs go weak and a sudden rush of colour surge up her throat, vanishing just as quickly, leaving her face pale, which highlighted her green eyes. It was the unexpectedness of seeing him that had shocked her and left her trembling, especially as he'd been on her mind all week. Emma quite expected her mother to faint, especially when she saw her colour change (as she had when she had met Paul for the first time). Leaving Emma to wonder if this was a sign of her mother's love for Paul.

For Anna, it had been the sudden shock of seeing him again, and the effect it had had on her heart, leaving her to think she was behaving as though she was experiencing her first schoolgirl crush.

It took an almighty effort on her part before she managed to pull herself together and greet him in a voice, that only to Paul, who was highly sensitive to her every nuance, was full of emotion.

He'd been equally as affected by Anna's arrival and couldn't take his eyes off her. She looked even more beautiful than usual that evening, with her glorious auburn hair worn loose, skimming her shoulders, as she'd worn it when younger, and just how he remembered it.

He wanted to put his hands deep into those glorious waves and pull her towards him and kiss her until she was breathless and helpless in his arms, instead, he just smiled at her, his smile hiding his lustful thoughts and his longing, knowing he must be patient. Something, he'd told himself often over the past week that he must be, believing the time would surely soon come when he would be able to make love to her as he'd once done all those years ago.

Anna tried to gather her composure, unaware of his lustful thoughts, but at the same time full of her own. He looked so handsome and virile she wanted him; therefore, it was with some considerable difficulty she managed to avert her eyes from his and sat down at the table next to Sam and Emma, with Paul sitting opposite, and Molly beside him. After greeting Emma and Sam with a hug and a light kiss each, she surprised everyone, including herself, by leaning across the table to lightly brush Paul's cheek with a kiss.

He wanted nothing more at that moment than to reach out and hold onto her, before taking her outside, where he would kiss her soundly, but he knew he couldn't do that and had to make do with returning a light kiss of his own. Needless to say, Emma, Sam and Molly had all watched the scene, open-mouthed each aware their matchmaking efforts might not be needed after all.

With her emotions only just under control and her composure regained, Anna tried to make sensible conversation, but with Paul's eyes staring at her, she found it virtually impossible to concentrate, to the secret amusement of the others.

Paul was in awe of her, unable to take his eyes off her, much to Anna's chagrin and to the delight of Sam and Emma, both keenly aware of the sexual tension simmering between Emma's parents.

Anna made, as she thought, appropriate responses to all their questions as to how the week had gone at the television studios but, as she confided later to Molly, she couldn't recall what the conversations, or questions, had been about, her head and heart too wrapped up in her own lustful thoughts of Paul!

Molly, with her normal astuteness, had seen for herself how much meeting Paul again had meant to Anna and how he appeared to be feeling the same. It was obvious there was a potent mix of chemistry between them and, if they *were* still attracted to each other and all the signs *were undoubtedly* there, then how long, she wondered, would it be before they both realised they shared the same feelings and came to their senses and acknowledged them? The sooner the better she thought. Perhaps then, they would put themselves and everyone else out of their misery!

A little bit of scheming wouldn't go amiss, she thought and, with Emma and Sam as her trusty cohorts, Molly was sure between them, they would get Anna and Paul together! Mrs Molly Matchmaker was, of course, in her element!

It was Molly, out of all of them, who knew how much Anna, had grown to love Gordy and how she'd devoted herself to him and how she'd gone into her marriage with him, not with love, but gratitude to start with.

Their marriage might have been one of convenience in order to save her from being the butt of spiteful gossip, but Molly also knew the man sitting opposite Anna had fathered Emma, and had once been the love of Anna's life. If her senses were to be believed, Paul was still as keen now to make her his wife and, with them both free agents, there were no reasons, not as far as Molly could see, why they shouldn't get back together, perhaps even to marry, but then Molly knew she was just an old romantic at heart!

As she sat watching the people she loved enjoying their meal, Molly wondered whether it had been fate, destiny or providence that had brought them back together. But no matter what or who had been responsible, she knew Anna and Paul needed time to adjust. It couldn't be easy for them, not when so many years had passed, especially as Anna had lived with and loved another man.

The rest of the evening passed happily enough, with Emma and Sam in high spirits, well aware, as Anna had been, of Paul quietly watching her.

They'd all made their own plans for the weekend.

First, Emma and Sam were to meet the vicar to discuss available dates for their wedding and then later, they planned to meet up with some of their friends from university, as well as a few of Emma's old school friends from the village.

Molly's plans were laid as well. The next day she was to be one of the judges at the local village show in the afternoon and, in the evening, she was going to the theatre in Stratford-on-Avon and then afterwards, she planned on staying overnight at a friend's house and didn't intend to be back in the village until late on Sunday afternoon, just in time for their planned supper all together.

With everyone making plans that didn't include either him or Anna, Paul saw the look of disappointment on Anna's face. Taking decisive action, he told everyone he'd already made plans for the next day. Anna looked at him in surprise; this wasn't the Paul she knew and remembered. When they'd been younger, he would have deferred to her wishes as to what they would do with their free time, not that she minded him taking charge.

She looked across the table and raised her eyebrows to indicate her surprise, just as he reached across and took her hands in his.

'I have need of your advice, Anna, if you don't mind?' he said. 'I need to visit a cottage I own in Coombe Norton, to see what needs doing. The tenants have just moved out and I'm undecided as to whether I should sell it or rent it out again. If you come with me and have a look, maybe I'll make the right decision?'

Anna couldn't resist having the chance to spend the day with him; it was an ideal opportunity to get to know him again and to find out whether her feelings for him were real or if she was still living in the past. She nodded her head in agreement, at the same time, dazzling and bewitching him with the beauty of her eyes, those cat's eyes he remembered so well from when they'd been younger.

Anna smiled at him, oblivious of the others at the table, but the fates were watching and they weren't about to concede victory to Paul quite as easily as he would have liked!

Emma and Sam stayed behind at the pub after they'd eaten their meal, to talk to some friends, leaving the others to return to the cottage.

Molly, pleading tiredness, went straight to her room, leaving Anna and Paul alone in the kitchen. He leant against the old pine dresser, watching as Anna made coffee, liking what he saw. Her slender body was virtually unchanged since her younger days and, with her hair shining and tumbling down onto her shoulders, she looked about twenty-five years old, not a woman in her mid-forties. There was elegance to her posture he hadn't been aware of before. He could sense she was a woman in control of her life, one not prepared to let a man run it for her.

Even after all the years that had passed, Paul knew he wanted her as his wife. He wanted to look after her, but he also knew it would have to be on her terms as he'd sensed she was no pushover!

Suddenly, the urge to hold her close overwhelmed him and, without hesitating, and with his heart thumping in his chest, he crossed the short distance between them and held out his arms to her. Without hesitating, she moved into them, her face upturned for his kiss, her arms around his neck, pulling his face down that he might reach her lips.

Paul kissed her, his tongue pushing its way into her receptive mouth, tasting her, his heart pounding so hard it echoed in his ears, not wanting to let her go.

Anna was equally affected as Paul by that first kiss. She returned it and, tasting him, she held him in a tight embrace, their joint passion in danger of spiralling out of control as they clung together. For a while, time stood still as they were transported back over the years, each remembering the passion they'd once shared that had resulted in Anna becoming pregnant. She could feel his mounting desire as his erection pressed hard against her, his hands roaming over her body; caressing her buttocks as he pulled her closer, whispering the words of love she'd longed to hear, words she'd never thought she would hear from him again. She matched her movements to his, her passion just as strong, wanting him desperately and at that very moment!

She wanted to tear his clothes off and for him to do the same to her. She wanted to be naked with him as they made love. If only Sam and Emma hadn't chosen that very moment to walk into the house, that's exactly what would have happened.

They hastily drew apart as they heard the front door opening, but it was obvious to the young ones they'd interrupted something and, from the looks on Anna and Paul's faces, their entrance had been not only untimely, but also unwanted!

Emma and Sam looked at each other and grinned, as Paul and Anna quickly took up their positions as far away from each other as the dimensions of the small kitchen would allow. Paul sat at the table, trying to hide his embarrassment, looking far from his normal suave and composed self, his face smeared with Anna's lipstick, while she was flushed and breathless, busy at the sink, until she managed to regain her composure.

After coffee, they'd all chatted for a while, before Sam got up to leave to say his own goodnight to Emma, leaving Paul and Anna alone once more. Suddenly the atmosphere changed, reverting back to the electric one of earlier and, while Emma and Sam were out of the kitchen, kissing in the hallway, Paul managed to pull Anna down onto his lap and kiss her again, this time in a more light-hearted way, even though he had an erection that would come to nothing, he only knew he didn't want to take his hands off her!

After saying their final goodnights, Sam and Paul took their leave, returning to the pub to sleep, leaving Anna and Emma to clear up before they too went to their beds, Anna to dream of Paul and what might have happened had Emma and Sam not returned when they did, as for Emma, she dreamt, as always of Sam, and their future life together.

Anna's sleep that night was disturbed by her recurring dream of that fateful Christmas Day, when mayhem had erupted and she'd walked away from Paul. She woke, sobbing into her pillow, his name on her lips, but this was only a dream of the past. Finally, she slept and this time, her dreams were of Gordy, the gentle man who had loved her in his undemanding way and who'd made her happy when she'd been in despair, never questioning her about her love for Paul, and who'd been the perfect father to Emma.

The sun was shining when Anna woke the next morning, the weather promising to be a day full of sunshine. To her surprise, considering her marathon session of dreaming, she felt remarkably refreshed, it was as if her heart and soul had been cleansed, knowing Gordy had given her his blessing, her instinct telling her he was happy for her now Paul was back in her life.

Today was the tomorrow of yesterday, and who knew where her future lay? No matter what lay ahead, Anna intended to face whatever she had to, with faith and optimism and, thankfully, her heart was already feeling lighter than it had for some time.

At last, she could honestly say she felt happy, as she made herself ready to spend the day with the man she loved, the man she'd once thought had forgotten the love they'd had for each other.

# Chapter 21

As Anna sat in her bedroom getting ready for Paul to arrive, she thought about her dreams of the night before and how they'd seemed to be so real, especially when she'd dreamt of lying entwined in Gordy's arms in what seemed to be the finale to their life together, and how his image had finally faded away into a mist, to be replaced by Paul and an intense and passionate bout of lovemaking. It was no wonder then that later she woke with her body covered in perspiration and the bed in a complete shambles. In her fevered state, it had taken a tepid shower to cool her down and some time before she'd finally fallen into a deep and restful sleep, waking later to the most glorious morning.

She waited until Sam and Emma had left the cottage before getting ready for her outing, feeling like a teenager again. With her hands trembling with excitement she applied a light film of make-up. Her hair, she left loose and flowing and, once dressed in her smart, yet casual clothes, she could easily have been mistaken for a much younger woman, rather than the forty-six-year-old Paul knew her to be.

As for Paul, she knew he too was approaching his fiftieth birthday and was wearing his years well. She wondered, for what seemed like the hundredth time since meeting him again, what it would have been like to be married to him when they'd been younger.

Would she have her own business as now, and be the strong businesswoman she'd since become? Somehow she doubted it. Walking away from Paul had given her a different life from the one she'd originally wanted, but now, in retrospect, it seemed to have been her destiny to make a life with Gordy and her beloved child. Her only true sadness was that Paul had been denied the opportunity to be a father to Emma, by circumstances beyond their control.

Anna made her way down the stairs just as Paul arrived. His manliness very nearly overpowering her and, for a moment, she felt as though her legs would give way under her, but Paul, sensing her emotions, instinctively placed his arms around her and, thankfully, she leant against him loving the way it felt to be in his arms. She could have stayed there forever, but her senses brought her back to reality and she moved away, making her way to the kitchen, with Paul following close behind, not about to waste any time in being with her. His sleep had been equally as fitful as hers, as well as full of his sexual longing.

As soon as Anna stopped walking, he reached out and pulled her into his arms, intent on kissing her. As his face closed down on hers he searched for her lips and Anna was lost! His kisses were deep and satisfying and, if she hadn't lightly pushed him away, she was sure they would have made love there and then, on the kitchen table!

His eyes, as love-hazed as hers, raked over her face and, for a few moments she was tempted to let her emotions take over and rush him upstairs, but she knew they had to take it easy and let their relationship flourish in other ways, apart from leaping into bed. She knew if they truly loved each other, and what they felt for each other really was love, and not just lust, then lovemaking would be a natural progression, but not at that moment in time!

Anna wanted to be sure of Paul and his feelings for her before she committed herself fully to him, knowing her feelings were different now from when she had been younger. But since those earlier days, she'd matured and altered, due in the main to her experience of being abandoned, pregnant and unmarried at a time when it was socially unacceptable to be a single mother. That and, not knowing what the future held for her and her expected baby had been totally responsible for her reluctance now to rush into having sex, even though her body ached with her desire to have him inside her.

Accepting Gordy's proposal of marriage had given her respectability, for which she would be forever grateful. Then there'd been his kindness, and how much he'd cherished her and Emma.

Paul was unaware that morning of just how much he had to overcome before Anna gave herself totally to him, she might kiss him, but how long would it be before she would let him make love to her? And would he come up to the standard Gordy had set for her? He had no way of knowing.

As for Anna, she only knew her life would have been quite different if Paul had followed her. But would they have stayed married? Would he have remained faithful to her, or for that matter, would she have stayed faithful to him? How could she answer? Speculating on what might have been, especially at that moment, as she was standing in the kitchen with him looking down at her, was pointless, but for a little while she did wonder.

Anna took a good look at Paul as he stood in front of her. He was certainly as handsome as she remembered, even though he was twenty-five years older. It wasn't fair, she thought, men could age without being criticized for having a few wrinkles and silver threads in their hair. Unlike women, who had to keep themselves in tiptop condition, but was this more to please other women?

Paul certainly looked distinguished, especially with his hair flecked with silver. Anna smiled to herself as she eyed him up and down. Even though he was dressed in smart casual clothes, he still looked like a banker. There was something rather sexy about the blue denim jeans and the black leather jacket he wore with such panache it turned her on! There was no doubt in her mind she still loved him and, just as suddenly, she knew she was prepared to wait, to be sure he felt the same way before giving in to her sexual urges, but it was going to be hard.

Paul reluctantly released his hold on her, after dropping a kiss onto her head. He knew he loved her; she was all he wanted. He wanted her to love him in return, but there was a hesitancy about her that was different from how he remembered and it was this reluctance he found hard to understand, or to equate to the passion he had sensed when she'd returned his kisses. As much as he wanted her, he knew he had to go easy and trust in his instinct if he was to win this fair lady again.

Without giving Paul another chance of getting her into a clinch Anna reached for her jacket. Understanding her tactics Paul smiled, and let her lead the way out of the cottage, knowing he would have to bide his time; both of them unaware Monica and Jim were watching from the pub; or the look of surprise they'd given each other as they saw Anna leaving with the handsome man who'd stayed the night with them at the 'Ring O'Bells,' nudging each other, as they saw and noted the loving glance he gave Anna, as he put his arm about her waist!

In all the years they'd been at the pub, they'd never known Anna go out with a man on a date, but this man looked as if he might have claimed that right, as they watched them walk to his car! Silent and bemused for a few minutes, they continued to watch with interest as Paul drove out of the village, leaving them both wondering if this man was a possible contender, for the role of *the* man in Anna's future life.

Anna and Paul sat in companionable silence as he drove to Coombe Norton, where he had bought his first cottage. For reasons he couldn't explain, he'd kept the cottage, even when he'd moved to Gloucester, where he'd bought another house for himself, renting out the cottage to any young couple needing a first home. The last couple had moved on, only a week ago, and Paul wanted to see it before the agents re-let it. He knew it probably needed re-decorating and maybe some of the furniture and curtains needed replacing. It was this that had prompted him to ask Anna for her help. He thought, being a woman, she would have a flair for decorating and, after seeing the pub and the cottage, and what she'd done to both those places, he was certain she would be able to help him.

He drove slowly along the high street, giving Anna the chance to look over the market town, finally parking in a space at the side of an old cottage, which immediately captivated her.

It was charming. Not quite as old as her pub, but obviously built in the same local golden stone. It had a small front garden full of sweet scented flowers.

A climbing rose in full bloom was making its way over the porch, just skimming the small windows of the upstairs rooms.

Paul produced the biggest door key Anna had ever seen from out of his jacket pocket, using it to open the solid oak door, before ushering her inside. It was without a doubt the prettiest cottage she had ever been in. It was beautiful. An intricately carved, dark oak wooden staircase wound its way up to the bedrooms and, from her first glances she could see old beams and panelling abounded everywhere. Paul, she thought, must have been lucky in his choice of tenants from the condition of the interior. It looked as though they'd lavished as much care on the old cottage as if it had been their own. Even the old oak furniture he'd bought many years ago gleamed, and the smell of beeswax and lavender polish lingered everywhere.

Once they'd viewed the other rooms downstairs, Paul left Anna to climb the stairs and explore the rooms upstairs, as he went into the kitchen.

Once she had seen the bedrooms and bathroom, she made her way back down to the kitchen where the aroma of freshly brewed coffee enticed her into sitting at the wooden table. Even the kitchen was charming, as well as functional, with an old cream Aga sitting in an alcove, where previously there would have been a fireplace or an old range cooker. It was all very similar to the kitchen in her cottage at Little Coombe, but this kitchen made her want to cook. Anna sighed. For the second time in her life she'd fallen in love, this time with another old building!

Paul watched her face, enraptured by the expressions that had flitted over it as she'd taken in all the charms of the cottage. He was thrilled by her delight. Before he could ask what she thought needed doing, she pre-empted him, by saying how perfect it all was.

'Don't you think it needs redecorating?' he'd asked her, quizzically.

'Certainly not,' she'd replied, her eyes quickly scanning the kitchen and the back hallway that she could just see through the open door.

'It's absolutely perfect,' she said, rather wistfully. 'I just wish I could live here.'

Paul stood up. 'Well, that can always be arranged,' he said, not looking at her as he spoke.

'What do you mean?'

'Well, you could marry me and we could move in.'

'Marry you and live here?' Anna said, startled! Not so much at his proposal, but that he would want to live in the small market town again and in this cottage. He seemed to be such a man about town, one she thought who would perhaps prefer to live in a city apartment, possibly a penthouse like her own, rather than a small and cosy cottage.

Paul felt hurt at first, mainly at her dismissal of his proposal, thinking for a while he might have misread her previous reaction to him. Maybe he'd imagined the intensity of her kisses, misunderstanding her body language, as well as her feelings for him.

Anna looked across to where he was standing and, for a few seconds, she saw the fleeting pain of her rejection cross his features and suddenly, she felt full of remorse. What had she done? She'd snubbed this dear man who, for the second time in his life, had proposed marriage to her. Before she could make amends and say 'yes please, I would like to marry you' he'd turned away from her and the moment was lost.

Paul rinsed their cups in silence and, for once in her life, Anna didn't know what to do or say. He was certainly giving her the cold shoulder treatment and, for a moment or two, she was tempted to retaliate by storming out of the cottage and going to the car in her pique, but something prevented her.

She stood patiently waiting, while he finished what he was doing. And, as he was about to leave the kitchen Anna had other plans. She took his hand in hers and then, with him following, made her way out of the kitchen and up the staircase to the first bedroom, which she'd previously assumed to be the master room.

Paul was astounded at her actions, his only thought was, what a woman!

As soon as they went into the bedroom and with definitely no preamble, Anna let go of his hand, took off her jacket, tossing it onto an ottoman, before reaching out and pulling him down to join her on the bed.

For a few moments they lay together in silence, with not even their hearts to be heard thumping. Paul, leaning on his arm, looked down at her. Neither of them moved, each waiting for the other. Anna looked deep into his eyes and then, at last, taking the initiative, she reached out for him. Within seconds they were in each other's arms.

In between kissing, they managed to remove each other's clothing and only when they were both totally naked did they immerse themselves in each other, with Paul now taking the initiative, but not before he'd reached into his jacket pocket and removed a condom from the packet he'd purposely bought before the weekend, hoping he would have the chance of making love to her.

Their caresses and kisses were soon leading them to a point of no return but, this time, as Paul entered her, Anna gave her body and soul to the man she'd never stopped loving.

Without a doubt, Anna was his woman, as Paul had known all those years ago, and this time, he wasn't going to either forget her or lose her!

# Chapter 22

Anna and Paul spent the rest of the day in the market town, where they walked hand in hand to the shops in the main street, buying supplies that Anna cooked for their lunch. It was a simple meal. Paul had busied himself laying the table and uncorking the bottle of wine they'd chosen together. It was just normal everyday living that thrilled them as they basked in their renewed love. Afterwards, they'd curled up together on the comfortable old sofa and talked. It was a time for being honest with each other and, although they knew they were in love, they also knew they both had their careers and commitments to think of, before they could be together. Anna told Paul of the offers she'd received for another cookery book and, most exciting of all, her chance to go into television presenting. Paul then told her of his future plans. As a senior financial manager at the bank, his responsibilities were enormous with his work schedule already planned for several months ahead, but he made light of his work commitments. Anna could see it wasn't going to be easy for them to make a full-time commitment to each other for some time and, realising this, she purposely skirted the issue of his proposal. She knew she loved him, but she also knew she was unprepared for marriage at the moment: it was too soon. She wanted to take a chance on the new career already beckoning her. When she gave her answer, it would be because she was ready to give up everything she'd worked for; prepared finally to devote her life to him, and to him alone.

It was late in the evening when they left the cottage and returned to the village, with no decision made as to their future; it was enough for Anna to know she was in love.

Paul had wanted them to spend the night together in the old cottage, but with Emma expecting her back, Anna declined; not that she didn't want to spend the night in his arms, or that she didn't want to make love to him again, that could wait, she wanted to be with their daughter and so reluctantly, Paul locked the cottage door and drove them back to Little Coombe, content to have had at least a few hours with the woman he loved.

He was quite certain if they both worked hard, they would be able to make their lives work in tandem, all it needed, was for Anna to want to be with him more than she wanted her career. He wasn't prepared to lose her, just because of their work commitments, but he knew, as far as Anna was concerned, further talk of marriage would have to wait. He was afraid of frightening her away if he were too persistent. With this in mind, he decided he would woo her and court her and eventually, when the time was right, he would make her his, knowing this would always be on Anna's terms!

The next day they walked and talked and, before they knew it, Molly was opening the door on the Sunday evening, to a meal cooked by Anna and Paul, and then, all too soon, they were all saying their goodbyes, except for Anna, who intended staying an extra few days at the cottage to be with Molly.

Paul kissed her goodbye, holding her close, kissing her with such intensity it made her go weak at the knees with her desire for him. Anna knew if she were to just say the words, stay with me, he would have! But the time wasn't right, not yet and, with the longing for more than kisses in both their eyes, Paul walked to his car and out of her life, but this time, Anna knew they would be seeing each other soon.

It was some time before she could escape to her room, as Molly was interested in all that had happened while she'd been away, wanting to know how the weekend had gone for Emma and Sam and then of course, for Anna and Paul as well, although from the look in all their eyes, she could see it had been more than a success.

Eventually, Anna was alone and able to re-live the events of the past few days; thankfully, her dreams that night were based on reality, not just her imagination and on what had once been. For the first time in a long while, she had a personal life that excited her. As for her future? Only the fates know the answer to that question!

The week that followed was busy as usual. Paul phoned each evening and soon they were into the routine of telling each other how their day had gone and what had happened, Anna even started to discuss some of her business problems with him, knowing he would understand and, of course, they always talked of their longings for each other, deep longings fuelled by their absence, that were becoming more intense day by day, with Paul wondering for how much longer he could go on living without the woman he loved sharing his bed. Even Anna's resolve to keep her career going full blast was starting to weaken.

Two weeks passed, quicker than either could have imagined. With Paul eager to see her again, he urged her to spend the following weekend with him in London. Fortunately, Anna had a meeting arranged for the following week at the television studios to discuss the new television series programmed for early autumn.

As it was a show planned around her and her cookery books, Anna had to be there. Knowing this, Paul suggested she should stay in his apartment and not the hotel she'd originally planned. To his delight, she agreed. He could hardly contain himself when, a few days later, he saw her walking down the station platform towards him. Regardless of those looking on, he'd pulled her into his arms and kissed her soundly.

After opening the door to his apartment and thrusting her luggage inside, he lifted her into his arms and carried her over the threshold, kicking the door shut behind them, carrying her through to the large master bedroom, where he placed her carefully on top of the huge bed, which he'd obviously planned on them sharing later.

After kissing her and whispering his words of love, Anna gently reminded him they were due at the theatre and any idea he might be harbouring of them making love, would have to be placed on hold until later!

Anna liked his apartment, after he'd shown her around, even though for her taste it was too masculine. Paul had made her laugh when he'd agreed with her, telling her he'd had nothing to do with choosing any of the furniture, or furnishings, as everything had been chosen by the colleague who'd sold him the property; telling her she could have carte blanche to choose anything she liked when they went shopping the next day, anything that would improve the ambience of the place, as he wanted it to be just right for her!

Anna chuckled at his pseudo-attempt at enticing her into his web! And so, anticipating their tryst later, they left for the West End, where they were to see one of the latest hit shows.

It was a wonderful evening and after a delicious after-theatre dinner, followed by congenial conversation with some of his friends and colleagues, they returned to his apartment.

Paul had pulled her into his arms and kissed her as they went in the lift up to his penthouse apartment. He'd held her close and kissed her, his hands roaming over her wanton body, one leg pushed in between hers, caressing her, so by the time they'd reached his front door, they were both so sexually excited in their haste to make love, they could hardly wait; leaving a trail of clothes from inside the front door to the bedroom, in such a hurry to get to the huge bed that awaited them.

Anna couldn't believe how happy she felt being with Paul in his home, or her feelings as they made love. There was no doubt about it, he was definitely experienced in the art of lovemaking and, momentarily, she felt a pang of jealousy, until she realised she was equally as experienced. Consoling herself that at least hers had been with just one man!

As for Paul, he couldn't believe Anna was at last in his life and, this time, he was determined she was going to stay. He intended to persuade her to marry him, as soon as possible, it was what he wanted more than anything else and, if he had to change his working life to ensure it would happen, he would, and gladly. Looking down at her asleep in his arms, he knew she was the most important person in his life and, for a while, he regretted all that had happened over the years that had kept them apart, and nothing more than thinking he'd lost her forever.

Mentally shaking away his morbid thoughts of the past, Paul pulled her close, loving the way she snuggled into him as he kissed her sleeping head resting against his shoulder;

her hair, with its auburn waves, spread over them like a protective mantle, reminding him of how they'd slept years ago, before his mother had tried to get rid of Anna from his home.

The next morning, after a leisurely breakfast and some good-natured bantering, they decided to drive across the city to Richmond. The weather was wonderful, perfect in every way. After walking along the riverside for a while, they stopped and enjoyed a drink at one of the prettiest pubs in the town, taking their time, enjoying each other's company and then, hand in hand, as lovers do, they walked along the quaint high street, admiring the shops and the contents.

Paul tried to steer her towards a jeweller's shop he knew of, but Anna pulled him away, until they came to an antique shop they were both keen to enter and explore; it was there he managed at last to buy her a gift, to remind her of their day: an antique silver photo frame. He'd laughed as he'd presented it to her, telling her she would need it, to show off one of the many photos she'd taken of him during their walk, a memento she would have loved many years ago, especially when she thought he'd forgotten her!

They returned to his apartment early in the afternoon and, after another session of lovemaking, and a short recuperative and peaceful sleep in each other's arms, they went to a small Italian restaurant, just a stone's throw away from his apartment, for yet another memorable meal.

They spent Sunday, like millions of others, relaxing and reading the papers after they'd cooked and eaten breakfast; generally behaving like any other married couple. Later, Anna had to look over her notes for her planned meeting the following day at the television studio, leaving Paul to prepare for his working week. He had to be in Geneva later in the week, after a quick trip to Paris the next morning.

As Anna would be returning to her own apartment after her meeting, they arranged to meet in two weeks' time, when Anna came to the city to record the first show. Inwardly, they both knew it would be the longest two weeks ever, a lifetime when you are in love and before they could be together again, but Anna knew she had plenty to keep her occupied; her present business interests were important to her and, with her new career taking off, she felt like a juggler, trying to keep all the balls in the air at once.

At least she knew lack of money wouldn't be an obstacle in her and Paul's life together, because they'd already discussed their finances honestly with each other, and knew each of them was wealthy enough for them not to have to work.

Paul's wealth, initially from the inheritance he'd received from his parents', had increased ten-fold, merely by his judicious investing.

As for Anna, her initial wealth had been her inheritance from Gordy, which she too had increased, even further, and all by her own efforts.

Knowing they were both solvent was, as far as Paul was concerned, a big plus, it would enable them to walk away from their present commitments and make a life together; all it needed, was for Anna to say she would marry him, and when. But Anna wasn't ready yet. And neither was she prepared to walk away from her commitments, or to say the words Paul wanted so desperately to hear. She needed to be quite sure he really was serious about their relationship, before she gave him the answer he so badly wanted, afraid something would happen to mar her happiness, as had happened before.

As for Paul, he knew he had to tread carefully where Anna and her career was concerned. He knew she'd worked hard to get where she was and it was going to be difficult for her to give up all she'd worked for, but he wanted to marry her. He loved her.

At least he had the sense to realise he would have to be patient and wait until Anna was ready. But hadn't he already waited for her long enough?

# Chapter 23

The next morning, they left Paul's apartment together. Paul to go to Paris and, from there, the morning after, to Geneva, for a meeting of international bankers. As for Anna, she was going to the television studios for a pre-production meeting and a rehearsal for the new programme.

They shared the taxi taking Paul to the airport, kissing each other goodbye, after making promises to talk later that evening, before going their separate ways.

For Anna, a new and exciting part of her life was about to start and suddenly, she felt a thrill of anticipation well up inside her as she reported to the reception desk. Within minutes, she'd been taken under the wing of a highly efficient researcher and was soon deeply involved in the process of making a television programme.

Working in television was going to be a new and exciting world for her, far different from her normal working life, so it was no surprise to Anna to find, at the end of the day, she was mentally and physically exhausted. She'd planned on returning to her own apartment in the Midlands that evening, instead, at the suggestion of the producer, who'd invited her to a meal that evening, she changed her mind and booked herself into a small and luxurious hotel near the studio. Spending the evening with the production crew she knew would be an ideal opportunity to get to know the people she would be working with and, once refreshed, and after a change of clothes, her tiredness was soon forgotten, leaving her to enjoy the evening, which turned out to be fun. Talking and laughing with her young colleagues, she couldn't wait until later, when she would talk to Paul and tell him of her day. To her dismay, her mobile phone remained silent. Paul's number unavailable when she tried to contact him later as she got ready for bed. She then began to worry, wondering what could possibly have happened to prevent him from contacting her as he'd promised.

As she was staying overnight in the city, the producer persuaded her to go to the studio again the next morning, to meet more of the staff involved with the show, which at the time seemed to be a good idea, until later that morning when, deep in a discussion with one of the studio technicians, she just happened to look up and there, on the opposite side of the studio stood Paul.

He was standing next to the young woman Anna vaguely recognised as one of the young researchers she'd met on her first visit.

She excused herself, and made to cross the studio, sure in her own mind Paul had come to see her, when suddenly, another producer from the show stopped her in her tracks, to ask a question. As soon as she could, she turned to go to Paul; to her surprise, he was just in the act of putting his arms around the girl. The next minute, he was holding her in a loving clinch and then, much to Anna's further surprise, she saw him kiss the young woman in such a familiar way she couldn't believe what was happening. Why, she asked herself, was he in the studio, when he was supposed to be on his way to Geneva? And what was his relationship with the young woman?

Anna's mind churned over as she tried to think logically. From how he was behaving he couldn't possibly have been looking for her, surely!

He wouldn't even have expected to find her at the studio, as she was supposed to be back in her office in the Midlands and, so far, even Lesley her assistant didn't know where she was. He couldn't have gone to Paris either, so where had he been? And then suddenly, Anna had a seminal thought, as to who the girl might be. She was about the same age as Emma, in other words, young enough to be his daughter! Was that possible? Could she be the result of one of the many dalliances he hadn't admitted to, or was she just another female, the latest no doubt in a long line of attractive companions he might still be involved with?

Before she could escape and get across the studio floor to reach him, Anna saw him leaving, with the girl holding onto his arm. By the time she'd reached where they'd been standing, there was no sign of either of them, they'd vanished into the warren of sets and corridors that made up the studio, and then suddenly, Anna remembered the girl's name, it was Zoe! But when she asked some of the others in the studio if they knew where she might have gone, they just shook their heads, unable to tell her, leaving her with no option other than to wait and see if Paul contacted her that evening, when perhaps, he would then be able to explain his strange behaviour.

Before leaving to catch her train home, Anna tried several times to contact Paul, to her consternation there was still no reply, either from his mobile, or home phones. The only thing she could do was to leave messages, even calling his office at the bank to ask where he was, which is where they told her he was on his way to Geneva and couldn't be contacted, leaving her even more exasperated knowing this wasn't the truth.

Anna was becoming more and more angry, as well as frustrated, until she realised neither emotion was going to do her any good, she would just have to have patience and be open-minded as to what Paul was up to, which at that moment was against her inclination. So much, she thought, for his words of love, or his promise to call her.

There was no news the next day, or the following. By the third, Anna was beside herself with worry, finding it impossible to concentrate on her work, even to her wishing she'd stayed in London. At least she had a key to his apartment and, if she didn't hear from him soon, she decided she would go back and stay there, a thought she quickly dismissed; realising he was a free agent and could come and go as he pleased, she might be in love with him, but she certainly wasn't his minder and neither did he have to keep her informed as to his whereabouts! As a last resort, she checked again with the studio, to see if Zoe was there, but even she seemed to have vanished, fuelling Anna's thoughts she was with Paul and they were probably up to no good!

During their talks, once they had become intimate, Paul had made no mention of his previous lovers and Anna hadn't pried, fully aware, from his expertise in bed, that in his past he'd probably had many women; a fact she would have to ignore if they were to be happy!

Being jealous of his past would not be the recipe for them having a happy relationship; it was also quite likely he felt the same about her love life with Gordy. But from how he'd spoken, while they'd been wrapped in each other's arms, he'd given her no indication this was the case.

It seemed to Anna, from her limited experience of falling in love, that men and women viewed previous relationships in an entirely different manner; was this fundamentally the difference between the sexes? Or was it merely the way human nature worked? The male of the species could have as many sexual partners as they wished; sowing their seeds in every direction, ensuring their genes populated the world profusely, while females were expected to keep themselves for the one male they thought would provide the strongest genes for their eggs.

Because Paul had made no mention of his past conquests, such as Angela, Anna was completely unaware of their existence. Therefore, she knew nothing of his special relationship with Angela's daughter Zoe, or that she'd always kept in touch with him, after her mother and Paul had split up. There'd been no talk either that Angela had finally married another man, with whom she was now living in a state of blissful happiness!

Zoe had been upset at first when Paul and her mother had gone their separate ways as she'd always viewed him as a potential stepfather adoring him as she had.

To his credit, knowing and understanding Zoe's feelings, he hadn't abandoned her when Angela had issued her ultimatum. He'd kept in touch; being supportive and encouraging, especially as she grew up and went to college and then to university, where she gained a degree in media studies. It was partly through his connections she was now doing an internship at the television studios where Anna's new programme was being filmed, and where she hoped, eventually in the future, to become a presenter herself.

Anna decided to ring Paul's office yet again, expecting this time to be fobbed off once more with the stock answer that he was away on business and couldn't be contacted! But this time, to her surprise, she was put through to his personal secretary where she learnt he'd cancelled his trip to the

Geneva meeting. Anna was stunned by this news, knowing it was the most important meeting he'd ever been invited to.

His secretary told her Paul suddenly had urgent family and personal business to attend to, all of which Anna thought to be very strange, considering he had no family left alive to worry about.

There was nothing more his secretary could tell her, leaving Anna to believe he would appear sometime soon. But why, she asked herself, hadn't he contacted her? Why hadn't he left a message with the studio, or even with his secretary for her to call and explain? It was a complete mystery.

Taking stock of the situation and briefly allowing jealous feelings to cloud her normally sound judgement, Anna decided he must have had second thoughts on wanting to marry her. Perhaps disappearing was his way of avoiding having to tell her he no longer wanted her, as his wife, maybe asking her to marry him had merely been a ruse to get her into his bed.

Suddenly, she felt overwhelmed. Instead of fighting her impulse to cry, she just let her tears fall, silent rivulets that ran unheeded down her cheeks, grief-stricken at the thought that, as suddenly as he'd come back into her life, so it seemed he was out of it, their relationship over, before it had hardly begun.

Nearly three weeks passed, and again she was staying in her apartment at the weekend, pleading too much work to catch up on as her explanation to Molly for her absence from the cottage.

While in her apartment she'd been trying to catch up with some of her outstanding paperwork. For some reason she felt uneasy, her mind refusing to concentrate on the papers spread out before her on the coffee table.

Wearily, she ran her hands through her un-brushed hair, and then placing the papers in some sort of order, she walked restlessly over to the picture window to look out at her favourite view of the city skyline. It was this view of the city that had lured her into buying a home there and the fact it was only a five-minute stroll to the city centre. As she looked out now at the familiar scene, in some peculiar way, it soothed and comforted her. It was the familiarity of the scene she particularly loved. It not only gave her a view across the roof tops and spires of the city, but she could look down into the park where she'd sat with Paul as they ate their lunches many years ago and where they'd first fallen in love.

Buying the apartment hadn't been a luxury for Anna she'd bought it out of sheer necessity. The amount of travelling she was doing, as she went between the cottage in the Cotswold village, and the factory in the city, was eating into her life to such an extent Molly was unable to bear seeing her so tired at the end of the day.

It had been her that had suggested it might be a good idea if Anna had a base nearer to her office. Of course Anna saw the logic behind Molly's concern and agreed and, once the apartment building was finished, she moved in straight away.

Other young professionals had also bought the other apartments and at last, Anna found herself with a proper social life that until then had previously eluded her.

Her apartment had everything a young and upwardly mobile professional person needed. It had two large bedrooms, both with a luxurious ensuite bathroom, a large lounge with two enormous picture windows that looked out to the far side of the city, to where, in the distance, she could see where she'd once lived; a large, modern and well-equipped kitchen, with an equally large dining room and a small study. In the basement, as well as secure underground parking, there was a communal swimming pool Anna used most mornings before she went to work, and a gymnasium she never used at all!

The main entrance to the building was secure, with entry phones to each apartment and Anna loved it, even though her modern new apartment was in sharp contrast to the old-fashioned cottage she shared with Molly in Little Coombe. She also loved the peace it gave her, and the tranquillity of being up high and away from the hustle and the bustle of the city centre.

Since moving into the apartment, she'd made good progress with her writing and her latest cookery book and, like her television show, it looked as if it would be just as successful as the others.

She couldn't help but think of her visit to London and Paul's mysterious disappearance; it was constantly on her mind. She was still mystified as to where he could be and it seemed quite strange to her his office didn't seem to be at all concerned at his absence, his secretary always giving the same answer as before when she called to ask if he'd returned to work. Perhaps, she thought, disappearing for days and weeks on end was not an unusual occurrence for Paul Adams.

Anna looked out of the window at the city, quiet and still that Sunday morning, deep in thought, until the entry phone in the hallway suddenly rang and broke her reverie. She wasn't expecting anyone and was still dressed in her silk housecoat, even though it was after ten o'clock.

She walked across the room to answer, wondering if it could be Emma, coming on an unscheduled visit, as Molly, she knew, was away for the weekend.

'Hello' she said softly into the mouthpiece. Suddenly, her mouth went dry and her heart began to beat hard in her chest as she heard Paul's voice on the other end.

'It's me, Paul,' he said, as if she wouldn't recognise his voice. 'Can I come up?'

Anna hesitated, but for only a second, before activating the control to the door of her apartment.

By the time he'd raced up the stairs, in too much of a hurry to wait for the lift, she'd managed to rake her fingers through her hair, partly to try and tame the unruly waves and managing, only slightly, to control her breathing.

She opened the door; fully expecting the lift door opposite to open any second and reveal him, but suddenly, to her surprise he appeared at the top of the stairs, out of breath from his run. To her dismay, he looked ghastly.

He was unshaven, and from his dishevelled appearance, he couldn't have slept in days, or changed his clothing from the state they were in, recognising his clothes as those he'd been wearing when they'd left his apartment nearly three weeks ago.

He looked exhausted. His eyes were red-rimmed with fatigue but, without hesitating, Anna held her arms open and drew him into the apartment.

Paul clung to her as she helped him to walk into the lounge, fearing he would collapse at any moment in a heap on the floor.

Tenderly she led him across the room to the sumptuous leather sofa where he sat down, his head immediately falling against the plump cushions, where he closed his eyes and, unbelievably, within a few minutes he was fast asleep and gently snoring before she could begin to question him.

Afraid of waking him, Anna carefully removed his shoes and undid his clothing; lifting his feet onto the sofa, making him more comfortable, covering him with her precious cashmere throw and there he slept, solidly, for the next hour.

While he was sleeping, she showered and dressed, roughly drying her hair and tying it back from her face, making her look much younger than her years. Her line-free skin was translucent, except for the dark smudges underneath her eyes, the only evidence and indication of her lack of sleep and the worry she'd suffered since he'd disappeared, but now, with Paul asleep in her lounge, there was a renewed sparkle in them, along with a joyous feeling once more in her heart, her jealous feelings wiped away, merely by his safe return.

While Paul had been sleeping, she'd been speculating, as to what had happened in his life for him to arrive at her apartment looking as awful as he did. Not that it mattered, because he was with her! He was back in her life, where he should be and, for the time being, that was all that mattered!

The smell of food finally pervaded Paul's senses, waking him, leaving him slightly dazed as he tried to recall where he was.

Anna heard him moving and walked into the room, just as he was sitting up. He rubbed his eyes and smiled ruefully at her, smoothing his hands over his unshaven face. She went to sit in the chair opposite, but he caught hold of her hand and pulled her down to sit beside him. 'Darling Anna,' he said, 'thank goodness I'm with you. I began to think I would never see you again.' Drawing her close to his chest, one hand reaching up to touch her face, looking deeply into her eyes as he did so, before pulling her face down that he might kiss her.

His kiss was demanding, yet with a gentleness that surprised her. She felt the roughness of his beard against her skin. 'Dearest Anna,' he said, as they broke for air. 'I'm sorry

I couldn't get in touch with you, but it was a matter of life and death and imperative I didn't implicate you in any way. I promise I will tell you the whole story, when I've cleaned up and rested.' Anna kissed him back.

'Come and have a shower. There's a ladies razor in the cupboard; if you let me have your clothes I'll wash and dry them while we eat. There's a bathrobe in the cupboard you can use.'

Paul stood up.

'I'm sure you can manage without me.' She laughed, as he moved to walk into the bathroom, intent on taking her with him!

By the time he'd showered and shaved, his clothes had been washed and were now drying. Wearing the man's bathrobe he'd found in the cupboard, he had of course speculated as to whom it belonged, as it was far too big for Anna to wear, his train of thought was suddenly diverted by the smell of bacon cooking, and then the aroma of fresh baked rolls and coffee wafting towards him, acting like a magnet, drawing him into the kitchen, where Anna, looking even more beautiful than he remembered, was waiting.

Paul still looked exhausted, but at least he looked and smelt less disreputable after his shower and shave, more like the man she knew. After kissing her, he sat down at the table Anna had laid with a cheerful red gingham cloth.

There was a crystal jug, holding fresh squeezed orange juice that Paul poured and sipped, as he watched her stirring smoked salmon into the scrambled eggs she knew to be his favourite dish from their weekend together in London.

As well as the eggs, there was a dish of crispy bacon and a basket of freshly baked rolls and warm croissants, along with a jar of jam he recognised as coming from Molly's larder at the cottage.

Anna was bursting to know what had happened but with great restraint, she let Paul eat his fill first. By the time he was onto his second mug of steaming black coffee, she was unable to wait any longer for his explanation.

'What happened?' she asked him quietly, as he sipped his aromatic drink, obviously trying to gather his thoughts.

'It's a long story,' he said. 'Come and sit with me and I'll tell you what happened.'

With Anna curled up on the sofa beside him, so Paul began his extraordinary story.

First of all, he started by telling her about his relationship with Angela and her daughter Zoe. At this, Anna had gasped. He looked at her, making no comment on her surprise as he continued. He told her how he had met Angela many years ago, and how he'd used her, merely to satisfy his own sexual longings and how ashamed he'd been at his actions, explaining he'd been unable to give her his love because of his love for the woman he'd lost due to his accident and his parents' interference. At this point, he'd pulled Anna into his arms, kissing her gently, before continuing his tale, one hand cupping her breast as though for comfort, without any thought Anna's whole body was screaming out for him to take her and make love to her. He then told her how he loved Zoe, as a daughter, and would have been proud to have been her stepfather, but not at the cost of living a lie with Angela. Then he told her how Zoe had always confided in him and how she'd looked to him for advice as she grew up. At these comments he'd looked directly at Anna. He wanted her to know he would always be a father figure to Zoe, just as he knew Emma would always think of Gordy as her father, even though he was now back in her life. There was, of course, nothing Anna could do but to agree.

She said nothing, as he then told her of his affair with Zoe's mother and how distraught Angela had been when she knew the reasons why Paul would never marry her!

In fact, Angela had believed he would never marry anyone if he couldn't have his beloved Anna, the girl he'd lost and, knowing there would never be anyone else in his life, and that she stood no chance with him, she'd walked away from what to Paul had always been a lukewarm relationship.

Believing she would never find the right man for herself, Angela had thrown herself into bringing Zoe up on her own, as well as putting her energy into furthering her own career, knowing she would have to spend the rest of her life making her own money!

Angela was correct in one of her assumptions, it did take a long time before she found her 'Mister Right', but that's Angela's story and, for the time being it doesn't concern us.

Paul continued, concentrating on telling Anna the reasons why he hadn't been in contact with her and why he'd come back to her in the state he had.

Strangely enough, it was because of Angela and her husband Max, and an unscheduled trip to Spain!

# Chapter 24

Angela had been alone, except for rearing Zoe, for several years, man-free after her affair with Paul had ended, giving the opposite sex a wide berth until, quite by chance, while visiting old friends in London, she'd been invited to a dinner party with them. The hostess, knowing Angela would be arriving without a partner, had invited Max, a guest of other friends of the hostess, not particularly to meet Angela, but to make the numbers even at the table! Therefore, as a matter of convenience to the hostess, they were seated together.

It had been many years since Angela had felt such a *frisson* of excitement tingle through her body the first time she met someone new, but that was how she felt when she was first introduced to the man intended only as her dinner companion.

Her first impression of Max was that he was in full control of his life and didn't need a woman. But Angela, being a savvy woman, and always up for a challenge, found this man to be intriguing! She'd felt an exhilarating energy force flow through her, the self-same feeling she'd last felt when Paul had walked into her life. But this man, sitting next to her, exuded a different kind of power and strength.

His testosterone level was much more subtle, unlike Paul's, that Angela had always thought was responsible for his tomcat qualities! Her opinion was further enhanced by his inability to commit himself to settling down with just one woman.

Max obviously felt comfortable with her, unaware of her initial feeling he was a challenge. They fell into conversation straight away and it was an instant attraction. Both liking what they saw in the other, instinctively knowing, within days, they had each found the soul mate previously missing from their lives. To their complete and utter surprise and delight and, within days of their first meeting, they fell in love.

Max wooed Angela without telling her anything very much about himself, except he'd been widowed, many years ago, and had no children, or even close family. At the same time, failing to mention he was a millionaire, several times over!

It wasn't until the day of the wedding, at the local registry office in Angela's hometown, where Max had placed a diamond-encrusted wedding band on her finger, one that perfectly matched the engagement ring she'd originally thought to be rather gaudy, unaware at the time of its true value. It was then she began to think he wasn't quite as poor as she'd first thought! Max had just smiled at her, in a way that had left her wondering what sort of man she'd just committed herself and Zoe to?

At first, Angela thought the house Max lived in was rented, as he seemed to hold no affection for the pretty house tucked away in one of the smartest mews in central London. It wasn't until much later she found out he owned many such properties in and around London, as well as many others all over the world! But Angela didn't care what Max owned, or even how much he was worth, she loved him, mainly for all the qualities she'd first seen in him, exactly those she wanted in a man. First of all though it was because he loved her and Zoe, unconditionally.

He was kind and gentle and, most of all, loving and tactile. He demanded nothing from the two new ladies in his life except they loved him in return and that was exactly what they did, in fact they both adored him.

Zoe had been a young teenager at the time of her mother's marriage to Max and, with his help and love, she grew up to be a well-adjusted and loving daughter, exactly as any man could wish for. Zoe absolutely adored him and, even though she had a good relationship with her own father, Max and Paul were the two most influential men in her life.

Max was stocky in build, with dark soulful eyes that looked out at the world with an innocence that made Angela smile, for an innocent Max was definitely not!

He told Angela his ancestors had been Spanish. With his sallow skin and dark hair and eye colouring, that wasn't hard to believe, it also backed up his claim there was property in Spain that rightly belonged to him; property that had been fraudulently taken from his family many years ago. It was this claim that was responsible for him making frequent trips abroad, whenever his other business interests allowed as he tried to pursue his claims through the Spanish courts to get them back. It was on one of these trips that a chain of events had started that took Paul back into Angela's life, in a big way.

Max's considerable wealth had enabled Angela to buy and furnish a small manor house in Devon where, to his delight, Max suddenly found himself to be the local squire, and it was there the three of them lived an idyllic family life, deep in the Devonshire countryside.

As for Angela, even though her life with Max was blissful, she'd kept in touch with Paul, mostly through Zoe, but in time, and over the years, his letters became less frequent and those she did receive never mentioned a wife or children, leaving her to wonder if Paul would ever find the elusive lady he needed to make his life complete.

Meanwhile, Zoe had grown up to be a beautiful young woman.

After graduating from university, she'd applied to work with a television company. With Paul pulling strings in the background, she'd been lucky enough to get a position as a research assistant. It meant she had to start at the bottom of the ladder but with her qualifications and motivation, she knew she would soon be climbing her own personal ladder to success, eventually hoping to become a television presenter. She always watched, with great interest, all the other presenters that appeared on the shows she worked on, hoping to glean ideas from their work, as well as some tips that would enable her to further her own career, and that was how she came to meet Anna.

At the time, Zoe was unaware Anna was the missing lady in Paul's life, or that inadvertently, she would soon be playing a large part in his return to the woman he loved.

Max was abroad, on yet another of his Spanish trips, leaving Angela alone at home in Devon on the day a letter was delivered to the manor house, demanding a huge ransom, if his life was to be spared and his safe return to England guaranteed.

Angela couldn't believe her eyes as she read and re-read the letter. First of all she thought someone was playing a practical joke on her, a mischievous prank, perhaps from one of Max's many business friends.

Secondly, Angela knew Max had gone to Spain, on what he had assured her was to be a quick business trip.

As she was closely involved in all aspects of village life and, because of the activities planned in the village to celebrate the church's feast day, Angela hadn't travelled with him as she usually did.

As lady of the manor, and with Max only intending to be away for a couple of days, she'd stayed at home and, even though she'd heard nothing from him since he'd left, she was not concerned, as this in itself was not unusual. She thought he would be returning home the next day, but now it seemed serious and suddenly, she knew the letter was for real. Feeling very afraid and alone, she didn't know at first what to do, but once she'd realised the letter was genuine, her first thought had been to pay the amount the ransom letter had demanded, straightaway, anything to get Max home safely.

The letter demanded, not only a million pounds but also that Angela had no contact with the police, either in England or Spain, or Max would immediately be killed.

Once this part of the letter had penetrated Angela's mind, not unnaturally, she went into a panic. What could she do to get her beloved husband back home safe and sound? She tried to calm down, knowing she had to focus, telling herself panicking wouldn't solve anything.

Angela's first instinct had been to ignore the letter, believing it to be a hoax, but once she realised it was for real, the thought of a gang of murderers watching the manor, for she presumed there must be a gang, with someone perhaps tapping her phone line and monitoring her calls had urged her to rethink her strategy, believing all would be lost if the kidnappers knew she'd gone against their wishes. She then thought of Zoe. She had to tell her daughter what had happened and then perhaps, between them, they would be able to fathom out the best way to get Max home.

Taking a chance on her phone not being tapped, Angela quickly made several phone calls before she found Zoe who, after her initial reaction that her mother should contact the police and pay the ransom demanded agreed the two of them must try to be logical as they planned what they should do next.

They talked for some time, before Zoe suggested they should contact Paul. At first, Angela was against this idea until Zoe convinced her he would be the ideal person to help them. He travelled extensively in Europe, especially Spain and knew the Basque region, which was where Angela suspected Max would probably have been taken, as this was the area he visited most often in his quest to legalise his claim on the properties belonging to his family.

It was also where Max was well known as a millionaire and therefore, worth snatching. To Angela, his kidnapping, and the ransom being demanded, was sure to be used to swell the coffers of the terrorists in the region, who obviously would use the money to further even more mischief.

Angela left Zoe in charge of contacting Paul and asking for his help. At first this proved to be a problem, as he'd recently moved into a new apartment and, with the pressure of his work commitments, had yet to inform his friends of his new address and phone numbers.

By this time, Zoe was also beside herself with worry, trying to comfort her mother in between times, trying to track Paul down until finally, she struck lucky, managing to find out his whereabouts by devious means from his employer, by pretending to be the personal assistant of someone high up in the banking world!

Luck was still on her side when she found he was due to fly out the same morning to Paris. Hurrying out of the television studio, she was just in time to see him drive away in a taxi, the same one a gorgeous-looking woman, Anna, loaded down with luggage had obviously just got out of, and was now standing at the kerb waiting for someone to help her into the studio.

Zoe didn't stop to help, she was too busy flagging down the next taxi that came into view and, within minutes she was chasing after Paul.

She called out his name, just as he reached the check-in desk. He stopped and turned. And, as soon as he saw who it was, he'd stepped aside from the desk, ready to listen with horror at Zoe's story. It took only a little time, after hearing what had happened to Max, for him to be persuaded to help and, within minutes he'd phoned his office to cancel his meetings in Geneva, arranging to contact her the next day at the studio, knowing in Paris he would be able to make contact with an organisation that worked in the Basque region and where he knew he would be able to throw some light on what might have happened to Max, possibly even to where they were holding him. Also, it would give Angela and Zoe time to arrange a transfer of funds to Spain, for Paul to use for the ransom, not that he intended using it, if he could avoid doing so, as funding terrorists wasn't on his agenda!

Paul didn't arrive back from Paris until later that same evening and, after speaking to Zoe and Angela, he decided it was too late to call Anna. This, he realised had been his biggest mistake, when, a few days later, he thought he might never see her again! As it was, he didn't see or hear from her for nearly three weeks, the longest and most painful weeks he'd ever endured.

Paul knew the Basque area in Spain quite well, although it had been a few years since he'd last been there, and then only as a place to visit on holiday. He knew it was wild and rugged in places, an area, he was assured by his contact in

Paris, to be the most likely place Max's captors would have taken him.

It was also an area Paul wasn't about to rush into, not without some official back up. As he'd never carried a firearm before, or even used one, he knew he had to involve the law, knowing the people he would be dealing with were sure to be armed and dangerous. The thought of what might happen to himself and Max gave him some anxious moments, until he thought of Max, who by now must be worried sick as to whether he would ever see his wife again.

Paul's banking contacts in Paris had given him some information on those most likely to be of help and, the next day, nervous of what was expected of him by Zoe and Angela, he flew out to Spain. Thankfully, his plane was met by an interested contact, who turned out to know Max's possible whereabouts; even to where they might find some of the group that had kidnapped him, believing them to be hiding out in the hills.

He also stressed to Paul it would be difficult to reach them, as most of the journey would have to be done on foot. He'd further added the heat at that time of the year was unbearable, especially for someone used to an English climate, stressing to Paul how hard the going would be and perhaps he should leave Max's rescue to those more experienced in such things. It was the thought of Max being alone, and afraid of what might happen to him, that had spurred Paul on, leaving him wondering if anyone would have done the same for him had he been the captive.

By this time, it had been nearly two weeks since he'd arrived in Spain and had managed, at last, to convince his contact, and then the local police, he was indeed serious in his intention of going into the hills to look for Max, and then for them to agree to let him have several of their officers to help him.

When nothing happened, for what seemed like weeks, after he'd got the go-ahead, he began to wonder whether they would help, or were they about to dismiss him as a crazy Englishman, ignoring his pleas for help in rescuing his ex-girlfriend's husband!

It was only after several more phone calls to and from Zoe, the Spanish police in the area agreed they would get involved, and only then, when they finally understood Max was more than just a foolish tourist who'd unfortunately strayed into an area where he shouldn't.

They finally galvanised themselves into action, which came as a great relief to Paul, even so, the hours passed so slowly he began to wonder if anything concrete would ever happen.

With the police's knowledge of the local hoodlums, that lived and worked in the area, a plan of action was conceived. First of all, they insisted Paul had instruction on how to fire a revolver and how to shoot straight at a target!

Paul didn't think he would be shooting at anyone, not if he could help it, but to keep the police sweet and in a mood to help, he went along with their plans, knowing if the gang had any inkling the police were involved, Max's life could be in serious jeopardy and so would his own. He knew he was taking a great personal risk, but he had to do it, there was no other option, he owed it to Angela.

It was a dangerous and very unfunny time and Paul was definitely frightened; as to how Max was feeling, Paul could only hazard a guess.

By now, he'd been away from work for nearly three weeks, a good proportion of it spent despairing of ever finding Max, until at last, it all suddenly seemed to come together as some specialist terrorist police officers joined him at the small police station, where he'd been sleeping in a spare office.

Paul felt dirty and unkempt, a bathroom not being high on the priority list of the local police, who had their own homes to return to each night. But they'd fed him well enough. Everything about the police station was very basic, not designed for the likes of an Englishman who, rather bizarrely, was trying to save the husband of his former lover!

It was only much later Paul found out this particular gang were being sought by most of the police forces across Spain, as well as the rest of Europe. And it was only when the British government, via Zoe, had intervened, Paul stood any chance of getting help in freeing Max.

His general discomfort, and the strain he was under, made him think being a secret undercover agent would not be a career change he would consider in the future; it was one lifestyle that certainly didn't appeal to him at all. He liked his home comforts too much.

The select band of police officers that had arrived, were those who specialised in undercover terrorist work in the region. After quickly briefing Paul, and giving him the necessary instruction on how to use the hand gun, which they'd provided, and which Paul was quite terrified of having to use against Max's captors, he was ready; well, as ready as he ever would be.

The next morning, at the break of dawn, and after another sleepless night for Paul, they set off on foot.

By noon, the hottest part of the day, when everywhere in the countryside hummed with the sound of insects, and siestas beckoned, the police along with Paul, tried to find some cool shade among the scrubland at the bottom of a hill in which to hunker down and rest.

Paul reasoned it was going to take hours to climb up to where the caves were, for this was the area the police had assured him they would surely find Max.

By nightfall, they were nearly at their destination. After a hurried meeting, where everyone spoke in hushed tones it was decided, by the officer in charge, to be too dangerous to storm the caves that night. They would spend yet another night out in the open and wait until daylight before proceeding and, so it was Paul spent yet another sleepless night, this one under the Spanish stars, cold, hungry and very apprehensive, as to what the next morning would bring.

Early, just as dawn was breaking, Paul came to, to the sound of hushed voices. His companion nudged him to follow and, with his stomach in knots, he quietly edged forward over the rough ground. After a while, the leading officer motioned for him and the others to remain still and silent as he edged forward alone to see what was happening. Paul and his companions waited, until suddenly, the leading officer motioned them forward, gesturing with his hands for them to crawl on their bellies. On his signal, they silently inched forward to where Paul could see the lights of cigarettes from several men sitting outside one of the caves. As they got nearer, he peered through the gloom, but he couldn't see Max amongst the men, assuming, quite rightly, he'd been left in the cave.

In some ways, Paul thought Max had probably been the one most comfortable that night, as he'd been out of the cold of the night air that would soon turn into the heat of an inferno, as the sun rose and the day progressed.

Sure enough, as Paul and the officers slithered on their bellies nearer to the terrorists, the mist lifted, leaving them knowing it wouldn't be long before the sun started to beat down relentlessly on them.

Paul didn't fancy Max's chances of making an escape, not unless they could cause a diversion and get into the cave, where he presumed Max would be tied up, but he hadn't reckoned on the bravado of his comrades, or the talent of their stalwart leading officer. They too were all lying face down in the scrub, with the sun starting to beat down on them, the beginnings of a heat haze shimmering overhead, waiting for their leader's signal, when suddenly, seeing an opportunity to attack, the officers had leapt to their feet and raced across the intervening land, to where most of the gang were sitting, calmly smoking in front of the entrance to the cave.

Paul raced after them, his borrowed revolver at the ready, coming to a halt and aiming at one of the sitting men, for the gang had committed the unpardonable sin of not keeping a proper watch, feeling they were safe. Their sloppy behaviour was the price they were to pay for their capture.

Suddenly, it all began to happen in slow motion as far as Paul was concerned it was like a scene out of a spaghetti western being played out, except this wasn't acting, this was the real stuff.

The leading police officer and his men had the gang rounded up and handcuffed within minutes, all thankfully without a shot being fired.

Paul followed one of the officer's into the cave where they found Max, his hands and feet bound and tied; a piece of old and dirty linen stuffed into his mouth. He looked afraid as Paul approached, for Paul, in his unkempt state looked like one of the desperados. For a full minute or more, Max didn't recognise who he was, thinking Paul was one of the gang still intent on carrying out their threat to kill him. For a few minutes his blood ran cold. It was only when Paul called out to him by name that Max suddenly recognised his voice and visibly relaxed, knowing his nightmare was nearly over.

It took several hours for the police and their captives, with Paul helping Max, to walk back down the rugged terrain and reach the village from where the rescue had started. The only thing Max and Paul wanted, was to get out of the area and return home, as quickly as possible.

Thankfully, Max's millions spoke loudly and, within a few hours they were on a private jet heading for London.

Once in the city, their two hired cars drove in opposite directions, as fast as the limits allowed, one taking Max straight to Devon, where he was sure of his welcome. As for Paul, he was apprehensive. He'd been driven to the Midlands, knowing he had a lot of explaining to do, but wanting to do that face-to-face with Anna. His only problem, would she believe him?

As Paul finished relating the events that had happened in Spain, Anna could see from his face her fears were totally unfounded. She knew he'd acted out of concern for his friends and suddenly, she felt overwhelmingly proud of the caring and gentle man she held in her arms. As she looked at him, she resolved never again to allow jealousy to play any part in her relationship with him. She knew it had been his mother's jealousy that had deprived her of having him as her husband and his chance of being a father to Emma, but that was all about to change!

Paul held onto her, afraid at first he would never have her as his wife and know the happiness Angela and Max shared. As he kissed her, he knew he needed an answer to his question and so, for the third time in his life, he asked her the most important question any man can ask of the woman he loves.

'Will you marry me? Will you be my beloved wife? It seems as though I've waited a lifetime for you and I need to know your answer?'

Anna couldn't wait to accept; finally knowing she and Paul would become husband and wife and they would be together for always, and no one would ever come between them again. Raising her face to his, they kissed, a long and lingering kiss, knowing neither of them would ever again forget their love, the most precious gift they could give each other.

One month later, on a glorious summer day in the village of Little Coombe, Paul and Sam stood side by side in front of the steps leading to the altar. The old church was full of the heady aroma of freshly cut flowers, grown by Molly and her friends. As they waited, Paul looked around. He could see every pew was filled with old friends, including Molly, Angela, Max and Zoe, and everyone from the village, as well as his and Anna's colleagues, all waiting for the bride to arrive.

Just as the church clock struck twelve, so Jim, at last the proud owner of the 'Ring O' Bells,' walked Anna into the church, where Emma in her role of maid of honour waited. She was soon to be a bride herself but this day was her mother's.

Dressed in a pale lilac chiffon gown that floated around her young figure she walked demurely down the aisle behind Anna. Sam, in his role as Paul's best man, couldn't take his eyes off her.

As for Paul, his eyes were locked on Anna, as she made her way towards him, holding onto Jim's arm. She looked beautiful, especially wearing the cream silk dress she'd chosen with such care: it showed off her slim body to perfection and, with her rich auburn hair flowing free, framing her delicate features, and her emerald eyes, shining and so full of love, she took Paul's breath away.

Anna smiled as she passed the small bouquet of the palest pink roses, freshly picked early that morning from Molly's garden and hand-tied with a cream silk ribbon, across to her daughter to hold.

Paul looked to be the handsomest man Anna had ever seen, dressed in his wedding suit of the palest silver grey, a pale pink silk cravat completing his outfit.

Putting her nerves to one side, Anna took Paul's hand in hers and, standing in front of the altar, they made a lifelong commitment to each other. The ceremony everything they could ever have wished for.

Anna said her vows to Paul, knowing in her heart her beloved Gordy was looking down on her with love, wishing her every happiness with the man she'd once thought, a long time ago, had forgotten her. But now all that was in the past and, as Paul said his vows, they both knew the love they shared now would never be forgotten.

As they became husband and wife at last, the fates finally smiled.

# Epilogue

When two people fall in love there are never any guarantees of a 'happy ever after.' Because falling in love is an emotion of the senses, an emotion, which can be triggered by a simple touch, or even merely by a look.

It's an emotional response to a stimulus that cannot be seen. But for the end result of love to have that elusive 'happy ending,' there needs to be much more. Will that first light touch progress to full-scale caressing? Will that first quick glance, which causes a catch in the throat, turn into the deep, soul-searching of two pairs of eyes?

True love needs two people to be utterly selfless for it to flourish. A strong and abiding love takes time to achieve, and is not for the faint-hearted. Some people fall in and out of love easily, and are therefore less likely to find or keep a lasting relationship. Being physically and mentally attracted to someone doesn't always guarantee a lasting relationship.

If you are the type of person who finds themselves attracted to many people, and believe they've found true love each time, you are just giving way to an emotion that isn't mature or sincere, but then I hear you say, 'What about the thunderbolt of lightning that sometimes strikes, that "coup de foudre". Is that ever the "real thing"?

The short answer is I don't know. My love grew slowly and gently and is still enduring. Perhaps these days, sudden rushes of passion and being able to satisfy the urge instantly, are the reason why so many relationships sadly fail at the first hurdle, and why, one in four marriages are said to end in divorce.

Maybe divorce happens because there was no substance to the emotions involved, or those first feelings of passion were misconstrued; mistaken for love, when in fact they were merely lustful longings that only took the act of sex to satisfy them. Real and abiding love is different. It's like a newly planted seed. It needs tender loving care before it germinates, finally becoming a beautiful flower.

Leaping into bed within minutes, or hours, of that first meeting with someone who you find sexually attractive and acting immediately on these feelings of passion, merely to gain sexual satisfaction is not, in my opinion, a recipe for lasting happiness. One has to know and understand a partner, and their character, before lovemaking becomes ideal and lasting.

As for Anna and Paul, their story is about a love that endured, even though the fates had decided to interfere, sending them on separate paths, until finally, those same fates relented and their love was finally allowed to flourish and grow, never to be forgotten again.